DEATH OF
THE NAKED LADY

A MARY MALONE MYSTERY

Marlene Chabot

Mary Jo
Enjoy
Marlene McNeil Chabot

Other writings by Marlene Chabot

NOVELS
China Connection
North Dakota Neighbor
Mayhem With A Capital M
Death At The Bar X Ranch

Anthologies
Why Did Santa Leave A Body?
"A Visit From Santa"

Festival of Crime
"The Missing Groom"

SWF Stories and Poems
"The Gulper Eel"

DEDICATION

This book is dedicated to my family, John, Scott, Amy, Kathy, Ava, Greta, and to all my loyal followers. Without your support and encouragement over the years, this second Mary Malone Mystery wouldn't have come to fruition. I also want to add a special thanks to my Aunt Shirley. If it wasn't for my husband's and my visit to her home one October day and her suggestion to take a leisurely stroll along the beach at Park Point, I would've never stumbled upon the theme for this story. Thanks a million. God Bless!

ACKNOWLEDGEMENT

Many thanks to Karlajean Becvar for the many hours spent proofing and making suggestions for this novel.

ISBN-13:978-1523351091
ISBN-10:1523351098

First Edition:

Photo provided by
Marlene Chabot

Printed in the United States of America

PROLOGUE

When the stork dropped off the Malone household's fourth bundle of joy, namely me, thirty-some-odd years ago, Mother insisted I be called nothing short of Mary Colleen. To her dismay, the proclamation didn't take root. The minute I entered pre-school, classmates, teachers and family alike referred to me simply as Mary. I didn't mind. Honestly. Perhaps they should've called me Jane. You see, I'm as plain Jane as you can get. I fear trying new things of any sort including new boyfriends, diets, and jobs. Of course, being the youngest of four children doesn't help either. Everyone assumes things are handed to you, the baby, on a silver platter, but it's not necessarily true. This baby has fought tooth and nail for everything she has, which at this moment doesn't amount to much.

I'm a teacher by trade or was until this past spring when, to my shock, Principal Drake from Washington Elementary handed me an envelope in which contained terrible news, blasting my *schoolmarm* foundation to smithereens. Mandatory school district cut backs meant I wouldn't be returning to my classroom in the fall after all.

Great, I thought. How's this gal with a master's degree supposed to support herself now? Not by running home to Mom and Pop. No way. So, I did what any sane, single woman would do. I said, *"Adios,"* to my job, sublet an apartment in downtown Minneapolis with a widowed aunt, and dusted off my resume, taking whatever job got tossed my way, which included a PI case intended for my brother. And in the midst of all the drastic changes in my life, I even found a steady guy, or so I thought.

Unfortunately, life doesn't remain the same. Just when you think things can't get any worse—wham— you hit another detour. The case is over, my pocketbook's still bare, and the so-called boyfriend's rarely there. Maybe I should curl up in a ball in the La-Z-Boy, binge out on Kemps's flavor of the month— Pumpkin Pie ice cream and wait for opportunity to knock. I'm told it works for famous starlets. Why not me?

~1~

The wind howled like a Banshee this moonlit night, tossing thunderous waves weighted down by debris and driftwood against mighty Lake Superior's shoreline. The horrendous noise made Ethan Tucker shiver to the core. Where's my comforter? Before he could remember, another loud crash pierced the quiet of his bedroom and thoughts of dead pirates rising from the depths of the lake to seek solace with him flooded his brain. Why did Jacob, his friend, find it necessary to share shipwreck and ghost stories on Halloween? The thin cotton sheet Ethan used to cover his noggin was no good. It didn't block out anything. He lifted the sheet a smidgen and cautiously peeked out to discover where his comforter might be hidden.

"No! No! It's still not right." Fingertips of one hand tapped out a feverish funky tune along the furrowed ridges of my fair forehead while a mean-looking neon pink pen, recently added to my collection thanks to a shopping spree at Ace Hardware, quivered in the other awaiting the next command from my meager brain cells. What would be the fate of the fiction staring me in the face? Would the fourth penned page of this preteen novel be tossed like an old pair of panties or saved to see another day? Seconds ticked by. The ax finally fell. "Scratch it. It's crap."

But the dreadful decree remained unfulfilled due to an unexpected outburst bellowed from the bowels of the kitchen.

"Mary, got time for tea and cookies?" The inquiring voice belonged to none other than Zoe, my roommate.

Startled by Zoe's untimely words, my shaky hand released the chunky pen imprisoned for the past hour. While I remained in somewhat of a semi-trance, I watched the pen dive straight for the aged-desk and add yet another unique nick to its wardrobe. There you go, Mary. If the book doesn't pan out, you can always work for a furniture factory, making new pieces look old. According to all those home makeover shows, distressed furniture's in high demand these days.

While I pondered an eight hour shift in a furniture factory versus no job at all, Aunt Zoe's shrill voice battered my thoughts yet again. "Mary, I'm waiting. A simple yes or no will do."

"I suppose," I harshly replied. The nasty tone wasn't meant for my widowed aunt who has shared a dwelling with me at the Foley Apartment Complex since I received a pink slip in my teacher's mailbox four months ago, even though her daily interruptions and other quirks do tend to slither under my skin. It was meant for me, and rightly so. My writing wasn't moving along as fast as I'd hoped. Extra income wouldn't be sliding into my checking account lickety split from book sales to cover bills when requests for a substitute teacher or an assistant at Singi Optical weren't forthcoming. Perhaps a hot refreshment would rejuvenate my mind and body. Even though I'm wearing a long sleeve shirt and sweatshirt, I'd been shivering for quite a spell.

Aunt Zoe's short, spiked, fiery red head crowded in on me as she leaned forward to deliver cookies and a cup of steaming tea.

My shoulders automatically stiffened. Whenever my aunt's involved with food, turbulence seems to follow in her wake. Today didn't prove otherwise. In the process of handing things off, her elbow nicked my shoulder and a few drops of liquid spilled on my neck. I reacted accordingly and jumped. "I'm sorry, Mary. How clumsy of me. I'll grab a tissue to dry you off." She quickly set the tea and Oreos down on the desk near my elbow and moved towards the tissue box on the night stand.

After counting to ten, I hastily produced a fake grin for my aunt's benefit. "Don't bother, Auntie." I raised my hand to the back of my neck and swiped the droplets of moisture off. "See. No harm done. I'm fine."

"You sure?"

"Absolutely." *Just don't do it again*, I thought, bending my head towards the tea resting by my elbow. "Mmm, smells wonderful. A cranberry-blend if I'm not mistaken. Thanks for your thoughtfulness." I curled a hand around my cup, took a sip, and then set the cup back down. "Autumn has finally made its grand entrance, hasn't it?"

"It certainly has."

"I love fall."

Aunt Zoe tilted her head forward. "Could it be because a certain someone's birthday's coming soon?"

"Maybe. But the red and yellow hues of leaves, the vibrant mums, and grocery bins overflowing with pumpkins, cranberries, squash and apples thrill me too."

"Hmm, yes," she agreed, "I know what you mean, especially the food in the grocery bins. So, what have you been up to, Niece?" she inquired as she continued to steal a glance over my left shoulder, "Making birthday plans? Or catching up on your letter writing?"

"Neither. No money for a party and I left snail mail behind years ago. What writing I do nowadays is via the computer."

Her bright painted nails poked at the loose sheets of paper on my desk. "Then what's with the pages of scribbled notes? Working on another case, huh?" Without waiting for a reply, which is par for the course where my dad's sister is concerned, she rambled on. "Funny, because last night I decided to make a suggestion in regards to our low cash flow. I think it's high time we posted a sign in the building telling our fellow apartment dwellers this Sherlock Holmes' team is available anytime, day or night."

I peered up at my aunt's chunky cheeks. The pumpkin-colored rouge she wore mimicked her thick coated lips and nails. "Sherlock Holmes? I thought we were trying to be more like Miss Marple." I waved my hand. "No matter. We're not taking on another case. One near death experience at the Bar X Ranch was enough for me, thank you very much." As far as I was concerned, the topic on sleuthing had been tabled permanently.

Unfortunately for me, Auntie didn't appear to think so. *What can I do to derail more of her sleuthing schemes?* Offering up my written words for her to inspect suddenly came to mind. "Here. Take a look at this. It's actually my first day's attempt at writing a saleable novel. If I can hit a homerun like J.K. Rowling did with Harry Potter, the future of this unemployed teacher won't be so bleak."

"Well, if my opinion counts at all, it appears you're off to a gang-buster start."

I only wish.

Auntie fanned her plump face.

Probably having another stupid hot flash, I thought as I crushed my arms to my chest. How many does this make? A thousand? God must really enjoy tormenting women. Maybe if He had warned Eve women coming after her would suffer because of her stupid decision in the Garden of Eden, she wouldn't have been so anxious to eat the dumb apple in the first place.

Leaving my thoughts on Eve behind, I stiffly replied, "It doesn't feel like it. I'm still having trouble creating the right setting. The novel must be extremely vivid if I want kids emptying bookstore shelves the minute it's released."

"Cooling your brain cells, Mary, ought to do the trick. It helps the juices flow to the surface." She inched her way towards the thin, grey metal vent mounted on the bedroom ceiling. "I'll stop the heat from flowing in here."

Cool my brain cells this time of year. Is she crazy? "Please don't," I quickly pounced. "The room's already too chilly for me."

"Hmm? My hormones must be out of whack. Every time I enter this room I swear someone's stoked the furnace." She stepped to the side of the desk and shoved back the knitted sleeves of her pumpkin-colored top, exposing the tiny lion tattoo below her left elbow.

I stared at the orange and black animal. It's not the first time I'd seen it, but I hadn't gotten up the nerve to inquire about it yet. Maybe it simply reminded her of the many safaris she'd been on. "Where does your story take place," she continued, "in a foreign land? If so, it's right up my alley. You know how much traveling Edward and I did over the years."

I hesitated with my reply. "Duluth."

"Oh, sorry, it's been several decades since I visited Minnesota's northern region. I don't remember much."

Yes! Her words were music to my ears. We already spend 90 percent of our waking hours with each other as it is. There's no way I'd give up the other 10 percent so she could co-author a book with me. But I knew Dad's sister, she doesn't give up easily.

Seconds later the rhythmic tap, tapping of her pudgy, orange-painted fingernails against the edge of the desk proved me right. Her mind clicked away. She'd soon be shelling out her secret thoughts. When they finally came, it wasn't much. "Why, that's easy to resolve."

What? She's got a simple solution. Dare I ask? Even though I pride myself on my inner warning system being fairly accurate, since moving in with my aunt I've caught myself ignoring it more and more. Instead of closing my ears to her hairbrained notions, I actually tune in. Maybe it's the teacher in me. Surely one of Auntie's ideas will eventually pan out, right? I bit the bait. "It is?"

"Sure. Doesn't your mother have a relative living around Canal Park?"

"Canal Park?" My fingers flew back to my furrowed forehead where they had been feverishly performing earlier. What relative could she be referring to? *Think, Mary.* Thankfully, not too many seconds ticked by before piano movement on my forehead kicked in and jarred my memory. "You must mean Lizzie, my second cousin. Actually, she lives in the Park Point area."

"Is that the quaint little community one gets to by crossing the Aerial Lift Bridge?"

I nodded. "I think so. I haven't been to Duluth since grade school." My mind reeled back in time, but all I saw were mountains of licorice-colored coal resting on the banks of mighty Lake Superior waiting to be hauled on board rusty Michigan-bound ships. I slipped out of my cushy office chair, scrambled to the nightstand where my cell phone had been placed before I dropped off to sleep last night, and picked it up. I flicked it on, chose contacts, tapped my parents' number, and waited for someone to answer.

"Hello."

I lucked out. I had reached my mother. If Dad had answered, he wouldn't have had a clue where to hunt for the info I needed and instead of getting Mom he would've told me to call back when she wasn't so busy. "Hi, Mom. You got time to talk?"

"All the time you need," she replied, "especially if you're calling to share info on a new man you've met."

Good grief. Sometimes I think my mother's more worried about my being single the rest of my life than I am. "Sorry to disappoint you, Mom, but I've nothing to report. No available bachelors have knocked on my door recently. Nope, I haven't heard from David lately either. And, no, I'm not hooking up on the internet with some kook, no matter what Uncle George thinks I should do."

I inhaled deeply. "Mom, please let me get a word in. Okay? I called to tell you Aunt Zoe and I thought we'd take a drive to Duluth and pop in on Cousin Lizzie, but I don't know how to reach her. Do you? Great." I turned my attention to my roommate for a split-second and pointed to the paper and pen on my desk.

Getting the message, she picked up the spiraled writing tablet and pen, and then handed them off to me.

"Thanks," I mouthed as I patiently waited for my mother to dig though her address book and return to the phone.

"Sorry, it took so long, dear," she said clearly out of breath. "I forgot I had left the address book by the phone in the basement. Okay, got a piece of paper and pen handy to write this down?"

"Yup. Go ahead." She gave me the number and I repeated it back to make sure I had it right. "Got it. Thanks."

"Say Mary, while you're up in Duluth, you and Zoe should think about going to the rose garden and the aquarium if you can fit it in."

"We'll try. Love you too. Bye." I pressed *END* and faced Aunt Zoe again. "My mom says the mutt misses us and we should think about coming by next week for a home cooked meal."

"Hmm. It's certainly a new twist on an invite; telling us your brother's dog misses us."

I laughed. "What's so hard about saying she and Dad are curious to see how we're fending for ourselves?"

Aunt Zoe's somber face broke out in a broad grin. "I don't know, but what the heck, we're getting another free meal. Something us single gals look forward to, right?"

On cue, my stomach growled. "You got it." Neither one of us would ever make it through the first hour of a reality cook-off show, but I gotta say my baking expertise isn't too bad, considering I've attempted desserts about four times in the last ten years. I glanced at my wide-banded, leather Timex watch. Noon already. I guess I'd better satisfy my stomach's complaints. I picked up my cup of tea and headed for the kitchen. "Hey, Roomie, is there a slice or two of pizza left over from last night's supper?"

Aunt Zoe stepped in behind me and headed in the same direction. "Gee, I don't know. I can't seem to remember. This menopausal brain of mine seems to be on forget mode lately."

It's been more than just lately. Since I didn't want to upset the applecart this early in the day, I kept my thoughts hidden from view. "It's all right." I waltzed into the kitchen and marched straight to the fridge. If I couldn't find any pizza, I'd stuff my size 16 body with a baloney and cheddar cheese sandwich, and whatever snacks happened to be lurking in our almost bare cupboards.

Unfortunately, my determination to find nourishment for my tummy in the fridge got cut short by a rap, rap on our door. This isn't the first time I've been interrupted at meal time by such nonsense, and I wondered if this was the big Man's way of subliminally telling me I should start taking my dieting more seriously. *Nah. He's got bigger fish to fry.* I just picked the wrong apartment building to live in. Reluctantly, I released the grip I had on the fridge handle and glanced over at my roomie who had plopped herself at the table. "Were you expecting someone?" I asked.

"No. Were you?"

I shook my head. Since no one had buzzed us beforehand from the main lobby, I assumed whoever knocked lived within the confines of the Foley, probably even on the same floor as us. Oh, no. It better not be Rod Thompson, the FBI agent who lives in 403 one door down. I've been avoiding this particular throwback to the Vikings for several weeks. He thinks we have a thing going, but we don't. The relationship is complicated. There's another guy I'm more interested in. *Whoa. Cool your jets, Mary. Maybe the person isn't a renter.* Visitors have been known to sneak through the building's double set of doors via the kindness of a resident exiting or entering the premises. *Ah, yes, so much for security.*

Auntie lowered the newspaper she had brought to the kitchen and studied me. "Do you want me to see who it is?"

I waved my hand like one does to shoo a pesky fly. "No, you stay put. Looks like you're already glued to the Enquirer." I spun on my heels, trotted down the narrow hallway leading to the door, and unlatched the safety chain. I hated to keep extra security in place all the time, but a woman can never be too careful, no matter where she lives, and I sure as heck didn't want friend or family finding one of our fabulous bodies' laying inside a chalk drawing at some point in time.

When I finally cracked the door open onto the fourth floor hallway, whopping whiffs of curry, broccoli and garlic whizzed past as a female neighbor poked her tiny, friendly face in the available space. *Thank you, Lord.* Rod Thompson didn't disturb our lunch after all. I threw the door open. "Margaret, come in."

~ 7 ~

The petite Italian native, a longtime Foley resident, stood before me clothed in a navy-blue cotton pant set and a green butcher-style apron with a fall leaf motif edged in rust-colored ruffles. Margaret's paper thin hands, along with what I presumed to be an apple pie, partially obstructed her mid-section.

I ignored the pie temporarily. I wanted to discover whether the resident of 402 wore the pink Isotoner slippers Foley renters used to identify the nonagenarian when congregating in the lobby, or if she favored a more fashionable pair for this floor. I snuck a glance at her feet. Nope, apparently she wears the same ones.

Margaret shifted her stance a bit. "Oh, dear, what's the matter, Mary? Did juice from the pie drip on your carpet?"

Shoot. I need to learn to be more discreet. "Ah, no. I thought I spotted the penny Aunt Zoe dropped the other day. It's hard to tell what you're seeing with this ugly mishmash of browns."

"I understand. Last year, the Foley residents banded together and demanded the management change our outdated carpets. Do you know what management did?" Since I didn't know if she expected me to answer, I kept my mouth shut. "Absolutely nothing."

"Really? Sounds like what happened to me at my other apartment. When I first moved in, management promised me a new dishwasher. On move out day they examined the dishwasher and asked how long since it stopped working. I told them on day one six years ago."

I backed up now to allow Margaret entrance into our home. Well, to be more precise my brother's abode. Matt, who is a PI, is letting my aunt and I sublet his apartment while he's on assignment in Europe for the Delight Bottling Company. The arrangement has been beneficial for Aunt Zoe and me, but there's a downside. Matt doesn't know when he'll be returning to the States. It could be a couple months from now or next year. As much as I love my brother, I'm hoping it will be the later rather than the former.

"Say," I said, as I closed the door and stepped closer to Margaret, "weren't you scheduled for a Senior Fall Color outing today?"

The elderly woman's thin mouth sagged. "*Si*, but the bus trip got cancelled." She shifted the weight of the pie from her right hand to her left so she could perch her wire rim glasses snug against the bridge of her nose.

"What happened?"

"The usual—not enough seniors signed up. If they'd only forget about their aches and pains for a day or two, they would find out how much fun it is to be alive."

"Sorry the trip got cancelled. I know how much you look forward to them. But, it worked out in the end."

"How so?"

"Well, if you had taken the trip, Aunt Zoe and I wouldn't be having the pleasure of your company or the enjoyment of your treat."

Margaret Grimshaw's olive green eyes twinkled brightly. "I knew you'd appreciate the pie."

I gushed. "Oh, Margaret, any dessert you create I love. But how did you know apple pie's my favorite this time of year?"

"Did someone mention apple pie," Aunt Zoe asked, stepping into the living room. "Oh, Margaret! What a pleasant surprise. Where have you been hiding? You haven't been ill, have you?"

"No, just busy as usual— running to painting classes and helping out with funeral luncheons at church." She tapped the deep wrinkled lines on her forehead with an arthritic finger. "I was about to tell Mary how I knew she'd enjoy fresh apple pie."

"Sorry I interrupted," Aunt Zoe said. "Go ahead."

The elderly woman's eyes twinkled again. "That's all right. I guessed. It's no ordinary apple pie though," she corrected, "A scrumptious apple pie requires a special sauce drizzled over the top crust." Her slim hand disappeared into an apron pocket and quickly produced a small jar labeled caramel.

"Ah, yes," my mouth salivated wildly, "I'm ready to taste it." I quickly latched on to her arm. "Let's go have a piece," and steered her towards the kitchen.

"You two did have lunch already, didn't you?" Margaret quizzed.

"Of course," we fibbed, knowing the apple pie would be our lunch.

After our neighbor set the pie on the table, she scanned every inch of the kitchen. Her careful examination of the room made me wonder if she had expected to walk into another one of Aunt Zoe's cooking fiascoes. Well, she needn't have worried. I scoured the kitchen from top to bottom yesterday after Auntie had another one of her mishaps. When Margaret's eyes finally focused on us again, she said, "No, Gracie, I see."

What? She wasn't concerned about the condition of the kitchen. So I'm fallible. My hunches don't always turn out to be 100 percent accurate. "Gracie? Nope, afraid not. My folks haven't asked us to watch her since they went on vacation this summer." The dog's living with my folks, but she actually belongs to my brother who saved her from euthanasia a couple years ago. I pulled a chair away from the small table for our visitor and then I went about retrieving dessert plates, forks, knife, and spatula.

"I think the real reason we haven't been asked," Aunt Zoe stated, "has more to do with my brother's health. Mary's mother wants him to get his walking in. Caring for a dog makes exercise mandatory."

Margaret sat and drew her chair closer to the table. "Yes, most of us do tend to put off things until it becomes absolutely necessary, don't we? Which reminds me, Mary, Gertie Nash wondered where you were this morning."

I released the hold I had on the silverware drawer and pressed my hand over my heart. "Me? Please tell me you're joking." I met Gertie, an extremely heavyset woman with tattoos up the kazoo when I first began working at the Singi Optical store this past summer. The middle-aged woman lives in the Foley, but on a different floor, thank God. Ever since she's met me, she's tried to convince me to help her cousin, Butch, who found himself in a jam years ago. Supposedly, he wants to clear the air once and for all and prove he was framed for stealing a well-guarded pickle recipe from Minnesota's number one pickle factory. I've told Gertie over and over again my brother Matt's the only private eye in our family, but she doesn't seem to get the message. Probably because this past summer I cracked a tough case at Reed Griffin's horse boarding ranch, originally meant for my brother, and Aunt Zoe made sure our fellow residents heard all about it.

My neighbor's washed out eyebrows arched severely. "I'm not joking, dear. Didn't you get an invite to her cousin's book launch? It took place in our community room."

I set the items I'd collected on the table and pulled out a chair. "For Butch the jailbird?"

"That's the one."

"I did but I tore it up. Oops!" Somehow I miscalculated the distance between me and the chair and my butt smacked the piece of furniture harder than I'd intended. But guess what? I didn't feel a thing. Maybe I should rethink dieting and continue to eat whatever I please.

Margaret's hands reached across the table. "Mary, are you all right?"

I pointed to my tush. "Sure, I'm too padded to get injured," I joked. "So, what's the title of the book Butch is pushing?"

Margaret clasped her deeply-veined hands together. *Ghosts that Haunt the Hennepin County Slammer."*

I tried to smother a laugh, but it came out rip-roaring instead. "Definitely a must read for everyone on my Christmas list."

Aunt Zoe shared one of her exasperating glares.

"What's wrong? Did I say something I shouldn't have?"

Dad's sister twisted her head slightly from side to side. "It's what you didn't do, Mary. You purposely ignored a chance for us to meet a real live author. Why, you know how much I love to read."

Yes, I certainly do. Any romance novel or National Enquirer placed in your path is fair game. I ground my teeth. I didn't appreciate being forced to explain my actions. "You won't be happy until I tell you the reason for not going, will you?"

She shook her head back and forth.

"I didn't think so. If I had shown up at the book launch, Butch would've gotten the wrong idea."

"How?"

"Butch wants me to help him solve a problem he's had for a long time, and I've been ignoring him."

Aunt Zoe released a loud sigh, something she does when she's not happy with me. Her pudgy hands grabbed the knife off the table. *Oh, oh. Watch out pie you're about to be obliterated.* As soon as Auntie thrust the knife into the pie, luscious cooked apples gushed over the tin's sides destroying the delicate crust Margaret had prepared.

Two seconds after the first messy incision had been made, I took charge. My stomach couldn't handle anymore destruction. I tore the knife from my aunt's firm grip. "Here, let me finish up. Margaret perhaps you'd like a cup of tea," I said, hoping my dad's sister would pick up on the hint. "The cranberry blend Aunt Zoe fixed earlier has a wonderful flavor."

My Aunt shot out of her chair. "Yes, Margaret, let me get you a cup. You'll like it."

"Where did you find the tea?" she asked.

"The new tea shop around the corner."

"Is that so?" Our ninety-some year old neighbor released a tiny grin. "I haven't had the opportunity to visit it yet. Are the owners friendly?"

"Very." Aunt Zoe promptly poured hot water into a teacup, added a teabag, and carried the cup back to the table where our neighbor patiently waited. Once the tea got handed off, Auntie slapped her derrière back on a kitchen chair and returned to our earlier discussion. "I've been mulling over what you said, Mary, about Butch."

Not the book launch again! *Can't she just let it go?*

"You made a terrible mistake in not going to his doings."

I felt my eyebrows twitch nervously and wondered if anyone noticed. "You're saying you'd have preferred to see me bugged by Butch?"

"Absolutely not. I just thought since you're working on a novel..."

"A novel?" Margaret quickly set her tea aside. "It's the first I've heard of it."

Auntie shielded her mouth with her hand. "Oops. I guess the cat's out of the bag so to speak, isn't it?"

Yup. No thanks to you. In the rush to clear my mouth of pie, I accidently chomped down on my tongue. I hate when that happens. It takes forever to stop hurting. I squeezed my eyes shut till the pain passed. "Yeah, well, I kinda wanted to keep it under wraps, you know, until further along."

Margaret gently tucked loose strands of stately white hair behind her ears. They had freed themselves from the bun-style hairdo at the back of her head. "I understand. I'll wait till you're ready to share." She turned to Aunt Zoe. "Were you reading anything interesting before I popped by?"

"As a matter of fact—"

"Hold on. I've changed my mind, Margaret." There's no way Auntie's repeating a crazy three-headed cat tale even if it meant opening up about my book. "I know you won't go blabbing to other people in our building." *At least I hoped not.* "I'm writing a preteen novel."

The nonagenarian folded her petite hands. "How exciting. Where does it take place?"

"Duluth."

"Such a grand place for a story. Ships coming and going on Lake Superior all hours of the day and night, the Glensheen Mansion built in 1908, Grandma's Marathon, the zoo, and the railroad museum."

"Yes," I interjected, "and my mom mentioned a rose garden and a natural water aquarium too."

"Ah, yes—the Great Lakes Aquarium," our neighbor said, "It wasn't there the last time I visited. So, have you two given any thought to when you might take your road trip? According to WCCO's meteorologists, fall colors are supposed to peak the next week or so in northern Minnesota."

"Actually, we were talking about the trip right before you arrived," I shared, "My second cousin has a place up there, but I need to check with her and see what date works for my visit."

My roommate shot up from the table with such force her chair almost toppled. "But what about me? You know, so you and I could do some sightseeing. Why did you tell your mother the two of us were going for a drive if you didn't mean it?"

"Well, at first I thought it would work, but I've changed my mind, Auntie. If I'm doing research, there won't be any time for fun. Besides, if the school needs me to substitute, I'll have to turn right around and come back. I might only be up there a couple hours."

Aunt Zoe pouted. "But, Mary."

I flung my hand out indicating the topic wasn't on the table any longer, a stupid mistake.

Dad's sister marched off in a huff, leaving behind a trail of anger as she did so. Embarrassed, I looked at our elderly visitor who remained seated and searched her deep-seated eyes. Did she think I was as rotten as I felt? I tried to cover my mean deed with words, suggesting Aunt Zoe's mood swings were par for the course. "Sorry about that. She'll be fine once she cools her jets."

Margaret Grimshaw studied my face. "Who are you trying to convince, me or you?"

I had no answer. Instead, I turned on the radio to soothe my soul and then studied the linoleum floor's black and white checkered pattern. Perhaps if I stared at the floor long enough, things might revert back to when Margaret first arrived and the atmosphere was pleasanter.

The classical music on the radio faded and the host of the program broke in. "If anyone has any information regarding the whereabouts of Darcy Hawthorne, a first year college student at the University of Minnesota Duluth, please contact the Duluth police immediately." Then he quickly passed on the hotline number and the music resumed.

My heart sank. Another missing college student. Five Minnesota students went missing last year. When would it end? I turned the radio off. It hadn't worked its charm like I'd hoped. Now my mind will be flooded, the rest of the evening, with thoughts of missing undergrads and why no one's found them.

Margaret shook her head. She appeared to be as bothered as I by what we heard. "Such terrible news!" she said, easing herself off one of our not so comfortable kitchen chairs. Why, the girl's parents must be devastated. What could have happened to their daughter? Do you think she ran off with her boyfriend, Mary?"

"Possibly. For her parent's sake I hope that's the case."

"Me too."

"Of course, they'll be mad at her when she first reappears. That's to be expected. But years down the road, they'll laugh about her crazy stunt and be thankful she's still alive."

"Well, dear, I'd better run along before an angry tenant tosses my washed clothes in a dirty corner of the laundry room."

I stood and escorted Margaret to the door. "I'll call you tomorrow. Thanks again for bringing over the apple pie. It was scrumptious."

"Your welcome."

As soon as I shut the door behind my elderly visitor, the apartment took on the atmosphere of a morgue, dead silence rang out.

If you've ever lived in close quarters with someone you've quarreled with, you know exactly how I felt. Life sucks. Ill feelings abound. Unfortunately for me, Aunt Zoe's feelings resonated louder than mine. I felt like I was already six feet under. What little I ate at supper stuck in my throat. Sure I could've easily remedied the situation, but I didn't feel like it. Auntie's not coming to Duluth and that's final. This single gal deserves R&R by herself. There's no law that says I have to vacation with my roommate. We're not an old married couple.

Wednesday

Margaret's last words to me yesterday stung like a bee. I didn't sleep a wink. I kept weighing the options. Do I let Aunt Zoe ride along to Duluth with me in Fiona, my VW bug I named after my great Irish aunt, or do I leave her to sulk in this apartment? If I left her here, she'd only be able to get around town on foot or by bus, too scary to even think about. With her notoriety for being easily confused, there's no telling what street corner she'd eventually end up on. It could be along Hennepin Avenue where the strip joints are banded together or on the corner where all the derelicts hung out. Neither painted a pretty picture.

Of course, it didn't help I hadn't gotten in touch with Cousin Lizzie before popping into bed last night either. Every time I attempted to reach her I got nothing but an earful of static. If I bet, which I don't, I'd say odds were ten to one my octogenarian cousin never set the earpiece in her landline cradle properly. I remember Mom saying Lizzie has severe arthritis in her hands.

Hopefully someone's alerted my cousin to her problem by now. That is if she's an early riser like our elderly neighbor across the hall. I studied my hands for a moment before I threw back the flannel sheet and quilt and slipped into my moccasin-style slippers. *What would I do if these fingers of mine became crippled,* I wondered. My stomach didn't wait for a reply. It rumbled loudly. Ignoring the obnoxious noise would only garner more complaints, so I put off the call to Cousin Lizzie, wrapped my salmon-colored floor-length terrycloth bathrobe tightly around me, and strolled to the kitchen.

Hmm? No hint of fresh brewed coffee hung in the air. That's odd. Auntie always makes a fresh pot of Folgers the minute her size 6 feet hit the floor in the morning. She says her zip for the day comes from her sips. My body on the other hand gets its zing from plain ol' Florida orange juice. No doubt it's because it's loaded with sugar. I breezed out of the kitchen and continued towards the living room, Aunt Zoe's bedroom quarters.

She selected the room, not me. I offered Matt's bedroom when we first moved in here. According to her she's slept on mountaintops and in teeny, tiny sailboat quarters, so it didn't really matter where she laid her head anymore. "Besides," she added, "a working gal needs to get her beauty rest," referring to me. My aunt hasn't held a job since she married Uncle Edward-a very wealthy fellow- forty years ago. However, since the almost penniless widow has moved in with me, reading the daily *Want Ads* has become an obsession with her. Maybe one of these days she'll come across something of interest. I can only hope.

Inching ever nearer to the largest room in our abode that my aunt has managed to transform from cheap modern to Moroccan to Spanish within a short span of five months, I wondered what weird decorating scheme I might fall upon this morning after perceiving her to be in such a foul mood last night. Perhaps she threw caution to the wind and created an extreme makeover.

When I finally dared look in the living room, I released a sigh of relief. Nothing had changed. No spinning windmills or other foreign objects protruded from the floor or ceiling. Matt's long, dark sleeper couch sat upright with used bedding neatly stashed near it. *Huh*? Obviously, Aunt Zoe wasn't as angry with me as I imagined. The room did lack one particular element, her. Unless she'd recently read how to become invisible, which is doubtful. My dad's sister soaks up romance novels faster than I can scarf down a handful of chocolate chip cookies.

"Wait a sec." I strolled to the hallway and looked down towards where I originally came from, my bedroom. I'd forgotten about the bathroom that sits next to it. Auntie spends a considerable amount of time primping in there. The door stood open. No occupant. *Great!* Where could she be? I ran my hand through my just-out-of-bed hair. *Settle down, Mary. Your roommate couldn't have gone far. She doesn't own a car. Maybe she needed more space to think.* "Sure, that's it. I bet she's across the hall unburdening herself to Margaret Grimshaw." Why didn't I think of that sooner? I could've saved myself a lot of stress.

My stomach roared again. *Okay. Okay. I hear ya.* I turned around and retraced my steps to the kitchen to scrounge up a bowl of cereal and a glass of Vitamin C.

***

Aunt Zoe swept into the apartment an hour later dressed in bright-green jeans and a rust-colored top humming an old, familiar cowboy tune, *Whoopie-Ti-Yi-Yo.* Pleased to see no foam dripping from her mouth, I begged her to reveal where she had been.

"Reed came by," she shared as she sashayed into the living room. Auntie's known Reed Griffin for a couple months. She met him this past summer when I offered to look into a horse problem at his ranch. They've been dating ever since. "We went down to the corner coffee shop for a spell. I needed to talk to someone."

I crossed my arms and clutched my sides. "I'm so relieved to hear that. You don't know how many crazy notions have been buzzing around in my head since I got up and discovered you weren't here." My arm reached for hers as she plopped her frame on the couch cushions. "Can you ever forgive me for yesterday?"

She flicked her wrist. "It's forgotten, Mary. I'm just as much at fault. Reed explained how important it is for a creative person to be by themselves when doing research. 'Distractions only hinder concentration,' he said."

Way to go Reed. Keep plugging away for me. I sauntered over to the La-Z-Boy and took possession of it. "Well, I'm glad you're back to your old self, Roomie. I'm bursting at the seams."

"Oh, boy. I guess it's time to find a decent diet and stick to it, huh?"

"Forget the diet. My clothes aren't the problem. I've got good news to share."

Her amply colored lips parted. "Really? Has one of your man friends finally proposed?"

~ 17 ~

I laughed. "Oh, Auntie, you're such a romantic. You didn't miss any proposals. Rod's not even in the ball park. And who knows when David will ever get up the courage to stroll down the aisle. No, I'm afraid there's no men involved in this bit of news. It pertains to my Cousin Lizzie. I finally spoke with her."

"Oh," her easy smile flipped to a heavy frown.

"Get this, Lizzie told me she was about to call me."

She pulled her shoulders up. "Whatever for?"

"Mom informed her of my plans to drive up her way, and she thought she should warn me she's not at her apartment."

"Well, I don't blame her. I'd be traveling this time of year too if a certain person let me join them." She gave me a disgruntled look.

I glanced at my stocking feet resting on the raised section of the La-Z-Boy. "Lizzie's not tromping around just anywhere. She's been at a health facility the past week recuperating from double-knee surgery. Isn't it great?"

Aunt Zoe pressed her fingers to her forehead. "Why would such a tidbit please you? There's nothing marvelous about having two knees operated on at the same time. Unless…"

"Yes…" I encouraged.

"She's on a high dose of Oxycodone or Vicodin. When you're taking those painkillers, nothing bothers you. I mean nothing. Or so I've been told."

Hmm. I wonder. Could she be speaking from experience? I didn't say anything. I knew the correct answer would eventually reach the matter between her ears.

She dropped her hands to the couch and gave me a stern look. "I'm not on the right path am I?" After confirming what she suspected with a polite nod, a huge smile enveloped her apple-shaped face. "You're not going to Duluth."

I hate to tell people when they're wrong, but this time it was imperative I do so. "No. I still plan to go. Cousin Lizzie needs someone to care for her dog, Winnie. Apparently the poodle doesn't do well being kenneled at a pooch care facility so her married daughter Sarah, who resides in South Dakota, offered to stay with the dog till Lizzie's doctor released her. But the daughter's time schedule changed. Her hubby needs her back home as soon as possible."

"So, in other words your original plan hasn't changed after

all. I'll still be stuck here by myself."

"Not unless you want to be. Lizzie told me *we* should make ourselves at home while she's gone."

Dad's sister bounced off the couch cushions, scrambled to where I perched, and threw her arms around me. "Oh, Mary, you've had a change of heart. Thank you. You won't regret it. We're going to have so much fun. You'll see." Then she rapidly shifted gears and loosened her possessive grip on me. "I mean, I'll have fun."

"We'll all have fun," I corrected.

Aunt Zoe tapped her foot on the well-worn carpet. "Wait a second. You make it sound like more than two of us will be taking this road trip."

I eased out of the La-Z-Boy and hovered over my aunt. "Yup, that's right. Do you have a problem with more people?"

The cold stare coming from her grayish-blue eyes said it all. "It depends. I know it's your car and your project, but how many others are you planning to squeeze into Fiona? Is Matt's dog, Gracie, in the equation?"

"Nope. No pets. Just one more human."

"Oh, then we must be taking your mother along."

"I hadn't thought of that. I suppose we could've, but I asked Margaret Grimshaw. You two have become quite close since moving in here. I thought you'd enjoy her company."

Auntie nodded. "Most definitely. She's easy to talk to and likes to share so many things with me." *Like food*, I thought. "Oh, but what about Petey, her parrot? I don't think he can be by himself for too many days."

"Margaret loaned him out for mating purposes, remember?"

"Vaguely." She gathered her 140 pounds off the couch and spun towards the door.

"Where are you going?"

"To see if our neighbor feels up to a trip."

Pleased with the way things had successfully turned around without much effort on my part, I felt a smile sweep across my face. "Save your energy, Auntie. There's no need to traipse across the hall."

"Oh, I know Mary, but I'd rather ask our neighbor in person than over the phone."

"You don't understand. She's already agreed to go."

"Well, then I guess there's only one thing left to do."

"What?"

"Start packing, girl. We're going on a road trip and it ain't with Bob Dylan or Prince."

Thursday

It took a bit of persuading on my part last night, but Margaret and Aunt Zoe eventually got on board with my plan to exit our metropolitan jungle at the crack of dawn. I'm sure the rush hour traffic stories reported on the daily news plus the horror stories I've shared about bumper to bumper cars flooding the roads factored in their decision making because neither of the women has been a working stiff for at least thirty-five years.

At promptly 5 a.m. I awoke with thoughts of showering, sneaking in a bowl of stale Cheerios, and packing before fleeing the Foley with the gals. Of course, like other parts of my life lately, the jelled plan went awry the moment I rolled out of bed.

Instead of showering first, my mind passed *GO* and flew directly to packing. I ended up squandering a whole twenty minutes determining how many garments to take. Dumb, I know. Five minutes should have been the max. I only own enough clothes for a week. At least no one can ever say my abundant wardrobe put Barbie dolls to shame. By the time I backed away from the narrow closet, it looked like Mother Hubbard's bare cupboards.

I picked up the pace a bit as I left the bedroom and wandered into the bathroom. *A quick shower should help rein in some lost time*, I thought. Wrong. The old plumbing at the Foley fought back.

Sure I heard the pipes gasping, croaking, and sputtering earlier, but it didn't concern me. The pipes made racket every morning. Talk about a body being rocked to the core. The second the frigid water sliced through my skin, my sweet lips let loose with a blood-curdling scream, and I immediately fretted I had awakened neighbors.

No cops showed up, so I must be in the clear. Lucky me. Wait, I'll rephrase that. If the cops are single and cute, by all means let them kick down the darn door.

But I digress. I must confess the biggest wrench thrown into this morning's well-oiled plans— the urgent phone call. It came as we locked up. A first grade teacher begged for a sub and this gal readily accepted. "You betcha. I can do it," momentarily forgetting I had now shifted our get-away time to peak evening rush hour traffic.

When it finally dawned on me what I had foolishly done by accepting the sub job, I could've kicked myself from here to Alaska. Driving in heavy traffic, especially a section of interstate I've never driven before makes me extremely nervous. I would never share that with my companions though. All they needed to hear was we were taking off later in the day. Fortunately they'd understand the delay. I had no choice. I needed cash and Washington Elementary, where I had been proudly employed once, happened to be desperate for a sub.

While Rosalie, the needy teacher, expounded on my arrival time and her lesson plans, I foolishly thought about what could be done with the few hours we'd have this evening after we reached our 2 ½ hour destination: a leisurely stroll around Canal Park. If only I had taken the time to borrow the Wicked Witch's crystal ball, my brain cells could've been wasted on trivial matters instead, like how to lose weight and still pig-out on my favorite foods.

The minute I got off the phone, I notified Margaret of the change in plans and then I disappeared to the quiet of the kitchen to jot down what the teacher had said before I forgot.

Two seconds later, the dull humming of the fridge disappeared into the background, replaced by Aunt Zoe's messing with the coffee pot. I suppose she figured she might as well make a fresh pot of brew for herself since she'd be in the apartment for at least another nine hours. I've never seen anyone go through as much java in a day as this woman does. You've heard of nicotine fits? She has caffeine fits. Too bad no one's gotten up enough nerve yet to tell her that supposedly cutting back on caffeine helps relieve menopausal symptoms.

In a way I didn't look forward to the coffee preparation being finished, I sensed what was coming next, the interrogation. "When are you expected at school? Did it sound like it's going to be a rough day?"

You might as well get her questions out of the way. There'll be no peace until you do, Mary. I laid the putrid purple pen I absconded from the bank the other day on the table and lifted my head slightly. "I gotta be at school by twelve. From what the teacher said the afternoon should fly by. When the kids come back from their lunch hour, they have three half hour classes: computer lab, science and art. Then I wrap up the day by reading the kiddies *The Lion King.* It'll be fun. I love using different voices for each character. The little ones eat it up."

"Gee, I wish I could hear you."

"Tell you what, I'll borrow the book from the library and give you a private performance."

"Wonderful. I can't wait." The coffee maker finished its process so Aunt Zoe went to fill her mug. Thankfully, her busyness gave me ample time to finish the note to myself and decide what to do with the rest of my morning.

"Any chance we might have lunch together before you put on your teacher hat?" my roommate asked when she returned to the table with her freshly brewed java.

I released a huge yawn. "Not unless you're thinking of eating lunch at ten-thirty."

"Forget it then, here's a new suggestion, Mary. Go back to bed. Catch a few more Z's. An article I recently read said the younger the kids are, the more they wear a person out."

Isn't it interesting how people who have never had a child or worked with one seem to think they know all the angles? Personally, I'd rather be worn out physically by little ones any day of the week than worn down mentally by older ones, including roommates.

I glanced at the wall clock. Another minute slid by. A nap definitely wasn't on my reworked agenda, but it couldn't hurt especially since I'd be driving several hours this evening. "You're right. A snooze is in order." I stood and stretched my arms above my head as far as they would extend. "There's plenty of time to change out of these jeans and pack a sandwich before I leave."

~**4**~

Although I wasn't delighted with rearranging my plans this morning, I must admit subbing first graders sounded mighty appealing compared to the usual boring routine of eating, sleeping, and being forced to listen to Aunt Zoe's up-to-the-minute gossip concerning both residents and movie stars. After hearing her babble away non-stop, the thought of a pleasant classroom experience excited me.

The second I entered the hallowed halls of Washington Elementary I spotted a woman I had been purposely avoiding for the past four months, Gertie Nash. Darn, there's nowhere to run. I couldn't escape her two-hundred pounds of flesh. Her body blocked my entrance into the school secretary's office.

Known for her complete color coordination from head to toe, Gertie reminded me of lemon meringue pie today, a dessert I could easily pig out on every day of the week but didn't relish thinking about in this setting. I couldn't tell you how long the woman's been appearing in public like this since I haven't known her long, but I did wonder if she had a good wig connection before spray on hair coloring came into vogue. Cheryl, a fellow teacher of mine, relied on one of three wigs on her bad hair days, Monday, Wednesday, and Friday, the mornings after she had partied late into the night.

Gertie spoke first. "Why, Mary, what are you doing here?"

"Funny, I was about to ask you the same thing."

The heavyset woman's tiny feet propelled her backwards into the office a few steps, barely making room for me. "I volunteer once a week in my grandson's classroom. It gives him more Grandma time," she explained. "Oh, my, gosh, Mary, you should see little Billy when I show up." She thrust her wide hands in the air. "His eyes almost pop out of their sockets."

"Cute. I bet his teacher reacts the same way."

"Ah huh."

Apparently she didn't catch my sarcasm.

"You wouldn't believe how excited Yolanda is to see me. Some volunteers are just too incompetent for her, if you know what I mean," and then she winked. "So, tell me, are you a volunteer too? Maybe we could rideshare."

After four months of unemployment, I finally appreciated the fact I didn't get over to Washington Elementary too much. There's no way I'd get caught dead or alive riding around town with Gertie. "No, I'm not a volunteer. I'm filling in for Rosalie Cunningham, a first grade teacher."

The middle-aged woman rubbed her thick hands on her jeans. "Oh, right. I forgot. When we first met, you told me you were a teacher. Say, I felt bad you didn't make it to Butch's book signing. He really wanted to talk to you about his problem."

"Something important came up," I lied. *Like not wanting to be there.* "Sorry I missed it." I eyed my watch. "Oh, my, gosh, where's the time gone? The kids will be arriving soon. I better get signed in. We don't want Rosalie's students wandering the halls."

Gertie let loose with a snort. "Yes, you definitely don't want to keep those little darlings waiting. No telling what mischief they'd get into." She bumped my arm for emphasis. I nodded. "Now remember, don't forget about Butch. I still want you to meet him."

"Believe me, I won't forget." *But I wish I could.* "I'll look over my schedule as soon as I get the chance," I said, knowing I wouldn't.

Georgette Swift, the school secretary, smiled sweetly at me as she plucked a clipboard off her overloaded desk and handed it and a brand new Bic pen to me. "Here, Mary."

"Thanks." I bent over, hurriedly scribbled my name on the sheet of paper attached to the clipboard, and then passed the clipboard back to Georgette, minus the pen. "There you go." The newly acquired Bic pen felt good in my hand, but only for a mere second. Number cruncher Georgette doesn't let anything slip by her. "I see you're still collecting pens," she teased. She held out her well-manicured hand and waited. I obliged. As soon as the pen hit her hand, it disappeared into a desk drawer. Thinking I had completed the sign in process, I turned to leave, but Georgette delayed me further. Apparently she had another tidbit to impart. "Did you hear the latest news flash?"

"You mean about the missing college student up north?" I said.

"Nope, although she was mentioned again today too."

"What is it? What happened?" Gertie questioned excitedly.

"There was a huge jewel heist."

"You're kidding." Wanting to know more, I inched nearer the secretary's desk again. "Here in Minnesota?"

"Ah, huh."

"Don't tell me Lubeck's at the Mega Mall got hit?" It's the largest jewelry store in our state.

Georgette rifled through a bundle of notes on her desk. "No. It's… it's someplace in Grand Marais." She snapped her fingers. "Darn, my mind's a blank. I can't seem to recall the name."

Gertie's abundant body drew closer to mine. "Does the name Clarity Diamonds and Gems ring a bell?"

The secretary banged her hand on the desk. "Yup, that's it."

"Well, I've certainly never heard of them," I quietly stated, hoping no one gave me grief over my limited knowledge of jewelry companies. As it turned out no one cared.

Gertie's whale of a mouth opened wide as she extended her flabby arms over Georgette's desk. "Wow! Clarity got hit. I can't believe it. Why, those thieves tapped the mother lode. Thousands of gems pass through Clarity's doors every year."

"Hold on," I said, "I thought precious stones brought into the U.S., including diamonds, always ended up in New York for cutting."

"Not all of them," Georgette said, "Many states have businesses offering cutting and polishing. In fact, Minnesota has two cutting facilities."

"And, Clarity happens to be one of them?"

Gertie plopped her large hands on her hips. "Nope. Clarity manufactures jewelry. They create the coolest gem jewelry like the necklace my Ralphie gave me last Christmas. See." She slid her thick hand under the one inch silver floral design dangling from a chain around her neck. The diamond chip in the center of the daisy looked like a speck of dust.

Speck of dust or not, jealousy didn't care. It reared its ugly head. *Gertie's got you over a barrel, Mary. You're nowhere near finding a permanent man.* My hand flew to a pumpkin designed earring on my earlobe. Why should my ears be decorated with fake gold? I deserved to have big fat, gaudy diamonds displayed on my body just as much as the next woman. "Nice," I mumbled.

Gertie must've digested the thoughts swirling in my noggin. She patted my arm briefly. "Don't you fret, Mary, one of these days the right guy will come along. You'll see."

I slipped my hand out from under hers. I didn't want sympathy, especially Gertie's. This gal just needed a crash course on how to meet the right guy. I offered a brisk good-bye and sped off to Rosalie's first grade classroom where I could forget my boyfriend woes for the afternoon at least.

The moment I entered the ill teacher's room, I set my belongings aside and hurriedly glanced at the daily lesson planner sitting on her desk, making sure I understood what needed to be covered for the day. According to Rosalie's notes, I'd barely have to lift a finger to earn my wages. What a waste of money. The school could've saved a bundle by hiring a babysitter instead. *Just be happy they didn't, Mary.*

My first official duty went off without a hitch, getting the children under control when they returned from recess. In less than ten minutes the kids were raring to go. If it had been winter, they'd have taken at least a half-hour to settle down.

I quickly gave the order to line up single file and then whisked the students down the hall to their first class of the afternoon, computer lab.

The school hired a permanent instructor for this special class a couple years ago, so I planned to relax and let the man do his thirty minute spiel on his own. Of course it didn't take long for this single gal sitting on the sidelines to figure out this class isn't all it's cracked up to be, especially when a hunk of a man wearing Brut cologne walks past said female every two seconds. Talk about losing control. There's no denying the guy's one hot dude. I just can't believe he and his wife have a fourth adoring child on the way.

When the bell finally rang for the students to move on, this gal was ecstatic; my sweaty palms couldn't have remained hidden from the instructor's view much longer. Not much escapes his roving eyes.

The twenty-five first graders must've sensed my predicament too. They flew out of the computer lab in nothing flat and vanished into the smelly bathrooms not far from there.

Upon returning to Rosalie's classroom, I handed the little darlings a science test, one their teacher had prepared. Oh, the moaning and groaning. You'd thought I'd told the kids chocolate didn't exist.

Twenty minutes later the art teacher took over with a leaf project. The kids traced, cut, and glued paper leaves together, creating a fun mess. All part of the school art experience.

Once art wrapped up, I quickly gathered the children into the reading corner where I'd have exactly a half-hour to read the *Lion King* or so I thought. A light tap-tapping coming from the classroom door immediately cut into the reading time. *Probably office personnel handing out take-home forms before the buses come*, I thought. Instead of getting up and trying to maneuver through the maze of children surrounding me on the floor, I pointed to the door monitor child. She could see who desired entrance into the room.

An unidentified person about five feet four in height leapt into the room before the girl had a chance to ask anything. I say about five feet four because the high-formed mask covering the face and the unique lion skin draping the upper body threw me for a loop. *Oh, no. It can't be Aunt Zoe. She wouldn't do this to me, would she? You're not thinking rationally, Mary. How would she get here? She doesn't drive. Okay. So, maybe the teacher I'm subbing for planned this and forgot to tell me.* After accepting the second scenario, my jumpiness smoothed out considerably.

In the meantime, as I sorted things out, the kids took it upon themselves to investigate the new arrival and welcome him or her into their fold by tugging at the fringes of the pretend lion's clothing. I have to tell you, twenty-some kids surrounding any type of lion real or otherwise can be extremely dangerous. Our visiting lion had a heck of a time trying to keep from being bowled over.

"All right kids step back. Miss Malone has to get the lion's name first before we can visit with him. Remember, we don't talk to strangers even if it's a lion."

The lion roared and then indicated it wanted me to come closer. I suspected so it could share words out of earshot of the children. I inhaled deeply, worrying what I might hear. This could be an ambush. What if the masked person happened to be a single dad who didn't have visitation rights? *There's always the option to jump back if they're loony, Mary. True.* Here goes nothing. I nervously scooted forward.

"After you left for school," the female voice whispered, "I remembered bringing this lion stuff back from Africa and thought how neat it would be for the kids to see."

What a low blow. How dare she use the kids for her defense? She's supposed to be hanging out at our apartment. I pressed my sweaty fingers firmly against my temples. "Auntie, you shouldn't be here. If someone saw you, we could be in a heap of trouble. The school has strict security policies in place nowadays." I pictured the principal arriving any minute and booting us both out the door without allowing me to explain about my aunt's eccentric shenanigans.

"Why, Mary, I'm surprised you'd think I'd just waltz in here unannounced. I stopped in the office first."

I swallowed hard. "You did?"

"Of course."

"What kind of story did you offer the secretary?"

"I told her you were expecting me."

"Figures. I'll be lucky if they ever let me substitute here again."

Aunt Zoe let out another roar. For the sake of the children I suppose. They laughed on cue. "See how the kids eat this up, Mary. I know you said you'd get the book from the library, but I just couldn't stand missing out on seeing what joy the students get from hearing you read, and seeing a big lion to boot."

I had a devil of a time controlling my anger. "I'd shove you out the door this second if I knew the kids wouldn't go home upset. By the way, how did you manage to get here? Did Reed drive you?"

Before I got an answer, several children latched on to Aunt Zoe's arm right below her lion tattoo and pulled her towards the reading corner. "Come on, Mister Lion. We've got a special spot saved for you."

Oh, boy. If I didn't do something by the count of three, there's going to be pandemonium. There's nothing worse than being forced into the second or third tier of a circle when something or someone interesting shows up. Everyone wants the front row seat. Luckily, the perfect remedy came to mind. I patted the chair by mine. "Children, this seat's reserved for Mr. Lion. He's on his feet all day and needs a good resting spot."

Aunt Zoe got the hint and said in a deep husky voice, "Thank you. I appreciate the chair, Miss Malone. My paws get awfully tired wandering around the jungle from sun up till sundown."

The children who had been trying to control the lion immediately dropped to the floor where the others were already sitting. Then Aunt Zoe wiggled her costumed body down onto the tiny seat. "Why, this is purrrfect for me." The kids laughed again.

"All right children," I said, "It's getting late. If you want to hear the whole story, you'll need to settle down."

***

"Come on, Mary. Grab your things and we'll skedaddle."

"I can't."

"Why not? The classroom's emptied out."

I pointed to the desks, chairs, and trash. "We've got to straighten up first. Then I have to write a note to the teacher so she knows exactly what her class accomplished today."

Aunt Zoe leaned up against a student's desk. "I understand about the note but why is tidying up the room the teacher's responsibility? Isn't that what a janitor gets paid for?"

I swiftly corrected her in regards to the title she provided in case one of the two school janitors overheard. One never knows who is touchy about their job title these days, and I certainly didn't want anyone taking it out on me. Subbing is part of my livelihood. "The person you once knew as janitor is now referred to as a maintenance engineer, Auntie. He's expected to fix any breakage, as well as control the flow of heat and air conditioning throughout the building."

I picked up a student's chair in the front row and balanced it on the desk it belonged to. "On top of that, the maintenance engineer is supposed to keep the washrooms and hallways spotless, empty wastebaskets and sweep all the floors. Whatever's left is the teacher's job."

"Hmm. I guess I better get cracking then." She swiftly moved to the back of the room and lined up the desks in neat rows.

When the desks and chairs were taken care of, I grabbed the metal wastebasket and bobbed up and down collecting scraps of paper the kids had dropped on the floor during art class. Of course, at the exact moment my butt mooned the classroom door, Georgette popped in to speak with me. "Good, I'm glad I caught you, Mary." I immediately straightened up and turned towards her. "Oh, Miss Zoe, I see you're still here too. I have to tell you the outfit you came to school in was simply delightful. Even the principal commented on it."

Oh, boy.

"Thanks."

Georgette tapped her narrow chin with her index finger. "As a matter of fact, I know someone who may want to borrow your getup."

"Really?"

Before more words exchanged concerning the lion outfit, I cut in. "What's up Georgette? Do you need a sub for tomorrow too?"

"No. Not that I'm aware of. But there happens to be an after school event scheduled for teachers tonight, and I wanted to make sure you were sticking around. Rosalie did mention the Mother—Daughter dinner, didn't she?"

"Ah, no. I don't recall her saying anything about it."

Georgette's hands flapped in front of us. "Oh, dear. Well, do you think you could fill in for her since she isn't here? We need all the help we can get."

I don't mind subbing, but a dinner function is another story. If I said, "Yes," I had no idea what I'd be getting myself into. It could be serving supper or worse—making it. Aunt Zoe's grayish-blue eyes pressured me to say, "No," but there's a fly in the ointment. I knew the teachers depended on the fund raisers for school trips, having been a full time educator at this particular school, and I couldn't possibly leave them in a bind. Of course, I also wanted to stay in the good graces of my ex-colleagues so they'd keep me in the sub loop.

Georgette must've sensed I was dragging my feet. She sweetened the pot. "Of course, the school would compensate you for your time." She bent at the waist and smoothed out the pleats in her navy blue knee-length skirt while she waited for a reply.

Compensation. A word this gal couldn't resist. I rested my hands on my panted waist. "Okay, sure. I'd be happy to help. What task did Rosalie volunteer for? Keep the coffee flowing? Fold fancy napkins?" These were minimal jobs I knew I could handle.

Aunt Zoe rudely interrupted. "But what about me? How am I supposed to get home, Mary?"

"How did you get here?"

"Your mom and dad made a surprise visit."

"Oops? I guess I never got around to telling them about our trip. Georgette, could you see if Gertie is still here? She lives in our building."

"Sure. I'll use the intercom." The gray-haired woman spun on her heels and sped out of the classroom, leaving flying paper in her wake.

"What if Gertie already left, Mary?"

"Call Reed. I'm sure he wouldn't mind coming to your rescue. In the meantime, we'd better let Margaret know our travel plans have changed again."

~5~

Friday

"Hey, Roomie, are you ready to hit the road?"

Aunt Zoe tossed her red-spiked head back and scanned the living room one more time before plucking a small brown paper bag and large chartreuse-colored Gloria Vanderbilt suitcase off the couch. "I guess. My mind's a bit fuzzy."

Whose isn't? They assigned me to waiting on tables at the mother-daughter function last night and then somehow I got demoted to pot scrubber. "Here's another pan, Mary." "Oops, sorry forgot one." By the time I left school, I felt like I had been driven crazy by Cinderella's stepsisters. But what's Auntie's excuse? After Gertie dropped her off, she sat in front of the TV all night.

Oh, no. Did she pick up a bug from one of the little darlings yesterday? I hope not. She's been so looking forward to this trip. I set the cheap beat-up suitcase I owned next to the TV stand and felt my aunt's forehead. "I think you might be running a slight fever. Maybe we should take your temperature."

She stepped back. "I don't have a fever. When I have one, you'll certainly know. I can't crawl out of bed, I'm as pale as a ghost, and I act like I'm ready to depart from this world."

I shook my head. After my close call with death at Reed Griffin's horse ranch this summer, I didn't want to think about death in any shape or form hanging out at anyone's doorstep, including mine. "You swear you're feeling all right, because there's no way we're leaving this apartment if you're not? Your health is more important than a dog and a silly writing project."

Dad's sister held up her hand like she wanted to take the pledge to swear off liquor. "I'm positive. There's absolutely nothing to fret about. I didn't sleep a wink last night, that's all."

"Hot flashes again or leg cramps?" I asked as I led her wildly clad body towards our entranceway.

"Neither."

I looked at her sternly. "Then what's the problem?"

"I'll explain later. Margaret's probably wondering where we are."

I peeked at my watch. "You're right." When I collected the keys off the narrow table, I again noted the brown bag Auntie clutched to her chest. "Bringing Uncle Edward on this trip?" Aunt Zoe's husband Edward died while they were on safari in Africa and she had him cremated there. The ironic thing is she keeps his ashes in a carved wooden bowl he purchased the day before he dropped dead unexpectedly. Lately, my aunt's taken it upon herself to disburse a few ashes wherever and whenever the mood strikes her.

"No. He has to stay here and guard our apartment."

"Ah, right." *Like ashes protect anything, including ones meager belongings.* I blew out a sigh of relief. Dead people should be buried six feet under and nothing less. I didn't want to hear the pitter patter of a ghost during the night. I jabbed the bag again. "If you've got goodies in there, you'd better be prepared to share with your two traveling companions or there's going to be a mutiny before the day's out."

My roommate let loose with a huge sigh. "It isn't edible."

"You're fibbing, right?"

Auntie shook her red head as we scooted out the door.

"Darn. I thought you bought us a huge bag of peanut M&M's to munch on."

"Don't tell me you've already forgotten what happened this summer when you spilled M&M's in your car?"

I poked our apartment key in the keyhole and locked up. "Ah, no. How could I? It's not every day a horse sticks its head in a car window and eats the steering wheel."

"Thank goodness that incident's behind us."

Not according to my bank balance.

As we crossed the fourth floor to Margaret's apartment, another renter stepped into the hallway and startled us. Crap! Remember how much I didn't want to run into Gertie? Well, seeing Rod Thompson, the FBI agent I mentioned earlier, is ten times worse. How did I forget he departs for work around seven?

"My, my, my," the Nordic male voice boomed down the dimly lit hall, "if it isn't Lucy and her sidekick Ethel." (He's referring to now-deceased actresses Lucille Ball and her cohort Vivian Vance.) "I love the tiger theme you've got going there, Zoe. And Mary, look at you. Wow! You're sufficiently clad this morning. I'm impressed."

I ground my teeth. Leave it to Rod to get a dig in where he could. He happened to be in Matt's apartment twice without my knowledge and both times he found me in my undies. Why did this throwback to the Vikings, a blond, clean-shaven man dressed as slick as they come in a crisp Brooks Brother's navy blue suit, have to keep bringing up such embarrassing moments in my life? *Because he likes to see you squirm, Mary.*

"So, what clandestine mission are you two sneaking off to today?"

Boy, would I love to get in this guy's face. If only I stood another whole eight inches taller. "Rod, I told you I'm not listening to anymore of Matt's work related messages. Solving the crimes at the horse ranch happened to be a onetime deal. It wiped me out."

His face tightened considerably. "Glad to hear it. Tracking down bad guys is a job for professionals who have been properly trained, not for amateurs." His hand swung out in a wide arc and landed on our luggage. "What's with the suitcases then?"

My lips remained sealed for a moment. I had to carefully choose my words before they tumbled into Rod's world. Sharing about the book research would definitely supply the guy with a lifetime of joke material. Hmm? What to say? A few plausible replies passed through my brain cells.

In the end I played it safe and cut to the core. "We're going to my cousin's."

"She lives in Duluth," Aunt Zoe pleasantly added.

"Well, just don't get into any hot water while you're there. You won't have good friends like me to save your skin or to keep gossip at bay back here at the Foley." He set his hand on my shoulder like he owned it. *Two can play this game,* I thought. I reached for my purse's shoulder strap and pretended to adjust it. Rod got the hint and removed his hand.

"There's no need to worry about us Rod," Aunt Zoe kindly shot back, "How much trouble can one dog be?"

Rod scrunched his face up. "You're babysitting a dog?"

"Yes," I snapped, "anything wrong with that?"

"Ah, no, of course not. But you had mentioned a cousin."

I shook my head. What a dope he can be sometimes. How the heck does he function at the FBI? *Oh, right, I forgot he's a computer geek. His world revolves around silence not humans.* I forced a grin. "The poodle requires attention while my cousin recoups from surgery at a health care facility."

"Ah... Mary, speaking of attention, isn't it about time for the two of us to chow down again at Ziggy Piggy's Barbecue joint and squeeze in a little line dancing to boot."

I squirmed. Rod didn't notice.

"Let's talk this Sunday night and arrange it, okay?"

Is he crazy? Yes, I love Ziggy Piggy's fattening food, but I hate line dancing and he knows it. This past summer when Rod dragged me on Ziggy Piggy's outdated dance floor to get even with me, my legs tangled up like a pretzel and I fell on my fat fanny. Then again if I hadn't fallen, David Miller, an undercover cop using the name Clint Russell, would've never offered me assistance. The hunk, a spitting image of a young Clint Eastwood, swept me off the floor literally and offered to buy me a drink. What gal in her right mind could refuse such an offer?

Rod moved towards the elevator. Apparently he didn't need a reply.

Too bad Aunt Zoe deemed it necessary. "Don't bother calling, Rod," she spit out, "We won't be here."

He waved and then vanished into the elevator.

"Do you think he heard me, Mary?"

"No, but it looks like others did." Several residents stood in the hallway giving us cold stares. At least our traveling companion didn't share their sentiments.

"There you are," the elderly woman said, dressed all prim and proper in a plain beige pant suit. "I wondered what happened to you. You're usually so punctual."

"We bumped into Rod," I explained, "We couldn't break loose."

Margaret smiled. "I understand, "On days I'm in a hurry, he drills me to death."

~**6**~

It took a while to figure out how to squeeze everyone's belongings into Fiona's tight trunk but we finally succeeded. *Yay.* We were on our way. Well, not quite. A tiny hiccup occurred. No, Gertie didn't get her claws into me before we pulled out of the Foley's underground parking nor did anyone buzz me to sub. But after driving a mere two blocks from the apartment building, it dawned on me perhaps I should check the gas gauge, something I had planned on doing yesterday at the end of my short school day. Of course, as you and I both know, an early departure didn't pan out for me. Events beyond my control kept me in the school kitchen till after nine o'clock: too long a day for anyone to still be on their feet including this chick. I only managed to stay awake on the drive home thanks to thoughts of stuffing my face with a huge bowl of chocolate caramel delight ice cream while watching a favorite sitcom on TV.

All I can say is it does pay to check your fuel gauge before driving any distance. Fiona's tank displayed empty. If I hadn't checked when I did, my companions would've been stranded on the freeway while I hoofed it in my too tight tennis shoes to the nearest gas station.

While I stood at the gas pump taking care of the car, I noticed Aunt Zoe fiddling in the front seat with the brown bag I originally thought contained goodies. When I finally returned to the driver seat,

I discovered what she had been up to. "I guess silk flowers aren't edible."

"I hope not. You'd get too much indigestion."

"Even though you told me there wasn't any candy in the bag, Auntie, I secretly hoped there was," I fluffed the flowers up a bit, "But this surprise is even better. I meant to do something about the empty vase, but hadn't gotten around to it yet. Thanks for sprucing up, Fiona."

"You're welcome. I knew you'd be happy to see the flowers."

Margaret leaned forward in her seat. "Where did you find such beautiful rust-colored mums Zoe? I'd love to get a similar bouquet for the flower pot outside my apartment door."

Auntie scratched her spiked hair. "I'm not sure where they originally came from. I found this bunch in the laundry room wastebasket."

"The wastebasket? But they look brand new," our elderly neighbor crisply stated.

I shifted the car into drive, stepped on the gas, and eased into the flow of traffic. "Maybe someone's significant other thought they were ugly and decided to stuff them where the other party would never find them."

Aunt Zoe threw her hands up in the air. "Anything's possible I guess. Thankfully, their loss is our gain."

I agreed wholeheartedly. "You've got that right."

I clicked on the left blinker indicating my intention to merge onto the interstate. When my hand came back to rest on the steering wheel, Auntie quietly placed her hand over mine. Since she doesn't drive, I had no idea what she wanted. She soon filled me in. "Dear, I don't think you're going the right way."

"What makes you say that?"

She released my hand. "Interstate 94 is up ahead. You said I'm supposed to help you watch for 35W."

"Sorry. I guess I should've explained our route a little better before we took off. We have to be on 94 first and then connect with 694 going west."

"Well, that still isn't 35W."

"I know. I know. Let me finish. After we get on 694, then you need to keep your eyes peeled for 35W."

Aunt Zoe sat back and allowed her head to press against the upper part of the car seat. "Oh? Well, I guess I'll read until we get on 694 then." She reached in her huge Zebra print purse resting in her lap, pulled out a novel by Danielle Steel, and opened it to where she'd left off.

"Mary, what time did you tell your cousin we'd be arriving?" our companion in the back seat inquired.

When one's back is to the party asking questions, especially in a car, it's nice to know one can maintain a friendly conversation by simply adjusting the rearview mirror. When I peered into the mirror, I caught our neighbor working on a multi-colored crochet project. "I think I mentioned eleven. I wanted us to have ample time to stop at the welcome center and also get a morning snack at Tobies in Hinckley."

Aunt Zoe stopped reading. "I don't know about Margaret, but I've always got room for sweets." Her stomach growled loudly in agreement. "What did I tell you?"

"I have no objection in regards to munchies," Margaret said in her defense, "But we don't have to stop to buy any goodies this morning, ladies."

"Why not?" Auntie and I said in unison.

"I took it upon myself to pack homemade treats for us. I hope you don't mind."

I shot a glance my aunt's way. "I don't mind, do you?"

"Heavens no."

"Good," Margaret replied, "It didn't make sense to stop at a bakery when all of us live on shoestring budgets these days."

I smiled to her in the mirror for her benefit. "Thanks for the thoughtful gesture, Margaret. The snack must be in the blue cooler bag I put in the trunk, huh?"

"*Si*. I assume you won't have trouble finding a good spot for our break, Mary."

"I'm sure I'll find the perfect place."

With our thoughts on morning treats out of the way, Margaret began humming and swiftly returned to her crochet project. I on the other hand directed my attention to my front seat passenger. "Auntie, I believe it's time to clone Margaret. If we don't, we're going to be stuck in a hollow somewhere starving to death."

"Watch out, Margaret, you'd better run for the hills while you can," Aunt Zoe teased. "I don't think I can stop my niece from following through on her devious plan."

The three of us had a good laugh and then silence ensued.

Fifteen minutes later I interrupted my fellow traveler's thoughts. "Do you gals mind listening to the radio while we're tooling along? It helps break up the monotony."

"Fine with me," Margaret said, "I always use the radio for background noise when I'm at home."

"What about you, Auntie? Will it interfere with your reading?"

"No. Not a chance." She reached for the radio scanning dial. "Do you prefer a talk show, or one with suitable music?"

I lifted a hand off the steering wheel. "You pick. I need to concentrate on exiting onto 694. The traffic gets a bit hairy around here."

A couple minutes after Aunt Zoe had selected WCCO, a Twin Cities radio station, the early morning talk show host got interrupted by a fellow news reporter. Must be some earth shattering news worth sharing that couldn't wait till the top-of-the-hour, I thought. Since there were no political offices up for grabs this year, I assumed it might be about a major flu epidemic this coming season or a foreign country having invaded a neighboring country. But the news flash didn't pertain to either.

"This just in—Troy Shell, president of Clarity Diamond and Gems Company, announced that police think the jewel theft of the Grand Marais manufacturing plant took place around the middle of the night when only a skeleton crew is on duty. All employees are being questioned. Information regarding any leads and how much the thieves got away with is still not being disclosed."

When the Clarity story ended, Margaret rested her hands on the back of my shoulders indicating she required my attention. I turned the radio volume down slightly and stole a look in the rearview mirror. "What is it Margaret? Do you need to take a break?"

"No, dear. The reporter happened to jar a trivial matter I had stashed away. Do you remember the story about the people who busted into a jeweler's car last year? It occurred at a rest stop in southern Minnesota."

"Yeah. Hey, didn't that take place around October too?

"*Si.*"

"The jeweler and his companions had been returning from an international gem and diamond show in Chicago," I explained to Aunt Zoe since she wasn't in the country at the time. "The thieves must've scoped them out the minute they arrived at the show."

Aunt Zoe shifted her large-boned body so it faced me. "Do you recall what ended up being the final tally on the stones taken, Mary?"

"Roughly a half-million, I think."

Auntie let loose with a piercing whistle.

"It wouldn't surprise me if the same greedy bunch hit the Clarity Diamond and Gem facility," Margaret said, "Criminals on the prowl tend to repeat their actions over and over."

I tapped my hands on the steering wheel. "I bet whoever stole the gems from Clarity's has already dashed across the border into Canada. There's no way they'd be stupid enough to hide out here and get arrested. It doesn't make sense."

"But what if you're wrong, Mary?" Aunt Zoe daringly stated. "If the crooks think it's too dangerous to slip away, maybe they're still hanging out up north somewhere until things cool off a bit. Anyone know how far Grand Marais is from Duluth?"

"About a hundred and ten miles," I informed her.

"And how long does it take to get there by car?"

"Approximately two," Margaret hastily shared.

"Hmm. That's less road time than we're putting in today, right?"

I nodded. "What's going on in that head of yours, Auntie?"

She grinned. "I think Clarity's going to be forced into announcing a mighty hefty reward."

The elderly woman sitting behind me finally released her pressure on my shoulders. "*Si*, Zoe's right, especially if the investigation continues to stall."

"Ah, now I see where this conversation's headed. Don't you dare say another word, Auntie."

She ignored me. "But, Niece, if we found those diamonds we'd be set for life. All we have to do is combine Margaret and your sleuthing skills with my diamond and gem knowledge. How hard can that be?"

"I don't care how hard it is or isn't. Count me out. There's no way I'm hunting down the people who pulled the Clarity theft off. They're in a bind. Who knows what they're capable of?"

Margaret agreed. "Cornered people can become extremely dangerous. If you want a safe case, Zoe, see what Gertie's nephew wants instead."

I squeezed the steering wheel. "Whoa! Slow down, Margaret. We're not going in that direction either. Although, I wouldn't mind tackling a case involving searching for say a lost relative. It could prove to be quite lucrative too."

"Searching for someone — like Matt's case concerning the elusive Brad Harper?" Margaret questioned.

"Yeah," I replied. As long as it doesn't involve the kind of danger Matt found himself in once he got too close to Harper."

The nonagenarian sighed. "According to Matt, every case has its pitfalls."

Aunt Zoe tapped my arm. "Why did you tell Rod Thompson you weren't taking on another case, Mary, if you really planned to?"

"I've learned to tell Mister Thompson exactly what he wants to hear. When a person's scrimping to make ends meet, you take whatever you can get unless it sounds extremely dangerous. Anyway, don't worry, Auntie. No one's hounding us to help them with any case, so what I told Rod is true for the moment."

~7~

With only ten minutes left of drive time, we stopped for a short break at Duluth's scenic overlook welcome center. While there, we took advantage of the facilities: perusing mounds of free brochures, devouring Margaret's homemade cinnamon rolls, and attending to our personal needs.

Fifteen minutes later, upon merging with the interstate traffic again, I warned everyone our exit should be coming up soon. "Be on the lookout for the Aerial Lift Bridge sign. That's where I need to turn off."

Driving straight ahead to the town itself now everything appeared neat and clean. So tidy in fact, new people to this northern region would never suspect one of the worst floods on record washed out parts of Duluth and its zoo just a couple years back.

Aunt Zoe suddenly nudged me and directed me to the right lane. I obeyed and zipped off as she suggested. Guess what? We weren't heading for the Lift Bridge. If I continued along the street she readily recommended, the VW and the three of us would eventually be taking a cold bath in Lake Superior. Maybe Uncle Edward, Aunt Zoe's deceased husband, had it right. She wasn't good with directions. *Hmm? Perhaps I'd better switch out the front seat passenger for the ride home. Surely Margaret won't mind.*

The very next intersection I came to I scanned the surroundings and spotted the Lift Bridge. Unfortunately, because of road construction, there didn't seem to be a way to reach it. *Better stop and figure things out.* I moved up a block, gently squeezed Fiona between two cars, left the car running, and grabbed the Duluth city map from my aunt's lap where it had been resting since leaving the welcome center.

Two seconds later a well-chiseled police officer rapped his knuckles on my window. *What does he want? I didn't break any driving rules.* I tossed the map back on my aunt's lap, pushed the button to bring the driver's window down, and immediately laid on the charm. "Good morning, Officer," I said with my best cheesy grin, "Beautiful fall day, isn't it?"

The mid-thirty, light-skinned cop tugged on his dark-blue cap visor, said "Yup," and then shot a grin my way. It didn't last long. "I'm going to have to ask you to move your car across the road, Miss. You're parked in a *no parking zone.*"

"I am? Wow, I had no idea." I whipped off my sunglasses and glanced along the curbing where the car idled. Sure enough a rectangular sign sat next to the car, the same height and size as seen along the streets in busy downtown Minneapolis, warning drivers this particular spot wasn't available for regular parking, just deliveries for Little Angie's Cantina. *Ah, crum!* I turned back to the officer, batted my eyelashes like Aunt Zoe did when she first met Reed, and begged for sympathy. "Officer, you aren't going to hand a newly-arrived-visitor a ticket, are you? I only pulled over because I'm lost."

He lowered himself a smidgen and locked his gray heavy set eyes on mine. "You've got nothing to worry about, ma'am. I don't pass out tickets to first time offenders, I give warnings. So, where exactly are you ladies headed? If it's not too far, you can follow me."

Aunt Zoe leaned her head closer to mine. "We need to cross the Lift Bridge," she informed him.

"Going to Park Point, huh?"

I nodded.

He pointed south. "Turn at this next corner. At the end of the block hook a left on Lake Avenue and continue towards the water. You can't miss it."

"The first road I'm turning on isn't one-way, is it?" I only asked because I didn't want a black and white to pull me over the minute I reached the other side of the bridge due to another stupid mistake.

"Nope, it's two-way."

"Okay," I set my sweaty palms on the steering wheel again, "appreciate the help."

The charming cop tipped his hat. "No problem. Enjoy your time here, ladies."

"We will," my companions and I pleasantly chirped.

I popped the window back up and swiped my forehead. "Whew. That's too close for comfort. I'd better be more alert to the signs around here. I can't afford to donate anything to the city of Duluth."

Aunt Zoe patted my knee. "Certainly not. If you're going to give money away, it should be to Minneapolis. We dwell in that city after all."

Margaret coughed.

"Are you okay back there?" I asked, knowing full well what Margaret meant by the fake cough. Another zany comment had spewed forth from Auntie's mouth.

"I'm fine," she said, "I must've gotten a bit of yarn fuzz in my mouth."

I stared into the rearview mirror and gave her a quick wink.

Auntie continued on oblivious to the prattle between Margaret and me. "He seemed nice, didn't you think, Mary?"

"Who?"

"The cop. And he was good-looking to boot."

"I didn't notice," I lied, "I came to Duluth to do research not check out guys."

"I'm just saying…"

I glanced in the side mirror to make sure the coast was clear before I pulled out of the parking spot and made a quick right at the end of the corner. "Aunt Zoe, I know where you're going and I'm not interested. We're only here a few days. A woman needs more time than that to figure out what a man's agenda is or if he's the real deal."

"But look at me and Reed. The first day I set eyes on him I knew we were meant for each other."

Margaret rushed to my defense. "You're in the minority, Zoe. Look how long it took Mary and David to figure each other out this summer."

"A lot of good it did. Their relationship's stuck on hold. What my niece needs to do is check out other options while she's waiting."

"Then let her jump into the lake when she's ready," the nonagenarian suggested, "A woman can never be too careful in this day and age."

"Amen," I added.

~8~

When we got to Lake Avenue several cars were already lined up ahead of us waiting for the all clear signal to go across. Better them than me, I thought. I'd probably jump the gun, lurch forward before the bridge locked, and end up ten feet under visiting the fish.

"Oh, look Mary. The bridge is finally coming down," Aunt Zoe exclaimed.

"I'm glad I'm not sitting in the control booth," I said, "Make one wrong decision and you're tuna."

"But if you did work up there," Margaret said, "think of the fantastic view you'd have of Lake Superior. You'd be able to see down into every cargo ship, sailboat, or other watercraft traveling through."

Hmm. That means I'd see all those good-looking muscular guys hard at work. Nah, I still didn't want the job.

As I followed the other cars across the lift bridge now, I tried to recall Lizzie's exact instructions for getting to her apartment. "Drive straight ahead on Lake Avenue till you see Franklin Park. That's where Lake suddenly merges with Minnesota Avenue. Once you're on Minnesota, watch for the apartment sign."

The instant I caught sight of the street sign leading to the Del Rosa Apartment complex, I began to worry whether Cousin Lizzie remembered about her keys. If her daughter didn't drop them off with the apartment manager, I'd have to drive back to the main part of Duluth and find the facility she's staying at. My roommate and I, and I suspected Mrs. Grimshaw too, certainly couldn't afford to stay in a hotel.

I took a right turn off Minnesota Avenue onto Huckleberry Lane too sharply and almost smacked into a faded olive-green 2 foot sign boldly heralding our arrival at the complex. The close call forced me to straighten the car tires a bit before taking a left onto the actual premises, seeking an empty *guest* slot, and parking.

I plucked my purse off the floor by the gas pedal, pulled the key from the ignition, and then peered in the rearview mirror. The mirror thing's a habit of mine. Before I duck out of a car, I always check to make sure I look presentable. I'm not a narcissist if that's what you're thinking. No way. I just never know who I might run into. It could be a parent of a student I taught or an old boyfriend.

Yikes. I bet I scared the heck out of that cop back there in Canal Park. My not so stylish hairdo was lacking any fluff thanks to the strong winds that skipped through the parking lot at the welcome center. Too lazy to dig out my comb, I lifted my hand to run it through my hair. As I did so, I noted a fenced off marina across the street. It stuck out like a sore thumb against the backdrop of the seemingly idyllic surroundings.

The second I stepped out of Fiona, I pointed out the marina to my companions. Both wondered aloud how noisy it got around the Del Rosa apartments in the summertime with boats jetting in and out of the area at all hours. With no resident present to give us an answer, we promptly moved from the parking lot to the lengthy walkway, lightly covered by maple leaves. Five newly planted red maples were to blame. They dotted the landscape leading up to the outer entrance of the light-sand colored four story brick building.

Three men, two in their late twenties and one in his early twenties, rounded the corner of the building as we were preparing to go in. Two carried rakes the other some tarps and string. All wore short cropped hair and were dressed in similar garb: short sleeved shirts, jeans, and sandals. They greeted us with a hasty "Good morning," and then hustled off.

"Must be cleaning the grounds before the snow comes," I said.

"Which could happen any day," Margaret added, crossing her arms over her buttoned down sweater.

Upon entering the first set of glass doors, I quickly scanned the metal buzzers mounted on the left wall, looking for the one labeled manager. A woman with a sing-song, jazzy voice immediately answered. "Hello. This is Virginia Bagley. How can I help you?"

"Virginia, this is Mary Malone. I'm taking care of Lizzie Connor's dog for a few days. Did her daughter leave apartment keys for me?"

"Excuse me. Who did you say you were?"

I rested a hand on the top of my head for a second. "Mary Malone. Lizzie Connor's cousin."

"Ah, yes. Her keys are sitting right here on my desk. Just give me a sec. I need to release the lock on the inner door for you." A loud grinding noise soon penetrated my ears, forcing me to step away from the door for a second. "Okay. You should be able to pop into the main lobby. The elevator's on the left. Do you know Lizzie's apartment number?"

I hooked my hand on the handle of the unlocked door and pulled it open a bit so it didn't return to lock position. "Yes."

"Good. I'll meet you on the third floor by her apartment."

I replied with a jazzy tone of my own. "Okay." Then I signaled the gals to follow close behind, swung the door open as far as it would go, and marched over to the waiting elevator.

"What about the suitcases?" Aunt Zoe asked after the elevator doors had already encased us, "Aren't we bringing them up, Mary?"

I flicked my hand. "Nah. I'll get them later when I bring Lizzie's dog outside. I'm sure the dog's bladder's ready to burst after being kenneled so long."

The minute we stepped off the elevator unto the dark-chocolate carpeted hallway, I caught sight of a woman, roughly the same height as myself, five-feet six, standing midway down the hall in soldier-like attention mode. *Gotta be Virginia*, I thought. I pointed the seventy-something woman out to my companions. "Can you believe it?" I whispered, "She moves faster than the building's transportation."

"And a speeding bullet," Aunt Zoe quietly joked, "Maybe she's the manager by day and superwoman by night."

"Shhh, she'll hear you," I warned.

Sensible Margaret added, "Maybe she's a marathon runner. Duluth is known for Grandma's Marathon you know."

"It's quite possible," I said. "Some runners have kept on going into their late eighties."

The well-coiffed bleached-blonde, clothed in a two-piece dark-brown pantsuit, greeted us with open arms. "Ladies, welcome to Duluth. I hope you enjoy your stay." When her hand dropped to retrieve an item from her pant pocket, thin gold bracelets encircling her wrist clinked together. "Here you go, Mary."

I curled my hand to accept the keys and noted the expensive looking stones gracing three of Virginia's fingers. *Nice. Either she treats herself or someone else does.* "Thanks." Thinking my business with her had concluded, I expected Virginia to leave, but she didn't budge from her spot. *Perhaps she wants to pass on a message to Lizzie since we'd be seeing her soon*, I thought.

Virginia Bagley's heavily rouged face grew taut. "I have to skedaddle, got a pot of stew on, but don't hesitate to call if you have any questions regarding Park Point or the surrounding area."

"Wait! What about rules concerning dogs?" I inquired, "Where do we exercise them?"

"Oh, yes, I forgot you'd need to know that since you're watching Lizzie's poodle. Well, many tenants take their dogs for a stroll along the beach; it can be accessed directly across the street from here. You just go up the sand dunes and over." She shook her head. "Although I don't think Lizzie does that sort of thing anymore, with her knee problems and her advancing age. But you're young, Mary. Winnie would love bounding up and down the beach with you."

"I don't know," I said, "The sand dunes we noticed on our way in here looked quite steep."

Virginia flapped her tightly-skinned hand, making her bracelets jingle again. "Nonsense. Don't be intimidated by them. They're not that hard to maneuver. The locals wouldn't take the shortcut unless it's to their advantage. And the walk is well worth the effort. Well, too-da-loo," and then she spun on her heels and zipped toward the stairwell.

Margaret drew up closer to Cousin Lizzie's door and poked an arthritic finger near the numbers attached to it. I hastily examined the area she directed our attention to, but didn't see anything. Either Margaret required new glasses or it's time for me to have my eyes examined. I didn't see a spider, box elder or any other tiny insect crawling around on the door. After inspecting Lizzie's door one more time, and still not finding anything I finally said, "Is there something wrong with this door?"

"Oh, no. I just realized it shouldn't be any trouble remembering which apartment we're staying in. It's the same number the Singi's have at the Foley." The Singi's, who live directly below Aunt Zoe and I, own the optical store I work at from time to time.

Aunt Zoe tossed her red head our neighbor's way. "Thanks for pointing it out. I can't tell you how many times I've paraded up to the wrong hotel room door only to learn the room hadn't been assigned to Edward and me."

Figures. I didn't dare add, *How about all the times you've tried to get into the wrong car?* The gem wouldn't be considered a joke and would only spark my aunt's moodiness.

Margaret finally inched back, allowing me access to the keyhole. I shoved the key in and the lock sprang open instantly not like some ornery ones I've had in the past. "All right, step in ladies. I'm anxious to see what my cousin's place looks like."

Aunt Zoe's hands settled over her heart the moment she caught a glimpse of the apartment interior. "My, what a charming upscale apartment your cousin has. It's decorated with such fine French flair." She inhaled deeply. "Mmmm, there's nothing like Paris in the springtime with the one you love."

Yeah, yeah. Whatever, I thought. *Not everyone's lucky enough to marry, let alone a rich dude.* Aunt Zoe moved further into the room allowing Margaret and me a better view of the fancy furniture she had gone gaga over. *Oh, boy. We shouldn't have stayed here. Her designing wheels are already spinning.* When we return to our humble abode in the cities my roomie's going to want to redecorate with France in mind, and there's no way I'll be able to stop her.

"I'm surprised Mom's never mentioned Lizzie's decorating style. It's really special." After realizing how my last words might have been interpreted by our Foley neighbor who has a super cute place, I hastily added, "Of course in decorating schemes it rates second place to yours, Margaret."

Her pale face displayed a tinge of pink coloring. "No need to score brownie points with me, Mary. Say what you like. I can take it. I won't fall apart."

I searched for a save. "But it's the truth. Tell her, Auntie." "Mary's right," she said as she continued to drool over each item, "Your Italian furnishings rate number one in my book too. I am a bit curious though; do you think Lizzie found her furniture in an antique store around here?"

"Probably not," I said, "A relative told us when Lizzie and her late husband finished their Peace Corp days in France they shipped a ton of stuff back to the States."

Margaret stared at the piece dè résistance, a French Provincial settee. "Obviously they had a knack for collecting the right pieces. This Louis XV replica is from the nineteenth century. The Grecian pattern in the wood framing gives it away."

My dad's sibling ran her pudgy hand across the smooth, red-brocade cushions. "It's amazing how well-preserved the fabric is."

"Like me," Margaret giggled.

Aunt Zoe's mouth remained agape as she took a few seconds to ponder Margaret's comment. "But you and the settee aren't anywhere near the same age."

"Close enough," she replied.

"So," Auntie began, "What would you say the age of—"

A soft whining winging its way from another room in the apartment swiftly derailed any further discussion of furniture. "I think that's the dog," our neighbor said.

"Yup, you're right" I replied, "She knows we're here. Why don't you two track her down and I'll hunt for the leash."

Margaret suggested she and Zoe investigate the kitchen and went off in that direction. Since I happened to be in the living room, I started there. Several seconds later, Auntie's voice boomed from the kitchen. "Winnie's out here and she's begging to be let out of jail. You'd better hurry with the leash."

"I'm trying." Finished examining the settee and matching chairs, I poked my head under the coffee table next, and then searched the hall closet. I found zilch.

"Mary," Aunt Zoe again, "The dog's going bonkers. Where's the leash?"

"I don't know."

"Too bad she can't tell you where it's at."

"Give me a few more seconds. I'll find it," I shot back. *No dog's going to make me look like an idiot.*

Our neighbor finally spoke up. "Mary, maybe we should give her a doggie treat to settle her down. When Petey's wound up, a cracker always works."

"Try it." Quite frankly, I didn't think anything would calm down Cousin Lizzie's antsy dog. The poodle had one thing on her mind, and only one thing, to release her tiny bladder anywhere but in her kennel. I wonder how long it'll be before she reaches her breaking point. Something tells me it would be sooner than later. *Yuk.* The thought of a kennel or kitchen floor flooded with pee revolted me.

Where could the darn leash be? I shoved the coffee table to one side, laid flat on the floor, and stared under the settee. *Ah hah.* One toy poodle's going to be extremely happy. A clump of dust surrounded the wayward leash begging to be claimed. I complied.

Holding the tightly coiled leash in one hand, I stood and straightened the coffee table, making sure to set the curved wooden legs directly over the circle imprints on the carpet. Hopefully Winnie hadn't peed in her kennel yet. After driving two hours on the freeway, and then almost getting a parking ticket when entering Duluth, I didn't feel like scrubbing the inside of a stupid cage. And I'd be the one stuck doing the dirty work since I'm the most agile.

I marched into the kitchen and waved the thin, black leather leash in front of the other women. "Let the pooch out. I'm ready."

The tiny silver ball of fluff watched Aunt Zoe's every move. As soon as the cage got unlocked, she nudged the door with her head and took off for our neighbor who happened to be resting comfortably in one of Cousin Lizzie's sleek, modern plastic and chrome chairs.

Margaret laughed. "I guess she knows who to come to for comfort."

"So it seems. Too bad it's going to be cut short." I knelt down, patted my hands on the cold tan linoleum floor, and said, "Down Winnie. Let's go outside." The twelve inch mutt immediately perked up at the mention of *outside.* She quickly joined me on the floor and yapped and pranced like crazy. *Getting a leash on this ball of motion could be my undoing*, I thought.

Catching a wound up poodle or any dog was an acrobatic feat of major proportions. It would be like trying to catch a youngster refusing to take a bath or snapping a picture of a hummingbird in flight. Thankfully, after some robust playfulness on Winnie's part, I finally got the upper hand and clipped her leash to the emerald-green collar studded with fake stones, encircling her neck. At least I thought the jewels were bogus. But what did I know? No one ever gave me jewelry. The few long term boyfriends I've had acted like Rocky Balboa, handing out cheap trinkets from a Cracker Jack box or a ticket to a boxing match.

"Good girl." While I struggled to get to my feet, I kept a firm grip on the leash. I didn't want a rambunctious dog tearing around an apartment knocking irreplaceable stuff off tables like Gracie did this past summer in our sublet apartment.

The second I got upright my stomach roared. Scared, the mutt jumped back. "At least my stomach knows what time it is," I told my companions, "How about doing lunch at Grandma's when I get back?"

Auntie appeared confused. "Aren't both your grandmothers deceased, Mary?"

"She's referring to a restaurant on the other side of the Lift Bridge," Margaret explained.

I displayed a grin. "Yup."

"Wuff, wuff. Wuff, wuff."

"Okay, Winnie, you're coming through loud and clear. Believe me, I don't want your bladder to explode either."

Saturday

I awoke with a start. An unrecognizable smell permeated the air. "No! I don't believe it. Not again." *She'd, better not be messing with my cousin's kitchen.* I refuse to clean up any more of Aunt Zoe's messes. I tossed back the off-white patchwork quilt, jumped out of bed, and ran to the kitchen. "Who's cooking—?"

Margaret Grimshaw greeted me in an upbeat tone while flipping something in a frying pan. "Good morning, Mary. I hope we didn't wake you." The mutt circled the elderly woman's legs hoping to catch a morsel of whatever she was making.

I quickly sucked in the needless worries I had fabricated in my mind and ran a hand through my tangled hair. "Of course not," I fibbed, "I've been up for a while. I just couldn't ignore the delicious aroma wafting into the bedroom any longer. I had to see what was cooking." Now that I knew Cousin Lizzie's kitchen hadn't been destroyed by one of my aunt's culinary disasters, I became aware of my bare feet and the well-worn two piece flannel PJ outfit clinging to my overweight body. *Oops.* In my haste to get to the kitchen I'd left my bathrobe and slippers behind.

Since I respected our prim and proper neighbor too much to appear at the table with my sleeping attire, I decided to make a hasty retreat. But before I could do so, Aunt Zoe lowered a copy of the

Duluth News Tribune she had been reading and said, "Mary, aren't you going to join us for breakfast?"

"Of course she is," Margaret replied, "She's the one who suggested blueberry pancakes."

I turned to face the two older women. "Yes, but if you recall I said I'd make them." Creating food according to directions found on a General Mills or a Kraft box was something this unemployed teacher excelled at.

Margaret shook her white head of hair. "I know you did, dear, but I've been out of bed since the birds first chirped. Once I'm up, it's hard for me to stay out of the kitchen."

And that's how I've added a few more pounds to my already voluptuous body in case you're wondering. Since moving into the Foley, Margaret's been there with her afternoon teas, desserts, and Italian meal invites. *Don't forget about the scrumptious caramel rolls in the morning.* Why, Auntie and I have become so spoiled by our Foley neighbor, I don't even know if we remember the correct procedure for obtaining a decent hardboiled egg. "Yes, but while we're here, I thought I'd repay you for the many meals you've made for us since we moved into the Foley."

"Well, if you feel so strongly about it, you can make supper."

Auntie smacked her hands. "Wonderful. What do you think you'll make, Mary?"

Open mouth insert foot. I coughed to cover a panic attack. "It's barely eight o'clock, too early to think about supper. I'll look through Cousin Lizzie's cookbooks later."

Margaret set a platter of finished pancakes on the table. "Breakfast is ready. Sit down."

"I will, but I want to grab my bathrobe and slippers first."

Our chef pulled out a chair and sat. "No, need to get covered up, dear. It's not like you're sitting at the table naked."

I glanced at my PJ's. "You sure? These jammies are rather holey."

Aunt Zoe patted the chair next to her. "Sit down, Mary. The pancakes are getting cold."

My stomach grumbled. "Okay. You win."

When I plopped down, Winnie scrambled under the table and remained there until I had downed my fourth, make that fifth pancake. Then out from the shadows she came, begging for crumbs. Too bad she chose the wrong woman. "No, Winnie," I said, "It's not good to have table scraps. You'll gain too much weight." I pointed to her food dish. She got the message.

"You're mean," Aunt Zoe said.

"Yeah, yeah. You're not the first person to tell me that. So, if I feed her like you want me to, do you plan to clean the upchuck she'll leave behind?"

Auntie shook her head.

"I didn't think so." I closed a hand around my juice glass, lifted it to my lips, and sampled the orange juice. Not my favorite brand but it would do.

My aunt quickly attempted to right things between us. "Mary, I thought you'd like to know I took the dog outside about three hours ago." Surprised by her bit of news since I assumed I'd be handling all doggie duties while here, I permitted a slight smile to emerge. Under her breath she added, "After Margaret suggested it."

Of course. I mouthed a generous *thanks* to our chef.

Aunt Zoe it seems wasn't quite finished filling me in. "So, I suppose she'll need to go out to do her duty in another hour."

"Not really, but I'm sure the exercise would be good for her as well as us." I pushed my plate away. If I had another blueberry pancake, I'd burst.

Margaret stacked her empty plate on mine. "Has anyone heard anything new on the jewel heist?"

"Not a peep." Aunt Zoe admitted, "I'd hoped there would be some news. I'm curious to hear the outcome."

I hurriedly cut the topic off at the knees. "Not me. How about the missing college student? Have they found her yet?"

"There's nothing in the paper regarding her either," Aunt Zoe replied.

"Huh? The police sure keep things hush hush up here. If those two incidents took place in the cities, a newsflash would be hitting the radio waves or TV screen every few seconds. Say, Auntie, how do you feel about taking a walk along the beach before I get too wrapped up in my research?"

She picked up a napkin and wiped her plump lips. "Sounds like fun, but we should include Margaret."

The elderly woman waved her petite age-spotted hands above the table. "Oh, no. I'd never make it over those sand dunes at my age. You two go and tell me about it when you get back."

Aunt Zoe appeared disappointed. "But I thought we'd planned to stick together like the Three Musketeers, 'All for one and one for all.'"

Our neighbor picked up the metal coffee pot sitting in the center of the table and refilled her coffee cup. "I'll be fine, Zoe. I'm going to attend a meeting for crossword puzzle lovers this morning. It's being held in the community room."

My aunt's usual perkiness returned. "Terrific. I'm glad to hear you're not going to be sitting here twiddling your thumbs while we're enjoying ourselves outside, aren't you Mary?"

"You bet. Its great news—Margaret's becoming an undercover spy. You can catch the local gossip about residents and fill us in. Who knows, you may hear some pretty intriguing tales, maybe even ones I can use in my novel."

Margaret let loose with one of her girlish giggles. "You never know."

I pushed my chair back and began to clear the table. "So, how did you hear about the meeting?"

"I couldn't get to sleep last night so I got up around two, put my housecoat on, and walked the whole length of the third floor hallway. To my delight, I found a small bulletin board mounted on the wall at the other end plastered with such interesting postings."

"You sure lucked out. Imagine you finding a group in this building who gathers together to discuss crossword strategy. The Foley doesn't even have that." I filled the sink with hot water and squirted a couple drops of Palmolive dish soap in it. There's no time like the present to get dirty dishes out of the way, although Auntie never feels that way. She keeps waiting for a fairy to appear and wave her magic wand.

***

A tiny spark was added to Aunt Zoe's gait the moment she caught sight of the blue sky tinted with a hint of pink overhead. "This weather's unbelievable. I never thought I'd be going without a jacket up here this time of year."

"Don't get too excited," I warned, "The weather forecast suggests the possibility of light snow in this area by next Wednesday."

"Ish. Let's hope they're wrong."

"Me too."

The corner where we needed to cross Minnesota Avenue to get to the sand dunes ended up having minimal traffic and didn't necessitate a mad dash with dog in tow like we had anticipated. A unique occurrence for a Saturday, something one would never observe in the big city. Busy streets can be so unnerving. One misstep and zap you're run over by a garbage truck or worse. After glancing in both directions, the three of us were on our way.

Winnie didn't take too kindly to the black tarred street and soon noticed the grass beyond it. She leapt onto the boulevard like a bulldozer and dragged me to her choice for a pit stop. At least she didn't wait to piddle on the beach. Auntie and I would've been treated to a sand storm.

While we waited for Winnie to complete her watering duty at the tree, Aunt Zoe and I stood guard on the sidewalk acting like two lost broads who didn't know what dwelling we were supposed to approach. The buildings in the area, made up of various styles and worth, included an A-framed cabin, a mansion, and two gray three-level stucco condominiums. Obviously, there were no set rules about what could be constructed on Park Point.

"Mary, take a look at the gingerbread place down there on the left."

I acquiesced to my aunt's request by twisting my head a smidgen. "It looks exactly like the witch's home in the tale of Hansel and Gretel."

"Yes, except this house is missing morsels to sample."

I nodded my head in agreement. "I bet it's the hottest place to Trick or Treat though. Maybe a sweet couple around Margaret's age owns it."

"The joke would be on you if the house's owner proved to be someone of your generation. Maybe we should stay here a while longer. Catch a glimpse of the owner."

"What, and give up our beach plans? I don't think so." Winnie finally finished and began prancing around. "Look, even the mutt's raring to go." I held my aunt's elbow and steered the three of us down the sidewalk to the plain, dark-green gabled house resting at the other end of the block half-hidden by overgrown Honeysuckle bushes. Behind the house there's supposed to be a narrow pathway leading to the beach.

"How did you find out about this particular route, Mary?"

"A resident at the Del Rosa told me about it when he saw me outside with Winnie last night. It's supposed to be easier to make your way through the sand at this location, the dunes are lower."

When we reached the front property of the gabled house, Aunt Zoe tapped her black, low boots firmly on the sidewalk and wagged her finger at me. "I think we'd better find a different path to get to the beach. I don't feel comfortable with this."

"Why not?"

"The backyard reeks of forbidden territory. I've got the willies just looking at the thick forest of low hanging branches, don't you?"

"I'll admit it's kind of creepy, but I'm not changing my mind. I'm committed to this path whether you are or aren't." I yanked the dog's leash and we trudged on.

A few seconds later Aunt Zoe caved in. When she caught up to me, she rubbed her crossed arms vigorously. "Are you certain you understood the man's directions? I've got this creepy notion someone's watching us. Mark my words, Mary, the minute we set foot on this path someone's flying out of there waving a gun in our faces."

"Don't be so paranoid. If there's anything to be worried about around the neighborhood, I'm sure Virginia would've warned us."

~10~

Despite Aunt Zoe's growing concerns someone would come running out guns a-blazing the moment we stepped on the path, nothing outrageous happened. Although there was a minor incident midway up the dunes. A certain playful six-year-old miniature poodle suddenly pooped out, plopped down, and refused to budge another inch. The mutt's drop in energy level probably had to do with lack of strenuous exercise on a daily basis. I can't picture my elderly cousin making her dog workout beyond the confines of the apartment's cement sidewalk, especially with bad knees.

Fortunately, a dog doesn't require much convincing to get it back up on all fours. But there was a problem, smart me had left the apartment without any doggie treats. *What are you going to do, Miss Swift? The pooch's supposed to zip around the beach, not snooze.* With no other motivational devices bouncing around in my pockets, I had no choice but to bend over and calmly gather the light ball of fluff in my arms. Well, I guess I could've ignored the dog. But then I'd have to listen to Aunt Zoe complain to everyone within earshot about how her mean niece permitted a poor mutt to suffer. Not just any dog, mind you, but a doggie whose owner was recuperating in a health facility.

Aunt Zoe fixed her eyes on Winnie and me and chuckled. "I suppose it's one way to get a stubborn poodle moving. But at your age it ought to be one kid on each hip, not a mutt."

"Thanks. I'll remember to tell that to the next guy I date."

Auntie's hand flew to her mouth. "Oh, Mary, forgive me. I know you've no control over the men you date and their thoughts on marriage. But things will turn around for you. Wait and see."

"I'm sure you're right." *The real question is how much longer do I wait? My biological clock for having kids grows shorter as each day passes. Sure a woman can resolve the child problem on her own, but having an absentee dad isn't worth it to me. I want the whole package or nothing.*

The added weight I carried forced my legs to exert more pressure on the mound of sand, causing my feet to disappear into the sand. Who needs a Stairmaster when you have a dog in your arms and sand dunes in your backyard?

Aunt Zoe shook her left foot and then her right. "When does this dune climbing come to an end?" she complained. "I feel like I'm walking in a sandbox."

I lifted my head. "Sorry, I didn't hear a word you said."

Auntie shook her feet again. "This darn dune's forcing so much sand into my shoes I feel like I'm playing in a sandbox. Why didn't we take our shoes off before climbing this monstrosity?"

"Hang in there. Once we get down to the beach we can find a level spot to sit and dump out our shoes."

The sand may have irritated our feet but reaching the dune's peak proved worthwhile like Virginia had said. Standing at the top we caught a breathtaking view. The sun's rays danced on the gently rolling waves of Minnesota's grand lake. When the water reached the shoreline, the rays were gobbled up.

Aunt Zoe raised her hand above her eyebrows. "What a sight!" she said excitedly, "Your Uncle Edward should be here. A few of his ashes could've been added to Lake Superior."

I gulped. "You insisted on leaving him home to guard our apartment, remember?" *Of which I was truly thankful.*

"Yes, I know. I guess I wasn't thinking. How many people can say their loved ones are a part of Lake Superior?"

Not many I hope.

"Well, what's done is done. We can drive up here with him another time.

Not with me you won't.

Oh, look, Mary—two cargo ships coming in at twelve o'clock. Memorize the scene. You might want to use it in your novel."

I set Winnie down and whipped out my cell phone. "No need to memorize anything. This little gizmo takes great pictures. Why, when I set pen to paper again, I'll have tons of reference material."

Auntie's hands fell to her sides. "I think you've lost touch with reality, Mary."

"What do you mean?"

"You can't take pictures with a phone."

I bit my lower lip. "You've been in the back country too long," referring to the many African safaris she'd taken with Uncle Edward. "These compact phones allow a person to do just about anything; take pictures, play games, send messages, and even browse the Internet highway."

"Internet highway? That must be one of Minnesota's newer freeways created while Edward and I were traveling abroad. Not much of a name if you ask me."

"It's not actually a highway you drive on."

"Then why call it a highway?"

Oh, boy. My idea of abstaining from explaining new technologies in communication to Auntie like Google Glasses and Apple Smart watches has just grown a bit longer. I'd better add drones to the list too. "I'll explain later." *At least I'll try.*

Content with my response, Aunt Zoe faced Lake Superior once again. "Minus the sand, I wouldn't have missed this view for anything."

I dragged a tennis shoe back and forth across the thick, whitish sand beneath it. "Why do we hunger for more fabulous natural surroundings when we become adults? It doesn't make sense. Minnesota offers so much at our fingertips, as well as our neighboring states. I wish I could be a kid again, even for a few minutes."

"Why would you want to go back in time, Mary? To see what you've missed?"

"Nah. I just want the thrill of sliding down a hill on my butt again."

Aunt Zoe giggled. "Slapping our bottoms on cardboard would work better."

"Do you see any lying around?"

"Nope."

I tucked the cell phone in a side pocket of my jeans for safe keeping. "Darn. Well, how do you feel about running down the hill instead?"

"Fine by me. I don't think I've reached the decrepit stage yet."

Winnie whined.

"Hush. You'll love this too, girl."

The instant my feet left the top of the hill, Winnie lurched forward faster than I anticipated and down I went face and tummy first like a sled, eating tons of sand along the way. It was a miserable way to reach the beach, but at least it was me who experienced it rather than my aunt. Her menopausal body couldn't have taken the impact.

Dad's sister arrived at my side shortly after my face slammed into the beach. Too bad the deeply concerned expression she displayed had nothing to do with my injuries.

"Honestly, Mary, what were you thinking? You said you wanted to slide down, but on your stomach? What a ridiculous idea. If this had been a race, you'd be disqualified for dishonesty."

Who said anything about racing? If she thought this gal was dumb enough to slide down on her stomach, there's no sense explaining the dog's to blame. Besides she wouldn't believe me anyway. I swiped the grit from my mouth. Then I got back on my feet, brushed my body off, and regained control of the dog. I didn't need another catastrophe. "Small dog disappears on beach. See news at nine," I uttered under my breath.

Winnie nudged my leg. Offering an apology of sorts I suppose. I rubbed her soft, fuzzy head. "I may look like I'm mad, but I'm really not. I suggested running not you." When I lifted my gaze to the left a tad beyond the poodle, Canal Park loomed off in the distance. The view was definitely deceiving. If I didn't know the water canal was in the way, I would've thought we could get to the park straight from the beach front. Before we wandered down the expansive beach, I plucked the cell phone from my pocket and took a selfie of Aunt Zoe and me with the water and sand behind us. When I finished, I immediately focused the camera on the Canal Park area.

It wasn't until I had my fill of snapping pictures of Canal Park that I realized I hadn't shared with Aunt Zoe how a person could actually get to Canal Park by starting on the beach if they didn't mind zigging and zagging a bit. You'd walk as far as you could along the beach and then hike back to Minnesota Avenue. From there you'd hoof it across the Aerial Bridge and continue on to Canal Park. Not so hard. When I spun around to tell her, I found her intently absorbed in other scenery, less than ten feet from us. Her lips tried to send a message. I couldn't make it out. I inched a bit closer to her. "I don't believe it, Mary. Please tell me I'm not seeing what I'm seeing."

I struggled with my words. "Sorry, I... I wish I could lie." Even though I'm thirty years younger than my aunt, I felt as terribly mortified as she by what we saw on this sunny fifty-degree morning.

A college-aged woman with straight, short-cropped reddish-brown hair shouted an overly-friendly good morning from her seat by a bonfire, clad in nothing more than her birthday suit. The naked woman was surrounded by three men. This definitely wasn't what I meant a couple seconds ago when I told my aunt Minnesota had a great deal of nature at our fingertips.

The men sitting with her greeted us with waves and smiles. They were clothed in scruffy wear from the neck down. Thick mustaches destroyed their upper lips and scraggily, dark brown medium-sized beards destroyed the bottom of their faces. I can't share the color of each ones hair because their heads were hidden from view with black wool stocking caps. I wondered if they got liberty from the foreign freighter they worked on, but no boats appeared to be anchored near the shore. It didn't matter I guess. It wasn't what apparently sloshed in the mugs of the rugged looking men that disturbed me the most, nor what they were smoking, but rather their companion, the young female.

Being an educator my mind raced a mile a nano-second. Who was this intriguing creature who didn't give two hoots about her decency? Had she just finished a morning bath? Did she live around here? Did a relative perhaps own the house over the sand dunes behind where they sat? What's she doing with these men? Had she skipped school to be with them? Did she share her body with all of them or one in particular? I had a hunch I'd never get the answers to those questions.

Not knowing if the foursome were a bunch of drug addicts or something worse, I politely lifted a stiff hand and acknowledged them from afar. That was the extent of my befriending them. Nothing more would be offered.

Aunt Zoe's hands shook uncontrollably after seeing the frank *hello* I delivered to the weird little group. "I know I've said I've seen a lot of things in my travels, Mary, but please tell me you don't expect me to traipse over there with you and get cozy with the foursome."

"Auntie, you've been out of the country too long. I'm not crazy. For all we know they're on the lam." I swung my body in the direction of Canal Park, grabbing Aunt Zoe's arm as I did so, and beat a mean path to town.

"Mary, slow down," Aunt Zoe yelled, "We've already passed a couple decent pieces of driftwood to sit on and my shoes still need to be emptied."

"I haven't forgotten," I shouted back, "I just want to get as far away from those people as possible."

"Do you think they'll still be there when we return?"

"I certainly hope not. I couldn't stand a repeat performance."

"Me neither. Maybe we should report them to the Coast Guard."

"What's the Coast Guard going to do? They handle maritime security and safety. I don't see anyone being harmed on this beach, do you? Besides, for all we know the woman could be a foreigner. They love to bathe in the nude."

"Still—" Whatever my aunt had planned to say next disappeared into thin air the second we stumbled upon another huge piece of driftwood, one sturdy enough to hold the two of us. She immediately rushed over to an end of the washed up wood, plopped down, and emptied her walking shoes.

I wound Winnie's leash around the other end of the driftwood before joining her. "I'll tell you what, Auntie, if what we saw bothers you so much, I promise to report it to the first cop I see." Of course, I had no intention of doing so.

"You mean it?"

I crossed my feet. "Sure." *There's no way I'll have to follow through,* I thought. *The chance of running into a cop along this quiet stretch of beach has to be one in a million.* I dropped the mutt's leash, told her to sit, and joined my aunt on the chunk of wood.

~11~

It took a good mile of traipsing along the beach front before reality finally kicked in. There's no point in trying to reach Canal Park when one of the walkers, namely me, thinks strolling three blocks is cause for celebration. The message sent from my eyes to the brain when we first hit the beach must've got mucked up somehow. Clearly, Park Point and Canal Park aren't so close after all. I took a couple deep breaths and exhaled. Maybe we could've managed another half mile if the constant repetition of feet sinking in the sand hadn't zapped our energy. I don't know. Right now feeling the way I do, an emergency crew would've had to airlift us out of here if we'd continued on.

I decided to break the sour news to Aunt Zoe who lagged further and further behind as time wore on. "I can't take another step, Roomie. Do you mind calling it quits?"

"Heaven's no." She pressed her pudgy hands to her chest and took in a few deep breaths. "Looks like our little friend here could afford to hang it up too."

I glanced down at Winnie. Her tiny tongue almost touched her fluffy chest. "Okay. It's magnanimous. We've done our bit to burn our breakfast calories off. Let's head back."

The mutt spun around and yapped loudly. I patted her head. "Happy to leave, Winnie?"

"Wuff. Wuff."

"Me too."

"Me three," Auntie chimed in.

It's surprising how simple thoughts of returning to the comforts of an apartment can rally the troops. The sand dune hike ended in a flash. Well, maybe not for Winnie. She repeated her earlier performance of sitting midway between the top of the dune and the bottom of it. Auntie offered immediate assistance but I said no. She had enough of her own weight to heft up the hill without adding the mutt's too. Besides, I wanted to demonstrate this thirty-something gal still had some stamina left.

As soon as I set the mutt down on solid ground, our next stumbling block stood before us, the forested pathway behind the dark green house. Would Aunt Zoe throw another tantrum or continue blissfully on? When she didn't release even a tiny whimper, I cheered internally.

Don't worry; her quiet attitude didn't last long. The moment her feet landed on the boulevard running along Lake Avenue she stirred up a huge ruckus. "Whoopee! Luck's on our side. I can't believe it, Mary."

"What luck?" Was she referring to Duluth's casino? *Unless*.... I pinched myself just to make sure I hadn't been walking around in a dream state since falling down the dune earlier. Nope. I wasn't standing knee deep in slot machines with alarms ringing and oodles of winning money falling at my feet. Darn. When I glanced at her again, I received a clue.

Her finger pointed the way. A pale, slender fellow with a young German Shepherd in tow had caught her attention. "See the guy with the dog?"

"Yup. What about him?"

"He's the cop who almost gave you a parking ticket."

"No way! He doesn't bear any resemblance to him."

"Oh, honey, I got a good look at him yesterday. It's him."

"But you barely saw him from your vantage point."

"Who needs a vantage point? I saw what I saw and no discussion will change it." She jabbed her forehead with a pudgy finger. "The man's face became imprinted on my brain the moment he appeared at your window."

My goose was cooked. I had to make good on a promise. Unless, I skedaddled before the.cop reached us. *Yes, that's what I'll do.* I tugged on Winnie's leash, notifying her of my decision.

Too late. Aunt Zoe out maneuvered me. She thrust her arms in the air to draw attention to us. "Yoo-hoo. Oh, yoo-hoo, Officer. We need to speak to you."

The man dressed in casual street clothes gave a sharp command to his dog and then he rushed to Aunt Zoe's side. When he reached her, the dog claimed Auntie's shoes while his master pursued more serious matters. "What's the problem ma'am?" he asked with concern in his voice, "Are you sick? Do you need an ambulance?"

"An ambulance?" Aunt Zoe shook her fiery-red head so hard I almost thought she'd lose all her hair, "I'm afraid that won't take care of the dreadful thing we viewed on the beach, Officer." She pointed in the direction we had recently left behind. "The terrible incident's upset me so much I can't even speak of it. My niece will have to fill you in." She stepped aside and I took her place.

The cop's dog immediately shifted gears and moved on to my tennis shoes. I've never had a great love for German Shepherds, they scare me to death, but at least he wasn't bothering Winnie. I had no clue how she'd react if he sniffed her. "I...ah, don't really know ahem... how to put this into words. By the way officer, what's your name? I never did catch it yesterday."

My aunt poked me in the arm. "You don't need his name. Get on with it."

Frustrated with my lack of gumption, I forced my tongue to reply. "I am." I couldn't help it if the cop's gray heavy set eyes threw me off kilter. Sure I could've taken in more of the view yesterday, but I had been too concerned about a stupid parking ticket to notice.

Hmmm. I guess he's good-looking in his own way. No beard or mustache—something I abhor on men I plan to get to know. He had thick wavy cinnamon-colored hair: nice to run ones hands through. The dimpled chin's adorable, but his smile needed a ton of work. I moved my gaze slightly downward. Neck proportioned to his head. Thank goodness. A Maroon and gold UMD hooded sweatshirt clung to his broad shoulders. No ring on the left hand. Always a good sign. Although, depending on their jobs, some men prefer not to wear one. And I don't blame them.

How about those boot-cut jeans, Mary? Ah, huh. They tweak him right where they should—definitely not a regulation uniform. If only I could whistle. *Earth to Mary, get back on track. Your interest lies in the city. Yeah, but he hasn't made a move for eons. For all I know he's six-feet under.*

"Duke, back off. Sit," the cop sharply commanded. The dog immediately obeyed. "Sorry about his sniffing."

"It's all right," I lied, "he's not bothering me." I know I said the dog scares me to death, but sometimes a gal has to play it cool when she doesn't feel like it, for example when an available male is standing alongside her.

"Glad to hear it," he said, "a lot of people would be upset with Duke. He doesn't mean to be a pest. It's just when he's in training mode his nose sniffs out everything."

"What's he training for?" Aunt Zoe inquired.

"Drugs."

A chill ran up my spine at the mention of *drugs* and before I knew it the mess at the Bar X Ranch rolled on the theatre screen situated in my brain. I didn't want to ever be involved in anything like it again. Of course, if David, the undercover cop I now date occasionally, was part of this case I might have second thoughts.

The off-duty cop finally extended a hand. I took it. *Oh, boy, you're treading deep water now, girl.* Liftoff's been engaged. My fingers tingled. I wonder if he felt it too. Probably not. Cops are taught to rein in their emotions. *Brain to body immediate termination necessary.* This gal doesn't need another wrinkle in her life.

"I'm Trevor Fitzwell. You've already met Duke." He slowly released my hand and then pointed to Winnie. "Cute poodle. I don't recall seeing her in your car."

Only because you were so determined to give me a ticket.

"I hope she wasn't stashed in your trunk."

My hand flew to my throat. "How could you think… Why, I'd never harm an animal."

Aunt Zoe graciously intervened. "She's not our dog, Officer."

The cop's penetrating eyes took on this strange look. "Oh? For a runaway she sure seems well cared for. Let me check to see if she's got any information on her." He stooped to look. As he ran his hand around Winnie's neck, searching for her tags, he said, "I bet this poodle's a show dog. Her collar looks mighty expensive."

His assumptions were getting crazier and crazier by the minute. I had to put a stop to them. "Winnie's not a show dog and she's definitely not lost. She belongs to the woman we're visiting."

"Ah…" Another half-smile bounced off Trevor's face as he stared directly into my orbs. "I didn't mean to upset you, Miss, with the trunk remark. I just wanted to lighten things up."

I didn't care to comment.

He cleared his throat. "I guess I need to work on my joke delivery a little, huh? So, what happened on the beach? Did someone bother you?"

I shook my head. "No."

"Did you ladies witness a crime being committed?"

I wrung my hands. "Ah, we're not exactly sure."

"Care to elaborate?"

Aunt Zoe shoved me aside. Evidently she couldn't take my dallying anymore. "For goodness sakes, girl, you act like you're having a tooth pulled. Trevor, I mean Officer Fitzwell, we caught three men and a woman sitting around a huge bonfire."

Trevor's brown bushy eyebrows rose a few inches. "Oh? Okay. Thank you for making me aware of it. Many people don't realize they have to have a special permit before building bonfires on the beach. I'll check it out and make sure your information's passed on to the officers who patrol this area."

Winnie had begun whimpering the minute Aunt Zoe took me out of the loop, and I worried the German Shepherd and she might be heading for a show down, but then all was freakishly quiet. What happened? I glanced down. No fight was about to ensue. The mutt had simply found an interesting tidbit on one of Trevor's shoes. I yanked on her leash. Licking yuk wasn't okay in my book. When Winnie moved, I noticed Trevor's shoes. *Cowboy boots. Shoot!* Another horse lover. He probably rides whenever he has the chance. After solving the case at the Bar X Ranch, I promised myself I'd stay as far away from horses as possible. *I guess that takes care of my dilemma with getting involved with someone new.*

I raised my head and cast my eyes on Trevor's smooth face. "I'm afraid my aunt hasn't shared the whole story, Officer."

"She hasn't?"

"Nope. She left out a tiny detail. The woman was naked." There I finally spit it out.

Officer Fitzwell ran a hand through his thick hair. "Naked? You sure?"

I nodded. "Most definitely."

His face drew serious. "Perhaps you two should stay away from the beach for a while."

"Why?" I asked, "Afraid we'll run into them again?"

"It's possible. They might be drug addicts or—"

"Or worse," Aunt Zoe jumped in. "Why, they could be those precious gem thieves you're hunting for, couldn't they?"

"Ah, you heard about the crime on the news I assume."

Aunt Zoe smiled. "The president of Clarity Diamond and Gems made a statement over the airwaves about two hours ago, but he never mentioned if there might be a reward for info."

"Oh? I hadn't heard the most recent update yet, but it's good to know you ladies are aware of the situation. No telling where the thieves have taken shelter." The thirty-something off-duty cop slid his sweatshirt sleeve up, peered at his watch, and then let the sleeve fall back into place. "Looks like Duke and I better move on. I'm on duty in another hour." He tugged on the dog's leash. Duke got the message and stood. "Remember, ladies, keep the warning about the beach in mind."

"Don't worry, Officer," I said, "There's no way we want to hook up with dangerous criminals such as druggies or diamond thieves."

~12~

"*Ciao,*" Margaret said, tilting her stately white head in our direction. "Good timing, ladies. I just got back a few minutes ago from the crossword puzzle meeting."

"Was it worth going to?" Aunt Zoe queried.

"*Sì.*"

Instead of quizzing Margaret further on the meeting, I whizzed straight past her, and set Winnie on the kitchen floor by her water dish. It wasn't until the dog began to lap up water that my mind questioned how the nonagenarian got into the apartment. I was certain I took the key. I poked a hand in my pant pocket to check. Yup, the key's still lodged there. Oh, great. I must've forgotten to lock up. I left the dog behind and poked my head in the living room. "Ah, Margaret, do you mind explaining how you got in?"

She flicked her hand. "I bumped into Virginia Bagley out in the hallway. She let me in with a master key."

"Oh?" I breathed a sigh of relief. I hadn't inadvertently left Lizzie's apartment open, allowing anyone to stroll in. "So, Margaret, did you learn any new words like *selfie* and h*ashtag?*" I quizzed, "They might crop up in a crossword puzzle."

"As a matter of fact I did. Thankfully, someone explained what they meant."

"Did you pick up any interesting tidbits concerning the Del Rosa?" I continued.

"*Si*. Love's in the air." Not exactly the answer I had hoped for, I thought to myself. Margaret continued on, "A ninety-year old couple is tying the knot in the community room on Halloween. The groom used to be a sea captain."

"Hey, Mary," my aunt blurted out, "I bet if you told him you're writing a novel, he'd be willing to share scary tales of life on the Great Lakes with you."

"I'm sure he would. Maybe I can weasel his phone number out of Virginia if I see her later. So, tell me, Margaret, did you hear anything juicy I might be able to use right now?"

"Not really. A woman said she thought she had seen Virginia's son recently. But someone straightened her out real quick."

"Oh?"

"According to him the manager's son died long ago."

"How sad," I said. "I wonder if she has any other children."

Winnie dropped to the floor by the elderly woman's feet, panting like crazy. "Well, I guess I don't have to ask how your walk went. If the dog's behavior is any indication, I'd say you went beyond what you should have."

"You got that right," Aunt Zoe heartily shared as she pointed to me. "The kid here was the first one to throw in the towel."

"You know perfectly well you were exhausted too. You just didn't want to admit it."

Our neighbor kept her eyes glued on the poodle. "Poor little, Winnie. You couldn't tell anyone how you felt, could you?" Margaret lightly tapped the cushion on the settee, inviting the dog to join her.

Winnie turned her back on her and waddled to the kitchen to lap up more water. When she returned, the elderly woman tapped the cushion again. "Come on, Winnie. I'm waiting." The mutt tried to join her but her little legs didn't cooperate.

Probably too tuckered out, I thought.

Aunt Zoe quickly stepped out of her shoes, bounded into the living room where Margaret sat, lifted the dog up, and placed her on the woman's lap. Once Winnie settled in, Auntie plopped her own weary bones in a chair and immediately stretched her short legs out in front of her. "You don't realize how fortunate you were to stay here, Margaret."

Her thin eyebrows arched. "Why would you say such a thing, Zoe?"

"Mary and I experienced a humdinger of a nightmare on the beach. And in daylight yet."

"Non capisco."

"Huh?" My aunt scrunched up her heavily-penciled eyebrows and gave me a questioning glance.

I slipped out of my grungy tennis shoes and joined the two women. "She said she doesn't understand."

"You sure? When did you learn Italian?"

I shook my head and gave Margaret a *see what I mean* look. "It doesn't matter when I learned Italian, Auntie…"

Our neighbor interrupted. "I don't understand why strolling along a beach front could end up being so awful for you. It's a gorgeous day and people at the meeting said the beach is a nice, quiet reflective place to walk."

"No complaints about the weather," I declared as I sat on a straw-woven chair, an eighteenth-century French design according to Margaret Grimshaw.

Aunt Zoe pressed her stubby fingers together. "Nor noise."

"And it's a super spot to sight freighters on Lake Superior," I continued.

"Definitely reflective," my aunt added.

The furrows on Margaret's high forehead grew deeper. "What's wrong with you two? Behaving so dramatic? You act like you're in one of Alfred Hitchcock's thrillers for goodness sakes. I hate it when the shocker gets slipped in at the end. I hope you're not intending to do the same thing. If you haven't noticed, I'm a lot further up the ladder to those pearly gates than you. I could be dead by the time you get to it."

"I don't know about Auntie, Margaret, but I didn't mean to keep you waiting. Here's the scoop—"

Aunt Zoe jumped up. "Stop!" she demanded, "The information you're about to divulge might be too lethal for someone who wears a pace maker or takes heart medication."

I shook my head. "Auntie, you're making our tale wilder than it actually was. Even a person with a heart condition could handle what we saw."

"Fine. Suit yourself." she smacked her derrière back down.

Margaret squeezed into the conversation between Auntie and I, that was heading nowhere fast, before I had a chance to say something I might regret. "Zoe, I can assure you I have no heart problems."

Auntie pressed her hands against her chest. "Sorry, I wouldn't have brought it up if I had known, Margaret. It's just, you know how it is. There's the apartment grapevine. Things get said. People tend to share which tenants have had or have serious health issues. Perhaps I got yours mixed up with someone else's."

"Well, I've never considered my problems serious, even though others might," the nonagenarian replied. "But I guess it's comforting to know someone besides me cares about my welfare."

I flung my hands out. "Margaret, I hope you don't think we don't care."

"No, no. How could I ever think that? You two treat me like a family member. Now, kindly tell me what happened."

Complying with our neighbor's request, I purposely skipped over the little business where I flew down the hill on my stomach; she didn't need to hear about that, and went directly to the smug group enjoying a blazing bonfire. "Well, we had barely planted our feet on the beach when we caught sight of a foursome sitting around a bonfire, three scruffy looking men and a lone female. The men looked like they had had one too many already."

"What about the woman?" Margaret inquired.

"She was naked," Aunt Zoe hastily supplied, "Talk about disgusting."

I rubbed my hands together, preferring to think of more pleasant things.

Margaret's hand flew to her mouth and remained there for a few seconds. I suspected she covered the lower section of her face to hide her true feelings. "That's the awful thing you were so upset about?"

"Why, yes," my aunt and I replied.

"Ladies, nudity has never bothered me. European's believe bodies are beautiful, not something to be ashamed of."

"Probably because of all those Renaissance artists your parents introduced you to," Aunt Zoe interjected.

Margaret's lips curved into a miniature smile. "How old do you think I am?"

The instant Auntie realized her faux pas, an apology tumbled forth. "Sorry. I... I didn't mean it the way it sounded."

"I'm sure you didn't," the older woman politely replied.

"It's that darn puritanical upbringing from way back when," I pointed out, "If the early settlers along the east coast hadn't gotten involved, we'd have a healthy outlook on the body like the rest of the world. Why, as old as I am, I still get embarrassed every time I spot a woman changing into a bathing suit in a health club locker room. Pretty dumb, huh?"

Aunt Zoe whipped her hand in the air. "At least we know who to blame regarding our thoughts on nudity. The serious problems affecting our country and others get covered up faster than we can snap our fingers." She rubbed her thumb and index finger together, but didn't produce a sound.

Margaret cleared her throat. "Ladies, I think we've strayed way beyond the circle of the four on the beach, don't you agree?"

"You're right," I said. "What else would you like to know?"

The nonagenarian tapped her hollowed cheek. "I'm wondering why the woman's companions weren't in their birthday suits too. Surely they must've joined her in the water. Think back about what you saw, excluding the nudity of course. There's always more to a scene than one realizes. After the initial shock wore off, weren't you curious what the four of them might be up to?"

"You bet," I said. "A ton of scenarios tumbled around in my head."

"Like what," our neighbor hastily inquired.

"Oh, illegals dropped on the beach; druggies; diamond thieves; gun smuggling."

Margaret rubbed her thin arthritic hands together. "Does this mean what I think it means? Regardless of the nude woman you'll continue to walk the beach to see what's cooking?"

"You mean dig up dirt? No, Margaret," Aunt Zoe announced in a decisive tone. "Indeed not. Trevor warned us the beach could be dangerous and to stay away. And that's precisely what Mary and I intend to do."

That's what she thinks. When I'm by myself, I'm taking another look.

"Who's Trevor? Where does he fit into the picture?" our neighbor inquired, lifting her petite hand off of Winnie who was snoring.

Aunt Zoe whisked her pudgy hand across her stretched out jeans. "He's the cop who almost gave Mary a ticket yesterday. "I think he's eligible, but Mary's still insisting she's not interested."

Margaret glanced my way. "He was rather good-looking I thought." I ignored the comment. I didn't come up here to have a sexagenarian and a nonagenarian behave like matchmakers. "Tell me, was the nice gentlemen policing this side of town on foot or driving?"

"On foot, but not on duty," I rushed to explain. "We ran into him on the sidewalk directly across the street from here. He was training Duke."

"Duke? Is that his partner?"

"I don't think so," my aunt hurriedly replied, "He's a dog,"

"Zoe, maybe you're not aware of this being out of the country so much," Margaret said, "but many policemen have German Shepherds for partners."

"Is that so? How does the dog call for backup if his partner is in danger?"

"Some sleuth I am," I said, rudely interrupting the two-way conversation that was going nowhere. I have a feeling Margaret didn't mind. Her face lightened up considerably.

"What's the matter?" she asked.

"I never thought to ask Officer Fitzwell why he picked this side of town to do drug training with Duke."

Margaret pressed a hand to her cheek. "Oh, dear. Another policeman involved with drugs."

"Afraid so," I smoothly replied. "But don't fret, he's not working undercover. He's only teaching the dog to sniff out the dope." I eased myself off the chair. "Well, if you two don't mind, I'm going to collect my purse and writing supplies from the bedroom, and then drive to the library to do research."

"What do you plan to do about lunch, Mary?" Aunt Zoe asked as I started for the guest bedroom.

I ran my fingers through the hair at the nape of my neck. "No sweat. I'll only be gone a couple hours. When I get back, I'll whip up a baloney sandwich." *A half hour of which I intend to spend on the beach alone doing some serious sleuthing, but they didn't need to know that.*

"Mary, dear," Margaret soberly began, "You never mentioned your cousin at breakfast. We're still visiting her this evening, aren't we?"

"Yes, of course. Sorry, I didn't mean to leave you in limbo. I'm thinking we should probably arrive at the Shoolinger Nursing Home facility after the supper hour. It'll give us plenty of time to chat with Lizzie before her painkillers wear off."

"Going after supper's an excellent idea," our neighbor said, "Our stomachs won't be complaining while we're there."

"Speaking of supper, I want you both to know I haven't forgotten I'm in charge of it tonight." *But I sure hope I remember where I spotted Lee Yu's Chinese takeout yesterday.*

~13~

When I went back to the beach this afternoon, I found pieces of charred wood and ashes where the foursome had been sitting and not much else except for several cigarette butts and a light-blue headband made out of cotton decorated with Monarch butterflies. Fortunately, the cigarette remains and headband supplied enough samples for future DNA testing. I whipped out 2 clean pint size Glad storage bags I had tossed in my purse, and a Kleenex. I used the Kleenex to pick up the items. The cigarettes were dropped in one bag and the hair item in the other.

As excited as I was to share what I discovered on the shores of Lake Superior, I decided it best to keep my findings a secret until it became necessary to share. Who knows, I might just get credit for helping catch the jewel thieves.

"Thanks for getting takeout," Margaret said, cracking a fortune cookie open. "I don't remember when I last ate chow mein, Mary".

"Me neither," Aunt Zoe chimed in, patting her stomach, "I'm stuffed."

"I'm glad you both enjoyed the meal." I glanced at the kitchen clock. Five-thirty. Oops. We better get going to see Lizzie. "Let's stack the dirty dishes in the sink," I suggested, "I promise to wash them when we get back."

"Sounds good," Margaret replied, "I'm sure your cousin has already finished her supper."

The second we entered Cousin Lizzie's small private room, where she had taken up temporary residency, we got blasted out of our socks by a blaring TV mounted near the ceiling in a corner of the room.

Unaware of our arrival, Lizzie sat motionless in a tall beige leather-padded chair positioned kitty-corner from the TV. From where I stood only the upper portion of her powder-blue floral nightgown could be seen. Her outstretched legs, covered with a yellow blanket, rested on an ottoman the same color as the chair.

The minute I cleared my throat to announce our presence, Lizzie's salt and peppered tightly curled head of hair bounced in our direction. Upon seeing the three of us, her well-lined elongated face lit up like a bonfire. She quickly reached for the remote control and lowered the TV volume to a whisper. "Cousin, how nice of you and your companions to stop by," she stated in a soft mellow voice, "The days are so long and dull here without Winnie. Tell me, does she miss me?"

"Of course she does," I cheerfully replied, hugging Lizzie whom I last saw about ten years ago at a family reunion in the Twin Cities. After I released my grip on her, I parted with the bouquet of deep-purple mums purchased at a nearby store, a cheer-up gift from the three of us. "What dog wouldn't miss a master who spoils her rotten?"

Lizzie took the flowers from me and set them aside. "Guilty as charged. So, did you find all her toys and treats?"

"Uh huh." Auntie reached over and pumped Lizzie's hand. "Hi, I'm Zoe, Archie's younger sister. And this is Margaret Grimshaw. She lives across the hall from us at the Foley." Margaret stepped out from behind my aunt's back and clasped Lizzie's hand.

Lizzie stared at our neighbor for a second. "Why, you must be the sweet lady who cooks those wonderful Italian meals for Matt." She gazed at me and wagged her finger. "If I'm not mistaken, it looks like you've tasted a few of her meals too, cousin. Your face looks fuller." She drew back a sleeve on her flannel nightgown, exposing an arm thinner than my neighbors. "I should cook more Italian dishes. It might put some additional fat on me too. Hey, Mary, copy a few of Margaret's recipes for me, will you?"

"Certainly," I said, "if she's willing to share her state secrets."

The nonagenarian's eyes filled with mischief. "Before you get an answer out of me, I want to know who blabbed about the meals."

"It wasn't me," I hurriedly admitted, "Must've been my mom."

"Your response is too quick to be a lie," Margaret said. "I guess I'd better be nice and let you have a look at my cookbook when we get back to the cities. By the way, Lizzie, I met the most delightful group at your apartment building today."

"Oh? Which one? Quilting? Painting? Writers? Del Rosa has so many."

"I'm into crossword puzzles."

"Ah, yes. I attend their meetings occasionally just to pick up new vocabulary words. What did you think of the members? I found the majority of them tend to gossip."

While Margaret shared her thoughts with Lizzie, I jotted down a quick reminder to myself concerning Margaret's recipes, slipped pen and paper back in my purse, and drew out a well-used deck of cards found at Lizzie's apartment.

The room suddenly stopped buzzing. "What have you got there, Mary?" my cousin asked.

I fanned out the cards. "Oh, I thought you might feel like playing a couple hands of gin rummy. A little birdie told me it's your favorite game."

A brief smile spread across her face "You must be referring to Virginia. Well, I can't think of a better thing to do while cooped up in a nursing facility. Deal me in. I'm raring to play."

I set the cards down on the narrow hospital table standing by the bed and pushed it over near Lizzie. Then I scanned the room to see how many chairs there were: two.

Lizzie realized the problem almost as soon as I did. "Don't fret, Mary. I'll get a nurse to bring another chair." She picked up the little white buzzer resting on her lap, pressed the button for the nurses' station, and then requested an extra chair.

"While we're waiting," Aunt Zoe said, "I've got something really silly to share." *Oh no. Don't go there.* Determined to tell her tale, Aunt Zoe's eyes settled on mine. "This story came to mind after our walk on the beach yesterday."

Hmm? Must not be the three-headed cat tale.

"A fifty-year-old woman from the Mid-West, Autumn Frederick, said she likes to clean house in the nude. Isn't that the craziest notion you've ever heard?"

Cousin Lizzie smacked her hands together. "Well, it certainly puts a new twist on housecleaning. Cleaning in the nude? How goofy is that? What if she has a visitor?"

"I hope she doesn't live at the Foley," I said.

After we shared a good laugh, Auntie drew serious again. "Maybe she doesn't have any neighbors."

"She probably lives on a farm," Margaret added, wiping away laughter tears, "Did she explain why she does it, Zoe?"

"Oh, yes. According to Autumn, cleaning in the nude's such a freeing experience."

I picked up the cards and shuffled them. "I know experiencing new things keeps us on the young side, but I'm not shedding my jammies to houseclean. PJ's free me enough."

My cousin grinned. "Well, we certainly got our chuckle for the day thanks to you, Zoe. If you ever have another silly story to share, I'd love to hear it."

Oh, oh. Lizzie doesn't know it but she just opened a can of worms.

A stern-looking nurse with dark-brown hair severely pulled back into a ponytail strode into the room with the requested chair. As she made her way across the bare linoleum floor her clean white shoes squeaked with agitation. A nametag attached to her crisp navy-blue scrubs screamed Charice Hawthorne, LPN.

"Why, Charice," my cousin sputtered, "I thought you'd be long gone."

"They were short-handed for the next shift so I volunteered," the fortyish nurse stiffly replied.

"Well. I'm glad you're still here. This is my cousin Mary. She's the one who solved those horrible murders at the horse ranch down in Cottage Grove this summer."

Nurse Hawthorne set the chair down and crossed her sleeved arms. "Oh, yes, I recall reading a news article pertaining to the case. It sounded gruesome." Her sickly-white face somehow managed a slight grin. "Nice to meet you."

Lizzie prattled on before the word *likewise* could tumble out of my mouth. "My daughter had to get back to Sioux Falls so Mary and her companions were kind enough to drive up from the cities to take care of my poodle."

The nurse's piercing greenish-brown orbs stayed with me. "It's good to know Lizzie has someone else to rely on."

I squirmed. The woman made me feel like a saint, which I wasn't. "Actually, Lizzie is my second cousin and it's been years since we've seen each other. It just happened we both needed a favor at the same time."

"Oh?"

Lizzie's hands flew out in front of her. "Say, Mary, maybe you can be of help to Charice."

"I doubt it. I'm not skilled in nursing."

"Her situation has nothing to do with nursing."

"Oh, I just assumed—,"

Lizzie grasped my hands. "It has to do with a missing person."

"Not the girl we've heard about on the news?"

"Why, yes, Nurse Hawthorne's seventeen-year-old daughter. The police still haven't come up with any leads yet and she's been missing a week. It's like the earth swallowed her up."

Of course. That would explain the nurse's unfriendly attitude and sickly appearance. "Who was the last one to see her?" I quizzed.

"Trudy Almquist," Nurse Hawthorne swiftly replied, "Her dorm roommate. My daughter moved on campus in August."

"Here at the University of Minnesota Duluth?" I asked dryly.

The nurse rubbed her long thin hands together nervously. "Yes. According to Trudy, Darcy had recently started dating some new guy, but she had no idea who he was or if he even attended school there."

Aunt Zoe interrupted. "And you believe the young girl's story?"

Darcy's mother shook her head. "My daughter and Trudy have been friends since third grade. What reason would she have to lie?"

"Has your husband thought of hiring a private investigator?" I asked.

"It's just Darcy and me. My husband died in an auto accident four years ago."

I pointed to the wedding band. "Sorry I leaped to the wrong conclusion."

"It's all right. It's my way of saying I'm not in the market," Marjorie explained.

"I understand." And I did. A few of my college chums do the same thing. Been there, done that. Don't want to walk down the aisle again.

The nurse's hand went to her pale throat. "I'm wondering…"

"Yes?"

"Is there anything I personally can do before getting a PI involved?"

"You bet. Inquire where around campus your daughter liked to hang out. Request a copy of her class schedule. And see if Darcy mentioned any males in particular she seemed to be attracted to."

A tiny smile emerged. "Thank you." Nurse Hawthorne began to leave now, but then changed her mind. "Miss Malone…"

"Uh huh?"

"Have you had much experience hunting someone down?"

My hand flew to my chest. "Me? I ah…" Someone hastily pinched the skin near my elbow. I turned to see if Margaret was the culprit or my aunt. Aunt Zoe, I should've known. Margaret wouldn't touch a fly. I suppose Auntie didn't want to see me blow a chance to take on a new case. If I counted all the children over the years who hadn't returned to the classroom after recess or going to the bathroom, the number's astronomical. But the woman wasn't speaking of that type of scenario. Hers was more serious. *Oh, what the heck. She didn't know I'm an unemployed teacher.* "Yes, I guess I've done a bit."

"I know it's a lot to ask and I hardly know you, but could I hire you to find Darcy?"

I pondered her question. Over the past five years 20 college students have disappeared in the Midwest. Some never found. Statistically speaking at least three students go missing each month throughout the country. The nurse's story tugged at my heartstrings. A missing child of any age, whether runaway or kidnapped, was a parent's worst nightmare. Hawthorne's daughter could be anywhere in the world by now and the longer she's out of the picture the harder it'd be to trace her.

Wasn't this exactly the type of case I told Aunt Zoe and Margaret I'd be willing to take on? But I couldn't. I had a major problem. I didn't want the money I had put out for my master's degree in education to slide down the drain. I had to keep my foot in the door—meaning subbing. If I didn't keep reminding the administration of my availability, no one else would. I patted the nurse's stiff shoulder. "I'm sorry, Charice, I'd like to help but I can't. My plate's full. I'm on call at two different jobs in the cities already. I think you'd be better off hiring someone from this area; a person who knows the terrain and can call in favors."

The nurse's hooded eyes looked as though they might spring a leak. "I see. Perhaps you could recommend someone else then."

"Not really," I replied with a gentle touch, "however I'd be happy to contact my private eye brother. He's overseas right now," I explained as I strolled to the doorway with her, "but he has a ton of connections here in Minnesota. Just leave your number at the nurse's station and I'll pick it up on my way out."

Nurse Hawthorne's bottom lip quivered. "I will. I can't tell you how much your help means to me, Mary. I've been feeling so boxed in lately."

The minute she disappeared from view Aunt Zoe spoke up. "Mary, how could you turn a deaf ear to that poor soul? You're like the Tin man, no heart."

Margaret came to my rescue. "Don't be so rough on your niece. I'm sure she thought the offer through very logically before giving her answer, didn't you Mary?"

I sat down on the chair Nurse Hawthorne had just brought us and stared out the window. There was nothing to see. It was too dark, like the story I just heard. "Yes, I definitely weighed everything very carefully."

~**14**~

Sunday

The morning sneaked in without fanfare. Not even a hint of fog according to the view from the bedroom window. A truly perfect day and this gal knew how to spend it.

"Mary," Aunt Zoe called, "breakfast is ready."

"Coming." Picturing the huge warm breakfast Mrs. Grimshaw most likely had prepared for us, I stepped back, dropped the cream floral sheers I had been holding, and reached for the black dress flats sitting by the white wrought iron double bed Aunt Zoe and I were sharing. As soon as my feet eased into them, I popped open the bedroom door, and zipped into the kitchen.

It wasn't until after savoring a third helping of thick cinnamon coated French toast, a second slice of crispy bacon, and a few glasses of overly sweet OJ, that I realized my thoughts on how to spend the morning had yet to be revealed to the other two seated at the table. It's time to spring it on them I guess. However my syrup saturated mouth needed to be blotted first; otherwise my sticky lips would utter pure nonsense. I plucked up the napkin resting on my lap and gingerly swiped my lips. "It's such a gorgeous day let's skip services at Our Lady of Mercy."

Aunt Zoe's fork rattled on her plate. "Skip Mass? Never! The church is only a couple of blocks from here. Just because it's a beautiful day, doesn't mean we're entitled to skip services. The Lord always comes first, Mary. If you don't want to go to church that's fine, but I still intend to go," under her breath she added, "No wonder there's so many empty pews in church. The younger generation looks for any excuse to skip services."

Thankfully our wise old neighbor refrained from admitting her feelings outright. Instead she questioned me further. "Are you suggesting we skip church entirely, or do you have another one in mind?"

Contrary to what some people might think, this thirtyish gal doesn't miss Sunday services no matter what's going on, burning in hell wasn't an option for me. Of course, if I can't get up from my death bed to attend, I understand there's a special dispensation. "Another church," I swiftly replied, "I thought we might want to check out the Cathedral of Our Lady of the Rosary while we're here," then I hurriedly added, "I heard the architectural style's Italian in nature."

Our Italian born neighbor, who I thought would be delighted to learn her homeland played a part in the church design, merely tapped her boney finger against her thin lips. "What's the real reason for the sudden change in plans, dear? That malarkey about Italian style architecture doesn't fool me."

"Okay, okay. Blame it on Julie, one of Lizzie's apartment neighbors. She said when the city isn't shrouded in fog a person can get a wonderful panoramic view of Duluth from a higher elevation, especially in the fall."

The nonagenarian poured herself a second cup of coffee. "Ah? It's the view."

"Well, yes. But believe me I was thinking of you when I suggested driving up there. You never had the chance to enjoy Lake Superior like Auntie and I did yesterday."

She shared a tiny smile. "*Si,* you're right. I didn't see the naked lady."

"All right, I deserved that. How about looking at my suggestion another way then? You get to see Lake Superior and a cathedral." I folded my hands underneath my chin. "And not just any cathedral but one that overlooks the world's largest fresh water lake," meaning Superior.

"Oh? What lake is that, Mary?" Aunt Zoe asked.

Don't worry I didn't show my true thoughts even though it's hard to contain them. "Think about it, Auntie," I said, "What body of water did we see when we walked on the beach?"

Her eyebrows rose a few inches. "Ah."

"So, is everyone okay with the cathedral?"

"*Si*, I'm fine with it," Margaret replied. "It's been years since I've been to one."

I glanced at my aunt. "You're the driver, Mary. I'll go wherever you want."

Julie had imparted one other tidbit last night concerning the college campuses of UMD and St. Scholastica. I purposely put it on the backburner until after Mass. No need to lay out everything at once. Besides, I knew I'd be inundated with more questions than I cared to handle at the moment, and I didn't have time to explain.

As much as I wanted to share everything with my companions, sometimes it's best to leave certain things unsaid. For instance, when Julie tossed the University of Minnesota Duluth— Darcy Hawthorne's college—into the friendly mix of conversation flowing between the two of us, a sharp chord resonated deep within me. Ever since I refused Nurse Hawthorne's soulful plea for help, I've felt guilty as hell. People think of me as a caring person and yet I didn't even offer a smidgen of assistance. I cut her off at the knees. How could I be so callous?

Call it morbid curiosity or guilt, but after church I plan to traipse across UMD's grounds to get a sense of where Darcy hung out. Who knows, maybe I can help in some small way. At least I hoped I could. According to info I read late last night while combing the Google highway, many missing college students never return to campus. A sad statistic I'd never share with Charice Hawthorne. What happened to the majority of them? Their bodies were found floating in a river or lake: cause of death— accidental drowning. Maybe Darcy's story will turn out different. She'll be a returnee—A lucky statistic. I said a quick prayer for her.

***

We arrived at 28th and East Fourth Street an hour later. Thinking the best view of Lake Superior and Duluth's neighbor, Wisconsin, would be on the steps outside the cathedral I was surprised to discover otherwise. The locations of the Catholic school and the church parking lot actually proved better. Both neatly nestled near the edge of a huge rock formation.

According to the clock on the car dashboard we had exactly ten minutes to look at the view and snap pictures of Lake Superior before mass started. Since we were already in the parking lot, I chose to lead our group to a safe spot at the edge of the lot instead of wasting time crossing the street to reach the school.

When I led Margaret away from the car, I hadn't noticed any camera in her hand and quickly inquired about it.

"I've got it right here, dear," she pressed her small purse against her bosom, "How about you Zoe, did you bring yours?" No one answered. "I thought she left the car when we did, Mary."

"I did too." I glanced over my shoulder. Aunt Zoe appeared to be fussing with Fiona's trunk. "Did you forget something?" I yelled.

"My camera and purse."

I'll never understand her. Why didn't she say something when we got out of the car? I yanked the key from my pant pocket and pressed the *OPEN* symbol on the car remote. "There you go."

Five minutes later, we heard the bells in the church tower peal and tucked our cameras back in the car. "Perfect timing," I said, "We'd better get going."

The first portion of Mass moved fairly quickly; the priest had finished his sermon from a gospel passage in Luke, and waited along with the church community for the prayer petitions to be read. Normally it's the deacon's task, unless no deacon is present then the lay person who read before the gospel handles the petitions.

But there was a deacon assisting the priest today, and the usual petitions, one hears most Sundays, seamlessly glided off the young man's tongue. "Remember parishioner so-and-so who recently died, those who are gravely ill, and those in the military..." Then the deacon stopped, took a deep breath, and with a slight catch in his throat added an extra prayer request. "And let us remember to keep a missing girl from the community in our prayers too."

A person didn't have to be a PI to figure out who he meant. Margaret, sitting to the left of me, tapped my hand, and Auntie, situated to the right of me, gently jabbed my rib cage.

An hour later we blessed ourselves with holy water, peacefully passed through the church doors, and slowly retraced our steps to the parking lot where we could reflect upon the missing girl.

Margaret commented first. "I was surprised to hear the deacon include Darcy Hawthorne in the petitions. Perhaps her mother attends this church."

I shook my head. "Not necessarily. Maybe someone who knows the family requested the prayer."

The petite woman quietly accepted my thoughts on the matter. "I suppose."

"I don't know," Aunt Zoe interjected, "If you ask me, it seems a bit odd."

Margaret's thin eyebrows shot up the same time I felt mine do so. "You mean the type of prayer request, Auntie?"

Her hands flew to her face. "Heavens no. I was referring to the fact that no one on a campus the size of UMD knows anything about Darcy's disappearance. It's as if the earth swallowed her up."

"She may have been swallowed up," I stated, "but I have a hunch someone assisted, like the mysterious boyfriend. Why hasn't he come forward?"

"Maybe he's on the lam from the law," our neighbor suggested.

I nodded. "You might be right."

With nothing more to add about Darcy or her boyfriend, we began to search for Fiona. "There it is Mary," Aunt Zoe said, gesturing off to the right, "It's tucked between those two black Cadillacs."

"How about that. The mafia's protecting Fiona." A Cadillac may be beyond this gal's meager budget, but having the VW surrounded by two big burly ones certainly can't hurt.

"The mafia?" my aunt said, "Where?" She glanced every which way before wrapping her trembling hand around the handle of the VW's back door. "Am I the only one who can't spot them?"

Unfortunately, yes. "I was speaking metaphorically, Auntie, not literally." I pressed the *OPEN LOCK* symbol on the car key fob and we got in."

"That still doesn't explain your reference to the mafia."

I rested my hands on my cheeks and titled my head towards the ceiling. *I wonder if Dad dropped Aunt Zoe on her head when she was a baby.* "The two Cadillacs are the mafia. They're big impressive and have Fiona squeezed between them."

"Ah!"

"Okay ladies, does anyone want to take more pictures before we take off? It may be your last opportunity, especially if I get called to sub in the Cities."

"I don't care about pictures," Aunt Zoe said, "But do we have to go straight back to the apartment? It's such a nice day I'd rather go for a walk."

"I don't need any more pictures either," Margaret stated, "However I do like Zoe's idea. Surely there's a park nearby."

Little do they know a stroll's exactly what I had intended. I adjusted the rearview mirror and then poked the key in the ignition. "How about meandering through one of Duluth's fine college campuses?"

"Would that happen to be UMD?" Margaret inquired.

"Uh, huh." Someone finally left space in the parking lot for me to back up. I took advantage of it.

As soon as Fiona fit snugly between the two cars in the exit line, Aunt Zoe breathed down my neck. "Say, isn't that where Darcy Hawthorne attended college?"

"Yes."

"Ah, the game's afoot," Margaret proclaimed, pressing her thin hands together.

"Maybe," I murmured.

~15~

None of us walked that much in our daily routine, so I thought it wise to limit our stroll on the UMD campus to the administrative offices and a couple dormitories. Since I didn't expect to discover anything about Darcy Hawthorne's disappearance on this visit and wasn't involved in the case, I mainly studied the height of the dormitories we passed by and looked to see if there were any blind spots between them and the admin buildings. In a kidnapping case, it's best to take everything into consideration.

"It's a beautiful campus, isn't it," Margaret said, gazing out over the college grounds.

"Yes," I replied, "and with the leaves changing colors it makes the surroundings even more spectacular."

Aunt Zoe bent down, picked up a few oak leaves off the grass, and stood again. "Did you ever consider going to UMD for your teaching degree, Mary?"

"Not really. I wanted to attend a college a little closer to home."

"I sure hope the police find Darcy Hawthorne soon," Margaret said, walking a few steps ahead of us, "It'd be a shame if she never got to fulfill her dreams."

"I agree." We had already covered as much ground as I'd thought appropriate for my companions and was about to suggest we return to the parking lot when my stomach took control and let everyone know my breakfast had worn off. "Well, ladies, shall we go? I think it's time for lunch."

Aunt Zoe stretched her arms out in front of her. "This was a great excursion, but to be honest with you, my stomach and feet put me on notice ten minutes ago."

"Why didn't you say something?" I asked.

"I figured you'd be getting tired and hungry soon too."

"Well, you were right."

"There are enough leftovers from last night," Margaret shared, walking back to the car, "We shouldn't need anything else."

"The perfect ending to an outing," I said, "serving up Chinese food."

***

Late evening, as we prepared for slumber, Principal Drake from Washington Elementary phoned. He wanted to know if I could fill in for the remedial reading teacher. Apparently she had been called away unexpectedly by a family emergency out East. "Boston or Connecticut. I'm not sure which," he informed me, "And I have no idea how many days Lucinda will need you to fill in. It could be one day or a week." I gritted my teeth. Why this week? My research was moving along nicely. Plus I had promised to take the gals to the Glensheen Mansion in the next day or two, and I also wanted to do more solo snooping on the beach.

The minute I got off the phone, I shared the bad news with my companions. Margaret took my hand and gently patted it. "There's no need for the long face, Mary. Wipe that frown off. You warned us school might interfere with this trip. So, do what you have to do. Zoe and I will keep the place humming till you return."

Aunt Zoe chimed in, "Yeah, we don't need to go back. Besides, if we don't stay who's going to take care of Winnie."

"And Lizzie," Margaret added, "Didn't she say something about being released from the Shoolinger facility on Wednesday?"

The palm of my hand slapped my forehead. "How could I forget?" I whipped out my cell phone again. "I'm calling Principal Drake back. I can't possibly sub. Caring for an elderly relative takes precedence over any sub job."

Our nonagenarian neighbor protested. "You'll do no such thing. You're forgetting your part time jobs pay the bills." She lifted

~ 95 ~

her thin arms and rested her aged-hands on my shoulders. "Lizzie will be fine. As soon as she gets discharged, one of her apartment neighbors can pick her up. And when she gets home, Zoe and I can make sure she's well attended too."

"I know she'll eat well, but caring for an invalid can be quite strenuous. You sure the two of you can handle the challenge?"

The older women pushed me towards the bedroom. "Yes," they replied, "Pack what you need and get going. It's almost eleven."

~16~

In my haste to get out of town in a moonless, foggy night, it didn't take long before my bearings got twisted around especially without the assist of a certain gadget, namely GPS. *No problem,* I thought. *Isn't there always a Mc Donald's or Holiday Gas Station just around the bend that can steer people straight?* "But what if it isn't the case, Mary? What if after driving several more blocks, there's nothing but darkness?" *Phooey. Darkness isn't dangerous. I'll just pull off to the side of road, sleep till dawn, and then drive like a maniac all the way to Washington Elementary.*

I tightened my grip on the steering wheel and pictured Principal Drake's face when I bopped into the school building wearing a grungy T-shirt, tight fitting jeans and tennis shoes. Not a good scenario if I wanted to remain on the substitute list.

I turned on the radio to boost my sagging confidence. There had to be a way out of this unfamiliar town shrouded in fog.

"This is KQDS with your news at the top of the hour. The investigation concerning the theft at Clarity Diamonds and Gems is continuing by police as they widen their search to the Duluth area where an ex-employee once lived. It's believed that at least two suspects are now wanted in connection to this crime."

The way things are going in my life I could use a few jewels to prop me up. Just then what appeared to be a gas station cut through the veiled fog. I couldn't say much for the lighting surrounding the building and pumps, but the weak welcoming glow didn't matter. I merely required decent directions for the freeway, nothing else. I quickly scrubbed ugly sleeping arrangements and clothes aside.

Al's Gas and Garage sat on a corner of what appeared to be a desolate area of town. But then eyes do play tricks when the night is thick with fog, and Halloween's nearing. Nothing moved on Al's lot as far as I could tell except the *OPEN* sign attached to the door of the station. It flickered on and off like Bate's Motel sign in the movie *Psycho.* My hands sweated profusely even though the evening had cooled off considerably. *Do you really want to chance running into a character like Norman Bates, Mary?*

While I killed time gathering up enough gumption to venture out of my comfort zone, someone pounded their knuckles on the car window. Startled, I shivered just like Ethan Tucker my fictional character did. *You're being silly, Mary. It's got to be the attendant. Who else could it be?*

I faced the window and partially rolled it down. Bad mistake. A gun was thrust in my face.

"Get out of the car."

Wouldn't you know a million cars a year get stolen in the U.S. and I end up joining the statistics. Frightened out of my gourd, I squished my tush together so I wouldn't pee in my pants and just sat there.

"Didn't you hear me? I said get out of the car."

"I… I heard you. Give me a sec. I gotta unhook the seatbelt." I closed my hands around the car keys, the nearest thing I had to a weapon. The cop who taught a defense class for women at Washington School last year would be so proud of me. *I can get out of this jam. My keys can save me.*

"No. No. You're not taking those. Leave them where they are," a deep baritone voice demanded, as he shoved the gun closer to my cranium. "Close your eyes and get out."

Some people might think I acted like a chicken giving Fiona up without a fight. But doggone it, a gal's gotta do what a gal's gotta do to survive. I didn't lay on the horn. Mainly because I didn't know how the guy would react. He might just shoot me in the head accidently. And with no mace or other hardware to shake him off, I chose to save my skin. Besides, no car was worth losing a life over even if the bank still owned a huge chunk of it. I released the lock on the door, closed my eyes and stumbled out.

"Back up! Back up!" the man yelled. I heard the car door slam. The engine was gunned.

Good, he's going, I thought, but the car didn't speed off. I kept my eyes squeezed shut, afraid the stranger might back up and run over me if I didn't obey.

Something got tossed at my feet. Hopefully it wasn't a dangerous critter. The car door slammed for a second time. Then boom, Fiona roared to life and I heard a car window come down. "If you value your life," the hijacker yelled, "forget what you saw on the beach." The window zipped back up. Then I heard Fiona peeling out of the lot.

Forget what I saw on the beach. "Oh, my God! This fella has got to be one of the guys Aunt Zoe and I saw on our walk." My eyes popped open. The darkness was still there. Unfortunately, I needed to know what had been thrown out of the car. It could've been trash, but I had a hunch it was more important than stupid candy wrappers. After two minutes of groping around on the ground, I found what I hoped was the object. It was a bag of some sort. I thrust my hand into the bag. I couldn't believe my good fortune. The thief had given me back my purse. Either the guy, almost totally hidden by his high-collared coat and cap, was new to thievery, or he didn't have need for anything beyond a simple means of transportation—A get-away car perhaps.

I shook like a leaf during a prolonged storm, but I was bound and determined to continue sleuthing. No one scares me out of something I'm determined to do. Why, I'll be on that guy's tail like grease lightening. *With what? The thief took your wheels.*

The instant I calmed down a solution began percolating in my brain. I just needed to put it into action. I plucked my purse off the ground and ran to the station entrance as fast as my legs could carry me. The door was locked. But how could that be? If there weren't any employees on duty, why was the *OPEN* sign on?

I dug through my purse for that oh, so familiar small rectangular object we all can't possibly live without. When I found it, I set it in the palm of my hand and pressed a button. A bright light instantly came on. Yahoo! Whoever invented a light display window for the cell phone was a genius. I owed him big time. But right now, recent calls stored on the phone had my undivided attention.

Thankfully, I hadn't deleted incoming or outgoing calls for over a month. I quickly scanned the area codes, found an odd one that didn't match the rest, selected it, and hoped the right person on the other end answered.

"*Ciao*. I mean hello."

"Oh, Margaret, thank God it's you and not Aunt Zoe."

"What's the matter, dear, your voice sounds strained? Is Fiona acting up?"

Warm tears flooded my vision. I wiped them away as quickly as they came. "No. No driving problems. Fiona's been hijacked."

"Oh, no!"

Aunt Zoe's voice buzzed in the background like a hornet. "What's she saying?"

"Something about being hijacked," Margaret repeated.

"Hijacked? You mean kidnapped? Oh, God, it's my fault. I shouldn't have let her drive back to the cities solo."

The conversation on the other end needed to be cut short before things went from bad to worst. "Margaret, tell my aunt to calm down. I'm fine. The car's gone not me."

"She says her car was stolen, Zoe, that's all."

"That's all," she bristled, "then why's everyone so excited?"

"Shush, Zoe. I need to find out where Mary's at so we can send a car. Do you have any idea where you're at, dear?"

"I don't know what street I'm on if that's what you're asking. The fog's too thick, but I can give you the name of the gas station I'm stranded at."

"Mary, you're not thinking clearly. Ask the gas station attendant where he's located. You're inside, with him, aren't you?"

"No. I'm standing in the middle of an empty lot."

Margaret released a sigh. "*Non Capisco*. I don't understand. Why haven't you gone inside to get help?"

"There's no attendant. The station's locked up."

"Oh, my. We need to get you out of there right away," she said with a shaky voice. "Give me the name of the station? The Duluth police should be familiar with it."

I sucked in the fog. "The sign says Al's Gas and Garage."

~17~

Why is it when you don't want to get involved with someone, they keep popping up on your doorstep like a lost puppy? An adorable one at that I might add.

The troops finally arrived on the scene approximately ten minutes after my phone call to Margaret. Well, Officer Fitzwell, Trevor, did anyway. I don't get it. Do I have a homing device hidden on my body somewhere or is my brain somehow connected to his and sending out periodic notices: *damsel in distress.*

"You're sure Johnny on the spot," I eloquently noted as my stress level dropped considerably upon seeing the cop.

"What do you mean?" he asked in a low key, marching towards me. "I was sent out as soon as the station received a call about someone's car being hijacked. There's thick fog to contend with you know."

No kidding. That's why I'm in this stupid jam. I shifted away from the cop slightly. "I'm not referring to that. I'm speaking of the uncanny way you have of showing up exactly when I need a cop. Aren't there any other police guarding this fair city besides you?"

Trevor Fitzwell sounded ruffled. "Newbies don't question what shift they're put on or where they're sent."

I set my fingers under my chin and rubbed it. "So, in other words, the police chief sends rookies out on cases they deem aren't a big deal. Am I right?"

Thanks to the fog I couldn't tell whether my remark caused Trevor to grin or cringe. He turned towards his car lights, whipped out a small notebook and pen. "Look, what happened to you is a big deal, so let's get the questioning out of the way, okay?"

I nodded.

Standard police questions immediately flew out of his mouth one after the other. Were you hurt? Did you get a look at the person? Male or female? How tall? Did he reek from smoking or drinking?"

Forcing someone to reflect back on nasty stuff that occurred only moments before is tough. I almost fell apart. Remember I said almost. There's no way I'd allow this rookie cop see the fairer sex in emotional turmoil.

I sucked in precious air and bravely poured out answers. "The person sounded male, but not positive. He used a gun to force me out of the car. I didn't see much. Clothing hid the face pretty well. I didn't smell any cigarette smoke or alcohol. The car door slammed twice. I'm thinking a possible accomplice. There's one more thing your superiors should know. This wasn't a simple carjacking." I paused. "The guy warned me to stay away from the beach." *Just like you.*

"Are you finished?"

"Not quite. Where the heck's the attendant for this place? The station door is locked, but the *OPEN* sign's on."

Trevor rested the white pen against his lips. "If I'm not mistaken, this station's been closed for some time. "Maybe a squatter's been using it." He went over to the door and tried it. It didn't budge.

I tapped my foot. "What about druggies or diamond thieves?"

"You're quick on the draw for a…"

"A what? A doggie sitter?" *If he only knew.* "Can we get going now?"

Trevor slapped his notebook shut. "Okay, I guess we're finished here. Let me just call this in and we can be on our way."

The fog had gotten even thicker by the time Trevor signaled me to join him in his car, and I wondered if I'd ever make it to the cities tonight. "Where would you like me to drop you off?" he asked, "somewhere in Park Point?"

I clicked my seatbelt in place. "How about the cities?"

He shook his head. "You're joking right?"

"Nope."

"I can't take you that far. Duluth police department doesn't run a limo service. It exists to uphold the law."

Someone's a bit testy tonight. Could he have gotten chewed out by his superior officer right before chasing here? I rested my hands on top of my purse. "Well, Minneapolis happens to be where I'm headed. I've got an early morning job scheduled and can't afford to be late."

"Another doggie sitting job?"

I grit my teeth. "No." What is it about me? Is it the pheromones I give off? I keep tangling with macho men who think they know all the moves. Before I could come up with another bright idea, my cell phone rang. Probably Margaret or Aunt Zoe checking to see if I've been chopped into small pieces and scattered around Al's yet. I plucked the phone from my purse and put it to my ear. "Hello."

"Niece," Aunt Zoe said in the high-pitched voice she tends to use when nervous, "did any cops show up yet? They told Margaret they'd be there as soon as they could."

"The cavalry has arrived. We're leaving the station as we speak."

"What are you talking about? Oh, never mind. Which station—police or gas?"

"Gas, why?"

"I called Reed and told him what a pickle you're in. He's already on his way, but wondered if the cops could provide you with a ride as far as Hinckley."

Hmm? Would the straight arrow cop bend the rules for a shorter drive? "Hold on." I turned to Trevor. "How about a ride to Hinckley? It's closer than Minneapolis."

"Depends on the time."

"Does it really matter?"

"Yes."

And men think women have to be so precise. I glanced at my lit cell phone. "It's quarter after eleven in our time zone."

"You're positive?"

Good grief. What's this guy's problem? "Yes. I've never gotten in trouble for being late for anything because the time on my phone's off a second or two."

He tapped his hands on his steering wheel. "Okay. I guess I can give you a lift."

Shocked at his response, I waved the phone in front of me. "Wait a second. Don't you have to buzz your superiors to get their approval?"

He shook his head. "I don't think so. I've been off the clock for fifteen minutes."

Aunt Zoe piped up, "Mary, can you hear me? Are you getting a ride or not?"

I placed the phone near my mouth again. "I can hear you. It's a go for Hinckley. Tell Reed to look for a blue squad car outside of Tobies. That is if he can see it in this thick fog," I mumbled. Then I clicked the phone off and tossed it back in my purse. "Hey, Officer Fitzwell, can you do me a teeny-tiny favor?"

"Aren't I already doing you a huge one?"

I yawned. "Yeah, but this is even better."

"How so?"

"I get the impression work days are pretty dull around here for a newbie, am I right?"

"Maybe," he replied a little too quickly.

"Well, here's your chance to let loose then. Turn the siren on and let's peel out of here." I whipped my hand through my hair now as if I had no cares in the world, just waiting for Fitzwell to make his move. But nothing happened. No siren blared. I dropped my hands to my lap. "Ah, come on. There's no one to stop you. And you'll be rid of me a lot sooner too."

"Whoa. Let me get this straight, you're suggesting a law officer break the law for you?"

I cleared my throat. "Those are your words not mine, but it shouldn't matter. You're the one who said you're *off-duty*. Not me."

"I hate to break it to you, Miss Malone, but no rules are being broken here tonight. I don't relish being raked over the coals by my superiors for someone I barely know."

"So—you would break the rules if you knew someone longer?"

"Give it a rest," he said as he jerked the car into motion and drove down the entrance to the highway. "Unless of course, you want to be handcuffed and hauled into jail."

This cop didn't know me well. He doesn't get the last word no matter what silly threats he blows my way. "Officer, if someone can get tossed in jail for simply making a suggestion, the jails would be full of politicians and you know it."

Fitzwell tightened his grip on the steering wheel. "Darn. You're one smart cookie."

"I know." Good thing it was dark in the car, he never saw my Cheshire grin.

~18~

Two days of subbing had already whizzed by, and according to the latest report coming from Principal Drake's office it sounded like I might have to stick around till the end of the week. Despite the glad tidings, it didn't put me in any mood for throwing an "I'm in the money" party.

I had a headache the size of Niagara Falls. Fiona, had to be found pronto. The only thing I had to drive for the moment was my brother Matt's Topaz, a stinker of a clunker, and it was already five years past its delivery date to Gonzo's car graveyard. Only a mechanic knew how much longer life could be squeezed out of it. And I wasn't a mechanic. I just prayed it'd get me back and forth to school and up to Duluth again. I dragged my fingers across my forehead. Of course, thinking about Margaret sitting in close quarters with my aunt for days on end didn't help either. It added tremendous pressure on my noggin too.

Dear God, please don't let Margaret end up in the emergency room. The sweet woman doesn't deserve it. Aunt Zoe had to be driving her crazy. A duo of complete opposites living together for an extended period of time can cause a major strain on the body, I ought to know. Margaret happens to be an excellent cook and housekeeper, keeping everything in its proper place. Aunt Zoe, on the other hand, knows nothing about housekeeping or cooking thanks to the many servants her wealthy husband supplied her with up until he landed in Boot Hill ten months ago. And she certainly doesn't leave her things in any one spot for long.

A blaring radio bombarded me the second I walked into the teacher's lounge. I hadn't expected that. The room is usually so tranquil. I had gone there with the intention of seeking fifteen minutes of refuge to contemplate ways to resolve my woes. Apparently I picked the wrong room.

My first impulse was to shut the darn thing off, but I changed my mind. News on the hour would be forthcoming any second, so I set my attention to other things, like goodies to munch on. Perhaps someone brought bars or a cake for the teachers to eat. Snacks always comfort me when I'm overwrought with problems I have no solutions to, like a missing car. "Ah, what do we have here?"

Scrumptious chocolate cupcakes with mile-high orange frosting sat smack dab in the middle of one of the tables. "Yum." Someone must be celebrating their birthday. I strolled over to the table where the cupcakes were sitting, picked one up, and settled in at another table.

The moment I sat down another substitute teacher came in and joined me. "Do you mind if we listen to the news?" she asked. "Before I left home this morning, I heard something on the radio about a body being found in Duluth. My eighty-five year old grandmother still lives in her own home up there, and I'm worried it could be her."

"Hmm. I haven't heard anything," I replied. "Been too busy. Maybe it was a drifter they found. The temperature has been dropping way down at night." As I clamped my mouth around the cupcake that would surely add five-pounds to my already overweight hips, my cell phone rang. I swallowed hard, wiped my lips with a napkin, pulled the phone from my pant pocket, and moved to a corner of the room. "Hello."

"Mary, it's your roommate. Is this a bad time to talk?"

"No. I'm in the teacher's lounge the students aren't around. What's up? Is everything okay with you and Margaret?"

"Margaret and I are fine. It's Nurse Hawthorne."

"What happened? Did the police find her daughter?"

"Yes."

"Wow! That's wonderful news. I'm sure she's relieved to have her back home."

Aunt Zoe didn't say anything right away. "I... I don't know how relieved she is."

I put the phone a little closer to my mouth. "What do you mean? Why wouldn't she be?"

"Her daughter's body washed up on shore sometime during the night."

"What?"

"Hold on. I'm too upset to talk. I'll let Margaret explain."

Crackling sounds came across the phone, then, "Mary, dear, I know you flatly refused to help Nurse Hawthorne when she asked for your assistance in finding her missing daughter, but she's wondering if you'd help her now. You know," Margaret said in a dry tone, "investigate Darcy's death. Apparently the police think she's committed suicide. Nurse Hawthorne doesn't agree. She swears it doesn't fit with her daughter's personality."

"Charice thinks her daughter's been murdered?"

Margaret cleared her aging throat. "*Si.*"

From a missing daughter to a dead one. Tracking down a killer changed everything. Did I want to risk my life on another murder case? *No, absolutely not. Too dangerous.* Besides, my car had been taken at gun point. The cords in the back of my neck stiffened. I rubbed my neck. If Matt heard about this, he'd tell me not to get involved, to leave Darcy's death to the police. What should I do? Principal Drake said the school might need me to sub a couple more days. How do I get out of this current obligation without ramifications? Making the principal angry won't help my job situation. And if I take the case, where do I stay? There's no room for four at Cousin Lizzie's, plus I don't have a decent car at my disposal.

A picture of Charice Hawthorne's face the last time I spoke with her flashed across my brain and I came to a swift decision. "Tell her I'll take the case."

"Good. I thought you would. When should we expect you?"

"Possibly tomorrow, but there's one thing I need to know before I drive up there, Margaret."

"What, dear?"

"Do you need to get back down to the cities or can you stay in Duluth a while longer?"

"I'm fine where I am. There's no need for me to return to the Foley yet. Petey's gone and my next doctor appointment isn't until January."

"Glad to hear you're available. I like running things by you. See if you can find me a cheap place to rest my weary bones, okay?"

"*Si.* Zoe and I'll pester the tenants until we come up with a solution."

"Thanks." I switched the phone off, set it down, and returned to my half-eaten cupcake. No reason to let it go to waste.

"They found a young woman," the other substitute teacher informed me, "Not a drifter. They think she may have been a college student."

"So I heard. That was a friend from Duluth who called."

"Oh? Does she know the family?"

"Vaguely." When the rest of the cupcake disappeared, I gave the sub a lame excuse about getting back to my students. But I'd no intention of going there. I had something more pressing to attend to. I rushed out of the teacher's lounge and zoomed towards the office. Principal Drake better be available.

~**19**~

Wednesday

Did I ever mention that things occasionally work out in my life? And I do mean occasionally. I can count the times on my stubby toes. My good fortune came in the way of Lucinda, the remedial reading teacher. She had caught the red-eye late last night and would be back in the saddle at Washington Elementary early this morning. After receiving the grand news from Principal Drake, I packed my bags, said too-da-loo to the city, plopped myself behind the Topaz's steering wheel, and scrambled back to Duluth.

Margaret and Aunt Zoe, minus Cousin Lizzie's poodle, had just sauntered out to Del Rosa's parking lot when I neatly tucked the washed-up Topaz in a slot. "Going for a walk," I readily asked as I lazily exited the car.

Aunt Zoe rushed forward leaving Margaret on the sidewalk by herself. "No. Your cousin was just released from Shoolinger a few minutes ago and Virginia offered to help us pick her up." My aunt pointed to the lower level of the apartment complex. "She's bringing her car up from the garage."

Three minutes later the grinding gears of the garage door started up and I realized if we didn't move we'd be flattened beyond recognition. I latched on to my aunt's arm and lead her back towards Margaret just as a cardinal-red Mazda RX-8 buzzed around the bend.

The driver braked hard, missing us by less than a foot. Whew! I checked my pulse to make sure my heart hadn't gone into overdrive. Where the heck did Virginia Bagley learn to drive like that? I thought she grew up on a farm.

A car window rolled down and the building manager poked her bleach-blonde head out. "Sorry about that. I didn't mean to scare anyone. I just can't seem to control my lead foot when I climb into this car."

Must be rough, I thought, *Fiona is missing and the best I can do is chase around town in Matt's ugly, sluggish cramped car. It's not fair.*

Marge finished what she had to say about speeding and focused on me now. "Oh, hi Mary. When did you get back from the cities?"

"About two seconds ago. Would you like me to take my companions over to Shoolinger instead?"

The Del Rosa manager shook her oval head. "Nah, go unwind, we won't be long."

"Thanks. I could use the rest. I got up much earlier than usual." I scooted around the car to the front passenger door and helped Margaret get in while Aunt Zoe took care of herself.

After the nonagenarian got situated with her coat and seatbelt, she asked me not to take off yet. Apparently there was something she wanted to retrieve from her purse. Of course I complied. I don't make a habit of ignoring elderly people's wishes. "Here Mary, you'll need these," she said as she snapped her purse shut and handed me Lizzie's keys."

"Thanks. I didn't even think about Lizzie's keys." I shoved them in a pocket of my light-weight jacket. "Hey, what about tonight? Have you figured out where I'm supposed to stay?"

"We'll talk about it when we return," she replied.

Virginia tapped her jeweled wristwatch with her mauve painted French cut nails. "We've gotta go, Mary, we're running late." She revved up the Mazda's engine giving fair warning of her determination to leave, and then zipped out of the parking lot, leaving me to fend for myself. Thankfully I didn't have much to haul in this time, just the basic crime fighting essentials: Matt's old fashioned Cannon camera and his Microcassette recorder.

***

Winnie wailed the minute the apartment door cracked open. Her whimpering sounded different somehow, like she anticipated the person crossing the threshold to be Lizzie, not me. Pets sense this kind of stuff, so I've been told. Too bad humans don't.

"It's not Mommy," I softly announced, thinking the information would calm her down. It didn't. It made matters worse. She wailed even louder. Not wanting to face irritated neighbors, I set my things on the dining room table and went directly to the kitchen and the kenneled pooch.

The second the kennel got unlatched Winnie flew to the door and sniffed everything in sight, including my grungy tennis shoes. Obviously, she didn't believe what I said and had to check things out for herself. Too bad the mutt's not a bloodhound, she'd be a huge help with the Darcy Hawthorne case. *How about Trevor Fitzwell's young German Shepherd?* "Nope. Afraid not." His dope sniffing would do me no good either. I should've borrowed Gracie. Matt said if she hadn't been with him on a couple of cases he would've been a goner. But then again, two dogs in one apartment, I think not.

Through sniffing, Winnie reverted back to whining. *Crazy dog, even Gracie doesn't make this much racket and she's bigger.* I had to get her to quiet down or there'd be no nap for me. A sluggish mind does not crack a case. One has to be as sharp as an eagle.

The ball of energy paraded into the living room. I followed close behind. Perhaps I could convince her to settle on the floor by me. I plucked the afghan off the settee, crouched down near the floor, and patted the plush, fresh smelling carpet. "Come here, Winnie. Snuggle in. Your mommy won't be home for a while yet." The poodle looked around, not sure what she wanted to do. I stretched out, hinting a little more. She marched closer, bit-by-bit. When the tip of her nose finally touched one of my hands, I knew I had her. "Good girl. Get closer."

Slumber didn't come soon enough for me. Before I had a chance to let loose with even one loud snore, the cell phone jingled. Since it wasn't the familiar tone set for my family, I figured I'd better get it. Perhaps the cops had tracked Fiona down. I threw off the afghan, scrambled to my purse, and plucked the phone from its hiding spot. "Mary Malone."

"Mary, its Charice Hawthorne. Are you in Duluth yet?"

I slid my hand to the top of my forehead and continued on into my hair. "As a matter of fact, I just got in. I planned to call you in a few minutes. *After my nap of course, but she didn't need to know that.* Look, I'd like to sit down with you and gather more background information on Darcy before I go banging on doors. Do you feel up to it?"

"Not really, but I know you can't do a decent job without my filling in the blanks. Why don't you meet me by the popcorn stand in Canal Park. I don't go on duty until five."

"Sure. I'll be there in an hour. Oh, and bring along one of your daughter's graduation pictures."

After I ended the call, I stretched out with the dog again, for what seemed a mere minute or two, when Winnie's fierce growl suddenly took charge. Apparently someone was attempting to get in. I tossed the afghan off and rushed to the door. "Who's there?" I timidly asked.

"It's me, Lizzie. Let us in, Mary."

Winnie shook like crazy when she heard her owner's voice. "Just a sec," I said. But before I dared unbolt the door, an antsy critter needed to be taken care of. I wasn't going to allow the frisky poodle to jostle her owner's newly replaced knees while I was around. I threw my arms around the mutt and hauled her to the kennel. She wailed. I ignored her. She'd be released soon enough.

I trotted back to the door, unlatched it, and cheerfully hugged my cousin. "Welcome home, Lizzie. "Here," I said, "let me take your overnight bag. I'll set it in your bedroom."

"Thank you, Mary. Home sweet home," Lizzie sighed, "It never felt so good."

Aunt Zoe stepped in after Lizzie and latched on to one of her arms. Margaret followed behind.

"Sorry the door wasn't unlocked," I said, "I didn't expect the gals to spring you from Shoolinger so soon. There's always so much paperwork to handle before getting released," drawing on my own dad's exit from a hospital a couple years back." I swiftly stepped out of the way, making room for my cousin and my companions to move beyond the doorway. "You must've been waiting out on the curb for Margaret and Aunt Zoe."

Lizzie stabbed the plush carpet with her cane, slowly maneuvering from the entrance hallway into the living room. "Good guess, but I wasn't quite on the curb. It's impossible to sneak out of that place. There are cameras everywhere you go. However, I did persuade a nurse to wheel me as far as the grand lobby on the ground floor. Watching the freshwater fish enjoy their huge aquarium is so relaxing." When Lizzie reached the brocade settee we all drooled over the first day we'd arrived, she turned slightly and scanned the room from top to bottom.

Concerned we innocently misplaced something in her absence, I said, "What is it, Lizzie? Did we disturb something we shouldn't have?"

"I'm not sure. The room seems to be much larger than I remember," she flatly stated, "Did you rearrange the furniture while I was away?"

"Aunt Zoe wanted to, but I told her to wait till you got home."

"She's fibbing," my aunt said, "I never suggested any such thing."

"It's all right if you did," Lizzie said, "I don't mind, really."

Margaret stepped alongside Lizzie. "The living room only appears bigger because you've been confined to a tiny room for so long."

"That's true. I know Sarah, my daughter, certainly wouldn't have touched anything while she stayed here. She leaves the heavy moving to her husband." Lizzie made herself comfortable on the settee, and her eyes soon flitted to an object on the floor near the TV. "I see Sarah must've purchased an ottoman and forgot to tell me. That's one less thing I have to worry about. Before I left Shoolinger, the nurses reminded me to elevate my legs as much as possible to reduce the swelling around my knees."

"Your daughter didn't buy the ottoman," Aunt Zoe stated dryly, "Virginia insisted you use the spare one she had instead of Sarah chasing around town looking for one to fit your décor."

Lizzie rested her long thin fingers on her chin. "Oh, dear, I hope Virginia didn't strain her back carrying it in here. It looks awful heavy."

"Virginia didn't deliver it," Auntie explained as she rescued the ottoman from its spot by the TV and rolled it over to Lizzie. "One of the building's handy men brought it down here this past Monday."

"Wuff. Wuff. Wuff. Wuff."

"Ah, now that's a familiar sound. Mary, where are you hiding my precious dog? Did you lock her in the bathroom?"

"No, she's in her kennel. I thought you should get situated first so she doesn't bowl you over. You don't want to end up back at Shoolinger, do you?"

"Good grief, no. I'm glad to be out of there."

Margaret spotted the two-tone crochet afghan I had left on the floor in my hurry to answer the door. She picked it up. "Lizzie, would you like this?"

"Yes, please. I'm a little chilly."

The nonagenarian handed it over with great care. "It's such a lovely piece of work. Did you make it?" she asked as she signaled for me to get the dog.

I rid myself of Lizzie's suitcase before slipping into the kitchen to unlock the kennel door. When I returned with the four-legged creature in my arms, I set her down on the settee and she immediately bounded onto Lizzie's lap like an excited child on a school holiday, licking her owner's smiling face, starting with the deep-wrinkled forehead. "I missed you too, but you need to settle down, you silly mutt." Lizzie placed her hand on Winnie's back and gently coaxed her to sit.

"She may not want to stay that way for long," I said, "We had been snoozing when you rapped on the door." I offered Winnie a doggie treat. She scarfed it up.

"Your poodle certainly didn't act wild around us," Aunt Zoe said, waiting for Margaret and me to corroborate her statement, even though it was a flimsy fib. *Uh, oh. I think I'm rubbing off on her.*

"No, never," the two of us neatly replied.

When Margaret's feet stepped back from the settee a bit, she stooped down near the carpet again where the afghan had been and scooped something up. Thinking one of my earrings had fallen out, my hands shot to my earlobes. Both silver hooped earrings were still in place. "What did you find?" I asked.

The nonagenarian held her hand out flat. "It's a tiny stone. Did anyone lose a gem from a ring?"

We looked from one to the other and shook our heads. Finally, my cousin said, "Maybe it fell out of one of my daughter's rings when she stayed here."

"Of course," I stretched out my hand. "Here, Margaret, give it to me. I'll put it in the glass dish sitting on the kitchen counter. The next time Sarah calls, be sure to ask her about it, Lizzie."

"I certainly will. Say, Cousin, I hear you're helping Nurse Hawthorne? Didn't you turn her down Saturday night at Shoolinger?"

I crossed the room and sat in the brocade chair nearest the door. "I did. When did you last see her?"

"I believe Monday evening. Why? What's going on?"

"Her daughter's body washed up near the northeastern edge of the beach here on Park Point sometime Tuesday night."

Cousin Lizzie's hands flew up. "The drowning victim the police found that's... that's Charice's daughter? Oh, the poor woman, what she must be going through."

Aunt Zoe hastily shared what she knew. "The police suspect suicide. But Nurse Hawthorne thinks someone murdered her daughter. She's requested an autopsy."

"But Charice knows the final results of an autopsy, including lab tests, can take anywhere from four to six weeks if done correctly," I added, "so she's asked me to help find the murderer before he gets away." I glanced at the intricate glass-domed clock ticking away on a side table. "Speaking of which, I'd better get going. Charice is meeting me down at Canal Park in a few minutes. Does anyone need anything while I'm out and about?"

Margaret and Lizzie said they couldn't think of anything. Aunt Zoe on the other hand sat with her roundish face scrunched up, deep in thought. A half-second later she said. "You're making a huge mistake going off by yourself. Wasn't one incident enough to scare you?"

"What's she talking about?" my cousin asked.

I ignored the question. "I'll be fine. It's still light out. Supposedly the goons don't come out until six or seven."

Aunt Zoe shook her fiery-red head. "I don't care if it's light out or not. After what happened Sunday night, who knows where the man may be lurking next."

"I agree," Margaret said.

Cousin Lizzie's face looked deeply concerned. "What incident Sunday evening? No one's mentioned anything."

Margaret squared her small shoulders and shared what she knew. "Mary's car was taken at gunpoint."

"What? You should've told me, Mary. Were you hurt?"

I shook my head. "I asked Margaret and Zoe to keep the situation under wraps. You had enough going on. I didn't want you to be burdened with anything else. Besides, there's nothing any of you could've done."

"You're right. So tell me, did the police find your car yet?"

"Nope. For all I know it could be sitting at a curb in Timbuktu waiting for an airport passenger."

"Or chopped up like I saw on a crime show last week," my aunt added.

Lizzie lifted Winnie off her lap and set her on the floor. "Well, Cousin, as much as you don't want to hear this from me, you need to heed your elder's concerns. Don't go running around Duluth by yourself. You may not have gotten hurt the last time, but it doesn't mean you won't the next."

Wow! I hadn't expected everyone to gang up on me. I had no choice. It was either do what they wished or I'd never hear the end of it. I shrugged my shoulders. "All right. All right. You can come with Aunt Zoe, but you have to promise to let me handle the investigation. Do you understand?"

Auntie grinned, exposing her generous overbite. "Of course, dear, I wouldn't dream of butting in. My lips shall remain zipped."

So she says. Her lips have this uncanny ability to stay sealed about as long as an alligator's does when supper's staring him in the face.

~20~

"There's a spot to park. It's right by the popcorn stand, Mary."

"Do you see Charice?" I asked, scanning the area.

"Nope."

"Maybe she left her house later than she planned." I pulled into the slot Aunt Zoe referred to, took the key out of the ignition, and grabbed the goody bag from the back seat I used when subbing. There were no fun classroom handouts in the bag today. Just a notepad, a tangerine colored pen I'd found at a Holiday gas station with SAVE the DATE and name of the lovely couple emblazoned on it, and Matt's recorder.

"What's the plan? Do we sit here till Charice shows up?"

"We could, but I'd rather get out and stretch my legs. I've been in this car way too long already."

When we stepped out of the car, a cookie truck drove by. I immediately thought of the truck of stolen Oreo's in Des Moines, Iowa last week and wondered where they ended up. I could use a few. My stomach rumbled. "You know what I could go for, Auntie?"

"What?"

"A package of Oreo Cookies."

"Sounds delicious, Mary, but there's no grocery store in this neighborhood. "How about we get a bag of popcorn? I haven't had lunch yet and I bet you haven't either."

"With what?" I showed her my jacket's empty pocket liners.

"No problem. The treat's on me." She whipped out her coin purse and stepped into the long line of people waiting at the cherry-red popcorn wagon. "My mother always said, 'Never leave home without money in your pocket.'"

Is that so? How come you never have any money when we're out and about in the cities?

I held my tongue. I wasn't about to lose out on a free snack. "Good advice. Just make sure the gal goes light on the salt and heavy on the butter." I got out of the way of the crowd and kept an eye out for Charice. Hopefully she would show soon.

She did, but not from the direction I'd expected. Darcy's mother approached me from behind. I only knew she was there because I picked up a whiff of *Cool Water* by Davidoff, my mother's favorite fragrance, and remembered catching the same scent on Charice at Shoolinger. "Sorry, I'm late," she announced as she tapped me on the shoulder, "I had to pay a bill at the shop across the way, and didn't realize how busy they would be. Should we find a place to sit?"

I pointed to the line of people waiting for popcorn. "My aunt came with. It looks like she's finally placing her order. Did you want anything?"

She swung her ponytailed head back and forth. "No thanks. I try to watch my calories." *No kidding.* In casual slacks the woman displayed a model-like figure, something I've dreamt of since good ol' college days. "Darcy loved cheddar cheese-coated popcorn," she softly shared, "It's her favorite snack, I mean, it was."

I made a mental note to remember that little tidbit. It could possibly lead me to the last place Darcy was seen alive. "Ah, here she comes," I said, referring to my aunt. When Aunt Zoe finally reached us, I led the two women to an empty bench near the lighthouse at the end of the pier no longer in use.

The minute we got comfortable, Dad's sibling tried to pass the popcorn around. "No, thanks," I said, "Charice and I don't care for any."

"Huh?"

I ignored my aunt's 'Huh' and pulled the notepad and recorder out of my bag. If I wanted Charice to trust me, I needed to convey professionalism not amateurish ways. I clicked the *ON* button for the recorder and began. "So let's go back about a month before Darcy went off to college. Did she have a set pattern for her day? Who was she dating at the time? Were you two getting along?"

The last question hit a raw nerve. Charice's limp arms clutched her body tightly. Her pupils grew considerably. "I don't see how our getting along has anything to do with her disappearance," she said, sounding angry, "I certainly had nothing to do with my daughter's death."

I patted her arm to soothe her. "I know, but it helps me understand her frame of mind when she left for college."

Charice inhaled deeply before dropping her neatly-trimmed hands to her lap. "Heated words had been exchanged between the two of us the day she left. My daughter had been out partying the evening before with her boyfriend, Zeke. Both had had too much to drink. I found them asleep on the couch entwined in each other's arms, woke them, and demanded Zeke leave. Darcy threw a hissy fit. Said I had no right to send her boyfriend home. I told her she needed to focus on college not on a one-night-stand with a boy who had no plans for his future."

"What...." Aunt Zoe interrupted, forgetting her promise already. I sent a stern glare her way. She caught it and slid a pudgy finger across her plump lips.

"What was Darcy's response?" I continued.

Speaking of her dead daughter brought tears to Charice's smooth, pale cheeks. She dug out a Kleenex from a pant pocket and dabbed at her face. "Once she set foot on campus, she said she was never coming home."

"Did she stick to her word?"

"Up until a week before she disappeared. I was at work when she finally broke down and reached out to me. She'd left a brief message. Said she was sorry for being such a brat and mentioned bringing a friend to our annual neighborhood Halloween party."

"Is there something significant about the party?"

"No. We just got involved with it more after my husband died. It's become something fun for us trying to outdo each other with the scariest costume." She pressed the crumpled Kleenex against her poncho style rust-colored sweater and dropped her head, "Darcy won hands down last year."

"Who did she go as?"

"One of those *walking dead* people."

Stupid, stupid question, Mary. Worried Charice might not be able to hang in there much longer especially after what I just asked, I said, "Perhaps we should finish our talk another day."

Tears scrambled down her cheeks again. "No, I'll be all right. I want to do this. It's just... it's just hard to speak of Darcy in the past tense."

We sat in silence for a few minutes, allowing Charice to get a handle on her grief. When she seemed ready, I probed further. "Let's talk about your daughter's roommate Tracy. She told you Darcy had been seeing someone new and you believed her. Do you still feel that way? Or could she have had something to do with your daughter's disappearance and eventual death?"

"I... I don't know. I want to believe her."

"What about your daughter's other friends?"

"I made a list of her friends and brought the photo you requested. Hopefully, there's something useful there." She reached for her medium-sized Coach purse, took out a brown envelope and handed it to me.

I clicked the recorder off. "I'm sure I will." I took what she offered, placed them in my goody bag, and then stood. Before we went our separate ways, I promised Charice I'd keep her informed as the investigation moved forward.

After Charice departed, I plucked the half-empty bag of popcorn from my aunt's pudgy hands, collected a handful, and stuffed it in my mouth. "I thought you didn't want any?" Aunt Zoe said.

How does one reply with broken bits of buttered popcorn still bouncing around the tongue? All I can say is don't try it when you're entertaining company. "I ...tried ...to be ...considerate ...of Charice." Thanks to the forced saliva action the rest of the popcorn in my mouth finally managed to find its way to my stomach, which worked out well because I had more to say. "She told me she didn't want any while you were purchasing it." I thrust my hand back in the popcorn bag now, but before I could withdraw more, someone rammed into me, making me the perfect target for a theft operation.

The perpetrator's quick fingers hurriedly hooked the shoulder strap of the brightly colored goodie bag slung over my right shoulder. *Mister you've no idea who you're dealing with.* Raised with two brothers, I fought back the best I could, losing the rest of the popcorn and my balance in the process, but not the bag. It remained in my possession.

Angry, Aunt Zoe took over where I left off. She swung her zebra purse behind her and then flung it forward in an effort to knock the would-be thief to the ground. She totally missed the target, and it took a while for her purse to calm down. "Are you all right, Mary?"

A bit shaken from the tumble, I said, "I think so. At least I landed on dead grass, not the parking lot." I stood and looked around. "What the heck was that all about?"

Aunt Zoe stared at me. "I have no idea."

"I hope he didn't get anything from my bag." I'd be in deep trouble if I'd lost Matt's recorder. My brother had no clue I was sleuthing on the side to pay bills. I opened the bag and took a quick peek inside: nothing missing. "Did you at least catch a glimpse of him?"

Afraid not," she hastily replied, "Are you sure it was a man? It happened so fast. I only saw a grey hoodie. Could it have been the same person who stole Fiona?"

I shrugged my shoulders. "Whoever it was, they took a big risk going after me in the middle of the day with so many people wandering about." I slid my hand through the bag handle and settled it on my shoulder again.

"Looks like your bag got torn when you fell."

"It did? Darn. Where?"

"The right corner towards the bottom."

I took the bag off my shoulder and examined the tear. "It's not torn. Someone sliced the bag with a knife." I trembled. Did the person intend to stab me or steal the bag? "Auntie, let's keep this incident under our hats, okay? I don't want Margaret and Lizzie getting all worked up."

"Got'cha," she swiftly replied, "Were in water up to our knees and it's going to be up to our hips before we know it."

~21~

Margaret and Cousin Lizzie cornered me the instant we returned to Del Rosa. It's understandable. If they had met with Charice Hawthorne instead of me, the reverse would've been true. "Charice's one strong woman," I shared, "She actually managed to get through the questioning without breaking down completely."

"Mary's right," Aunt Zoe added, "Why, when my Edward died, I was a basket case. No one could get anything out of me for weeks."

They still can't.

"She's in shock," Margaret reminded us, "The hailstorm will come soon enough. I remember Mary's brother behaving the same way when his wife Irene died."

I raised a hand to my forehead. "I must be a terrible sister. I don't recall him being that way."

Our neighbor hugged me. "You're being too hard on yourself. When Irene passed away, you were busy with teaching and attending classes for a master's degree. I on the other hand had been a widow for many years and had time to check on Matt."

"Matt was lucky to have someone so close by to talk to," I said, "According to Charice, she has only one living relative, a sister recently diagnosed with cancer who resides in Marquette, Michigan."

Cousin Lizzie spread her long thin hands out like she was about to take flight. "Well," she declared, "then we'll be her support group. It's the least we can do for such a caring nurse."

"I agree," Aunt Zoe piped up, "So, where do we go from here, Mary?"

"We need to follow Darcy's trail, specifically her last day on campus. See if she attended classes or skipped them. Her mom said she didn't have a car. Did someone notice her departure from campus? What means of transportation did she use?"

"I imagine you've already thought about who you want to interview first?" Margaret softly quizzed.

"Yup, it's already included in my agenda."

The ding-ding of the microwave timer interrupted the flow of conversation.

Margaret pushed herself out of a brocaded chair. "Lunch is ready. Why don't we carry this discussion to the kitchen, ladies?"

Winnie took Margaret's orders seriously. She jumped off Lizzie's lap and immediately flew to the eating area. My cousin laughed. "There goes my little puffball," she said, as she held out her arm for assistance, "I wish I could be that agile."

I slipped my arm around hers. "You've got an excuse, Cousin. What's mine?"

"Give me time. I'll come up with something."

The kitchen table held a variety of crackers, butter, and beverages. All it needed was the soup. Aunt Zoe approached the table ahead of me and pulled out two chairs, one for her and one for Lizzie. I left Lizzie by her chair and offered to help the chef, Margaret, who was standing at the stove ladling steaming chili into bowls. As each one got filled, I delivered it to the table. When all four bowls sat in their respective spots, the chef commanded us to dig in before lunch got cold.

Aunt Zoe sniffed the chili sitting in front of her. "Hmm. It smells delicious, Margaret. There's plenty of chili powder in it I presume? I always say there's nothing like spicy food to liven up a meal." She gathered a few soda crackers and crushed them over the bowl of chili like she was destroying her worst enemy.

"Afraid not," Margaret replied, "Some of our stomachs can't handle hot spices anymore."

"Of course. How inconsiderate of me." She patted her bulging stomach, "It probably wouldn't hurt me to cut back either.

As we continue on in years, the Tums seem to fly off the medicine shelf faster and faster, don't they?" The two older women agreed.

Curious to see if Auntie would appreciate Margaret's chili recipe since she just learned it lacked less chili powder than she preferred, I watched as the first spoonful of chili made contact with her orange painted lips. "Mmm. It's mighty tasty, Margaret. Do you ever make this for a large group?"

Margaret leaned into the table. "I've never taken it to a potluck if that's what you mean."

Oh, Oh. I wonder what scheme she's got up her sleeve this time. "What are you thinking, Auntie?"

She dipped her spoon back into her bowl. "Margaret's chili would be a big hit at one of Reed's monthly cookouts."

"Please tell me you're not planning to ask Margaret to make it for you."

"No. No. I'd never do that. I'd have you make a copy of the recipe and I'd make it."

Right. Just like she made fudge that never hardened. There's no way she's touching our stove. I'll flip the circuit breaker before I'd allow that to happen again. I set a few crackers next to my bowl and passed the rest to Margaret. "Anyone care to share where I'm going to be sleeping tonight. Since no one's mentioned what type of arrangement's been made yet, I hope it's nothing too drastic."

Margaret took a couple of crackers and set them on a napkin. "We tried getting the visitor room on the main floor for you, but its booked solid through October. According to Virginia, residents at the Del Rosa have more visitors this month than any other."

I nodded. "It makes sense. Everyone wants to see the fall colors, including us."

"Yes, but don't worry," my roommate added, swiping her mouth with a napkin, "We found you another place. And, believe it or not it's right here in the building."

Picturing a dark dank room swarming with centipedes situated smack dab in the heart of the underground garage, I barely managed to say, "Where?"

"Why, one floor up. Virginia offered her second bedroom."

"And why would she do that? She barely knows me."

"Apparently she was a teacher over a decade ago," Margaret replied, "and she misses the buzz of what's happening in the classroom."

"Did she teach elementary or high school?"

The nonagenarian wrapped her hands around a glass of water while she thought about my question. "I believe she said high school. Now, can we please get on with the case? You didn't say who you might interview first. I want to see if my hunch pans out."

I rested my spoon in the bowl of chili sitting in front of me, lifted my head, and glanced around the table. "I'm sure everyone knows who it is."

"How could I?" Cousin Lizzie announced. "I've been out of the loop so to speak."

Aunt Zoe shook her head. "Well, I certainly have no idea. You didn't mention anyone in the car."

Margaret's old eyes twinkled briefly.

I stared at the petite Italian woman. "Go ahead, tell them what you think."

Her reply came softly. "Trudy makes the most sense to me."

"Bingo," I hollered, "You win. I'm depending on her to lead me straight to Zeke, the ex-boyfriend."

"And," my aunt added, "when you pass *GO*, you'll collect the new boyfriend as well."

"That would be nice otherwise the case will be at a standstill." My stomach roared. I grabbed the spoon. I didn't know if the chili had cooled off sufficiently for my temperamental tongue, but I didn't care. It's going down. I'm not ignoring my stomach, even if it means burning my mouth and esophagus, twice in two days.

Lizzie took a dab of butter off the dish Aunt Zoe had passed to her and buttered a cracker. "Do you really think the roommate's involved?"

My spoonful of chili hovered three measly inches from the portal to my stomach. Maybe it wasn't meant to reach my innards. I'm supposed to be dieting. "Probably. You know what they say about a woman scorned."

"No," my roommate said dryly. Unfortunately, she wasn't joking.

I dropped the spoon back in my ceramic bowl. "I'll Google the phrase for you."

"When?"

Few people know this but when my stomach's in control, I'm a bear. "Right after I finish lunch," I snapped, picking up my spoon and shoving lukewarm chili into my mouth.

~**22**~

After examining the floor to make certain I hadn't left any traces of lunch behind for Winnie to gobble up, I didn't run to my laptop to Google the stupid phrase like I said I would. Don't worry I wasn't being spiteful, it's not my style. I just had more urgent things on my plate like lining up interviews with Darcy's friends.

As soon as the coast was clear, I made a mad dash to the guest bedroom and quietly closed the door. Sitting on the edge of the white metal bed now surrounded by the necessary solitude I desired, I dumped the contents of the goodie bag on the bedspread, and grabbed the cell phone from the interior of my knock-off Coach purse. This sleuth needed to formulate a strategy and fast. Time was slipping through my fingers like sand in an hour glass.

Examining the short list of names Charice had given me, I quickly assigned a high or low number to each name. The lower the number the sooner the person would be hearing from me.

Not surprisingly, Trudy still came up number one. The minute I gleaned information from her I could cast the net wider. But, would she be available to speak with me this evening? I held the cell phone in front of me and gingerly tapped out her number on the keypad. A gentle knock on the door stopped me from hitting the *CALL* button. "Yes?"

"Sorry to disturb you, Mary," my aunt said through the lightly-stained hollow door, "but I wondered if you had a chance to Google that information for me yet."

Even though I had a lot on my mind, I recalled how I snapped at lunch and didn't want to repeat the performance. Sure, Dad's sister's ignorant about certain things, but she didn't deserve the way I responded to her earlier today. "No, not yet," I kindly replied, "I'm in the middle of making an important phone call. But I promise to get to it as soon as I'm finished."

"Okay. I'll let you be then."

I hit the *CALL* button. Trudy's phone rang eight times before her voice mail kicked in. *Probably at a class or chowing down with a friend.* I left my name, number, and a brief message explaining what I wanted and then hung up. Hopefully she'll return my call before tomorrow. With nothing further to do, I grabbed the laptop and proceeded to the living room where Auntie and the others waited for me.

"There you are, Mary," Margaret said, "Did you reach who you wanted to?"

"Nope. I left a message."

Lizzie signaled for me to sit in the French antique chair closest to the settee where she sat. It wasn't the most comfortable, but I complied. "Zoe told me you don't need a regular camera to take pictures anymore. People use their phones instead. How's that possible?"

"Let me take a few pictures first." I dug out my cell phone, pressed the symbol for camera, and took several group pictures of the three older women. Then I tapped the symbol for stored photos and passed the phone around. "What do you think?"

My cousin set the phone in the palm of her hand and examined the photos. "Oh, my goodness. What will those computer people come up with next? So, where's the film stashed in the phone?"

"Phone cameras don't require film."

"Really?"

"Yup. So you don't need to waste money on developing pictures you hate ever again. You simply delete the ones you don't like."

Lizzie handed the phone to Margaret. "Well, how do you get a paper copy for a photo album?"

"Give me a second and I'll show you."

Margaret stared at the picture on the phone. "Isn't it amazing how quickly technology forges ahead? I can barely believe it. My generation didn't even believe man could get to the moon."

"Oh, you haven't seen anything yet," I took the phone back. "This little gizmo can do much more. For instance, if you want to save only a portion of a picture, you crop it."

Margaret seemed genuinely interested. "Do you mind showing us how cropping works?"

"Sure." I set the phone in the center of the coffee table. "See how much added space is above your heads?"

"Yes."

"After I focus in on the part I want to keep, I simply press the CROP button and the stuff I don't want vanishes."

"Very clever," Aunt Zoe said, "Say, Mary, as long as we're gathered together, can you show us the pictures you took Saturday and Sunday."

"It'd be better if I downloaded the phone pictures to my laptop instead. The viewing screen's much bigger." I set the laptop on the coffee table next to the phone and then left to retrieve a phone cord kept in the laptop storage bag. When I returned, I found the three older women squeezed together on the settee.

I immediately dropped to the floor near Margaret's feet, made the necessary connections between the phone and laptop, and explained the importing of pictures. "Once they're downloaded, I'll enlarge them one by one. When the photos have been transferred to the computer, you can also make all the photos you want. Of course, you'll need to be hooked up to a printer. "

The instant the first picture appeared on the screen the "Ooh's and aah's" began and continued to grow louder when the next new scene popped on the screen. "Wonderful shots," Lizzie remarked, "Lake Superior never looked so enticing. I'm looking forward to climbing those sand dunes again."

"I'm rather surprised the pictures turned out so good," I said, clearing the current picture and replacing it with another, "My thumb usually has a way of spoiling one or two."

A new scene appeared and an "Oops," escaped Aunt Zoe's thick lips. "I think your hand shook when you took the selfie of the two of us. I can't figure out what's supposed to be behind us."

I drew closer to the screen and analyzed the picture. *No it can't be.* How did those people around the bonfire end up in the shot? I scratched my head. "I have no idea either."

Margaret reached for my arm. "What's wrong, Mary? You look like you've seen a ghost."

I shook my head. I didn't want Aunt Zoe to learn what ended up in our picture. "I'm upset about the botched picture. I thought it would be a nice Christmas present for my folks."

"But you said you can crop out what you don't want," the nonagenarian kindly reminded me.

"I know. I guess I can attempt it later. Christmas is a long ways off." Maybe I'll use the photo for a gift like I said, but before I think about that I'm going to scrutinize the picture more carefully and make notes regarding the foursome around the bonfire. I cleared the screen. Everything I had on Duluth had been seen. "Okay, Auntie, "I'm ready to Google the information you wanted."

"What information?"

~**23**~

Thursday

Trudy Almquist called around nine last night and said her second hour class on Thursday had been cancelled. If I wanted to catch her at the dorm, it would have to be then.

No problem. "I get up by eight when I'm not working," I told her tongue-in cheek.

The minute I showed up on Cousin Lizzie's doorstep and announced my plans for after breakfast, Aunt Zoe begged to tag along, like the excursion to UMD was another exotic adventure. But I stood my ground. This time I insisted on going by myself. If Trudy felt too many people were beating down her path, she might get skittish.

Cousin Lizzie pointed to the cupboard under the kitchen sink. "Well, Mary, if you must go by yourself, at least take the heavy duty 6 volt flashlight I keep down there. I always say a weighty purse makes a handy whacking weapon."

I wasn't too keen on the flashlight theory. With my luck, I'd probably be the one conked on the head. But then again, it's safer than packing a pistol. I got up from the table and retrieved the flashlight.

As soon as I finished the breakfast of frozen waffles and sausage on my plate, I said, "Adios," and took off. No dishwater hands for me this morning. *Yippee*. There are definite benefits to sleuthing.

Trudy's scheduled free time worked out splendidly. Morning work traffic had already wound its dutiful way through Duluth's major arteries: London Road and Interstate 35. Twelve minutes later, I found myself in Burntside Hall, one of the dormitories we happened to walk past on Sunday. As I walked down the hall towards Trudy's room on the first floor, I reminisced about my own college days at Saint Cloud State University, fifteen years ago, and couldn't help but notice the young women students bustling past me today. They appeared to be as lively a bunch as my old freshmen classmates and me. Apparently some things never change. Too bad my friends and I can't turn back the clock and savor those moments again, minus the exams.

When I finally came upon Trudy's room, located near the end of the hall, I found the door slightly ajar and the college student I came to see bent over her desk studying intently. Not wanting to scare her, I knocked softly.

"Enter at your own risk," the lone girl studiously stated, continuing to be engrossed in the books spread out before her on a small, two-drawer maple-colored desk situated under a lofted bed.

I waited to see if she'd check out her intruder, me, but she didn't. Obviously, the ball was in my court. "Excuse me. This is Trudy Almquist's room, isn't it?"

"Ah huh." She spun around. An anemic-looking blonde with stringy shoulder length hair stared back at me. She wore slim-fitting jeans and a UMD sweatshirt. "Oh, sorry I ignored you, Miss Malone. I've got a history test tomorrow and I'm trying to cram. When you knocked, I thought it was one of the other girls coming in to borrow my blow dryer. Here, sit in my chair I'll grab the other one."

I ignored the chair for the moment. Instead, I soaked in the room, trying to get a feel for the person about to be interviewed. My observations didn't pick up much. No clothes tossed helter skelter or friends' photos tacked up on the cork board by the window. Just sheets of highlighted notes spread across a desk, and an unmade second lofted bed. I pointed to the empty bed. "I presume that bed belonged to Darcy."

Trudy glanced at the floor. "Yeah, her Mom said she didn't want the bed back. I suppose I wouldn't either if I was in her shoes. I still can't believe Darcy's dead. Things must've gotten pretty bleak for her to end her own life," she lifted her head and pinched her chin, "I mean that's what every ones saying she did."

Tired of standing, I finally plopped down in the chair Trudy had offered me. "Yup, you're right," I said, "Most people are assuming the worst. But did she commit suicide? You knew her a long time, Trudy. When she got upset about things, how did she usually react? Run off or stick around?"

Trudy's bare feet continued to swing loosely under her chair. as she filled me in regarding her deceased roommate. "She'd rant and rave for a couple days. Then things fell back into place and it was smooth sailing once again. Like when she broke it off with Zeke. In no time she had a new boyfriend."

I sensed a hint of jealousy, even though her rival had been dead a few days, which makes a strong motive to kill someone. *Drop the bomb, Mary.* "By the way, there's going to be an autopsy to determine the cause of death."

The news didn't appear to trouble Trudy's conscience one iota. Her fidgety fingers slowly shifted from her chin to the thin-metaled earring running through her pimpled nasal passage. "Mrs. Hawthorne requested an autopsy? Huh. I hadn't heard. Right after Darcy's body had been found, our resident assistant volunteered to pack up her belongings and deliver them to the Hawthorne's house. Charice said it wouldn't be necessary. She'd pick them up herself. But the stuff's still here."

"Where are her things being stored till she shows up?"

The barefooted girl flicked her thumb over her shoulder. "It's all in there." *There* meaning the second closet. "The police went through it. Looking for a suicide note I suppose."

I crossed my legs. *What luck.* I figured Darcy's dorm belongings had gotten hauled off to the main office for the police to pick up. Now I could look through the dead girl's things on my own schedule. I offered to take the stuff off her hands. "I'll return Darcy's things to Charice. She's got enough on her plate, with waiting for the final police report and planning a funeral."

Trudy's feet stopped kicking. She rubbed her hands in a nervous cleansing motion. "Gee, that's great. It's been kind of creepy having Darcy's possessions around. I keep expecting her to show up some night to get them."

"You haven't slept much, have you?" I said, staring at her sickly features. *Could she.be overdosing on drugs?* I wondered.

"I didn't realize it showed. You must be a nurse too."

" Nope," I slid my sweatshirt sleeve back and snuck a peek at my watch, "Mrs. Hawthorne hired me to look into the death of her daughter. She strongly believes Darcy didn't end her own life."

"So, you're a PI?"

"Something like that." I set my purse on my lap and pulled out a note pad. "Darn, I forgot to bring a pen. Could I borrow one of yours?" I actually had one, but I wanted to try and sneak off with one of Trudy's. Not for my collection. Fingerprints come in mighty handy when solving a case.

"Here."

"Thanks." I posed the plain non-descript pen between my fingers. How long had you known Darcy?"

The first year college student sat silent for a minute. She seemed stumped. "Since second or third grade, I guess. Everyone in our class treated us like outcasts. It's probably what brought us together. Two extremely shy girls and the runts of the class. But we sure showed them when we got to high school. We pretty much aced our way through all four years, earning partial scholarships in the end."

"I suppose you both had to find jobs to supplement the rest of your college fees?"

"You got it. It wasn't too difficult though."

"Did Darcy work on or off campus?"

Trudy twirled a number 2 pencil between her fingers. "She worked at UMD's Newman Center."

"Do you work there too?"

"No. Thanks to my aunt I found something off campus."

"What kind of work schedule did Darcy have?"

"She cleaned the Center on Monday and Thursday mornings."

"I understand the last day you saw her was a Monday. Morning or evening?"

Trudy took her time answering, like she wasn't sure. "Ah, Monday evening I think. Yeah, that's right. I ran into her before supper. She told me she was heading to the cafeteria and then going to the library to study."

Did she go to a bar with her new friend instead? I pressed the lime-green Bic pen against the notepad. "I understand Darcy and

Zeke's relationship got pretty intense around graduation time. Do you know if their break-up had to do with her attending college?"

Trudy cast her eyes to the thinly layered linoleum floor. "I really don't know. Could've been anything."

More than likely someone, namely you, got in the way. I uncrossed my legs. "How about the new guy she hooked up with after moving on campus?"

Trudy's head shot up. "The new boyfriend? There's not much to tell. Darcy kept that relationship on the Q-T. She'd only been going with him a short time."

Something's not right here. Why would Darcy, a friend since grade school, not want to talk about the guy she's dating? "Having lived in a college dorm, I know how difficult it can be to control ones curiosity, especially concerning a roommate's love life. Surely the boyfriend's name cropped up when Darcy chatted away."

Trudy folded her hands and rested them in her lap, giving the appearance of being relaxed. "Nope, I never heard anything and Darcy rarely used her cell phone around me."

This girl's no saint, Mary, don't give up yet. "How about purposely popping into the lobby when the guy was expected to show up?"

"As far as I know, he never came to the dorm. Darcy must've met him off campus. Like I said, she was very secretive."

Hmm? Trudy's a hard person to chip away at. Even though I wasn't getting anywhere, I trudged on. "Had Darcy been chummy with any other girls on this floor?"

"I couldn't say. Our schedules weren't the same so she may have hung out with someone else when I wasn't here. You could ask around. But I have a feeling classes and a boyfriend didn't give her much time for anything else."

"Did she ever mention she had plans for an upcoming Halloween party?"

She scratched the back of her head. "Which one? Our campus puts on a huge party and so does her neighborhood."

"I'm more interested in the neighborhood party."

Her hands fell back into her lap. "Ah, yeah. She said she thought she'd go this year as Paul Bunyan. You know the lumberjack? She already had gotten a red flannel shirt."

Purchasing a costume and making plans to attend a Halloween party doesn't sound like someone who is contemplating suicide. I quickly scribbled Trudy's reply on the notepad and then looked up. "Do you mind if we talk about Darcy's ex-boyfriend?"

"No. Why should I? What would you like to know?"

"I understand Zeke's hotheaded. Do you think he might have gone over the edge after the breakup?"

Trudy came on stronger than I anticipated. "What are you saying? Zeke had something to do with Darcy's death? No way!"

"It's just a thought. I'm not accusing him of anything."

"Well, let me set the record straight. Zeke's temper flares up easily, but he's not capable of harming anyone, especially Darcy."

No sense in messing around any longer. Go for the jugular, Mary. "You had a major crush on Zeke in high school, didn't you?"

The college student drew her arms to chest level and squeezed them. "What? Who said that? No way! Never! I couldn't stand the guy."

The play Hamlet came to mind. Well, I can read between the lines too. Surely the college student didn't think I was dumb enough to believe such strong protests. "Good to hear. If you had feelings for him, you might not want to share his whereabouts. I understand he works somewhere in Duluth."

The girl nodded. Her arms remained where they were. "Yeah, at the DECC."

"Never heard of it. I'm new to the area."

"DECC's short for Duluth's Entertainment Convention Center. It's close to Canal Park. Looks like the front of a ship."

"Hmm? I must've driven by it yesterday, coming from the Cities." I tore off a sheet of paper from my notepad, scribbled my cell number on it, and handed it to Trudy. Then I stuck the pen and notepad in my purse. "Anytime you want to talk, I'm available." I stood. "Thanks for your time. Good luck with your studies."

"Hey, don't forget about Darcy's things."

"I won't." When I crossed the room to reach the closet storing Darcy's belongings, I glanced out the dorm window and watched as harried students raced to their classes or back to their dorms. *At least they were still alive to enjoy life.*

~**24**~

After I slid behind the wheel of the Topaz again, I popped open my purse, took out the list of possible suspects and a pen that looked like it had been dipped in several vats of paint. I placed the list on my lap and circled Trudy's name. Then I grabbed the cell phone and made a couple calls, the first to the Duluth Police Department to get the low down on Fiona, the second to the DECC to weasel Zeke Henrik's schedule out of them. No word on the VW, but Zeke happened to be setting up for a huge convention and was expected any minute. Now, that's what I called luck. If I wanted to catch the guy off guard, I'd have to hustle.

I drove out of UMD and made a hasty retreat to the Lake Superior waterfront where DECC and the S.S. William A. Irvin sat a block apart on the same side of the street according to the DECC employee I had spoken with. I remembered seeing the Irvin with my folks when I was a kid, but had no recollection of Duluth's Entertainment complex. The ship, landlocked since the late '70's, used to carry iron ore and coal from Duluth to Lakes Michigan and Erie. It's a museum now.

When I passed by the front of the ship to get to DECC's main entrance on Harbor Drive, I noticed a huge makeshift sign flapping in the wind announcing the Irvin's October Haunted ship tours. *Hmm? Touring an old ship?* I never thought of that. I bet I could glean tons of material for my book. "Stay focused," I quickly reminded myself, echoing words I would use with young students, "Stick to the agenda at hand. An Unknown killer is still at large."

A mid-fifties dark-skinned woman with huge brown eyes framed in cherry-red reading glasses, cautiously looked me over as I paraded up to the DECC reception counter where she sat. When she stood to see if I required help, her huge gold hooped earrings swayed to and fro like pendulums.

Recalling how easy it had been to feed a bunch of malarkey to the staff and boarders at the Bar X Ranch while working on my first case, I decided to use it to my advantage here too. I withdrew a Kleenex from my purse and dabbed my nose. Then with as much emotion as I could muster, eyes downcast, I informed the woman I was Zeke Henrik's sister and needed to speak with him immediately. "Our Grandpa died of heart complications a half hour ago."

Her right hand littered with rings flew to her chunky cheek. "Oh, my. I'm so sorry. Let me see where he's at." She quickly flipped through a small folder and found what she wanted. "He's on the second floor. Do you want me to page him or would you prefer to go up there?"

I had no intention of questioning Zeke in an open lobby where anyone could walk in at any moment, including the police whom I wanted to stay ahead of at all costs. "Ah, I think I'd like a private place to speak with him. Is there anything like that down here?" I twisted this way and that for her benefit, pretending to look for an enclosed room.

"No, there isn't. But City Side Convention area where Zeke's at is huge. I'm sure you can find a quiet corner up there."

Continuing my deception, I dabbed my nose again and then headed to the elevator. The moment my feet stepped out onto the second floor my heart sped up. Why couldn't I have been born with nerves of steel like Superman? I had no idea what to expect of Zeke Henrik. Charice Hawthorne made him sound like a hopeless dropout. Was he Darcy's killer? When I tried to make contact, would he disappear into the woodwork or lash out at me?

Whatever bravery I felt when I first arrived at DECC was long gone. I was as nervous as Hemingway's six-toed cats, flitting from one private room to the next looking for my prey. When I finally arrived at the room I was seeking, I took a deep breath and waltzed in. Five young muscular men were busy rolling oval tables to the front of the room. I hung back and waited till one of the guys returned to collect another table, and then I pounced. "Pardon me. Do you know where I can find Zeke Henrik?"

The six foot, twenty-something fellow with a head of hair to die for in my favorite food color, dark chocolate, straightened his muscular shoulders and looked me over, assessing my question I presumed. Since the thick bushy beard and mustache hid him so well, his highly polished teeth barely peeked through his lips when he finally responded. "You found him. I'm Zeke. What do you need?"

I tugged on one of my pumpkin earrings and offered a smile. "Sorry, I didn't recognize you. But no one mentioned your beard. Can we find a quiet spot to talk?"

"What's this about?" he asked in a casual tone, "My hours aren't being cut back again, are they?"

My cheap imitation leather purse banged against my knees. "You've got it all wrong. I'm not here about your work schedule, Zeke."

The young man ruffled his thick head of hair. "Well, you sure as heck don't look like a new hire to me."

"Good guess. I'm here to talk about Darcy, not work."

"A cop, huh?" Zeke's voice had an edge to it. "I wondered how long it would take her mother to send one my way." He rolled up his navy-blue cotton shirt sleeves. "Look, can't we do this another time? We have two-hundred tables to set up before noon."

"I'm not a cop, but my time's precious too. Charice Hawthorne hired me to look into her daughter's death. The sooner I get the answers I need, the sooner I'll be out of your hair."

He stuttered, "But...but I thought the newspaper said something about suicide."

"Sadly, nothing's been confirmed. It'll probably be several weeks before the police know for sure. You dated Darcy for over a year; do you honestly think she'd take her own life?"

"Maybe," he slid his sweaty hand across his forehead, "I don't know. She was pissed off at everyone—me, her mom, even Trudy."

"Why did she split with you? And don't tell me because of her mom. I'm not stupid."

Zeke didn't respond. He just stared at his fellow workers as they rolled more tables passed us.

I applied more pressure. "How long have you and Trudy Almquist been seeing each other?"

His hazel eyes became hooded. His face grew grim. "It wasn't like that, okay? Trudy invited me over to her folk's house. a month after college began. When I got there, she told me Darcy was running late and started mixing drinks, two at a time. Booze and I don't hit it off. We never did. Before I knew it, I was stretched out on the couch half-out of it with Trudy sitting next to me clothed in hardly anything, clicking her phone fast and furious. I had no idea she'd sent the pictures to Darcy. What kind of friend does that?"

"Obviously one who envied what you and Darcy had."

He ran his long fingers through his hair.

"Tell me," I said, "did you ever try to get in touch with Darcy after she broke up with you?"

"Heck, yes. At least five or six times. She refused the calls." He rubbed his beard. "I had so much to tell her. Now she'll never know I'm getting my act together."

"You've gone back to school?"

He nodded. "Taking GED classes and working two jobs."

"I know this may sound trivial to you, but did Darcy like popcorn?"

Zeke laughed. "Oh, yeah. Couldn't be just plain popcorn though, it had to have tons of cheddar cheese topping on it."

I couldn't think of any other pertinent questions, so I handed Zeke my number. "If Trudy tries to get in touch with you, give me a call. I have a feeling you'll be hearing from her soon."

"Why would she call me?"

I started for the elevator. "She knows Darcy's out of your life permanently."

Zeke tailed me. "Wait a second. Are you implying Trudy might have had something to do with Darcy's death?"

I shrugged my shoulders.

When I returned to the lobby, I found the receptionist chatting it up with Officer Fitzwell, the last person I wanted to run into. If I kept a low profile, maybe I'd be able to sneak out without him seeing me. I tilted my head down.

"Officer, it's so nice of you to stop by and offer Zeke your condolences," the receptionist said, "I'm sure he'll appreciate it. His sister came a few minutes ago. Oh, why there she is." Fitzwell spun around. "Did you find him?" she inquired.

"Ah, no," I replied, without looking their way and swiftly strode to the nearest exit.

Officer Fitzwell tried to stop me. "Hold on there, Miss Malone," he called out, "I want to speak with you."

I increased the length of my footsteps, raised my hand to shoulder level, and waved. "Sorry, I'm late. No time for chit chat. My cousin just got released from the hospital and she's waiting for me." When the nearest exit approached, I charged through its double doors with the speed of a rhino, hoping the rookie cop wouldn't give chase.

Why did Officer Fitzwell come to the DECC anyway? Did he want to question Zeke about Darcy too or talk about previous run-ins Zeke had with the law? If it pertained to Darcy, maybe the police department didn't think things had jived either. Of course Officer Trevor Fitzwell could be here for another reason entirely. And that motive scared me. According to what he said in the cop car the night he drove me to Hinckley, he hasn't been on the Duluth Police Force long. Were he and Zeke involved with the group on the beach? And if so, was his story about training Duke a clever deception.

I unlocked the Topaz and took a quick peek over my shoulder before climbing in. To my relief no one lurked about. I could relax.

~25~

The interviews with Trudy and Zeke hadn't produced anything useful, but seeing Zeke's beard reminded me of the beach picture I hadn't cropped yet. Surely one of the four at the bonfire had a scar, birthmark, or tattoo that would prove beneficial. Odds were on the naked lady. Too bad I hadn't caught her backside. The more I thought about the warning I received, the angrier I became. What right did someone have to tell me to stay off the beach? It was public property.

I needed comfort food to calm me down. Anything coated in heavy chocolate or caramel, it didn't matter. I opened Matt's glove compartment. No sweet's there. And there wasn't any grocery store near the Aerial Lift Bridge either. "Wait a second." What about the chocolate factory near Grandma's? People were popping in an out of there in droves the other day. Yeah, that's where I'd stop. And afterwards I'd hunt for a pizza-to-go place.

"Hey, where's everybody?" I said, closing Lizzie's apartment door behind me. No one responded, not even a whiny dog. That's a bit strange. I continued on to the kitchen thinking everyone must've gone somewhere else in the building and I'd find a note for me on the table. Nope, no note. "Hmm." I guess I'd I better put the food in the fridge till I know what's going on. When I turned to put the box of pizza and dessert away, I heard a slight noise and then someone spoke.

"I'm here, Mary."

I stepped into the living room and found Cousin Lizzie, with cane in hand, making her way from the master bedroom to the settee. "Like some help?" I asked.

"Thanks, I'll be fine. I have to do this for myself." She sniffed the air. "Is that pizza I smell?"

"Ah huh. It's our lunch. When I didn't find anybody here, I figured I'd have to eat it by myself. Were you on the phone?"

Lizzie finally reached her destination and sat. "No, I thought I'd take a catnap while Zoe and Margaret walked Winnie." She raised her legs and rested them on the gold fabric covering the ottoman Virginia had lent her.

"Glad to see you're making use of the ottoman."

"I have to. I want the swelling around my knees to go down."

"Virginia Bagley sure goes above and beyond what's expected of a manager, loaning you a piece of furniture and putting me up in her apartment. At our complex we only get a glimpse of our manager if the rent's late."

"She's definitely unique. The last person to manage this building stayed out of the limelight like yours."

"Perhaps it's the teacher in her coming out, keeping abreast of the tenants' needs. How long has she been here?"

"About three years, I'm not really sure. Years seem to fly by the older one gets. Say, as long as you're here, Mary, would you be a dear and grab my ice packs and towel?"

"Sure. Would you like me to get a cup of coffee or tea for you while I'm in the kitchen?"

"No. I can wait till lunch."

A minute later I popped back into the living room with the wrapped ice packs. "Here you go. Anything else I can get you before I sit down?"

"Not that I can think of."

I moved away from the settee and dropped my bod into one of the fancy French designed chairs. "Did your doctor mention how long you'd have to use the ice packs?"

The octogenarian shook her head. "I suppose it depends on how long my knees continue to swell."

"And each person's recovery is different. We learned that when Dad had his heart surgery."

"Speaking of Archie, how's he doing?"

"Great, especially with Matt's dog staying there."

"Exercise is the key isn't it?"

"Yup." *And I needed to start doing exactly that if I wanted a slimmer bod.* "Lizzie, do you mind if I abandon you for a few minutes to check my e-mails? I stashed my laptop in the guest bedroom."

She picked up the remote control from the coffee table and clicked on the TV. "No, go right ahead. I love watching the Food channel."

So do I. But nothing's going to distract me from the mission I'm on, and with Margaret and Aunt Zoe out of the way, nothing should hamper me. I left the living room and swiftly made my way to the bedroom closet, retrieved the laptop from the overhead shelf, and turned it on.

When the folder appeared where the selfie had been stashed, I clicked on it. Soon, the photo filled the screen. I cropped it, leaving only four strangers to study. The men's beards and hats made it impossible to discover facial features or even to pin down ages. One of the males' hands did reveal scars though. They didn't appear recent. With nothing else noticeable on the men, I drew my attention to the lone female. Subject about seventeen or eighteen. Upper portion of body displayed no scars, but there seemed to be a tiny tattoo below her left shoulder, a rose perhaps. Lower half of the body hidden by leaping flames.

Maybe the girl's age triggered it, I can't say for sure, but I wondered if Darcy got a tattoo after she had left home. I never asked. It wasn't relevant. She went from missing to dead before I even got involved. I inhaled deeply. Who were these people? Why did they want Fiona? To leave town unnoticed? Could they be the diamond thieves everyone's looking for?

I plugged in a flash drive and saved the picture. Tomorrow I'd beg Virginia to let me use the printer in her office. I wanted a paper copy to carry around.

When I disconnected the flash drive, my stomach churned, reminding me of the pizza waiting to be eaten. I glanced at my watch. Twelve-thirty. Where did Margaret and Aunt Zoe walk to, the moon?

Obviously, we can't eat without them. It wouldn't be polite. I kept the computer on and decided to do some digging on the internet while I waited for the dog walkers to return.

Like I said before—the beach people might have been off a foreign ship. But it didn't mean they couldn't have rendezvoused periodically with other gang members once they were in port.

As soon as the heading entitled Jewelry Thefts popped on the screen, I began to pour through numerous Wisconsin and Minnesota news articles covering the past fifteen years, ignoring anything that dealt with small amounts of stolen property. I was only interested in the big fish and which businesses they hit.

Four serious incidents stood out enough to warrant further reading. The first, pertained to a young adult male, early twenty, arrested for stealing jewelry valued at 700K from his place of work, over a five year period. Most of what he stole still hadn't been recovered. The second incident contained info on a group of smash and grab robbers who made off with jewelry from six jewelry stores. No arrests. Police thought there may have been a regional gang connection. The third theft, the one Margaret and I had already referred to, occurred at a rest stop. 500K taken. No arrests. And the final incident spoke of a very sophisticated band of thieves headed by a retired police detective with a Polish last name, Razinki. He masterminded ten jewelry heists in seven states for well over a decade. Value of jewels: 5 million. Jail time knocked down to twelve years. Released a year ago.

I tossed all the heist incidents around in my head for a bit and mulled them over. The more I thought about the last operation mentioned, it seemed to be more along the style of the Grand Marais theft in Minnesota. And Razinki, the mastermind of the final heist I read about, was available to plan more.

As I thought through how thieves might have stolen the diamonds and gems from Clarity's Facility, I caught movement out of the corner of my left eye. The shadowy figure had been too high off the floor to be Winnie. I spun around, startling Aunt Zoe. How long had she been poking around in the bedroom? I backed up against the bed and blocked the laptop with my body. "Sorry if I disturbed you, Mary. I didn't mean to. I just came in to get my slippers. Are you working on some special project?"

"What? Oh, no. Just perusing ads and dreaming about all the things I can't afford." If I told Auntie the truth, she'd blow a gasket. Better to keep her in the dark for a while longer. I bookmarked the page and then cleared out of Google, forgetting the cropped picture of the foursome hadn't been closed.

Aunt Zoe peered over my shoulder for a mere second and caught the image on the laptop screen. *Great!* Shaking her fiery-red head, she said, "Where...where did that come from, Mary?"

Did I say it's not kosher to try to pull a fast one? Secrets have a way of coming back to bite you in the butt every darn time. "It's what's left after I cut us out of the selfie snapshot."

I waited for Auntie's jets to fire up, especially after seeing the naked lady on the screen again, but no smoke appeared. Her eyes remained tightly settled on the enlarged picture. "Strange, I never realized how much that girl looks like someone I should know. But I haven't the foggiest notion where I've bumped into her."

"Maybe you met her on one of your many trips. She's certainly not anyone I know. My friends have little tots running around." I put the computer on *SLEEP* mode and steered her towards the door. "Let's go eat. The pizza's getting cold."

"Pizza? Fresh or frozen?" she asked as I escorted her to the kitchen.

"Fresh, of course, with all the extras you like, onions, green peppers, black olives, mushrooms..."

"And pineapple?"

"Yup. And if you eat a good lunch, there's surprise dessert too."

~26~

Margaret Grimshaw picked up the paper napkin resting on her lap, brought it to her narrow lips, and blotted them daintily. "How did your meeting go with Trudy?"

My stomach softly growled in anticipation of the messy slice of rewarmed pizza that would soon filter down to it. "Not as well as I hoped. I suspect she knows much more than she's willing to share. But at least I came away with Darcy's belongings."

I'm surprised you found them still in the dorm," Aunt Zoe flatly stated while placing a second slice of pizza on her plate, "Shouldn't the police or Charice have collected them?"

"According to Trudy, the police already looked through Darcy's things."

My cousin's tongue became acidic. "Zoe, when would Charice have time to collect her daughter's belongings? She has more important things to do." Her knife slashed away at the pizza sitting in front of her, creating smaller pieces to chew. Cheese oozed everywhere, as it had done for the rest of us. It's what happens when cold pizza requires nuking.

When Lizzie finished destroying her pizza, she set her knife down and picked up her fork. Before sliding any food onto it, she leaned my way indicating she had something important to share with me. "You should consider using the kitchen area to go through the deceased girl's belongings. It has the most available work space."

"Thanks. I'd hoped you'd let me. The fewer people who know what I'm working on the better."

"*Si*, I agree," Margaret said, "I don't think it's wise to sort through Darcy's belongings at Virginia's. You never know who might stop by her apartment."

"Not only that," I added, "But Virginia speaks to so many people throughout the day, she might accidently slip and say something without realizing it."

"Where did you leave Darcy's things?" Aunt Zoe asked. "I didn't see anything by the door."

"I left the bag in the trunk. I'll get it after lunch."

Aunt Zoe's fork remained in her right hand as she rested her wrists on the edge of the table. "I'd love to help you sort through the stuff, Mary. You said I was quite helpful with your first case, remember?"

"Yes, I remember." *Too well I'm afraid.* The first night I'm hiding out in Reed Griffin's woods, hoping to catch the person responsible for removing horses from his property, she falls asleep in Fiona with a walkie talkie nestled in her hands and I ended up knocked unconscious in the middle of the woods.

"I'd like to help too," Margaret said solemnly, "but I don't want to get in your way."

"I appreciate the offers," I said, traipsing over to the microwave to nuke another slice of pizza for myself, "If I find anything that doesn't gel, I'll be sure to ask for your input."

"Speaking of input," Aunt Zoe said, stabbing a bite of pizza with the tines of her fork, "why don't you ask Margaret about the girl? See if she recognizes her."

The wrinkles on Cousin Lizzie's forehead reached new heights. "What girl? Someone you've seen in this apartment building?"

"The naked one," Auntie calmly replied.

Cousin Lizzie dropped her fork back on her plate. "From the beach?" The land line suddenly came to life, interrupting further flow of chatter. "Zoe, can you get that? It might be my daughter."

My Aunt's chair scraped the floor as she scooted away from the table to reach the phone sitting on the counter by the stove. "Hello... Yes, she's here... Just a minute." She then spun in my direction. "It's for you, Mary."

"Who is it?" I mouthed, thinking it might be my mother.

She covered the mouthpiece. "Officer Fitzwell. How did he get this number?"

Through my second suspect of course. "I don't know," I offered in a whisper, adding yet another lie to my sleuthing repertoire. *How many does that make?* I swallowed the half-chewed pizza still lingering in my mouth, quickly washed it down with Pepsi, and then asked Lizzie if I could use her bedroom phone. "Otherwise you three will have to be as quiet as mice," I said.

"Go right ahead. It's on my dresser, dear."

"Aunt Zoe, hang up when you hear me say 'hello'. Okay?"

She acknowledged my request. As I left the table behind, I overheard her say, "My niece will be right with you, Officer."

***

Officer Trevor Fitzwell can wait, I thought, looking at the extension phone. I stepped in front of Lizzie's dresser mirror and gave myself a brief pep talk. *Don't let anything jar you, not even the good-looking cop on the other end of the line. Play it cool.* I put a smile on my face, inhaled deeply, and picked up the phone. "Hello."

"Surprise. I bet you didn't think I'd be able to track you down so soon."

"A smart cop like you? Sure I did."

Fitzwell drew in a long breath. *He must be frazzled,* I thought. *Wish I could see his face.* When the rookie cop spoke again, his stumbled words could barely be understood as they floated through the phone lines to my ears. "Miss Malone, what's your relationship to Zeke Hendrik?"

Expecting the loaded question, I acted dumb. "I don't know why the receptionist at DECC thought I was Mr. Henrik's sister. Maybe she got me confused with someone else. All my siblings live in the Twin Cities."

The officer turned huffy. "Then perhaps you'd like to explain why you left a business card with him."

"When has it become a crime to let people know about a legit business?"

"You mean dog sitting?"

"Why, yes, of course!" I snapped, forgetting to remain calm and detached. "What else would I be advertising?"

"Look, lady, if you're up to something illegal, I'll find you and personally haul you down to this station."

"You'll find nothing on me, Officer Fitzwell. I'm squeaky clean. Save the jail cell for someone dangerous to society. But hey, as long as you've got me on the phone, I'd like to know what your police department's doing about my stolen car?"

No reply.

Ah-hah. I caught him off guard. "Are you still there?"

~27~

I thought I'd successfully managed to squelch further discussion of Officer Fitzwell's mysterious call since no one intruded upon me after lunch while I spent a good hour examining Darcy's belongings, but I was dead wrong. As the four of us got comfy in the living room to share in our dessert, the mouthwatering caramel apples I had brought home from the candy shop, and to view the cropped picture on the laptop, Aunt Zoe pointedly said, "We know the handsome lad called to ask you out on a date, Mary. Why won't you tell us if you accepted?"

"There's nothing to fess up to, Auntie. The subject's closed. Now, do either of you recognize the girl in this photo?" The question intended for Margaret and Cousin Lizzie's benefit. While I waited for their feedback, I took several sliced up apple pieces from a bowl, set them on my paper plate, and passed the remaining apples on to Aunt Zoe.

Margaret removed her wired-framed glasses and squinted at the computer screen. "Have we bumped into this individual somewhere?"

Hearing the nonagenarian's query, I was doubtful my cousin would shed any light on the girl either, but I tried to remain positive. "What do you think Lizzie?"

"I couldn't say. Since my surgery, the only thing I've been seeing way too much of is TV. Is she a well-known actress?"

"Nope, she's definitely not an actress," I confidently stated.

Aunt Zoe's face registered disbelief. "What makes you so certain?"

I stood up. Lizzie's poodle joined me thinking it was time to go out, but I wasn't going anywhere. Pacing back and forth actually helps me think more clearly. I don't know why. Maybe having been a teacher in the lower grades has something to do with it. I was constantly on my feet, moving from one student to another offering extra praise or help. "Well..."

"Because," Margaret explained, pressing her arthritic fingers against her cheek, "Mary knows I rarely watch TV and I haven't gone to a movie in years. I'm afraid the only thing we all have in common is Duluth."

I patted her shoulder. "Great job, Sherlock. You've earned your dessert."

Cousin Lizzie tapped the settee letting Winnie know she should join her. "You can rule out the campus and Grandma's. I haven't been to either in years."

I ran a hand through strands of hair hiding my high forehead. "Actually, there are only two places we've all been together, this apartment and the Shoolinger Nursing facility."

"I don't think we'll ever figure this out," my cousin murmured.

"Why not?" I quizzed.

"This building has over a hundred residents."

"How about Shoolinger?" Aunt Zoe asked. "Any idea how many nurses work there?"

Lizzie's salt-and-pepper permed hair bounced when she shook her head, signifying she had no idea.

Margaret put a few apple pieces on her plate and gave the rest to Lizzie. "Actually it's not as hard to figure out as one might think."

"Easy for you to say," Aunt Zoe rudely remarked. "Matt's shared snippets of cases with you over the years. You know how things get done."

I glared at Aunt Zoe. She had no right to speak to the eldest woman in the room like that. I leaned into the laptop screen and poked it for emphasis. "Having knowledge of Matt's cases has nothing to do with figuring out who this girl is. It's a matter of deduction, Watson. Margaret went to the crossword meeting; we didn't. The number of possibilities dwindles even more, leaving Virginia and four residents on this floor, one being male."

"What about the nurses at Shoolinger?" Cousin Lizzie inquired, drawing her sleepy mutt closer to her, "How many do you think we've actually been around?"

"Roughly five."

Aunt Zoe counted out loud. "Four plus five equals... Whoa. That certainly cuts down the number of people we've all been in contact with."

"Yup," I winked at Margaret, "And when you're working on a case, it's extremely important to whittle the number of suspects down. The less people to follow and interrogate the better it is. So, does anyone want to take another guess at who this girl might be related to? Otherwise I'm shutting my computer down."

"Her features don't match Virginia Bagley's that's for sure," Aunt Zoe said.

I nodded in agreement. "Anyone else care to take a stab?"

Margaret's fingers made a steepled gesture. "The girl's eyes bother me."

"Color or shape?" I swiftly inquired, thinking we were finally getting somewhere.

"The width between the eyes. Most eyes are set closer to the nose."

I quickly compared the distance between Aunt Zoe's, Margaret's, and Lizzie's eyes to those of the stranger. "You're right. I'm surprised I didn't notice it earlier."

"I certainly got a good look at Nurse Hawthorne's eyes," Lizzie lazily shared as she rubbed her snoozing dog's back. "I couldn't help it. I didn't have a choice. Vital signs get checked every hour. Her eyes don't seem to fit quite right with her small framed face. Do you understand what I'm saying?"

I excitedly exploded, "Of course." I jumped up and pecked my cousin on the cheek. "I'm such an idiot. I need to fetch an item from the guest bedroom." When I returned, I dumped the goodie bag's contents on the carpet, including the brown flat mailing envelope Charice had given me.

Cousin Lizzie leaned forward, "What on earth are you up to, Mary?"

I held the envelope up. "Charice Hawthorne gave me a graduation picture of her daughter along with other items, but I haven't examined them yet." I reached in the envelope, pulled out Darcy's picture, and held it next to the computer screen.

Margaret's hand smacked her thin lips. "Why, I don't believe it. The naked girl's Darcy Hawthorne."

"Oh, my God!" I said, "What have I done? I could have saved her?" Tears welled up in my eyes. I swallowed hard.

"Don't be so hard on yourself, Mary," Margaret said, trying to console me, "For all we know, Darcy could've been killed right after you saw her on the beach."

Aunt Zoe left her chair and trotted over to where I stood. Throwing her arms around me, she said, "We're going to find her murderer, Niece. They've got your car, and we've a picture of them."

***

The minute I returned to Virginia's apartment for the night, I waltzed into her kitchen, interrupted her dishwashing, and inquired if I could use the printer in her second bedroom. When an answer wasn't forthcoming, I added, "I'll gladly pay you. I know how expensive certain brands of ink cartridges can be."

Virginia's heavily made up face tightened. "It's not that," she said, grabbing a towel to dry her hands, "I'm just not sure how well the printer's working. You see I haven't used it in a long time. I mainly print off paperwork for the apartment complex and that requires the heavy duty printer in the manager's office."

"So, you don't mind if I try it, then?"

"No, go right ahead." She swiveled her hips and immediately went back to her dirty dishes.

With Virginia's permission out of the way, I hurried to the spare bedroom, plugged my laptop into the printer, and waited for the printer to warm up. When the printer finally stopped making weird noises, I assumed it was safe to print out a couple copies of the foursome on the beach. Of course, that's also when I realized there wasn't any computer paper to work with. I did however have a few blank sheets in a bag I left at Lizzie's.

I peeked at my watch: nine-thirty. Lizzie and my companions wouldn't be dozing off yet. I set my laptop on *SLEEP* mode and walked towards the apartment's entrance. "Virginia, don't lock up yet," I said on my way out, "I need to run down to Lizzie's."

~28~

Friday

The next morning I left Virginia's apartment fairly early, but not before notifying her of my departure. She was on the phone in the kitchen at the time and acted quite surprised when she caught my goodbye wave as I passed by. Perhaps she expected me to sleep another hour. But this crime busting gal had too much going on today, for such nonsense.

Wearing my usual dress down clothes of white tennis shoes, faded jeans, bright red sweatshirt, and stylish candy corn earrings, I whisked into Cousin Lizzie's apartment to get a quick pick-me-up of OJ. It's all I really had time for.

Aunt Zoe cloaked in a rose-colored silk kimono brought back from one of her many overseas trips, sat at the kitchen table reading the Duluth paper, like she's been doing every morning since we arrived here. Rollers the size of orange juice cans still adorned her short red do. The nightly head covering ritual took getting used to when she first became my roommate, but now it's just part of the ebb and flow of our everyday life.

Obviously my entrance into the kitchen had been too quiet. Auntie ignored me. Not wanting to scare her, I cleared my throat before grabbing a glass from the cupboard. She immediately lowered the paper to greet me. "Good morning, Mary. Did you sleep okay?"

"Yes. How about you?" I set a glass on the counter and then retrieved the OJ from the fridge.

"I slept like a baby. Margaret said she got up during the night, but I never heard her."

"Did the paper have any articles pertaining to the jewel thieves?" I filled the glass and put the juice away.

"It's been kind of hush-hush the last four days," Aunt Zoe said, "Maybe the police know where they're holed up."

I certainly hope not.

Auntie picked up the paper again. "By the way, Mary, Margaret's making omelets for breakfast, do you want one?"

"No. I thought I should start dieting. I can barely zip up my jeans."

"Suit yourself. She makes the best meals around. I suppose you'll be interviewing more people today."

"Not sure. Depends. I have tons of errands to get out of the way first."

Our neighbor shuffled into the kitchen wearing a bright orange and gold apron over black knit pants and a long sleeved yellow knit top. As usual, her white hair was arranged in a bun at the back of her head. "Good morning, Mary. Don't forget to get a photo copy of the beach scene. I'm anxious to see it blown up."

"Already done," I informed her, "Virginia let me borrow her personal printer." I pulled a folded sheet of typing paper from a pant pocket and opened it.

The elderly woman's neatly styled hair didn't stray a bit when she bent over to study the photo. "Yes, that size ought to do the trick." She went to the fridge, took out eggs and a carton of milk, and carried them to the stove. Then she dug through the cupboards, looking for a bowl and a frying pan. "You know, Mary, you're going to have a hard time tracking down those men shown with Darcy. If they weren't wearing fake beards to disguise themselves, their real ones probably have been shaved off by now."

"Hmm. I hadn't thought of that. Appreciate the input." I finished my juice and set the empty glass by the sink. "Well, I'd better get going if I want to get all my errands done."

Aunt Zoe poked her head out from behind the newspaper. "What time should we expect you back?"

"Plan to see me by noon, unless something delays me. Oh, and no need to plan lunch. I'll stop at the deli and pick up sliced turkey and a variety of cheeses for sandwiches."

"Good morning everyone," Cousin Lizzie chirped, as she slowly meandered towards the coffee maker, dressed in a thick, purple terrycloth robe and purple moccasin style slippers, "Why on earth are you discussing lunch? We haven't even eaten breakfast yet."

"Mary's got errands to run," Aunt Zoe explained.

"Well, she has one less to do," Lizzie announced. "She doesn't have to take me to my therapy session. I cancelled my appointment."

"Why would you do that?" I asked.

"Maybe you haven't noticed, but it's snowing out, Mary. There's no way I want to chance taking a tumble."

"No, of course not. Darn," I groaned. "My coat's in the car."

Lizzie shuffled towards the kitchen table with her cup of coffee and sat. "I hope your errands aren't taking you too far into Duluth. You know how reckless drivers can be in the first snowfall."

Yup, I ought to know. Had my first spinout the year I turned sweet sixteen. "I'll be extra cautious. I promise."

~29~

"Hello. Could you tell me if Charice Hawthorne is on duty today?" I asked a youthful volunteer when I entered the Shoolinger Nursing Facility.

The candy striper looked up at me with big, round greenish eyes and gave me the sweetest smile. "Why, yes, she is."

"What wing might I find her in?"

She studied the list of names on her clipboard. Then she stood and gestured to the right. "You'll find her in 1E. It's at the end of the hall."

"Thanks." I spun in the direction she indicated and briskly walked to my destination.

As luck would have it, the first woman I bumped into wasn't Charice, but a short, cantankerous-looking, heavy-set nurse whose clean white shoes seemed to be too tight for her feet. "Excuse me. I'm sorry to bother you, but I need to speak with Charice Hawthorne. Has her shift ended yet?"

"I certainly hope not," she grunted, "She just started an hour ago. Wait right here. I'll see if I can find her," and off she went in a huff.

A few minutes later Charice, dressed in a crisp white uniform, rushed down the hall to meet me. "Miss Malone, what are you doing here? The way the head nurse talked I expected to see a police detective."

"I'm sorry to bother you at work, but what I want to show you is extremely important. It's a picture I snapped this past Saturday on the beach at Park Point."

Before she glanced at the photo, Charice braced the left side of her face with her hand. "It's to do with Darcy, isn't it?"

"I'm afraid so." I pulled the folded picture out of a side pocket in my purse where I had tucked it and gave it to her.

Shock registered instantly. The paper rattled in her hand. "Why is my daughter naked? And why is she with these men? I've never seen them before."

I heaved a sigh. "I don't know. I was hoping you might recognize them. I'm thinking Darcy hooked up with one of the guys after she and Zeke broke up."

Charice handed the picture back to me. It felt damp. "Have you showed this to the police, Mary?"

Tears rolled down her slender cheeks. "Why would Darcy blatantly display her naked body to three men? She had to have been drugged. There's no other explanation. She was taught good Christian values."

I wasn't about to remind the distraught woman how easily kids get swayed by outside pressures when seeking acceptance, including trying dangerous substances. She didn't need to hear it. I took a Kleenex out of my purse and passed it to her. "I'm going to figure this out I promise," I waved the printout in the air, "And this picture's going to do the trick."

When I returned to the world outside the care facility, I found snow still falling at a steady rate. I'd hoped it would've let up by now. Although I treaded lightly on the path back to the Topaz, my feet almost slipped out from under me several times. Each near miss reminded me of my promise to drive safely. *I'll try, Lizzie.* But I still had more errands to run: get gas, buy groceries and drop off a photo.

It didn't dawn on me till I slid back behind the steering wheel that I had forgotten to tell Charice about her daughter's possessions. The ones I'd picked up when I questioned Trudy. I had tossed them in the car's trunk right before coming here. Too lazy to retrace my steps, I decided the items in the plastic bag, minus a class ring with the initials J.R. and a poetry book I wanted to find out more about, could stay where they were a while longer. No need to add to Charice Hawthorne's turmoil.

When I left the parking lot, a blue Ford Focus followed me out at a close clip and appeared to be traveling the same route I had selected. I didn't think much of it at first, but after stopping for gas and groceries the Ford slid directly behind me again. No doubt about it, I was being tailed. Could the guy who stole Fiona possibly be J.R.? Well, he'll be in for a shocker when I pull up in front of the police station.

To reach Superior Avenue I had to head down a slight incline which makes stopping at a lighted intersection on a slippery road, dicey at best. Since I hadn't been on this side road when the light actually turned green and I didn't want to chance sliding through a red light, I pumped on the brakes a couple times to decrease the car's speed, and give fair warning to the idiot following me.

The warning didn't matter to the driver of the Focus. He sped up and connected with the Topaz's bumper, forcing a domino effect. My car clipped the car in front of me. "Matt's going to kill me." *Good thing he's in Ireland.* I glanced in the rearview mirror. The fool who had hit me had fled the scene. I was left to take the rap.

The owner of the silver Toyota Corolla effortlessly glided his car to the side of the road. I followed his lead.

Shaken by the jolt to the back and front end of the car, it took a few seconds to register I'd need to leave the Topaz. Insurance information would have to be exchanged and extent of damage to the cars checked out. The cops might even have to be called depending on how bent up the fenders actually were.

Too bad the accident didn't occur by a bar; I felt the need for a 2 Gingers Whiskey coming on. I inhaled deeply and then reached for my purse. It wasn't on the passenger seat where I had tossed it after grocery shopping. Darn. It must've taken flight during the accident. My stuffs probably scattered all over.

While I kept my eyes focused on the car ahead of me, I leaned over to the right slightly, swung my hand back and forth on the floor until a purse strap got hooked on my hand, and sat bolt upright. Having the purse in my possession now, I thought about seeing if anything rolled out of its various compartments, but given the circumstances, I figured this wasn't the time to do so.

I pulled the key from the ignition and rested my hand on the door handle for a second, trying to gain strength to face the music. That's when I noticed the other driver ambling towards the Topaz. His eyes were fixed on the snow beneath his white speckled black oxford shoes. He wore a dark brown stocking cap, crisp black dress pants, and a bulky chocolate-colored knit sweater with what I presumed to be a light-blue dress shirt underneath, only the pointed collar showed.

I buttoned up my coat and zipped out of the car. "Sorry, I slid into you," I said, watching the man draw nearer. "It couldn't be helped. A guy hit me from behind and shoved me into you."

The Toyota driver raised his head. "It's you," Trevor Fitzwell said. "Why am I not surprised?"

"Ditto for me," I exchanged sarcastically, "I guess this is where we get to swap names and numbers, huh?"

"Yes, if we're going to do this by the book, which we are." He glanced at the back of his car and then the front of mine. "It doesn't look like we've had enough damage for another cop to inspect the cars. See what you think."

The guy kept showing up at the oddest times, which made me wonder whether he was enjoying himself at my expense or if he was in cahoots with the other driver. I walked to the front of the Topaz and stared at the bumper. It had only minor scratches, nothing more. I stared at the back of the Toyota. The car didn't display any dents either. Maybe there's something to be said about an older model car. "Huh. I sure thought I banged your car up good. Maybe my braking helped. So, what do we do now? Part ways?"

Trevor rubbed his bare hands together. "How about you follow me over to Starbucks? We can warm up with a cup of coffee and you can tell me about the driver who hit you from behind."

I tucked my license and insurance information in my coat pocket while I pondered whether Trevor could be trusted or not. I finally said, "I'm not a coffee drinker," thinking the straight-forward response would get me off the hook. It didn't.

He grinned. "Then have tea or hot chocolate. It's on me."

I thought about his request for a moment. Despite my not knowing whether he was a good cop or bad cop, I decided having him at my disposal would be to my advantage. If I was lucky, I'd glean info from him without him realizing it. "Actually, I should buy your coffee. You're saving me a trip to the police station. It's where I had planned to go next."

"Did anyone ever tell you you're exasperating?"

"No, not that I recall."

"Well, you are." He opened my car door and held it while I slid in. "We'll go Dutch then."

~30~

Aunt Zoe and Margaret would've been proud of me. I didn't disgrace myself while Trevor and I dawdled over cappuccino and chai tea at Starbucks even though I worried I might do or say something stupid.

When the guy's off duty, he can actually be a charming fellow, making this woman feel all mushy inside. I ought to know. This happened to be the third time I'd spoken with him, not as a cop but as a single guy, like someone I might have bumped into casually on the beach or the elevator. I even got him to reveal his hometown and how long he'd been on the Duluth Police Force. My sleuthing skills must be getting better.

"I've been working in Duluth for almost a year," he said.

"How's it going?"

"Not too bad I guess considering I left the small town of Dover behind for a city this size."

"Going from a smaller city to a larger one just takes time to adjust."

Trevor nodded. "So, I've been told."

I gazed into his gray, deep set eyes. "Where's Dover located? I've never heard of it."

"Southeastern Minnesota. Near Rochester."

"Rochester? I'm surprised you didn't take a job there. It's much larger than Duluth."

"I wanted a change of scenery."

Hmm? Did someone break up with him or vice versa? "Well, there's plenty up here; moose, bear, wolves, ships and water."

He glanced at his wide band wristwatch. "I have to leave here in a few minutes. So perhaps we should discuss the guy who hit you, the driver of the Ford Focus. You said he purposely banged into you. There are only two reasons I can think of that he'd do that, road rage or unhappy ex-boyfriend. Which is it?"

My fingers played with a short, thin silver-chained necklace butting up against the top of my sweatshirt. *Did he throw the boyfriend into the mix to find out if I'm available?* Well, too bad if he did. I don't give that type of information out until I'm certain a man's trustworthy, and this guy's still dangling in the wind as far as I'm concerned.

I dropped my hands to the table and tapped out a nonsensical sound with my short, unpainted nails. "I hate to burst your bubble, but it wasn't road rage or an ex-boyfriend." To push the conversation along and safely away from any more mention of a boyfriend, I swiftly divulged my take on the accident, knowing the revelation wouldn't have repercussions. "The accident had to do with the warning I received the night my VW was stolen."

I leaned back in the chair and thought about what I had just said. What if my explanation was only partially true? Someone knew I had Darcy's belongings. By getting rid of me, there'd be no ring to connect J.R. to Darcy. But the ring wasn't in the car. I had stashed it in one of Lizzie's many sugar bowls.

Trevor cupped his Styrofoam container with his chapped hands. "You're referring to what the guy with the gun said to you about staying away from the beach. Well, have you?"

I didn't realize how frequently my teacher skills would be put to the test when I took on a case. Pushed to the max, I could weasel out of anything. "Let's bypass that topic since your short on time, shall we." I dug in my purse, quickly produced the photo of the foursome on the beach, and set it on the table in front of him. "This is what I wanted to show the guys at your station. You do remember my telling you about the naked lady?"

He took a sip of coffee. "How could I forget?"

"Well, in case you thought you met a couple of dumb broads last Saturday, this proves we knew what we were talking about." I tapped the photo with my index finger. "Do you recognize the lady?"

Trevor crossed his arms and rested them on the table. "She looks familiar."

"She should. It's Darcy Hawthorne."

He leaned back in his chair. "Whoa! You found her like this a couple days before she washed up on shore?" He lifted the photo a few inches off the table. "This is important evidence, especially if the lab proves she didn't commit suicide."

"I know," I said, crowing on the inside, "So, take good care of it. I'm fairly certain when the coroner's report comes back it'll show she was murdered." I stabbed the picture with a finger again. "Probably by one of these three men. One or all of them could already be in your database. The beards don't help though. Perhaps you can stack up more brownie points with the boss by suggesting your sketch artist get involved."

"Couldn't hurt." He folded the photo up and tucked into his pant pocket. "You know you're too clever for your own good. I can understand why someone would want you out of the way, Mary."

Is that so? Well, I can hardly wait to hear what he has to say when I prove the same guys are mixed up with the stolen gems, unless he's involved. I flicked my wrist, "Nah, not really. I've just picked up pointers from my private eye brother."

Trevor sat in silence for a second or two. Maybe the mere mention of a private eye put him on edge. "Do you mind telling me why you met with Darcy's friends, Zeke and Trudy?"

I folded my hands in front of me. "I guess not. Since someone's determined to knock me off, you might as well know the truth." It's a good thing I'm part Irish. Spinning a yarn comes naturally to me. "Charice Hawthorne and my cousin go way back. As soon as we heard the details of Darcy's death, I offered to speak with them to see if they knew anything about her disappearance. End of story."

Trevor's mysterious eyes seemed to regard me with suspicion, but he held his tongue. He picked up his coffee, gulped down the remainder, and then left the table to discard his cup. When he returned, he remained standing. "I gotta go, but try to stay out of trouble, Mary, okay?"

My face burned. "Ah, yeah. Sure." *How am I supposed to keep out of trouble? It always seems to find me.*

***

I waltzed into Lizzie's apartment determined to keep the meeting with Trevor and the accident to myself for as long as I could. "I'm back," I announced. "Anyone ready for lunch?"

"We certainly are," Lizzie called out. "How were the roads? Pretty treacherous?"

I hoisted the grocery bag on my hip and kicked my wet tennis shoes off before trudging down the short hallway to the kitchen where I assumed my cousin was waiting for a reply. "Not too bad," I said, finding her at the kitchen table, "I just had to drive slower." I set the grocery bag on the counter, emptied the contents, and spread them out before me.

Lizzie watched while I prepared our soon to be lunch. "I talked to my daughter today."

"Oh? How's Sarah doing?"

"All right, I guess. She mainly called to find out how I'm doing."

I held up the glass dish holding the gem Margaret found. "Did you remember to ask about the stone?"

She folded her hands. "As a matter of fact I did. Sarah said she doesn't own any rings with green stones. I guess we might as well toss it."

"Maybe it came off Winnie's fancy collar. I didn't think to check."

"No need to. I already looked. It's not missing any. Say, Mary, there's a jar of kosher dill pickles in the fridge. Would you set it on the table? I'm sure everyone would like pickles with their sandwiches."

I scooped up the gem and pretended to discard it in the wastebasket on the way to the fridge, but I pocketed it instead. What's the harm in checking it out with a reliable jeweler? At least I'd know if the stone was fake or not.

~31~

Saturday

When I entered the kitchen, I found Lizzie and Aunt Zoe sitting at the table drinking coffee while Margaret busied herself with breakfast. Before I allowed myself to plop down on one of the chairs, a quaint reminder of the '50's, to relive my weird evening with the apartment manager, I poured a glass of juice for myself. "You won't believe what happened last night."

"What?" Aunt Zoe asked.

"I found Virginia standing in the doorway of the bedroom I'm using. Apparently my surprise at finding her there forced her into an explanation of sorts."

"What did she say?" Margaret inquired.

"She'd popped in there to look for material she'd bought to make a dress, but couldn't find it in the bottom dresser drawer where she thought she'd stored it."

"Her response sounds plausible," Cousin Lizzie said.

"I'm not finished. After I suggested she might have placed it in the closet when she made room for me, she spun around and went to look. No material. Only a quilt and a couple large hats for keeping out the sun sat on the shelves."

Aunt Zoe set her coffee mug down. "You don't think Virginia snooped through your suitcase, do you?"

"I can't say. If she did, she's one very subtle woman. When she left the bedroom behind, she gave me the impression she was embarrassed about her memory lapse. She mentioned having a *senior moment*."

"I know what that's like," Auntie blurted out.

I gave Margaret a knowing look, she smiled. "Anyway, the woman totally switched gears after that," I explained, "The next thing I know she's back to playing perfect hostess, telling me to find a seat, asking if I'd like a bowl of ice cream, and inviting me to watch an old episode of CSI. Not wanting to disappoint her, I gladly went along."

Aunt Zoe shared a disapproving look. "But, what about your veggie diet, Mary? You said whenever you felt the urge to snack you'd grab a celery stick or carrot instead."

I crossed my fingers and hid them from view. "I'll watch it more carefully today."

The instant Margaret set the filled platter of prepared French toast on the table, the scent of cinnamon wafted its way to my nostrils, turning my stomach to jelly. "*Buon appetito*," the nonagenarian said as she gently pulled a chair away from the table and joined us. "So, Mary, was there any other questionable occurrence at Virginia's before you retired?"

"I guess strange would be the right word. While Virginia attended to the ice cream, I poked around her living room. Unfortunately, I only had time to study her bookcase. It's a lovely white-washed piece chock full of books of every sort, coin collecting, antiques, and the stock market, but nothing suggesting she once worked as a high school teacher. A couple photos on the top surface added additional charm."

Cousin Lizzie's wild eyebrows instantly shot up. "Photos? Like her family? Virginia never talks about her relatives."

"Yes, family members. One frame held a picture of a much younger Virginia with a handsome man and a teenaged boy, another, displayed a different boy's high school graduation. Curious about the handsome dark-haired one in the second picture, I picked it up. Of course, Virginia came back into the room just as I did so."

"How did she react?" our Foley neighbor asked.

"She told me the boy in the photo was her grandson. Apparently he moved to Canada after high school. He had some sort of accident and nearly died. Nearly died," I stressed, "Not dead,

Margaret. The man and woman you overheard at the crossword puzzle meeting had the story wrong. Virginia's grandson is the one who had the close call with death, not her son. After hearing part of the grandson's story, I decided to dig deeper. I asked if his parents moved to Canada too."

"Well, did they?" Aunt Zoe asked.

"Nope, they reside in Miami. When Virginia retired, they suggested she move in with them but she didn't take their offer seriously. So, now she sits and suffers Minnesota's harsh winters along with everyone else."

"And every winter she probably wishes she were in Florida," Margaret said, holding her coffee cup in midair, "I can't blame her. When snow starts falling, I think about life in Italy."

"Hey, I'm the youngest here," I said, "and I'd go somewhere else during the winter if I could."

"Dear, do you think Virginia suspects what you're up to? You can't afford to have her leak whatever she's learned to the other residents. It would be disastrous. In order to do a decent investigative job, it's imperative information concerning Darcy remains hush, hush."

I took a sip of orange juice. "Believe me I understand how secretive I need to be. When I prepared for bed, I checked to make sure the other printed copy of the group was still safely stashed away."

Aunt Zoe leaned forward in her chair. "And—?"

"Apparently Virginia didn't find it. At least I don't think she did. I had unzipped the cover of an accent pillow sitting on the chair next to the bed, hid the picture inside the opening, and surrounded it with the polyester fiberfill."

Margaret set her cup down, picked the bottle of maple syrup off the table, and drizzled it over the second slice of French toast she intended to eat. "That's a mighty clever spot to hide an important document. Five points awarded to our ingenious sleuth."

"Maybe, maybe not. Since I couldn't be certain, I brought the picture down here. If any of you want to take another peek at it, go right ahead. I'm stowing it in my laptop bag."

I slid two slices of French toast on my plate, slathered them with butter, and patiently waited for Margaret to finish with the syrup. While I waited, I watched Winnie weave in and out of our chair legs, hunting for crumbs. Poor dog, she'll never find anything. If I could speak doggie language, I'd tell her not to bother looking.

Cousin Lizzie took the syrup from Margaret and handed it to me. "Here you go."

"Thanks."

"Mary, do you really think you have a chance of finding any of the men who were with Darcy? It's been a week since you saw them on the beach."

"I hope so for Charice's sake. She's counting on me Lizzie."

Margaret cleared her throat. "Think positive, Mary. You've got a photo and a ring."

"And a poetry book from J.R. I neglected to mention."

"Well, see, that's more information than you had when you took on the case four days ago," Margaret added.

"You're right." I eyed the last slice of French toast on the platter, waiting to be eaten by someone, and I contemplated whether it should be me. The button on my jeans said not to risk shoving any more food in. I guess I had my answer. I picked up my plate and carried it to the sink. "Oh, Auntie, before I forget, do you think you can set aside some free time this afternoon to run an errand with me?"

Her heavily rouged face lit up. "Of course, just let me know when you're ready to go."

~32~

"Where's this errand of yours taking us?" Aunt Zoe asked with her head angled to take in the view of shops whizzing by her side window. "You never did say."

"Actually, I've decided to stop at two businesses, one being a local jewelry store." I didn't mention the other place yet, for good reason. If I disclosed it beforehand, she might balk and try to talk me out of going there altogether.

The second the word's jewelry store floated out of my mouth, Auntie abruptly turned her attention to me. "Oh, Mary, I didn't realize our money situation had gotten so out of hand. Why didn't you tell me? I'd gladly sell the few gold chained necklaces I have to keep a roof over our heads."

As usual, Dad's sister presumed the worst. I shook my head. "I'm not selling any jewelry. The majority of stuff I wear is cheap imitation." I raised a hand to my earlobe. "Even these supposed sapphire earrings an old boyfriend gave me are fake."

"You could've fooled me."

"Glad to hear it. I want the jewelry store guy to treat us like we've got money to burn."

Auntie threw her head back against the headrest. "But, but we don't."

Aunt Zoe sure knew how to get under my skin. I took a deep breath. "It's okay. All you have to do is pretend the little gem we found on the carpet at Lizzie's belongs to you. I'll do the rest."

"Whatever you say, Niece, but I wish I knew what you're up to."

"It's better this way. You don't have to worry about blowing any lines."

As I crossed the bridge over Interstate 35, I spotted Padock's to the left of us on the corner of Main Street. I knew nothing about the store other than it was listed in the phone book and the nearest to Lizzie's. Since I didn't see a sign for parking around back, I assumed I'd have to park somewhere along the busy street. When the light changed, I turned onto Main. Halfway down the block I spotted a truck pulling out. I eased in and turned the car off.

Aunt Zoe immediately unbuckled her seatbelt and stepped out onto the sidewalk to wait for me to lock up.

"Now remember," I said when I joined her, "just go with the flow. It's all about pretending."

"No problem. You know how I love to act."

A few minutes later we swept into the store, appearing to reek of money, ready to impress anyone we might end up rubbing shoulders with. "Good afternoon," said the middle-aged, bald-headed man who greeted us from behind one of the four glass enclosed jewelry cases. He wore a black suit with a striped bowtie that pressed up against his Adam's apple. "Welcome to Padock's. How can I be of assistance to you two lovely ladies?"

"My recently widowed aunt has a question concerning an emerald that came from an old ring of hers."

"Of course. Did you bring the stone with you, ma'am?"

"Yes." Aunt Zoe slid her knit gloves off, reached inside her mega purse, and produced a tiny leather coin pouch. "I put it in here for safe keeping," she explained, fumbling with it until it opened.

The jeweler quickly prepped the counter in anticipation of Auntie's jewel. He took a thick white cloth from a drawer and placed it in front of her. "Just lay the emerald on this when you're ready." As he patiently waited for Aunt Zoe's trembling fingers to let loose of her jewel, he played with the loupe magnifier attached to a cord hanging around his thick neck.

"There you go," she said, finally releasing the object in her hand.

"Now, what exactly do you want to know?" he asked, "The emerald's value or if it can be put in another setting?"

Aunt Zoe eyed me for a moment, looking for help I suppose. I didn't offer any. I had none to give. "Both I guess," she replied weakly, "My doctor's given me about a year to live and I want to leave something precious behind for my niece to remember me by," she clutched both my hands for emphasis. "If I'm going to purchase a setting for this stone, I want to make darn sure it's worth it."

"I understand completely," he said, holding the loupe in one hand while sliding the cloth across the counter to a nearby lamp, "Do you have any idea where this emerald came from?"

Auntie pressed her pudgy fingers to her lips. "Why, no," she firmly stated, "My late husband's job took him all over the world."

At least that's true.

"Is it important?" my aunt asked.

"No. That's fine, ma'am," he replied in a comforting tone, "I can still figure out the value without that information. I must tell you though it won't be the exact amount. I'm not the stores trained. gemologist. He isn't in today."

"That's all right," Aunt Zoe said, "a close enough figure is fine."

The jeweler picked up the gem, held it under the bright light, and studied it with his magnifying lens for a few minutes. "The tiny flaws I see indicate it's genuine. The saturation's excellent. The coloring like this one, grass-green, is in high demand. Ah huh, I'd have to say the inclusion rating's about a WS." He manipulated the emerald a few minutes more and then finally set it back on the cloth.

"What does a WS rating indicate?" Aunt Zoe asked.

"A higher quality stone." His hand lightly stroked the gem. "I'd say your husband did a fine job in selecting this piece." He put the emerald on a scale now and glanced at a small chart resting on the counter. "In today's market this 2.0 carat emerald's worth at least $5,800 dollars. Enough to warrant a new setting I should think."

Aunt Zoe fanned herself. Either her hot flashes kicked in right at that moment or the dollar amount of the emerald shocked her. "Oh, my, yes that's quite within the range I wanted to spend."

"Excellent." The jeweler whipped out a catalog and placed it in front of us. "You can browse through this or I can show you what settings we have in stock. It's totally up to you. While you're thinking about what you'd like to do, you might want to consider a style that allows for additional stones."

Aunt Zoe poured over a few pages in the catalog. "My goodness! I didn't realize the variety of settings available. It's a bit overwhelming." She glanced my way. "What do you think, Niece? Should we settle on something from the catalog or take a look at what the jewelry store has on hand?"

I pushed my jacket sleeve back and peered at my wristwatch. "I'm afraid we can't make any decisions today, Auntie. We'll have to come back another time. You know how the doctor's office is about arriving late for an appointment."

"Oh, dear." Aunt Zoe touched the jeweler's hand slightly. "You've been so kind to me. I'd really like to have you help me when I come back. Perhaps you could give me your business card."

The jeweler gave her a thoughtful smile. "Certainly." He waited till Auntie got her coin purse out, then he slipped the card and emerald to her. "I'm here every day, but Saturday. Have a nice day."

"I'll try," my aunt said.

After walking a short distance from Padock's stone and wood structure, Aunt Zoe inquired about her performance. "Well, Mary, did I sound convincing enough?"

Pleased with our charade, I clapped my wool gloved hands. "Auntie, you should be nominated for an Oscar. I haven't seen you put on a performance like that since you did silly skits for my siblings and me when you babysat us." Anxious to get on to our next stop, I looped our arms together and we hustled off to Matt's car.

"Where to next?" Aunt Zoe giddily asked, sliding into the Topaz and buckling her seat belt, "I hope this place requires acting skills too: I'm just warming up."

"You won't need a voice, just your eyes." Before I started the car, I glanced all around, making certain no one suspicious happened to be lurking about. There didn't seem to be. "Okay, on to our next project." I twisted the key in the ignition, stepped on the gas, and pulled away from the curb.

As the car moved forward, Aunt Zoe stared out her side window and softly hummed "We're in the Money."

"Yup, we're deep in the money, Auntie. So deep you need to keep a close eye on your purse, unless you want it stolen."

She lifted her huge purse off her lap and squeezed it against her chest. "Don't worry, Niece. No one's getting near this emerald.

But I'm wondering how you propose to find the owner? An ad in the paper won't do. Anyone could claim it's theirs."

She's right of course. Why contact anyone? I'm quite certain the one who lost our precious emerald will find us soon enough.

~33~

The instant I caught sight of Al's Gas and Garage my knees trembled. Could someone possibly be waiting to attack me again? *Nah. That's impossible.* There's no fog and there's still plenty of daylight. Besides, those guys are too smart to stick around here for long. But just in case I was wrong, I remained overly cautious. I drove across the parking lot to the left side of the building, continued straight ahead until reaching the end of the cement garage, whipped the car around the building, hid it in the back away from prying eyes, and turned it off. Darn. I didn't feel any safer. Fear still gripped my insides even with the car tucked away. Maybe I should abort the mission. *Don't be ridiculous.* I just needed some chocolate to push me on. I checked my jacket pockets. Empty.

"I can't believe you brought me to this side of town, Mary. What a foolish thing to do. The only living creatures around here are rats."

"Yup, and some are bigger than others," I nervously teased.

My aunt pretended to cover her ears. "Blah, blah, I can't hear you."

I ignored her prattle and shifted my eyes from her to the decrepit garage. The minute I did so, my mind reeled backward to when I stopped here the last time with Fiona and a gun got shoved in my face. Maybe returning here was a horrible mistake. Scared senseless, I plucked the key from the ignition and fled to the concrete building without looking for signs of human activity underfoot in the lightly covered snow as I did so.

Instead of joining me, Aunt Zoe remained in the car stiff as a board. I'm sure the thought of rats, thanks to me, had to do with her resistance to move on. But even so, her behavior irritated me. You'd think she'd realize we'd be safer inside the building than outside where anyone could see us.

I waited near the building, hoping I wouldn't be out in the open too much longer. A few seconds later my aunt finally got up enough gumption to hop out and make a mad dash to the station's back door where I stood, keeping her eyes to the ground as she did so. As soon as she reached me, her hand flew to the ancient door knob. The door didn't budge. Auntie didn't look happy about her discovery. "Matt better have tools in his trunk," she said in a grumpy, high-pitched voice, "otherwise our drive here's been a total waste. Not that I don't mind."

"Oh, don't give up so easily. There's got to be a way in." I peered through the old style window and noticed the lock wasn't set. "Over here," I called, "I need your help."

"What is it, Mary? Did you find an opening?"

"You bet I did." I shoved the unlocked battered window up. "All you have to do is hold this in place until I crawl through. When I get in, I'll prop it up with something and then help you."

"Whew," Aunt Zoe said, brushing off the accumulation of snow on her pants as she stood on the cracked cement floor in the garage bay, "That was a tough squeeze. I hope we don't have to use that window when we leave."

"Me too." I knocked off the snow clinging to my pants while scoping out the room. "Not much light in here, is there?"

"Nope and there's not much room to move around either." Aunt Zoe tapped her foot on the cement floor. "It'll require a bulldozer to clear all the junk on this floor."

"Well, we don't have one. We'll have to make do with what God gave us. Stay put. I'll get Lizzie's flashlight from the car."

"Don't worry; my feet aren't going anywhere till I see your face again."

"Glad to hear it." I said, stumbling over to the back door to see if I could get out that way. Things were looking up. I managed to get the rusty handle to release its lock mechanism somehow. "Hey, good news, Auntie, we don't have to climb through the window when we leave after all."

"Thank goodness," she screeched.

The second I came back to the garage, Aunt Zoe forced me to reveal the reason I dragged her here. "All right, Mary, I want the truth. Did you expect Fiona to be stashed here?"

"Of course not, but you've given me something to chew on."

"I have?"

"Yeah, what if my car didn't end up on the banks of a foreign land? What if it's actually hidden in a garage somewhere in Duluth?"

Aunt Zoe's hand pressed her plump cheek. "How many garages exist in a town with a population of 86,000?"

I stamped my foot. "Too many I'm afraid. Let the police figure it out. We've already got an important job to handle."

"Finding which man killed Darcy, right?"

"Uh huh, and hopefully the jewel thieves."

"What? Mary, you said we shouldn't get involved in the jewel heist. It's too dangerous."

"We don't have any choice. I believe the men with Darcy were running from the law."

"How did you come to that conclusion?"

"Think about it. What crime would be so big an innocent person had to be snuffed out? And, why else would they steal Fiona?"

"Or warn you to stay away from the beach?" my aunt added. "So, have you shared your thoughts with Margaret?"

"Not yet. I'm still trying to narrow down the men in the picture. If I can prove they were hiding out here, then at least one of them is from the Duluth area."

Aunt Zoe's eyebrows raised a notch. "Oh, of course, it makes sense. If none of the men were from around here, how would they know about this deserted building? So, how do we go about proving they stayed here?"

"We need to look for fresh food wrappers and sleeping paraphernalia."

Midway through our search in the junk-filled garage bay, Aunt Zoe stumbled over our first piece of hard evidence. "Here, let me help you up, Auntie."

"I can't believe I didn't see those rolled up bundles."

"Don't blame yourself. They're dark and blend in with all the other junk."

She gripped my arm and stood. "At least I didn't hit the cement floor. When my friend tripped on a sidewalk last year, her face looked like someone had bashed it in with a bat. Not wanting to be seen in public after the accident, she remained secluded for over a month."

"Too bad makeup couldn't hide her horrible bruises."

"Yes, I felt so sorry for her." Aunt Zoe's eyes dropped to the objects at her feet. "What did I trip on anyway?"

I shined the flashlight on the thickly rolled fabric touching her shoes. "Just as I suspected, someone's been staying here," I bent down and checked out the sleeping bags. "The bags appear to be in good condition, not aged like the rest of the stuff around here."

"You mean people have been here recently?"

"It sure looks that way." I held the flashlight even with my waist and swept the light back and forth across the area ahead of us, looking for any evidence of meals. "I wonder how long those men from the beach hid out here before stealing my car."

"I'd like to know what they did with the vehicle they used for the heist. They had to ditch it somewhere along the route." Aunt Zoe gestured to a corner of the bay. "Mary, shine the light over by the metal cabinet again. I'm sure I saw a yellow wrapper, the kind Mc Donald's recently switched to."

When it comes to recognizing fast food wrappers, Aunt Zoe and I come out on top. Our takeout purchases beat cooking any day of the week. Of course, that might be why my hips are expanding at an exponential rate.

I focused the light on the area my roommate suggested. "We've hit the motherlode, Auntie. I believe you can skip this year's eye exam." I scrambled to the location and found empty popcorn boxes too. One box had a coating of orange stuff inside it. Charice Hawthorne said Darcy liked cheese-coated popcorn. Maybe Darcy was here, but when?

Our excitement soon soured when the window I had left propped open to enter the building slammed shut, followed by a loud pop, pop sound. My aunt shook me. "Was that gunfire? Oh, my God, do you think they've got us surrounded, Mary?"

"Stay where you are," I whispered. Pressing my body against the nearest wall leading to the window, I slowly inched my way towards it, and snuck a peek outside. There didn't appear to be any human movement. Just branches bending and leaves swirling about. But the window faced the back of the building, who knew what lurked out front. "I think a car backfired." *At least I hoped so.*

The moment we left the garage a familiar voice shouted, "Hands up. You're under arrest."

"Oh, crap," Aunt Zoe moaned. "My social security's going down the toilet."

"Calm down, Auntie. Officer Fitzwell's just joking." I tried to look into the cop's eyes, but his darn flashlight blinded me. "Turn off the flashlight, all right. The jokes over, Trevor, I can't see beyond my nose."

"I'm not turning it off until I have the two of you in the back of my squad car."

"Are you crazy? We haven't done anything wrong."

Another masculine voice, deeper and older spoke now. "Good catch, Newbie. Let's run them down to the station and book 'em."

"Hey, wait a second," I said. "You need to inform me of my Rights first."

"You hear that Trevor? I think the lady's ready to be cuffed."

"Okay, okay," I said feeling the heat rising in my cheeks, "At least tell us why we're being placed under arrest. It can't be because we're snooping around a long abandoned garage. Who would've squealed on us? A disgruntled squirrel?"

"Oh, she's a smart cookie like you said Fitzwell. You must be the kingpin's moll."

"What? I'm no moll. I'm just an unemployed teacher from the cities who happens to be spending time with a relative here in Duluth. I've never met any kingpins."

"She hasn't," Aunt Zoe blubbered. "I can vouch for that."

"Like your word is as good as gold, Grannie," the grouchy older cop said.

"Don't believe her story about being a teacher either," Officer Fitzwell said, "She's a dog sitter."

"Hey, I resent that. Just tell us why were under arrest."

"They're both crazier than loons, Trevor."

"Have you ever been up close to a loon when it makes its wail call?" I said, "It's pretty impressive."

"Okay, lady. You want to know what you're under arrest for? I'll tell you. You two thieves stole precious stones from the Clarity Diamonds and Gems facility in Grand Marais. And you're squatting on property that doesn't belong to you. Is that sufficient information for you?"

"Oh, you fellas have so got the wrong people," I said. "By the time you get this situation with us squared away, you're going to want to stick your heads in a sand dune. Come on, Auntie; let's take a free ride in the back of their squad car. You recently added that to your bucket list, didn't you?"

My roommate became more chipper. "Why, yes, I most certainly did."

~34~

"Have they given you their ringleader's name yet?" the sixty-something Sergeant in charge asked as he entered the police station's interrogation room carrying a manila folder.

Officer Fitzwell glanced at the floor, "No, Sarge. The two of them keep saying they're innocent, but I know they're in cahoots with the other three guys. They're just trying to throw us off. When I ran into them near the beach, they told me about the men. Then about a week later, the younger one there," Trevor points to me silently sitting alongside Aunt Zoe at a small table, "conveniently rams into my car and presents me with a photo of Darcy Hawthorne and the three males."

He didn't mention seeing me at the DECC. *Why keep it a secret.* I braced my elbows on the table, clasped my hands together, and rested my chin on the locked hands like I do sitting behind a teacher's desk studying the students as they go about their work with fellow classmates, wondering what they'll be when they grow up. The reverse is true of these men. I know what they do for a living, but they're acting like small fry. What they need is a little discipline. And this unemployed teacher would love to be the one to serve it up.

The Sergeant turned to Officer Fitzwell and his partner. "You two go get coffee, I'll take over now. When the men left, he pulled up a chair. "Which one of you is Mary?"

"I am."

He points to Auntie. "You must be Zoe. I suppose Mary dragged you into this mess, huh?"

"She most certainly did," she blurted out without thinking. "I warned my niece we'd end up in hot water if she kept going about her business the way she does."

He looked at me again like my picture had already been posted on the FBI's MOST WANTED list and broadcast nationwide. "I'm surprised you haven't asked for a lawyer yet. Most people do once we arrest them."

"Why should we? We're innocent," I replied in a disgusted tone.

He laughed. "You're innocent. That's a good one. You know how many guilty people come through our doors and use those exact words? Now, let's cut the crap, okay? If you're not guilty, why were you at a jewelry store getting a stolen emerald priced?"

"We didn't know it was stolen," I said.

Aunt Zoe agreed. "We found it on the carpet in her cousin's apartment."

The Sergeant's eyebrows jetted to a peak. "Is that so? A stolen emerald just happened to find its way to your cousin's floor and you discovered it. How stupid do you think I am?"

"It's the truth, Officer, whether you believe us or not. We only came to Duluth so I could do research for a novel and care for my cousin. Check out my story. We were nowhere near Grand Marais on the day of the theft."

"You didn't have to be," he said, "Maybe the men expected you to move the merchandise once they procured it."

"Officer, doesn't it seem a little dumb for me to walk into a jewelry store in the general region where the robbery occurred to find out the worth of one lone emerald?"

He rubbed his thick jaw. "Not if you're new to the fencing game."

I could feel my irritation rising to the surface. "I'm not new to any fencing game."

"Sir," Aunt Zoe chirped, "Mary doesn't know how to fence. If she did, she would've told me. I've known her since she was a baby."

Auntie's interference wasn't helping. I tried to rein in my anger, but found I was fighting a losing battle. My hand gave a mighty blow to the table. The thundering noise must've scared Aunt

Zoe. Her body jerked. "How about checking out my references, Officer? I've got tons. I held up my left hand and gripped one of its fingers with the right one each time I ticked off another name. Let's see, there's Principal Drake at Washington Elementary; Rod Thompson at the FBI campus in the cities; Sergeant Murchinak—"

"Don't forget your boyfriend David Miller, the undercover cop and Reed. He's a horse boarder," Auntie proudly explained.

The Sergeant rubbed his forehead so hard I was afraid the skin might peel off. "All right, all right. I'll check your references. If they come out clean, you're good to go."

"Finally, someone who's got enough sense to listen," I said.

~35~

"Mary, I'm glad you're finally back," Margaret said in a distressed tone, "I found an envelope addressed to you in Lizzie's mailbox."

"I'm glad we're back too," I said haggardly, as the two of us just released jailbirds dragged our weary buns across the threshold. Luckily Margaret and Lizzie didn't notice our downheartedness. The women didn't need to hear about our time spent in a police interrogation room. All I can say is it does pay to have friends in law enforcement. Otherwise, we'd be sitting in a jail cell stuffed in orange jumpsuits right now, and no one, not even my folks would attempt to send us a cake with a saw in it.

Cousin Lizzie got off the settee and slowly made her way to us. "There's no return address on the envelope, or a stamp. Someone living in the building must've poked it through the slot."

I took the small manila envelope from Margaret's petite arthritic hands and moved from the hallway to the living room. "A very clever person left this. Choosing bold print strokes instead of manuscript, so I couldn't compare handwriting even if I had a sample." The women circled around me, curious to see what the envelope held. I loosened the flap and stuck my hand inside. "Relax everyone. It's just a picture."

"Of what?" Aunt Zoe anxiously queried.

"Darcy and Zeke standing by the popcorn stand in Canal Park." I flipped the photo over. "Someone stamped this past Monday's date on it."

Margaret reached for the photo. "Zeke wears a beard? Why, you've finally got the break you've been waiting for, Mary." Silence engulfed us. The Italian woman handed the photo back and studied my face. "This should be cause for celebration. Why aren't you yelling from the roof tops?" She straightened her shoulders and wiggled a crooked finger at me. "You think someone's setting Zeke up."

I ran my hand through disheveled hair, thinking of our release from the pokey just mere minutes ago and how easy it is to end up there. "Possibly. I guess I'd better have another chat with him."

The nonagenarian gave an inquisitive look. "Another talk? How come we never heard about your first encounter with him."

I removed my jacket and slung it over my arm. "I didn't want you worrying needlessly."

"We know you're a grown woman, but you shouldn't leave the premises without telling us where you're going," Cousin Lizzie scolded. "It's too dangerous, Mary."

Aunt Zoe clutched my arm forcibly. "I'm concerned about this case. You need to back away, Niece. Darcy's killer's ruthless. There's no telling how many spies he has watching us. For all we know they had their eyes glued to us the minute we drove off to the jewelry store."

I shook my arm loose. "No one's scaring me off, including a rookie cop. I'm seeing this through." Winnie clawed my leg. "Down, Girl, no one's in trouble." I marched over to the coffee table, placed the note on it, and then I plopped down in one of Lizzie's exquisite chairs.

"May I ask what possessed you to go to a jewelry store?" our neighbor inquired, "Unless you want to keep it between the two of you."

I glanced at Aunt Zoe, hoping she'd remember to keep the arrest to herself, and then I tilted my head in Margaret's direction. "No, there's no reason to keep it a secret. The stone you found on Lizzie's carpet turned out to be a genuine emerald."

"But …but I thought you tossed it?" Lizzie said.

"I pretended to."

Aunt Zoe busted in, "Good thing Mary followed her intuition. It's worth almost 6 grand."

My cousin's thin lips jarred open. "Six thousand dollars? Holy tamale! Why hasn't Virginia notified residents to be on the lookout for it if it's worth that much?"

Margaret's fingers pressed her tiny forehead. "Maybe the person who lost it doesn't know it's gone yet. Could the stone have wedged in the groove of a shoe, Mary?"

"And fallen out in here?"

"*Si.*"

"It's unlikely. We always take our shoes off by Lizzie's door."

Winnie suddenly leapt on to Lizzie's lap and began chewing away. "What do you have in your mouth, you little stinker? Something you shouldn't have, I'm sure." After a few seconds of gently cajoling, my cousin finally succeeded in getting the poodle's mouth open. "A Kleenex? That's not good for you."

Hmm? Maybe I should rethink things. Winnie could've gotten ahold of the gem somehow. I tossed my jacket aside and scrambled to the door to collect a tennis shoe. When I returned with one, Auntie signaled she wanted to take a look at it. Not wanting to argue with her, I flipped it over and handed it off.

She set the shoe on her lap. Then she stuffed her hand in her huge purse and produced a stone the same size as the emerald the police confiscated.

"Where did that come from," I inquired.

"I found it on the beach." Auntie worked with the stone and the grove of the shoe to find a fit. She finally gave up. "The stone's too big."

"What about one belonging to a man?" the nonagenarian quietly suggested. "Like the one who dropped Virginia's ottoman off?"

"We have to find him," I volleyed back. "He could be one of the jewel thieves." I jumped out of my chair. "Margaret and Aunt Zoe, I want you to try and recall as much as you can about the man who came to the apartment the other day. While you're doing that, I'll find out when Zeke's scheduled to work at the DECC again." I dug the cell phone out of my jacket pocket and searched for the DECC number.

"Take Margaret with you when you go," Lizzie ordered. "She's been catering to me around the clock."

Margaret's aged forehead furrowed. "I'm perfectly fine, Lizzie. Mary needs someone more agile to chase around with her, like Zoe."

"No, you go," Aunt Zoe insisted. "You'd throw whoever's watching Mary off their game. They won't expect a woman in her nineties to be digging for answers. At least I know I wouldn't."

"Hush," I said. "I can't hear. Yes, hello. This is Zeke Henrik's sister. Could you tell me what time he works tonight? What? When did that happen?" The minute the conversation ended I turned towards Margaret. "Get your coat we're going to the hospital."

My aunt rested her hands on her lap. "What happened, Mary? Was Zeke involved in a car accident?"

"No. Someone beat him to a pulp late last night outside a local bar. He has three cracked ribs and a broken arm."

~36~

Sunday

"Mary, who do you think wanted Zeke harmed?" my Italian companion questioned as we slowly made our way down the well-lit second floor hospital corridor of St. Luke's. "Some drunk he teed off or a man involved with Darcy's murder?"

"My guess—the guy Darcy got wrapped up with."

When we reached the nurses' station, I asked the L.P.N. on duty if she thought Zeke Hendrick's was up to having visitors. She said, "Yes," and quickly directed us to his room.

Zeke glanced up briefly from the plump chair pressed against the hospital bed, gazed towards the doorway where we stood, and then his head drifted back to the cops and robber show on TV. *So apropos.* The guy lacked his handsome looks from a couple days ago. His thick hair was matted, the upper part of his face badly bruised, and his right arm covered in a cast. "What are you doing here?" he asked in a snarly tone.

"I could ask you the same question," I snidely remarked, slipping into his room without waiting for an invite. "I have a feeling your answer would be more creative than mine."

"It's your fault I'm in this shape you know. You led them to me."

"Oh, no. You're not shifting the blame to me. I'm not responsible for your situation." Zeke didn't respond. I picked up the conversation thread again. "I'm surprised the hospital hasn't pushed you out the door yet."

He swallowed hard, pointed to the top of his head with his left hand. "I got clobbered along with everything else. The nurses are making sure my noodle's working properly." He took a good look at Margaret. "Don't tell me you brought your grandma for protection?"

I grinned. "Margaret Grimshaw may look the part but she's no one's grandmother." I clutched the elderly woman's frail arm. "This lady's worked on quite a number of important cases with a well-known private eye in the Twin Cities." I was referring to Matt, but he didn't need to know that.

That piqued his interest. "Oh, yeah?" He turned to acknowledge the little woman. "Nice to meet you. Sorry, I didn't mean to include you in any ill will I have towards Miss Malone."

Margaret straightened her tiny body to its full height, looked him straight in the eye and said, "No need to apologize, young man. You're scared and we've come to help you."

Zeke snorted. "Ma'am, I don't mean to doubt you, but how the heck are you two dames going to do that when the cops don't even know where to look?"

I pressed my knobby knees against his well-padded chair. "We've got inside information they know nothing about."

He reached for the remote and cut off the TV. "Go ahead, I'm listening."

I whipped out the picture I had received in the mail and held it in front of his face. "Some photo, huh?"

His bruised face took on a tough guy appearance. "Where did you get that? Did you take it?"

"No, I wish I had. Why did you tell me you hadn't seen Darcy after the breakup? Were you two involved in criminal activity, like maybe a jewel heist?"

Zeke squirmed in his chair. "The jewel heist? If you know about it, why are you here?"

"We can't help you until we hear your side of the story," I shoved another picture in front of him, "Tell me about these guys with Darcy. Are they friends of yours?"

Zeke grew angry. "You must be kidding. I respected Darcy too much to ever see her display herself like this."

Margaret shared one of her more memorable smiles for Zeke's benefit. "Dear, exactly what were you discussing when someone caught the two of you huddled together like this?"

"Look, I told Miss Malone the other day I hadn't seen Darcy since we broke up."

I stared him down. "And how did that confession pan out for you?"

He braced his forehead with his left hand. "Okay, okay. It's true we hadn't seen each other since the breakup. But then boom, this past Monday out of the blue, Darcy calls. She told me she wanted to talk and asked if I'd meet her around ten. I'm thinking hallelujah, we're getting back together."

"When I showed up, she acted all nervous and jumpy, like she's expecting someone to pop up behind her any second. The minute I asked her what was wrong, she started bawling. Says she's in a jam up to her eyeballs. Somehow she found out the guys she'd been hanging out with were involved in a jewel heist. Now, they won't let her out of their sight. I told Darcy to sneak off to the police, but she refused."

"Did she say why?" Margaret asked.

"The men had threatened to kill her."

My hand flew to my forehead. "Whoa! Why didn't you report what you knew then?"

Zeke drew the back of his hand across his eyes, wiping away tears I assumed. "I wish I had. Darcy begged me not to. I'd been in minor scrapes with the law before and she thought the cops might assume I was involved."

"So much for staying away from cops," I said, "Since finding Darcy, they've been hounding you, haven't they?"

Zeke stared at his lap. "Yup, but who told you?"

"When I returned to the DECC lobby, I overheard a cop ask the receptionist where he could find you."

"Maybe he led the bad guys to me." I gave him a dirty look, but in my heart I knew he could be right. "Hey, I'm just calling it like I see it. If you don't like it, too bad. I just know the one time I needed the cops breathing down my neck, they weren't there. And wham, what happened? Two big bozos flew out of the woodwork and tossed me around like a garbage can."

"Did you recognize either of the men?" I asked.

"Nope, too dark. I couldn't believe those creeps insisted I knew where their stash got hidden. When I told them I had no idea what they were talking about, they beat me to a pulp." His face grew somber. He rested his chin in the palm of his hand. "You know if it weren't for the bar bouncer coming out to take a smoke, I'd be dead too."

He let go of his chin and swiftly moved his hand towards the photo. "Do you think this picture of the two of us got her killed, Miss Malone?"

I shook my head. "I honestly don't know. There's still a lot of loose puzzle pieces floating around. Until I can gather them all up we won't know the full story."

Margaret patted his hand. "Don't worry, Zeke, when we get the answers, we'll let you know."

"Do you mind if I keep the picture of Darcy and me?"

"No," I replied. "But put it somewhere safe where the cops wouldn't think to look. You don't want to end up behind bars."

With a few more answers concerning the case now, we left Zeke's room and headed for the elevator.

"Zeke really loved Darcy, didn't he Mary?"

I flicked a few stray strands of hair away from my eyes. "Yes. I think he would've done anything for her. It's too bad they broke up."

"You never shared the reason they split up. Is that because you don't know?"

"Oh, I know. Another woman got in the way."

"Ah."

~37~

On our journey back to Park Point Margaret inquired whether I planned to remain quiet about the photo I'd received in the mail or share the information with Officer Fitzwell the first chance I had. I told her I wanted to hammer out things a bit more before revealing anything further with him, never mentioning the real reasons being my recent arrest and reluctance to confirm his trustworthiness.

After dismissing the case, light-hearted conversation ensued. Margaret described in great detail her new crochet project, a sweater, she was working on. I politely listened, having no idea what a G hook or triple crochet happened to be. When she finished, I asked if she thought she might attend another meeting for crossword puzzle enthusiasts. Instead of replying, the nonagenarian produced a question of her own. "Did I ever tell you about the strange chat I had with a retired gent after the last meeting?"

I smiled. "No. I guess Aunt Zoe and I kind of took the wind out of your sails that day with our naked lady story. Did he try to get your phone number?"

She batted her age-dappled hand my way. "Don't get smart, Missy. I have enough man friends in Minneapolis. I don't need any more."

Maybe she didn't, but I could use a few in my age bracket. "Well, what did he have to say?"

"He asked if I knew what happened to the elderly grounds keeper Del Rosa's had for years. He wasn't pleased with the young crew who replaced him. 'All those three do,' he said, 'is stand around smoking or chatting up the young girls hired to clean apartments.'"

"Why would they need three men to do the job of one?"

The elderly woman folded her hands and rested them in her lap. "That's what I've been mulling over. From what I've seen, it doesn't look like there's enough yardwork to keep more than one person busy."

I tapped my fingers on the steering wheel. "Did the man happen to mention when the new crew took over?"

"I think he said over a month ago."

"Hmm, the plot thickens. Margaret, remind me to hug you when we get back to the apartment. We've got our next clue."

"Our next clues," she corrected.

I nodded. "You're right. We need to check out the grounds crew *and* the cleaners. There might be a connection."

"*Si,* maybe they work together."

"And play together. Perhaps that's why the cops haven't rounded up the men yet. The ladies provide lodging."

~38~

As I directed the Topaz into one of the ten designated *guest* spots at the Del Rosa, I caught sight of a dark-haired youthful-looking man clothed in a tan jacket and blue jeans dodging into the underground parking. Even though I was more than a hundred feet from him, I had the feeling he might be one of the three groundsmen we almost bumped into when we arrived here last Saturday. If I didn't chase after him, I'd probably lose any chance of ever finding out where the men were holed up.

Before I could set my plan into action though, there's one minute detail I needed to take care of, Margaret. I didn't want the nonagenarian harmed while I was in hot pursuit. I'd have to come up with an excuse for not returning to the apartment with her. But what could I say?

Luckily, it didn't take long for my noggin to devise a believable story. I stuffed the car key in my purse and then turned my attention to the elderly woman who was unbuckling her seatbelt. "Oh, darn. I forgot Aunt Zoe wanted me to give the car a thorough looking over today."

Margaret opened the front passenger door. "Why?"

"She insists she lost one of her favorite earrings in here. I told her I'd look, but I have a feeling it's a waste of time. Look, it's getting close to suppertime, you don't mind going up to let them know we're back, do you?"

My neighbor released a slight smile. If she suspected something, she didn't let on. "Don't worry about me, dear. We've been here long enough, I know my way around."

The minute she slipped into the building I made a mad dash to the garage. Of course, the man I so desperately sought had already disappeared. *Shoot!* By now he could be riding the elevator, roaming the woods on the backside of the building, or hiding in a car. I decided to check the cars first on the off chance the guy might have popped in one of them and be waiting for his buddies.

The one thing I didn't expect to find while examining the cars was a VW, the exact make and blue coloring as Fiona, parked in the seventh slot of the second row. Too curious to see if the VW had all the same features as mine, I totally ignored the license plate, trotted over to the car, leaned against the driver's door, and peeked in the window. "I don't believe it." The vase held the same fake mums Aunt Zoe put in my car. "What? Fiona's been sitting right here under our noses all this time?" *Dang. I had no choice. Officer Fitzwell had to be notified immediately.*

I shoved my hand in my purse, yanked out the cell phone, entered the words Duluth Police Stations and waited for the specific area I desired to pop up. Once it did, I pressed *CALL.*

A crisp, clear woman's voice instantly came on the other end. She followed proper protocol to the letter, gingerly asking how she could be of assistance. I rushed to explain my call. It was intended for Officer Fitzwell. "He's been working on finding my stolen car."

"I'm sorry, Officer Fitzwell doesn't come back on duty until next Tuesday." *I can't believe it. The one time I hoped he'd be available he isn't.* Not receiving any feedback from me on what I wanted to do next, the woman's polite tone continued. "If you'd like to speak with another officer regarding your car, I can transfer your call."

I pressed the palm of my hand against my forehead. "Here's the deal. I'm not calling to see if anyone found the car. I just discovered it tucked away in the underground garage where I'm staying. But before I use the Volkswagen again, I thought you might want to send a cop out to dust for fingerprints. You know, so you can catch the culprit."

"Give me your address Miss. I'll send someone to handle it as soon as possible."

***

The grumpy, mid-fifties officer standing in front of me, legs generously spread apart, acted like he had more important things to do than listen to my wild woes, like popping in at the donut shop down the street. I guess if I was in his shoes I'd rather be sitting at a Dunkin' Donuts dipping a sugary sweet or two in a cup of java than hearing the words flying out of my mouth, considering the supposed stolen car sat in the underground garage where said victim happened to be staying.

"Okay, Miss, let's go over the details once more. Why wouldn't you have known your car was down here?"

Aunt Zoe took one of my hands in hers. She probably sensed I was about to blow a gasket. "I don't live here. My cousin does," I said.

He pointed at Aunt Zoe. "You mean this lady here?"

"No, I'm her aunt. We're here caring for her cousin who had knee surgery."

"So, the two of you are staying with your cousin?"

"Actually, there are three of us," I said, wondering why I even offered the information. The cop rubbed his grayish-black eyebrows. "If the VW was stolen Sunday night like you reported, what did you use to get around town, your cousin's car?"

An exasperated huff melted off Aunt Zoe's lips. "Of course not, Officer Murphy, she doesn't own one, nor do I. Mary used her brother's."

"Look," I said, tiring of the questioning. "I don't know why we're quibbling over what car I've been using. It has nothing to do with the car sitting in front of us. I hope you're not insinuating I purposely stashed my Volkswagen down here and then reported it stolen. Why would I do such a stupid thing?"

Murphy tipped the front of his cap. "You'd be surprise what people do for insurance money, ma'am."

"Well, I'm not one of them. Ask Officer Fitzwell about the night the thieves left me stranded in a ghastly part of town. He came to my rescue. He knows how distraught I was."

"Now, now, calm down," he said, exposing a shy smile as he pulled a notepad from his back pocket, "Everything you've said is in his report. But it never hurts to have a victim repeat their story just in case an officer didn't record the facts accurately."

"Does that mean you're going to dust for fingerprints?" Aunt Zoe asked.

The cop nodded. "And take pictures."

"Ooh, how exciting, to witness the process in person," she exclaimed, "I've only seen prints lifted off a car on Hawaii Five-O."

"Well, this ain't a TV show, lady," he said rather brusquely, slapping his notebook shut and sticking it in his back pocket, "So, stand back and give me room to do my job." He rushed back to the trunk of his car, took what he needed, and returned where I stood.

Officer Murphy took photos of the cars exterior first. Then he set the camera aside and pulled out a special powder, brushing it on the door handles and other areas of the car. Wherever the cop discovered a latent print, he lifted it with what looked like clear tape, attached the tape to an index card, and then scribbled info down on the card.

After the cop finished with the car's exterior, he moved to the inside, repeating the exact same procedure but in the opposite order: lifting prints first then taking pictures. He also opened the trunk, pulled up floor mats, and dug through the glove compartment. I assumed to see if my keys or anything else out of the ordinary had been left behind.

It wasn't until Officer Murphy landed his feet on the garage floor again that I dared to ask him if he found my keys.

"Yup. They were under the driver side floor mat." He set the fingerprint kit on the cement floor.to free up his hands. Then he whipped out keys from his pant pocket and dangled them in front of me. "Here. I'm done with them. Take 'em."

"Thanks. So, are you all finished here?"

"Nope, I need your fingerprints too."

I didn't give him any guff. The station already took them earlier, but what the heck. This will really confuse them. Prints taken twice in one day, that's not too bad. I bet really active criminals have theirs lifted four or five times in a day, depending on the action they see when they're out and about.

Aunt Zoe, on the other hand, didn't like what she heard. She demanded to know why the cop thought it necessary to take her niece's prints. She hadn't done anything wrong. Stunned, the cop's wide jaw dropped open. His eyes fixated on Auntie as if she was an alien visiting earth for the first time.

Noticing the cop's strong reaction to Auntie's words, I skillfully interceded on his behalf. "Shush. It's okay. He has to eliminate my prints from the rest. Otherwise he won't be able to narrow the playing field."

"You mean find the culprit?"

"Exactly." I offered my right hand to Murphy first. After each fingertip got inked, it was carefully recorded on an index card. It wasn't until the final finger was recorded, the pinky on my left hand, that I politely suggested my aunt's prints and our other companion's be taken too since they both had ridden in the VW with me.

I could tell Aunt Zoe didn't want to cooperate after what happened earlier in the day, but I gave her the old thumbs up routine and then she smiled.

As crabby as Officer Murphy had been since arriving on the scene, I half expected him to blow a gasket over a layman telling him how to run his show. Luckily, his face didn't register any offense taken. He just whipped out more index cards and indicated he was ready for Aunt Zoe and anyone else I cared to toss his way.

~39~

After Officer Murphy left, the three of us took the elevator up to Cousin Lizzie's third floor apartment and showed off our blackened fingers. Looking at them, she jokingly said, "Leave and don't ever darken my apartment door again. I can't afford cops showing up to throw you in the slammer. I'd have to move out. My impeccable reputation would be tarnished."

The moment Lizzie finished her spiel someone knocked at the door. Margaret giggled and said, "Oh, dear, the police have figured out we've escaped from the penitentiary. Quick, hide us, Lizzie."

"I'll see who it is," I offered, trying to compose myself. "Officer Murphy probably forgot to ask me something." But the policeman I referred to wasn't standing in the hallway. It was Del Rosa's apartment manager Virginia Bagely.

"Hi, I hope I'm not interrupting anything, Mary."

"Of course not," I signaled her to enter.

She stepped in and waved a quick 'hello,' to the rest of the women in the room. The swift arm action caused the four thin jeweled bracelets she wore to slide to her bony elbow. "I heard I missed all the excitement in the garage a few minutes ago." She rested her hand on my shoulder. "Mary, I bet you're tickled pink to know your car showed up. I just can't believe it's been sitting in the garage all this time and no one reported it to me. Crazy, huh?"

I combed strands of fine hair over my left ear with my fingers. "Yeah, it's crazy all right."

Virginia leaned on the back of the brocaded chair where Margaret had positioned herself. "Did you inspect the car for damage?"

I nodded. "As far as I could tell, everything appeared fine. Say as long as you're here, Virginia, do you have a list of gals who clean for tenants in the building? I had promised Lizzie I'd find out."

Lizzie picked up the thread of the conversation, as if she was on my conspiracy team. Maybe Margaret filled her in. "Yes, my visitors are leaving in a couple days and even though I feel fine, the doctor insists I take it easy for a while longer."

"And so you should," Virginia said, "If you over do it, you might run into trouble. Besides it doesn't hurt to be pampered from time to time."

Lizzie smiled. "That's what my daughter said."

"Say, I'm on my way to the office. Why don't you join me, Mary, and I'll print out the list for you."

"Sure. Then we can get someone lined up before we leave."

***

Margaret about tripped over her pink Isotoner slippers trying to reach me when I waltzed through the door. "Well, let's take a look at the list," she said. "I'm anxious to see if we recognize any names."

"Where's my aunt?"

"In the kitchen making chocolate chip cookies," the nonagenarian whispered conspiratorially.

Remembering the last fiasco she had with baking I said, "I can't believe you allowed her in there. Are you supervising her?"

The little Italian woman stuffed her hands in the yellow apron tied around her waist. "*Si*. Don't worry. She's dropping spoonful's of ready-made mix on to cookie sheets and putting them in the oven, but I'm timing the baking."

"For heaven's sake, bring that list over here this instant," Cousin Lizzie ordered. She was sitting on the settee. "The suspense is aging me."

Since we were in her abode, I figured it would be smart to do as she asked. Besides, I'd already looked at the names of the cleaning gals while I rode the elevator up here.

"My goodness," Lizzie said, "such a long list of cleaners for an apartment complex the size of Del Rosa. I didn't realize they're in such high demand."

Margaret's arthritic finger poked at a name halfway down the list. "Well, surprise, surprise. Look who cleans here."

Before I could share my two cents worth, Aunt Zoe's voice disrupted our flow of conversation. "Okay, Margaret, I'm ready for you to set the timer."

I looked up from the list we were staring at and found my aunt leaning up against the wall that acts as a divider between kitchen and living room. A navy-colored butcher apron with blotches of dough clinging to it hid most of Auntie's dark pants. Seeing the wasted dough made me wince. There would be a dozen less cookies to devour. She does look kind of cute though. If Dad's sister played her cards right, she could be the next Pillsbury Doughboy or Doughchick. "Hey, what am I missing? No one told me Mary came back already."

"Sorry. We got too wrapped up with the list of cleaning people," I answered.

"*Si*. And we found one more clue for her case," Margaret added.

Cousin Lizzie straightened her tight-permed head. "You'll never guess who cleans for Del Rosa residents."

"Who?" my aunt asked.

"Darcy's roommate," I shared.

"Trudy?"

"Yup."

"I guess a certain someone's going to be seeing you again, Mary. How about tracking her down with me tomorrow?"

"I think it can be arranged." I'm sure Lizzie and Margaret can use a break from her never ending chatter.

~40~

Monday

Before I ended my full-time employment at Washington Elementary, fellow teachers tried to persuade me to break down and purchase a slick Fitbit device. It would enable me to see how much walking I did in a school day and how many calories I burned. If I found the numbers too low, I could simply do more walking after school. Sounded like an easy way to lose weight, but I never got motivated enough to purchase one. And now I'm glad I didn't. Heck, at the pace I'm going chasing down bad guys, I'll lose weight without watching one itty-bitty ounce of what passes through my precious lips.

Aunt Zoe huffed and puffed her way down the first floor of Burntside apartment, trying her best to keep up with my speed demon walking. I felt sorry for her, but I couldn't slow down. Not yet. This sleuth had only one thing on her mind, catching Trudy Almquist before she flew the coop.

"Mary, did you ever check to see if Trudy's in her dorm room?"

My cell phone pinged announcing an incoming message. I read it. "Yup. She's there. This text from the dorm's resident assistant just confirmed it." My cell phone pinged announcing an incoming message. I read it. "Yup. She's there. This text from the dorm's resident assistant just confirmed it."

"I suppose you didn't think about finding out when she cleans at the Del Rosa and saving yourself a trip here."

"The idea flashed through my mind for a split second. But Trudy could get away too easily there, hence, the trek here. Ganging up on the girl in her room leaves her nowhere to run."

As we neared the middle of the first floor hallway, I threw out a warning to my aunt. "We'll find Trudy's room just three doors down from here."

Aunt Zoe stopped a foot short of the girl's room. I thought to catch her breath, but I was wrong. She actually wanted to establish her body language. She pulled her shoulders back, adding a half inch to her height. Then she stuffed her hand in her jacket pocket, making it appear she carried a gun of some sort. "Okay, Niece, let's do it." Oh, my, gosh. Her words and actions seemed to be copied straight from a police show.

I knocked. Trudy responded same as last time. But this visit I had back up. Although it wasn't the kind of help one would desire if trouble with a capital T stared you in the face. Aunt Zoe and I stepped in the room. Knowing Trudy didn't seem to pay attention to whomever entered her room, I immediately announced us.

Fear registered in the college girl's eyes the moment she looked up from her desk. "Why, Miss Malone, I didn't expect to see you again."

"I'm sure you didn't. Look, it appears I'm interrupting your study time so I'll cut to the chase. "When I asked you what you did for a job, you never told me where you cleaned apartments. Why did you deem it necessary to hide that fact from me?"

She scratched her head. "I don't know. It didn't seem relevant to Darcy's death."

"Well, it is," I snapped. "And if you don't want to spend time behind bars, you'd better tell me everything you know right now."

Aunt Zoe added her two cents. "Yeah, Missy, don't beat around the bush. We know you're involved with what happened to Darcy. It's just a matter of time before we find out what actually went on."

The girl picked up a pencil and chewed on the eraser.

She's acting like a trapped rat, I thought. Good. Let her sweat it out. Her best friend's dead. The least she can do is suffer a little. I tugged my cell phone out of my purse and readied my hand over the numbers. "Well, how long are you going to make me wait for answers? I've been told I'm not a patient person."

"Mary, call the police," Aunt Zoe ordered, "You can see she doesn't plan to cooperate."

That did it. Trudy cracked. She tossed the pencil against the wall behind her desk and whimpered. "Everything was fine until I took Darcy to the Del Rosa to help me."

"What happened?" I inquired.

Trudy swept the tears off her face. I had my eye on the manager's grandson."

"You mean Virginia Bagely's?" Aunt Zoe questioned.

"Yes."

"But he set his sights on Darcy instead," I tactfully stated. "Of course, she only threw herself at him after you destroyed her relationship with Zeke. Too bad you interfered. You may have gotten his affection eventually." A woman scorned twice would be motive enough to kill someone. But did Trudy have access to a boat and the opportunity, I wondered? I moved closer to her desk. Thinking of the ring I found with Darcy's belongings, I dug deeper, "Would his initials happen to be J.R.?"

"Uh huh," she dabbed her nose this time. "Everyone calls him J.R., but his full name's Jarek Razinki."

The Surname jiggled a teeny memory stowed away, but not enough to validate whether it belonged with the puzzle being pieced together. Darn. This memory lapse couldn't have come at a worse time. "I thought he lived in Canada."

"He does, but he came down to Duluth almost two months ago to look for work. When he couldn't find anything, Virginia convinced him to take over the outside maintenance around the Del Rosa."

Aunt Zoe jabbed my upper arm excitedly. "Razinki's Polish. Virginia isn't Polish."

I pulled my aunt aside and in a low, gentle tone reminded her we were here to gather facts not analyze them. "You asked to come, so follow my lead. Don't deviate from it, all right?"

Auntie's heavy eyelids drooped. "Sorry. I'll try to stick with the flow." She spun towards Trudy again. "Does J.R. have scars on his hands?" *Now she's cracking eggs.* I gave her the *thumbs up* sign.

Trudy nodded. "He was trapped in a house fire."

"Did he ever say who started it or where he lived at the time?"

"No."

"Have you seen J.R. with a beard?"

"Occasionally. His two buddies and he like to goof around and wear fake ones from time to time."

With Auntie's few questions out of the way, I forged ahead. "Who are the other two guys he works with?"

"They only go by their first names Demetri and Lewis. J.R. said he met them at some sleazy bar in Grand Marais."

I glanced at my aunt. We were definitely working two cases. Zeke told me Darcy wasn't involved with the stolen jewels, but what about Trudy? Probing that topic could wait. I veered off in another direction instead. I whipped out the photo I received in Lizzie's mailbox. "I assume you took this picture. Why send it to me? Didn't you realize I'd question Zeke?"

Trudy squeezed her hands together so tight her knuckles turned white. "I was freaking out. I thought I might be blamed for Darcy's death since everyone assumed I was the last one to see her. Then I remembered the picture I snapped of them last Monday at Canal Park. I happened to be walking back from the lighthouse when I saw them by the popcorn stand. Zeke looked angry. Darcy couldn't stop crying. Every time Zeke thrust his arms out at her, she'd back away. Eventually she ran off down the street."

"Did he go after her?" Aunt Zoe queried.

"Not while I was there."

"What I'd really like to know Trudy is why you've conveniently thrown Zeke under the bus and forgotten about J.R.? Did you share the photo with his buddies? How about him? J.R.'s the one who had been hanging out with Darcy since she broke up with Zeke. You knew it and yet you told me you had no idea who her new boyfriend was. What other dark secrets are you holding on to?"

Trudy's cell phone suddenly rang. She picked it up and listened. Then she hung up. "You have to go. I'm late for a math class." She nervously slung her purse strap over her shoulder, plucked up the book and notebook sitting on her desk, and then ushered us out the door. The second she locked up she turned her back on us and sped down the hall.

She sure flew out of here like a wild cat," I said, watching Trudy disappear.

Aunt Zoe plopped her hand on her hip. "Niece, we've been conned. Today's Columbus Day, isn't it?"

"Yeah, so?"

"Well, one of the posters on the bulletin board in the lobby reminded residents that there weren't any classes on Columbus Day. So, who do you suppose got under Trudy's thin skin?"

"I don't know, but I'm betting it's one of the guys we're looking for. Come on, Auntie. We can't let her slip through our fingers."

~41~

If you ever find yourself on the heftier side of the scale, don't plan to chase down a slim eighteen-year old girl who used to be on her high school track team. You won't catch her. You'll just end up bent at the waist, hands tightly clasped to your midsection trying to keep your insides from trickling out along with other unmentionables. As hard as Auntie and I tried to get to Trudy before she split, we didn't succeed. She was long gone before our cheap tennies smacked the newly redone lobby floor.

The student receptionist on duty, bless her heart, wanted to know if she should call the paramedics for us. I told her it wasn't necessary. Bottled water or candy would be sufficient if she had either. She quickly obliged with a couple mints and water for both of us. We thanked her profusely and left.

"What do we do now, Mary?" Aunt Zoe asked, struggling to hook her seatbelt.

I opened my bottled water and took a sip before popping the key in the ignition. "I believe reconnaissance is in order." Refreshed, I settled my back against the car seat, ready to back up and take off. Unfortunately, Auntie's seatbelt had other plans. *If I don't take control, the two of us we'll be sitting here till doomsday.* I reached for the safety gizmo my aunt held in her hands and slid it into its teeny slot. It finally clicked into place. "There."

Auntie tossed a mint in her mouth. "Thanks." She smoothed out her light-weight jacket that had gotten scrunched up during the safety belt fiasco and then she placed her hands in her lap. "The military-like operation you're speaking of doesn't require guns and ammo, does it?"

"Not necessarily." I lightly tapped my fingers on the steering wheel. I was raring to go. Fiona had been backed out and straightened, but a guy in front of me blocked our way, keeping us from departing Burntside.

"Good, because there's no way I'm packing a Glock or a Beretta."

"Don't worry, Auntie, I'd never force you to carry a weapon." I'd be crazy to let her. Can you picture her with a gun? She'd probably shoot herself in the foot. As for myself, well, even though tracking down the bad guys makes me sometimes feel like the substitute teacher Miss Meadows in the movie of the same name, I'm never going to don pretty white gloves or '50's style dresses, nor do I plan to ever tap dance my way down the street while carrying a .38 special revolver in a cutesy little purse. It's not my style. It goes against the grain. But it sure would be nice to have a stun gun. Too bad Matt never purchased one for his business. When he gets back into town, I think I'll throw out a hint he needs one.

"Count me in then. I'm all for sneaking around."

"Great. We'll start with the manager Virginia Bagely," I shared, growing more impatient as each new second passed and the poky driver still hadn't indicated his intention to move along. "Come on, guy, what's the holdup?" If he didn't make up his mind in another second I'd show him where to go.

"You know it's too bad we have to leave the campus behind so soon, Mary."

"Getting cold feet already?"

"No, no. Look around you. It's like someone ordered up this perfect fall scenery just for us. The cooler weather hasn't dampened the enthusiasm of the trees one iota. Their vibrant-reds, rusty-browns, and golden hues still crave attention."

"You're right. My mind's been so wrapped up in this case I haven't taken the time to absorb what's around us. As soon as Darcy's death is resolved, I promise to bring you and Margaret back here."

I shifted my attention from the campus landscape to the car's clock. *Time's up, Buddy.* I pressed Fiona's horn to let the driver know I meant business. As soon as the horn blasted, a girl came running out of the dorm, jumped in the car, and gave the guy a serious kiss on the cheek. *Really Save it for later.*

Aunt Zoe keept her eyes glued to the young couple ahead of us. "You think she might be in cahoots with the three fellas and Trudy?"

"No idea. I've never seen this girl before," I joked.

Auntie turned towards me. "Very funny, Mary. I'm glad to see you've loosened up a bit. You were getting too squirrely for me. I almost thought I'd have to send in the troops to save you. So, how about sharing your thoughts on Virginia's possible involvement in this case? Remember she did hire Trudy, Demetri and Lewis."

"I haven't forgotten," I tapped my forehead. "That information's still stashed up here. Clearly Virginia's involved to some extent. How much, I don't honestly know. But I'm going to question her as soon as we get back to the Del Rosa." The car in front of us finally took off. I stepped on the gas pedal and zoomed out of the parking lot.

Aunt Zoe shook her pudgy fist. "Well, just so you know, Niece, I'm coming with when you interrogate, Virginia. You can't stop me. You could be entering a hornet's nest."

~42~

Aunt Zoe stood rigidly by my side me as I lightly rapped on Virginia Bagely's office door. "Hello. Anyone there?" I politely inquired. When no response was forthcoming, I knocked again. Still no reply.

"Try the door knob, Mary," Auntie whispered in my ear. "She could be on the phone."

The door wasn't locked. I decided to take a peek inside. "Virginia—"

"Well?"

"She's there. Her head's resting on the desk."

"Maybe she's napping."

I swung the door open. "That's one way of putting it."

"For heaven's sake, what is it?" Aunt Zoe pushed her short body past me and looked inside. "Oh, Mary! Why didn't you warn me? Call 911. The woman's dead."

Auntie's chalky white face disturbed me. It reminded me of Casper the Ghost, a cartoon from way back when. The woman was about to pass out. I felt bad about the quick decision forced upon me, but someone collapsing took backseat to a possible murder. Virginia won hands down.

I extended my arm across the front of the desk, gently wrapped my fingers around Virginia's wrist, and held them there for a while. "Auntie, she's alive." But what caused her to collapse? She never mentioned being a diabetic or having heart problems. I set her hand down and sprang into action, walking behind the desk where Virginia's body reclined. As my aunt joined me, I reminded her to touch nothing of significance in the process.

"What are you doing, Mary?" she whispered, "The cops need to be notified."

"Calling them can wait. I want to examine Virginia first and discover how she ended up like this."

Shifting the angle of my body so I could study the unconscious woman's neck and head better, I stooped down closer to the desk. "Ah, see that? There's a swelling at the base of her head. If Virginia wore a longer hairdo, I wouldn't even have noticed it." I did a fast turn around the office. "Auntie, do you see anything she could've hit her head on?"

Aunt Zoe carefully examined the items scattered around Virginia's head. "Not on her desk, unless applications and folders can be used as weapons. You don't suppose someone purposely clobbered her, do you?"

I nodded.

Aunt Zoe twisted her small frame this way and that, inspecting every inch of the room beyond the desk. Her eyes finally fell on an object of interest: a clear, crystal paperweight the size of a baseball. It sat right under our noses. Not literally of course. It had the place of honor on the four-drawer file cabinet sitting in the corner by the window. "Pretty handy device to render a person unconscious, don't you think?"

"I'd say so."

Aunt Zoe reached for the paperweight.

"Stop! Don't touch it," I cautioned. "Remember, whoever did this to Virginia probably left their prints all over it."

"You're right. I wasn't thinking. I'm not very good at detective work. I don't know why I talked you into letting me be here."

I clutched her hand. "You wanted to help protect me and I'm grateful." I turned my back on her and leaned in next to Virginia's ear. Using a soothing tone similar to a nurse's when a patient's coming out of surgery, I said, "Virginia, can you hear me? Virginia, wake up." No reaction. I glanced at Aunt Zoe. "Take the stairs to Lizzie's. Get a wash rag and ice. And whatever you do, don't stop to chat."

"But …but, Mary, I don't want to leave you by yourself. Whoever messed with Virginia could still be around."

"Get going. I'll be all right. I don't think they'll be coming back." As soon as Auntie left I chattered away in Virginia's ear again, hoping my words would bring her around.

Dad's sister didn't waste any time. She came back in a flash. She must've used wings to get from the office to Lizzie's and back in under five minutes. She's never moved that fast before. "Here you go, Mary," she handed me a freezer bag filled with ice and the wash rag, "Margaret thought it'd be best to put the ice in an enclosed container first than wrap the wash rag around it in case you had to hold it on Virginia's head for a while."

"Leave it to Margaret to think about freezer burn." I quickly wrapped the bagged ice and placed it on Virginia's swelling.

In a few minutes loud moaning came from the patient. "Ow… Ah… Oh, my head. It feels like a steam roller ran over it." She tried to lift her head but finally gave up. "What happened," she asked, before sliding a hand across the base of her neck and releasing another moan.

Aunt Zoe stepped to the side of the desk so she could see Virginia better. "Take it easy," she raised the woman's light-weight hand and patted it. "You'll be okay. Mary and I are here. We put a cold compress on the swelling."

Del Rosa's manager lifted her head slightly and rubbed her forehead. "They've got all my keys."

"Who?" I swiftly asked. "Your grandson?"

"No. Not Jarek. Those other two men he begged me to hire." Virginia held the ice pack in place while she straightened her body a bit. Then she rested her head against a grey hoodie draped over the back of the swivel chair.

You know how I'm always complaining that my aunt drives me crazy? Well, sometimes she catches important things that I miss, like drawing my attention to the grey hoodie that I hadn't taken note of. She did it slyly of course. Just jabbed my elbow and then touched the jacket.

Could Virginia have been the runner who tried to steal the goodie bag? "Ah, Demetri and Lewis."

"Yes, I didn't want to give them a job, but Jarek insisted. I knew they were up to no good the moment they put foot on the Del

Rosa premises. Those shifty eyes—exactly like my ex-husband's. I tried to watch them the best I could."

"Did they mention skipping town?"

Virginia tilted her head at an angle. "Not in front of me. The two of them just waltzed in here and demanded I hand over my keys. I told them I didn't have them. They didn't believe me. The next thing I knew they began to rifle through the desk drawers and file cabinets. I tried keeping my eyes on both of them, but it was impossible. Then whack, I saw nothing but stars. I'm worried about Jarek. His life could be ruined. Please find him before it's too late." Her ringed fingers circled my wrist almost breaking it, a desperate woman's attempt to save a loved one.

"Too late for what?" I inquired.

"I can't talk about it. I'm worried it might put Jarek in jeopardy."

"Virginia, I can't help him if you don't tell me what's going on. One of the men already killed Darcy."

She appeared bewildered. "But that's impossible. The news led us to believe she committed suicide."

Aunt Zoe snuck into the conversation. "That's because the police want to hold off sharing additional information until they receive the autopsy results."

"Depending on how backed up the testing lab is," I explained, "it can take anywhere from four to six weeks to discover the exact cause of death. Darcy's bereaved mother however wasn't about to wait on the sidelines for answers. Charice Hawthorne wanted immediate results. She hired me to look into her daughter's death. And believe me I'll do whatever it takes to find the real cause of death, including reporting what you and your grandson have been up to lately."

Our backs were to the door when its hinges creaked. "Leave her alone," a youthful male voice warned, advancing into the small office as he did so. "She doesn't know anything."

I spun around and immediately recognized the well-defined face and thick dark hair of Virginia's grandson whose photo I had studied in the picture frame resting on the bookcase the other evening. The only addition to his looks since graduation appeared to be his scraggy mustache. My eyes slowly drifted from his face to the scars on his hands. "You must be Jarek."

"Who are you?" he demanded, "What do you want? You'd better not be trying to blackmail Virginia. It won't get you anywhere. She's made a clean slate of her life. There's no extra dough sitting around in a safe somewhere."

"Blackmail," Aunt Zoe repeated, thrusting her hands in front of me. "What's he referring to, Niece?"

I didn't answer her. I was too busy processing recent files stored in my brain. Then like a bolt of lightning it all became clear to me. Everything fell neatly into place. Razinki, Jarek's last name, bothered me the first time I heard it, but I didn't understand why. Of course, Virginia's ex-husband had to be Tomasz Razinki, the former chief of detectives for Madison, Wisconsin who acquired over 5 million from jewelry and gem heists covering seven states. I had read about his famous escapades on the internet last Thursday. "Jarek, how long have you known Demetri and Lewis?"

His cold blue eyes bore through me. "About two months, why? What's that got to do with what you're doing here?"

I pressed a hand against my cheek. "We came to talk to your grandmother and found her unconscious. Those two men whom you brought to the Del Rosa knocked her out and stole her keys."

"What?" He flew around the desk and placed his hands on Virginia's shoulders. "Grandma, I'm so sorry. Are you all right? Do you want me to call Doc? He's only one floor up."

Virginia's smooth hand covered one of his. "It's not necessary. I'll be all right as soon as I take a couple aspirin."

"They didn't force you to do anything for them, did they?"

"Other than give them my keys, no."

His brows furrowed deeply. "What did they want with them?"

"Perhaps they want to flee with the jewels and let you get tossed in the slammer for Darcy's death," I said, then held my tongue for a few seconds, allowing my words to sink in. "Jarek, wise up. You don't owe them any favors. Tell us what those two men are holding over your head. If you don't, other innocent people could be in jeopardy."

He cleared his throat. "I don't understand. Who are you? The police? You never said."

Virginia shoved her swivel chair back and tried to stand. Too weak she sat again, training her eyes on her grandson. "Mary's been hired to look into Darcy's death. Please tell me you had nothing to do with it. I know you were involved with her. Why else would she have hung out here with Trudy?"

Jarek evaded the question. He brushed his thick hair away from his eyes. "Look, I liked her, but she didn't take me that seriously. She had recently ended a relationship and just wanted to have fun. So we did."

"Who suggested hanging out at Al's garage?" Aunt Zoe asked.

"Me. I knew Lewis and Demetri had used the place when they first got to town. Darcy thought of the garage as her home away from the dorm, away from her meddling roommate." He thrust his hands into his pockets. "If you met Trudy, you'd understand. She's the most conniving female I've ever known, throwing herself at any available male the way she does. I think she's got some sort of Daddy complex."

I lined up my body squarely with his muscled six foot frame. "Look, I have to know, was Darcy with you when you stole my car Sunday night?"

Jarek glanced at his soiled tennis shoes. "Yes. Lewis called and said I should follow you. He'd seen you snooping around on the beach again and worried you might be a narc cop. I couldn't believe it when you pulled up to the garage. How did you figure out where Darcy and I had been staying?" I didn't reply. If he thought I was that good at sleuthing, why shock him with the truth. "All Darcy wanted was a little quiet time to think before she returned to her studies. I thought if I scared you really good, you wouldn't waste any more time around here"

Anger welled up inside me. I wanted to bop Jarek in the jaw so bad, but I held back and dug my nails into the palms of my hands instead. "Oh, you scared the crap out of me all right, shoving a gun in my face."

Virginia pushed herself out of her chair. "You stole Mary's car and threatened her with a gun? Are you crazy, Jarek? Do you want to end up behind bars like your father and grandfather?"

Jarek grabbed her arm. "The gun isn't real. It's a harmless water pistol, Grandma."

"It doesn't matter. You still threatened her," Virginia shot back.

His hands flew out of his pockets and went right to his hair. "Look, I wanted to protect Darcy. She had nothing to do with the drugs," he shoved his finger in my direction, "I knew if this lady kept snooping around, Darcy would be caught up in it. Demetri and Lewis already served time in prison. They don't care what they do or who they hurt.

"The Saturday before Darcy died, Demetri suggested we all gather on the beach to kick back and relax around a bonfire, and we were doing just fine until one of the guys belted it up a notch, slipping drugs into everyone's coffee. Darcy went wild. Demetri and Lewis thought her behavior hilarious. I didn't."

"She threw off her clothes," Aunt Zoe mumbled.

"A naked lady on the beach," I said. "So, where did Darcy go after you dropped my car in the garage?"

Jarek ruffled his hair. "I don't know, I swear. She just ran off. Maybe stealing your car upset her. I tried calling her cell phone on Monday. She never picked up. Then Tuesday I heard her body had been found."

"Whatever possessed you to hook up with Demetri and Lewis in the first place?" I snidely inquired, "Could it be the cheap thrill of stealing gems like your grandfather did?"

"What's Mary talking about, Jarek?"

Her grandson's scarred hands balled into fists. "Ignore her Grandma. She doesn't know what she's talking about. Someone's filled her head with nonsense. Demetri and Lewis aren't involved with any jewelry heist. They just sell drugs and take odd jobs here and there. When I met them at the bar in Grand Marais, they told me a jewelry facility in town had recently lain off several workers, including them. Anyone angry enough over losing their job could've entered the plant and lifted those gems."

Virginia stared wide-eyed at her grandson. "Don't say anything more, Jarek. I'll get you the best darn lawyer I can afford."

~43~

"Shoot!" I said, as I hustled Aunt Zoe and me out of Virginia's office and onto to the elevator.

Auntie's thickly lined brows raised to new heights. "What's wrong? Did you stub your toe?"

"No. I forgot to ask Jarek what make of car he drove or if he knew Trevor Fitzwell."

"Well, go back in there and find out."

"No way. There's too much tension floating around in Virginia's office right now."

"Fine. Do you care to explain why you think that good-looking officer would be involved with Jarek then? He's training dogs to sniff out drugs, not buy them."

"Sure." I stabbed the elevator button. "What if that was just a ruse?"

"A ruse intended for whom?" she asked, searching my eyes for answers. "Surely not us?"

"Nosy neighbors. It's the perfect setup. Who would suspect a cop of being involved with dishonorable people?"

"But that would mean Trevor lived somewhere along Park Point."

"Yup. Otherwise his silver Toyota Corolla should've been neatly parked along the curbing on Lake Avenue when we ran into him that day."

Aunt Zoe got quiet for a moment, not easy for her. "You're right, Mary, Now that I think about it, I don't remember seeing any cars parked on the street when we got off the beach. Oh, dear, I don't like picturing handsome Officer Fitzwell as a bad guy, he seems so nice."

In all honesty, the few times I spent with Trevor he did seem like a decent fellow when he was off the clock, but Dr. Jekyll had his moments too. The elevator stopped on second. No one got on. Someone must've changed their mind. "Auntie, what if Jarek's meeting up with Demetri and Lewis at the bar in Grand Marais was an innocent coincidence? They all just happened to be there at the same time."

"Are you saying Jarek might not be in cahoots with them?"

"Possibly. Imagine for a moment what can happen to a person who has put a great distance, like Canada, between him and his druggie friends, and then the second he crosses the border into the U.S., without warning, he comes face to face with druggies again. The temptation's too great. He can't refuse. The ex-addict samples what's offered to prove to himself he can live without the stuff just like an alcoholic who's taken the pledge accepts a glass of wine at a party."

Aunt Zoe sighed. "And finds out he can't. The craving's back."

"Exactly. At least Jarek did tell us his drug buddies had been laid off at Clarity Diamond and Gems before he clammed up completely. Anyone who worked at Clarity's would know the layout of the plant and the work schedule."

"Including Demetri and Lewis," she said, tapping her plump cheek with her bright painted nail. "They probably were sitting at the bar, slugging down whiskeys, hatching their plans for the heist the night Jarek stumbled upon them. Once the men shared dope with Virginia's grandson, he busted his gut about his summer work plans in Duluth."

"There couldn't have been a more perfect union that night," I said.

The elevator door quietly slid open for our floor. We stepped out and strolled down the hallway two by two, like Noah's animals loading the Ark, chatting as we went. "What about the grey hoodie on Virginia's chair?" Aunt Zoe asked, "How do you explain it?"

"Grey's a common color. The jacket could belong to Jarek or maybe Virginia borrowed it. We know how speedy she can be for her age."

Aunt Zoe nodded in agreement. "And if she thought her grandson might go to prison for killing someone, well that's a whole different ball game."

"Right." I ran my fingers across my bottom lip. "I wonder…"

"Yes?"

"If Virginia came by the apartment on Wednesday to check on Lizzie after we left to meet with Charice Hawthorne in Canal Park, I don't recall hearing about it. Perhaps she phoned. Remind me to ask them."

"Hopefully I'll remember. So, how much of today's events do you plan to share with Margaret and Lizzie?"

"All of it," I stressed. "I want them to know how serious the situation has become. Maybe they'll have an idea where Demetri and Lewis might be hiding, I sure don't."

"What have you two been up to?" Margaret quizzed somberly, as we walked into the living room.

"Why?" I asked, not sure how to respond to the nonagenarian's tone of voice, usually so sweet and soothing like honey.

"Virginia Bagely just called. She's furious. She wants to know what gave you the right to ransack her place."

"What? We haven't been near her apartment. After we spoke with her and Jarek in the office a few minutes ago, we came straight up here on the elevator." I marched to Lizzie's kitchen and picked up the phone. "What's Virginia's number? Oh, never mind." I set the phone back in its cradle. "Aunt Zoe can fill you in. I'm going up to talk to Virginia face to face. I don't know how long I'll be." I left the kitchen and headed towards the door. When Winnie saw me traipsing to the door, she whined. "Go lay down," I ordered. "I'll take you out later," then I opened the door and raced to the stairwell.

#

When I first caught sight of the mess in Virginia's apartment, I felt I was viewing the aftermath of an F5 tornado. No wonder the woman went ballistic.

"Get out," Virginia snapped, "I don't want you here."

"I'm not leaving till we talk."

The lady didn't hesitate to go a second round. "Haven't you done enough damage for one day?"

I didn't budge. Things needed to be said. Unfortunately what little I offered in my defense didn't clear the air. The way Virginia continued to go on you'd never know she had gotten a blow to the base of her head just fifteen minutes earlier. She acted like a wet hen. Her thin-framed body strutted back and forth across the short-loomed beige carpeted flooring, while her lips spewed indecent words. My ears burnt from such profanity, but I couldn't get upset with her. She had every right to be angry. I'd be plenty mad too if someone had entered our tiny sublet abode at the Foley and tossed everything we owned helter-skelter, regardless of its worth. It's disarming to say the least. The home's supposed to be a sanctuary— a restful place away from all the turmoil in the world, not a disaster zone.

When the woman finally took a breather, I made one final attempt to reach the logical part of her brain. "I'm telling you we didn't tear your apartment apart like this," I rested my hands on my wide hips. "We didn't have the time nor do I know how to pick a lock. It's got to be Demetri and Lewis. Whatever they're looking for they aren't leaving the area until they find it."

She stared off into space. "What could they possibly want from me? I don't own anything of value."

Only jewels, I thought. I helped her pick up magazines, books, and other small items strewn across the living room floor, and then I gathered up the aqua-colored couch cushions and set them back where they belonged. "Maybe Jarek's the key. By the way, where is he?" I glanced towards the kitchen, "Is he in there?" She shook her head. "He should be keeping an eye on you after what happened, not gallivanting about town."

The woman who appeared so strong the first day I met her covered her eyes and released a wail. "Oh, my, God, he could be in more danger than I realized."

I took Virginia's arm, guided her to the couch, and made her sit. "Is it the drugs you're concerned about or something else?" She didn't reply. I tried another question. "Did you know I was meeting Charice Hawthorne at Canal Park this past Wednesday?"

She nodded. "I overheard the conversation you were having with your aunt when you stepped off the elevator."

"Did you share the information with your grandson or anyone else?"

"No, of course not," she replied tersely, "I acted on gut instinct when I decided to follow you. It wasn't until you pulled out the tape recorder that I became concerned. And then Ms. Hawthorne added to my worries when she handed you an envelope. I had to know what information she passed on to you."

I joined her on the couch. "You were afraid I'd find out Jarek had been involved with Darcy, is that it?"

Virginia fumbled with her hands. "Yes, that's why I tried to get your bag. In case you had anything that would lead back to Jarek. I know he didn't kill Darcy. I just know it. He doesn't have it in him to hurt a flea. Ever since he was little he hated seeing harm come to anyone, even an insect. It disgusted him."

"Well, you fretted for nothing. Darcy's mom didn't know about Jarek, Trudy never told her. It wasn't until I searched through Darcy's belongings in the dorm that I found a ring with the initials J.R. on it and a poetry book belonging to him. But how does one track down an invisible man with only initials to go by? You question one of your suspects a second time. Bingo. Jarek's name finally popped up."

The seventy-something woman sat up straighter. "May I ask who gave you the information?"

"I'm not at liberty to say. The person's still considered a suspect in my book. Let's talk about the jewels instead. Did you believe Jarek when he said he doesn't know anything about the theft in Grand Marais?"

"I don't know. Since you confronted him, I keep asking myself the same thing over and over. Was it just a coincidence his meeting Demetri and Lewis or was it planned? I realize the need for drugs can make anyone do crazy things."

"Even kill," I harshly pointed out.

Virginia's pale hand rested over her red painted lips. "Not Jarek. Never! You can't convince me otherwise."

I gazed at the woman who usually appears so put together. "You're positive you don't know where Jarek is?"

"I'm telling you I don't know. It's the truth. I sure don't want to see the boy going to prison. My heart would break in two. He's my only grandchild."

"One more question for you, Virginia. Then I'll take off. What's the make and color of Jarek's car?"

Her slim hands shot out in front of her. "Before I tell you, you've got to promise you're not going to pass the information on to the police."

"Look," I said, "I want to try and help him as much as you. The question isn't related to Demetri and Lewis."

"You swear?"

"Yes."

"He drives a blue Ford Focus."

So it was Jarek who banged into me. Finished with what I came here to do, I stood to take my leave. "Would you like me to get you a cup of coffee or anything else, Virginia?"

"No, thank you. I'm just going to tidy up. Trudy comes tomorrow and I don't want her seeing the apartment the way it is."

"Trudy cleans your place too?"

Virginia stood. "Why, yes." She's an excellent cleaner. Look, I'm sorry I talked to you the way I did. You know, when you first showed up here. I'll still see you tonight, right?"

"Of course." I took a few steps towards the door and then spun around. Before I departed, I wanted to verify another matter. I hadn't mentioned Virginia's ex being released from prison and was curious to see her reaction. For all I knew the woman and her ex could've orchestrated the heist from a safe distance. "By the way, I thought you should know Tomasz is roaming the streets again."

The newsflash jolted Virginia. Her well-manicured hands flew to her cheeks. "What? Since when?"

***

Margaret slapped the frozen Walleye in the warm frying pan. "What? Trudy cleans Virginia's apartment? Mary, you've got to turn Jarek and Trudy in. Why are you stalling? This case is getting more dangerous by the minute. Those two hoodlums you're trying to find already spent time in jail. When your brother Matt got too close to the criminals, he didn't go it alone. He'd lean on his buddy Sergeant Murchinak for backup."

"Not always. There have been a few times his stubbornness endangered his life."

Margaret's hard soled shoes squeaked on the linoleum surface when she turned to face me. "Hmm? I'm not sure if you're making that up to suit you or not. Obviously I haven't known him as long as you; you're his sister after all."

I pressed my fingertips against my chest. "You bet I am, and I want to prove myself too." I set the plates on the table. Then I added the silverware and napkins. I still had to get cups and glasses out of the cupboard. "I know I'm taking a chance by remaining quiet, but I don't have enough evidence on Trudy yet and Jarek's our only link to Demetri and Lewis. Besides, Officer Fitzwell doesn't come into the picture until tomorrow. He's been off duty since Sunday."

The elderly woman moved to the counter by the sink where four potatoes sat. She took a potato peeler out of her apron pocket, and began peeling them. "From what I've heard, you don't feel Officer Fitzwell's all that trustworthy. So, why even bother with him?"

I looked up from where I stood by the table with fingers hooked around three dainty coffee cups. "Aunt Zoe and her big mouth."

"She's worried about you, Mary. And quite frankly your cousin and I are too," she cut the peeled potatoes into small pieces and dropped them into a pot of boiling water. Then she added a dash of salt. "We're just lucky it wasn't you Zoe found unconscious today. You've already been in that situation this past summer. *Amico*, listen to me. Please heed the advice of three older women— back away and let the police do their job."

Cousin Lizzie and Aunt Zoe caught the tail end of the nonagenarian's plea as they entered the kitchen with Winnie. I sensed their thoughts on this case would be added as well. They had boxed me in. I had nowhere to go. Lizzie spoke first, "Yes, for all our sakes do as Margaret requests. Leave this case alone, Mary. Charice will understand if you explain how dangerous things have gotten."

Aunt Zoe stooped down and patted Winnie. "Tell her the death of her daughter has swept you into unforeseen circumstances beyond your control. You've decided to hand over what you know to the police so they can resolve the case."

When Lizzie moved away from Zoe to reach the table and chairs, her gait seemed to stiffen with each new step taken. *The drop in temperature must be doing a number on her knees.* I quickly pulled a chair out for her. "Thank you, Cousin." She clasped my hand. "I want you to know that if not finishing this case will cause you any financial hardship, I'll loan you and Zoe some money. I'd rather do that than attend your funeral."

I put up my hand. I didn't want to hear anymore motherly advice. I told Charice I'd find her daughter's killer and I meant it. Sometimes a person has to take risks in life and for me this case happened to be one of them. "Give me one more day. If things get a much hotter than they are now, I promise to throw in the towel."

Aunt Zoe's face brightened considerably. "Hallelujah. You're finally talking sense."

~45~

Tuesday

Morning had dawned with a promise of a thunderstorm by noon, according to Duluth's local news station, making me think a cleansing of sorts was in order for nature, as well as man. Start anew. Rid the town of the bad guys and move on. *Today I could make it happen. I really could.* But only if I could manage to hang on long enough to this slippery eel of a rotary landline, Lizzie refuses to relinquish, and dial somehow. I suppose if I wasn't so darn nervous about whom I was contacting I'd have a better grip on things. The call had to be made. No question about it. Other options didn't seem to be available to me anymore. But still—.

My hands finally finished the job they had been commanded to do and someone picked up on the fifth ring. Just before I spoke, I glanced at what I was wearing, the crummy PJ's with holes. Yikes. Well, at least I wasn't on FaceTime. "Hello, I'd like to speak to Officer Fitzwell please if he's there."

"Just a minute," said the heavy baritone voice responding on the other end. "I believe the meeting he's attending is winding down. May I tell him whose calling and what it's in regards to?"

I cleared my throat. "Ah, yes," the two simple words came out sounding squeaky, almost chipmunkish. Luckily the rest came out smoother. "Tell him it's Mary Malone. That's all you need to pass on."

"Okay. I'm going to put you on hold. You all right with that?"

Not really. I wanted to get this over and done with. My lips quivered. "Sure." In an instant the police station noise completely vanished. For some reason I thought my head would be filled with the theme song from *Criminal Minds* or *Hawaii Five-O* during the wait gap. Instead the phone lines became a vacuum of white noise waiting to suck in sounds at a moment's notice.

Someone finally picked up. "Hello, Mary." It was charming Officer Fitzwell. "I'm glad you called," he said, acting as if the latest incident at Al's Garage never occurred, "I had planned to phone you later this morning to share information with you."

I played with the small PJ hole near my kneecap, wondering what words he'd spit out of his mouth next. Maybe the lab results came back about Darcy. "Concerning what?" I anxiously asked.

"One of the sets of prints we lifted from your car belonged to Darcy Hawthorne."

"Uh huh."

"Wait a second. The news I just shared didn't seem to surprise you. Who told you? Did another officer from the station call you while I was off duty?"

I yawned. "Nope. I had a little chat with the guy who shoved the gun in my face."

"You what? If you know who he is, why didn't you bother reporting it? Or is that the reason for this call?"

"Not really. I wanted to give you the names of the men involved with the Grand Marais jewel heist. I understand they used to work at Clarity's."

The newbie cop remained silent. I went on. "You might want to write this down. The two men you're looking for are Demetri and Lewis. I have no idea what their last names are. Sorry."

Officer Fitzwell almost broke my eardrum. "How did you discover that? We haven't released a statement concerning them yet."

I didn't bother explaining myself. "I imagine the picture I shared with your department helped?"

"Yes, but we still don't know where they're holed up. I suppose you do though?"

"Nope. The people I've been in contact with have clammed up. I do however have another piece of info for you. Darcy Hawthorne was definitely drugged before ending up in Lake Superior."

Fitzwell stumbled with his words. "But…but how did you come to that conclusion?"

I ran my hand through my hair. "I'll explain later. Listen, I want you to know I plan to remain in close contact with you if anything further develops on my end. I can't afford to end up dead yet." I ended the call without a polite "goodbye," returning the receiver to its antiquated cradle just as Margaret walked into the kitchen.

~46~

"Well, Mary, what did Officer Fitzwell have to say?" Margaret asked, grabbing the newly brewed pot of coffee from the Black and Decker coffeemaker and pouring a cup.

I pushed the hair back behind my ear that had been dangling in my face for the past ten minutes and then brazenly plucked a donut from a box on the table. "Nothing much. He told me they lifted Darcy's prints off my car."

Finished getting her coffee, Margaret set the coffee pot back down where it belonged and picked her cup off the counter. "What about Jarek's prints?"

"He didn't mention any others. Maybe Virginia's grandson doesn't have a record on file as an adult, but only as a teen."

"Would it make a difference?"

"Definitely. Most juvenile records are sealed. Meaning the public isn't allowed to see them. Of course, circumstances involving felony offenses where a sixteen-year old was prosecuted as an adult is a different story."

"What about the other men? You did tell him about them, didn't you?"

I quickly swallowed the bite of chocolate donut teasing my tongue. "Of course. Officer Fitzwell, Trevor, seemed genuinely surprised I knew anything about Demetri and Lewis. But even so, he was kind enough to acknowledge the police department had already come to the same conclusion, and asked that I continue to be discreet about what I knew. The cops don't want the information blabbed about town."

"It makes sense. Otherwise the men would flee the area and never be caught."

"Yup," I scarfed down the rest of the heavily frosted donut and reached for another with my still messy hand. "These are really good. Sit down and join me."

"No. No. It's too soon after breakfast. I need to watch this girlish figure of mine," the nonagenarian joked.

"Okay. But there may not be any left for a snack later. You know how fond I am of chocolate."

"Yes, dear, I'm quite aware," Margaret said, setting her empty coffee cup on the counter by the sink before leaving the kitchen.

The nonagenarian's comment jolted me into action. *If she can discipline herself, so can I.*

I definitely didn't need the extra pounds. I placed the uneaten second donut back in the box, closed the lid, and marched out of the room.

***

"Mary and I are going to town in a few minutes," Cousin Lizzie announced not too long after lunch, "Are you two sure you don't want to ride along? You can help us pick out something for supper when I'm finished with physical therapy."

"Yeah," I chimed in, "while Lizzie's at her session, we can spend time in Enger Park or even the Rose Garden. It's your choice."

"I know the temperature's supposed to be in the upper sixties, but what about the rain they've been predicting?" Margaret inquired.

I whipped out my cell phone and searched for the Duluth weather report. "According to the latest update the storm's gone around us."

Aunt Zoe yawned. "No thanks. Good weather or not, I prefer to stay here and take a catnap."

I faced Margaret, "How about you? I bet you're dying to stretch your legs."

"Sorry, to disappoint you, but I really ought to finish the afghan project I've been working on before we go back to the Twin Cities."

"Virginia wants to buy it," Aunt Zoe hurriedly explained. "Isn't that nice?"

"Yeah. The color and design will look terrific with her living room furniture."

"It's not for the living room," Margaret corrected. "She wants to drape it over a chair in her bedroom."

"Ah? Well, I'm sure it'll look lovely in there too. I've never taken a peek in Virginia's master bedroom, but I imagine it's as tastefully decorated as the rest of her apartment." I glanced at my watch. "We'd better get going Lizzie if you want to arrive on time for your appointment."

When my cousin got up from the settee to join me, Winnie began to whine. "Go lay down by Margaret or Zoe," she ordered, "They'll take good care of you."

"Come here, Winnie," Margaret called from the chair she sat in, "I've got a cookie for you." She withdrew a Milkbone biscuit from a pant pocket and showed it to the dog. The poodle immediately left Lizzie's feet and bounded over to her new friend.

"Thanks," Lizzie said. "Okay, Mary, let's leave while the mutt's got food on her brain."

"All right. Ladies, if you need anything or want to suggest what to get for supper, just dial my cell number. I've left it by the phone in the kitchen."

Two hours later, when we came back to the apartment, arms filled with bags of groceries, we were shocked to find Lizzie's door standing open and the living room ransacked. "Demetri and Lewis," I muttered.

"Where's Winnie, Margaret and Zoe," Lizzie screeched.

Parading through the mess, we continued on to the kitchen where we found Margaret and Aunt Zoe sitting sat back-to-back on Lizzie's '50's retro-style chairs, encircled in heavy rope. They couldn't utter a word. The perpetrators had muffled their mouths with hankies to stifle calls for help.

We tossed the groceries on the counter and immediately went to work removing their gags and ropes. "Are you two okay?" I asked.

Margaret nodded. "It was two tall men," she managed to say, gasping for air as she did so, "Not much over six feet. I'm assuming the intruders were Demetri and Lewis. Their faces were covered with beards."

"Did they threaten you?"

"No. My hearts pounding a bit fast though," she admitted.

Aunt Zoe took a deep breath and pressed her hand to her heart. "Mine too."

Satisfied that her two houseguests were okay, Lizzie went off in pursuit of Winnie, leaving me behind to put the groceries away.

While I busied myself sorting out dry goods versus cold storage items and stashing them away, I pumped my traveling companions about the two ex-employees of Clarity. How did the men get in the apartment?"

"We didn't invite them in if that's what you're insinuating," Aunt Zoe said defensively, "They had a key."

"Ah? No doubt it's the master key on Virginia's missing keyring." I ran my fingers through my hair. "I can't believe the ordeal they put you through; getting tied up and having to watch as Lizzie's possessions got tossed about. I don't understand why those men showed up here. It doesn't make sense." I shook my head out of frustration. "Cousin Lizzie's never going to speak to me again."

Our neighbor clutched my arm. "Perhaps you should help Lizzie search for her poodle. We can talk more later."

The woman was right. I should be helping Lizzie. Her dog means the world to her. The counter was finally cleared of groceries so I tucked the empty bags away and went off to find my cousin.

"Come here Winnie," Lizzie frantically called from her bedroom. "Mommy's home. Where are you hiding? There's nothing to be scared of. Those mean men are gone. Come on out you silly girl."

When I stepped into Lizzie's bedroom, I found her standing in the closet examining its contents. "Is she in there?"

"No. I thought she might be. She hates loud noises and frequently snuggles in among my things."

Feeling lousy about the mutt, I quickly inquired what I could do to help. Lizzie suggested I check the guest bedroom. Before I marched off, I offered to look under her bed. "Sorry, no pooch." I stood and smoothed out the.bedding.

Lizzie shook her head. "I didn't think so."

As long as I had to cross the living room to get to the other bedroom, I decided to peek under the chairs and settee. A dog Winnie's size could easily squeeze under the fancy furniture: no animal. I continued on to the guest bedroom, hoping against hope she'd be there. After examining the open closet and looking under the bed, it became clear the little ball of fluff had fled the apartment. But did the poodle leave of her own free will or did the men take her as a hostage? If something happened to Winnie, I'd be up a creek without a paddle and overdrawn at the bank.

Five minutes later, Lizzie emerged from her room and joined the rest of us in the living room. She appeared disheartened.

I put my arm around her shoulder, offering support. "Winnie can't have gone far, Lizzie. Why, she's such a smart dog, she probably sensed the men were bad and disappeared into the hall the first chance she had. Look, Aunt Zoe and I've decided to walk through the apartment building floor by floor. We'll find her."

Her eyes brimmed with tears. "My dog's gone, my lovely home is a shambles, and my knees ache from therapy. It's too much to take in one afternoon."

I released my hand from her shoulder and patted her on the back. "Today's a bad day I agree, but it'll get better. I promise. We'll find your precious poodle."

"One of the men yanked her collar off," Aunt Zoe calmly stated, "I'm sure that's why she left."

"What? But why would he do that," Lizzie questioned.

I braced my hands on my hips. "I can think of one humongous reason. They thought Winnie's collar had been gussied up with precious gems stolen from Clarity's."

"Are they crazy? Why that's a preposterous notion."

"I don't know about that," I muttered, feeling sheepish. "When I first set eyes on your dog's collar, I thought it was embedded with real jewels too."

"Maybe China shipped Walmart the wrong collar order," Lizzie said tongue-in-cheek.

Margaret tapped her narrow chin as she sat down. "I have a feeling something happened to the jewels or a portion of them after the men hid them here in Duluth."

Picking up on the nonagenarian's train of thought, I said, "All right, I'll go along with your theory. And then for some unknown reason, Demetri and Lewis believe the gems unaccounted for have been moved to this particular building. But I don't understand why they thought the jewels might be stashed in Lizzie's apartment. Am I missing something here?"

Margaret took her glasses off and resettled them higher up on the bridge of her long narrow nose. "Several people knew Lizzie would be at Shoolinger for at least a couple weeks. Any one of them could've come in her apartment while she was gone."

"Trudy," Aunt Zoe shrieked, "The connection's got to be Trudy. She uses a master key to get into the apartments to clean."

I threw my arms around her. "You know you might have the makings of a good sleuth yet. Come on let's get the Milkbones and hunt down Winnie."

~47~

After pounding on several doors on the third floor, we finally found Winnie. She seemed happy to see us, if circling our legs a dozen times and yapping up a storm counted. "When I came back from the laundry room, I found her wandering the halls, acting terribly confused," the neatly dressed aged gentleman with a cane explained, barely opening his mouth as he spoke, "I hope it was all right to bring her in here. I rarely leave this apartment and wasn't sure who she belonged to. As you can see, she's not wearing a collar. I figured I'd phone Virginia after supper. You know, to see if anyone in the building reported a missing dog."

"Believe me," I said, "my cousin will be thrilled to see her poodle again. She was quite upset when she realized she had run off." I bent down and scooped Winnie into my arms. She thanked me profusely, licking my face like she was enjoying a huge bowl of ice cream.

"Your cousin's dog is a cutie," the man chuckled. "I sure enjoyed having her here. Say, do you mind telling me what the dog's name is, just in case I see her again?"

"Not at all. She answers to Winnie. What's yours?" I nudged Zoe's elbow slightly, hoping she'd take the hint.

"Gus," the bald headed man replied shyly.

Aunt Zoe turned towards the door. "Well, we'd better be off, Mary, before another search party's sent to track us down too."

"I hear yeah. Well, thanks for taking the dog under your wing, Gus."

"You're quite welcome." The old gent with sapphire-blue eyes and bushy white eyebrows gripped the door as we stepped into the hallway. "Ah, Miss, you might want to tell your cousin I gave the dog some water and fed her a little bacon. She looked awful hungry."

"Don't let this dog fool you," Aunt Zoe cautioned. "She gets plenty to eat and still begs for more."

"Like the young folks these days, eh," he said, gazing at me. "The ones they refer to as couch potatoes."

Aunt Zoe nodded. "Yes, yes. I know exactly who you mean."

I wonder if she realizes the two of us fit into that category. Naw.

Cousin Lizzie refused to set Winnie down once I handed the dog off to her. Holding the poodle securely in her lap, she gently scolded her. "You naughty girl. I thought I'd lost you. I'm never letting you out of my sight again. You hear me."

Winnie licked her hands and face.

"Excuse me Cousin, but I hope that doesn't mean she's sitting on your lap during supper," I said tongue-in-cheek.

"No, of course not, Mary. If that old man down the hall gave her too much bacon, she'll be snoozing long before we even set foot in the kitchen. Now tell me, what do you plan to do about Trudy and those awful men? I certainly hope you had time to concoct a plan to capture them while wandering the halls seeking out my poor little Winnie."

"As a matter of fact, I've formulated a plan of sorts. But in order for it to work, I'll need Virginia and Jarek's full cooperation."

"Do you think they can be trusted?" Aunt Zoe asked.

I tilted my head and pressed fingers to my furrowed forehead. "I don't know. I sure hope so because I don't have any other ideas up my sleeve."

~48~

Wednesday

Exactly a week ago today I drove back up to Duluth from the Twin
Cities to work on a case involving the death of Darcy Hawthorne.
Little did I realize at the time what a tangled web this.case would
become. The same drug dealers who snuffed out Darcy's life almost
destroyed Jarek Razinki's future in the process, and stole millions of
dollars' worth of precious cut gems. Trudy Almquist was no
innocent bystander as she would've liked me to believe either. She
triggered the demised of the deceased, not by her hands, but by her
mouth and one lousy picture.

      I approached Virginia's apartment with trepidation, not
knowing what I might find there this morning. I had opted not to
spend last night in her guest bedroom. Instead, I slept on the cushy
carpet in my cousin's living room with Winnie snoring peacefully
against my chest. After what happened in Lizzie's apartment
yesterday afternoon, everyone was a bit jumpy, including myself.
Even though I didn't have a gun to protect the three older women, I
could certainly make mincemeat out of someone's leg or arm with a
cast iron frying pan. Luckily, Lizzie had various sizes residing in the
cupboard next to the stove.

      After three short raps on Virginia's door, she cracked it open
and peered out. I could see she still had on her nightie and bathrobe.

Not wanting to embarrass her, I promptly shifted my eyes to her face. The absence of makeup didn't change her youthful appearance, lucky lady. I'd love to be blessed with those great genes. My face is already displaying wrinkles. "Hi," I said. "I'm sorry to disturb you so early, but I need to talk. Is Jarek around?"

"No, he went up the street to buy me a newspaper, but he should be back any minute." She swung the door open and invited me in. "I was just sitting down to breakfast. Would you care for anything?"

"No thank you. I already ate. Margaret made eggs and bacon for us." I heard the toaster pop up. "If you like, I can come back later when you're finished."

"Nonsense. You're here now. Besides, I'm only having a light breakfast. Come on and sit with me."

Virginia led the way to her tiny kitchen. "How about having a cup of coffee at least?" she asked pouring one for herself before she sat.

"Nah, I rarely drink the stuff. Go ahead and eat."

Virginia obeyed. She picked up a knife, slathered margarine and strawberry jelly on a slice of toasted wheat bread, and took a bite.

"Is this your usual breakfast?" I asked, pulling a chair out to sit.

"Sometimes I splurge and fry an egg or cook up oatmeal. Now tell me, what's this visit about, Mary? Your face looked pretty serious when you first walked in."

"I'm back, Grandma," Jarek shouted while closing the apartment door.

"I'm in the kitchen," she hastily replied, "We have company."

"Oh," Jarek said, popping his head around the corner to view the kitchen. "What's she doing here?" he snapped, "Hasn't she caused enough friction between us?"

"Calm down, Jarek. Mary just wants to have a little chat with us. She doesn't plan to stay all day."

"That's right," I said, feeling as loathsome towards him as he towards me. "How about sitting down and listening a bit. If you don't like what you hear, you can split."

He dragged a chair across the charcoal-colored linoleum floor and sat a distance from the table. Maybe he thought he'd catch something from me if he sat too close. After he got situated he glanced at the apple-shaped clock on the kitchen wall by the fridge. "You've got five minutes. Talk."

I rubbed my sweaty palms on my jeans. Hopefully everyone will play the game the way I'm setting it up. "First off, have you seen Demetri and Lewis since they knocked out Virginia and stole her keys?"

Jarek pressed the back of his hand against his mouth. "Nope. I think they've left town." He shifted his attention to the kitchen clock again. "Four and a half minutes and counting."

"I'm getting there. Your two buddies used Virginia's master key to get into my cousin's apartment."

Virginia's mouth fell open. "Oh, no. When did that happen, Mary?"

"Yesterday afternoon. They got in sometime after I took Lizzie to town for her physical therapy session."

"Did they tear her place apart too?"

"Oh, yeah. But they also left a present for us."

Jarek tensed up. He shot out of his chair. "What kind of present?"

"My two elderly companions were bound and gagged. Both could've easily died from heart attacks, considering their ages."

Virginia slammed her hand on the table, rattling her coffee cup enough to splash hot liquid on her hand. "My God, what can they be after?"

"Someone stole part of their jewel heist," I shared, "and they want it back. It's gotta be hidden on this property somewhere."

Virginia reached out for her grandson, "Jarek, I want you to know I do believe you weren't responsible for Darcy's death, but tell me the truth about the jewels. Did you steal them? Did you hide them around here?"

"Heck no, Grandma. I swear I don't know anything about the gems. I only hung around those two guys for the drugs. They told me if I squealed about their drug pedaling they'd toss me to the cops too. I do have a hunch who might know though."

"It wouldn't happen to be Trudy, would it?"

Virginia's grandson picked up his chair and set it next to the women. "Yes, as a matter of fact. She was in tight with all three of us."

"If that's true, how come she wasn't sitting on the beach when my aunt and I caught sight of you by the bonfire?"

He stared at his low-clipped nails for the longest time, as if the answer was written on them with invisible ink. "Trudy had met us down there. She arrived way before us and had already taken a swim. As soon as the bonfire got lit, she told us she had to run, too many errands to do. But she made a point of telling Demetri and Lewis she'd hook up with them later that evening at a bar downtown."

"Did you notice if she had a beach bag or knapsack with her on Saturday morning?" I asked.

Jarek scratched his head. "I don't remember maybe. Why?"

"Sand dunes make a great spot to hide treasure. Don't you think?"

He frowned. "I guess so."

"Just for the record, Jarek, I don't believe you're responsible for Darcy's death either. You said you didn't see her after she ran away Sunday night, right?"

"Right."

"Well, from information I've recently received, Darcy was still alive Monday morning. She met with her ex-boyfriend in Canal Park."

"She did? Why would she do that? She told me she never wanted to see him again."

"She was frightened and didn't know where else to turn for help. According to Darcy, some men were following her and had threatened to kill her. Your name never came up."

Virginia cupped her mouth. "Did Darcy say why the men were keeping an eye on her?"

"Apparently Demetri and Lewis discovered she knew about the jewel heist."

"Demetri and Lewis," Virginia bellowed. "Jarek, didn't I tell you when they showed up here I didn't feel comfortable around them? They gave off bad vibes."

He lowered his head. "I should've listened to you."

I shoved my hands into my jean pockets. "If Darcy had only blabbed what she knew to the cops," I continued, "your friends' butts would've been fried by now and she'd be alive."

Jarek rested his scarred hands on his forehead. "But she didn't. So that leaves only one reason for Demetri and Lewis to kill her. She refused to reveal what she did with their missing gems."

"The poor girl couldn't if she never took them," Virginia added under her breath.

I kept my opinion to myself regarding who might have had the opportunity to take and hide a bag of gems. I didn't want anyone being warned. "I came over here this morning to tell you both I've shared a few things with the police yesterday."

Virginia's grandson gave me an icy look.

I extended my hand to ward off any bad thoughts about to spew from him. "Hold on. I didn't mention you. I told you I wouldn't. But I do expect the cops to question me further in the next day or so, they'll want to know everything." I gazed at Virginia's antique wooden table. It had less nicks than Matt's desk. "I can't keep them away forever. Look, Jarek, you come off as a pretty decent guy. I'd rather not tell them about your involvement with Demetri and Lewis if I don't have to. So, clean up your act for your and Virginia's sake."

"I've already checked into a support group."

Virginia stared at her grandson. "You did?"

"Yup. I just haven't had a chance to tell you."

"That's a start," I said.

Virginia crossed her arms. "What about you, Mary? Couldn't you get in trouble for withholding information from the police?"

I looked directly at her grandson. "Jarek, have I ever seen Demetri and Lewis offer you drugs?" He shook his head. "So, there's no problem then. However, I do need your help, and it could prove extremely dangerous." I glanced over at Virginia.

Her small hands hastily encircled her grandson's larger wrists. "Think very carefully before you give your answer, Jarek. You could get yourself killed."

"Grandma, if she's right and Demetri and Lewis had something to do with Darcy's death, I'm willing to do whatever it takes to put them behind bars."

"Virginia, you may want to get paper and a pen so Jarek can go over the major points after I leave."

"I might as well pour myself another cup of coffee while I'm at it too," she said, moving towards the counter where the coffeemaker sat. When she returned to the table, she had a cup in one hand and a notepad and pen in the other.

"Okay, so here's what I'd like you to do, Jarek …."

~**49**~

Cousin Lizzie turned her attention away from one of her favorite TV programs as soon as she saw me walk through her door. "Did Jarek agree to your plan, Mary?" she anxiously asked.

"Yes. If he didn't, I don't know how we'd be able to resolve Darcy's murder and the jewel heist. He'll call Trudy today and pass along the message. Hopefully Demetri and Lewis will agree to meet with him this evening." I glanced around the small apartment, but didn't see my companions. "Where are Margaret and Aunt Zoe? I thought they'd be clamoring to find out what took place?"

"They said they wanted to get some fresh air."

I plopped down in one of the living room chairs and tried to get Winnie's attention. It seemed like forever since I'd given her any serious cuddling. But she was too busy pawing at the fabric covering the ottoman, a silly activity she'd taken on this past week, to even consider breaking away for me. Prior to today, I'd simply ignored what seemed a harmless game for her. Cats putter with loose strings and threads all the time. Why not dogs? "Lizzie, what's Winnie trying to get? She's behaving the way Gracie does when Matt hides a doggie treat between the couch cushions."

Lizzie cast her eyes on her poodle for a second. "Oh, dear. I hope I didn't spill something on it when I had a late night snack."

Winnie kept at it. Curious to see what the poodle wanted, I padded over to the ottoman, neatly tucked in a corner by the TV, and got down to her level to investigate. To my surprise I discovered the fabric holding the ottoman together wasn't part of the original construction, but actually a woven piece tightly secured with elastic underneath. The real ottoman was a well-worn brown piece of leather work. "Would you like to see what's inside, Winnie?"

"Wuff, wuff."

"Me too." I eased the two-strands of elastic out from underneath, lifted the fabric off, being careful not to tear it, and set it aside.

Lizzie gave up on her show and leaned over slightly to examine the side of the ottoman facing her. "I only see pencil-size holes in the leather on this side. Is there damage anywhere else, Mary?"

I scrutinized the other sides. "No major tears only several teeny ones."

Dying to find out what secrets Virginia Bagely's old ottoman held, I pried its lid up high enough to allow the hinges to click into place. Once it was secure, I bent my head down and gazed inside. Shocked by what I saw, my legs gave out and I landed on my butt. I tried to speak but no words formed.

Lizzie's face became a question mark. She hadn't seen what I'd uncovered. The lid hid it from view. "What is it? Are you ill, Mary?"

I forced my arms to move somehow and spun the ottoman around, giving her a clear view of its innards.

"Oh, my, word!" She rested her fingertips on her lips. "It's certainly not doggie food, is it?"

"What's not dog food?" Aunt Zoe inquired, briskly parading from the hallway to us in her stocking feet. "Did I pick up cat food by mistake? I'm sorry. The boxes are so similar."

"We're not talking about animal food," Lizzie plainly stated. "Just empty bags of popcorn and something else."

"Oh?" When my aunt finally caught on to what was being discussed, her mouth expanded the way an alligator's does when preparing to snap up its delicious meal. "What …? When …? How on earth?"

"*Mi Scusi*," Margaret said, trying to squeeze between Aunt Zoe and me, "What's everyone staring—?" Her thin-skinned hand landed on her cheek. "I don't believe it. You mean to say we've had the jewels all this time! Whatever possessed you to search the ottoman, Mary?"

I finally regained my voice. "Blame Winnie. I'm sure you've noticed how she's been acting around here lately."

"Yes, but I thought she was merely bored, dear," the nonagenarian stiffly replied. "Well, these jewels certainly clear up the mystery surrounding the emerald we found on the carpet."

"Yup, they sure do." I got off the floor. "You know what this means, don't you?" I pointed to the rubies, diamonds, and sapphires whose brilliance almost blinded us, "A certain someone who had access to Virginia's apartment stashed money away for a rainy day."

Aunt Zoe reached down and picked up a handful of precious cut stones. "Where are we going to hide these until we can collect our finder's reward?"

"The safest place I know," I took the gems away from her and returned them to the ottoman, "at the police station where they belong. I've got something else in my purse they might appreciate receiving too."

"Oh, what's that?" my cousin inquired.

"I returned to the beach the same day Aunt Zoe and I saw the foursome at the beach and collected cigarette stubs and a hairband. The cops can collect DNA from those items as well."

"What? I can't believe you went back there," Aunt Zoe said, "especially after Officer Fitzwell specifically said to stay away."

"You should know her better than that, Zoe." Margaret said as she moved from Aunt Zoe's side and planted herself by me. "But please tell me you're not foolish enough to go to the station by yourself, Mary?"

I closed the ottoman's lid and put the woven fabric back in place. "Nope, the police can come here." I glanced at my cousin. "Unless you'd rather they didn't."

"Considering the situation you've found yourself in Mary, I'm perfectly fine with your decision. You've made a wise choice. Besides, with all the excitement that's been happening around me since I returned home, I'm feeling no pain."

***

Officer Fitzwell showed up at our door at exactly one o'clock with fellow Officer Peter Gundersen. Both dressed in casual clothes like

I'd suggested. Peter, whom we had never met before, appeared to be close to Aunt Zoe's age which delighted me. The muscles around my mouth gave way to a smug smile. I couldn't believe Trevor actually followed through with my idea. Maybe there's more to him than meets the eye.

After we introduced ourselves, I explained about the break-in yesterday and the subsequent discovery of the gems in the ottoman. "According to the person I've kept in contact with, the two men you're looking for, Demetri and Lewis, may be hiding out on a boat in the Marina just across the way. Once they get their hands on what they perceive to be the rest of the jewels tonight, I'll let you know exactly how they plan to leave town. Just keep your eyes peeled to the fourth floor apartments facing the marina, that's where the arranged signal will be coming from."

Trevor's deep-set eyes rested on mine. "You're not the one delivering the fake jewels are you, Mary? For all we know Demetri and Lewis could be heavily armed."

Hmm. The guy seems genuinely concerned. How sweet. "Don't worry. I don't plan to put myself at risk. Someone who knows them has offered to pass the fake gems on."

Both cops stood, signaling it was time to take a spin around the block or to be more precise, to get a cup of coffee at one of the café's across the bridge in the Canal Park area.

Right before our so-called dates escorted us out the door, Aunt Zoe and I each slung huge gaudy purses over our shoulders, which we'd purchased two hours earlier at an antique store on Lake Avenue. They roughly held the same weight in semi-precious stones. The playacting had to be done. Demetri and Lewis could be watching our every move. Once we drove out of the neighborhood, we'd switch the real jewels for the phony ones Trevor had stashed in his car.

~50~

Virginia Bagely acted as jittery as a caged cat. She paced back and forth in front of her 21inch flat screen TV, clasping and unclasping her hands as she did so. Occasionally, she broke the repetition by swinging her arm out and peering at the gold watch snugly wrapped around her thin wrist, a gift from her grandson. If I hadn't known the real reason she couldn't settle down in her apartment tonight, I would've guessed the lady was off her meds or hyped up on caffeine. "Why hasn't he called, Mary? Something's happened to him. I just know it."

I was nervous too, but I wouldn't admit it in front of Virginia. Ever since Jarek left here at eight-thirty with the bag of fake jewels, guilt had been gnawing at the pit of my stomach non-stop. Sending someone off to certain death will do that to a person. I can't imagine what a top military officer feels like when he dispatches soldiers to the most dangerous war-torn countries in the world. Maybe that's why so many of them drink themselves into a stupor. I should've brought a bottle of vodka to Virginia's. Too late now. "Calm down, Virginia," I warned, "or you're going to have a meltdown. You don't want Jarek coming back and finding you a total wreck. He's smart enough to get himself out of a tight jam. It's only two minutes past nine. See." I shoved my cell phone in front of her face, "They didn't meet up till nine."

My words went in one ear and out the other. "No," she said, "he's in trouble. I can feel it in my bones. I bet Trudy double-crossed him."

There was a gentle knock at the door. I went to answer it.

"Aunt Zoe, what are you doing here?"

"The three of us wondered how Virginia was holding up. I told them I'd check on her," she explained, stepping into the tiny hallway without waiting for anyone to ask her in, "I won't stay long, I promise." As soon as she caught sight of Virginia in the living room, she quietly shared her thoughts with me. "Apparently, she's not doing too well, huh?"

I shook my head.

She leaned closer to me and whispered in my ear. "I've never seen her look so unkempt. She's going to need a long vacation after tonight. Maybe she and Jarek can go someplace together to help them reconnect. Preferably a quiet spot away from others."

I patted her pudgy hand. "I think you're right. Why don't you see if you can convince Virginia to sit on the couch. She may listen to you since you're closer in age. I haven't been able to get through to her."

Aunt Zoe trotted over to the woman and took one of her hands in hers. "How you doing?"

Virginia swiped her loose hand across her forehead. "Not so good. I keep thinking Jarek's been taken hostage or even killed. We should've heard from him. Why haven't we?

Auntie used a soft lilting tone with the overwrought woman. I hadn't heard her speak like that since she babysat me years ago. "I'm going to make you a cup of coffee. When I come back from the kitchen, I want you to sit down on that beautiful, comfy couch of yours and stay there. Do you think you can do that for me?"

Virginia released a heavy sigh. "I'll try."

"Good." Aunt Zoe let go of her hand. "I'll be right back."

"That cup of coffee ought to help you relax," I said.

Virginia began to pace again. "I hope you're right. I'm going crazy thinking about Jarek." Just then the cell phone resting on her coffee table rang. Relief rapidly spread across her face as she recognized the name of the caller listed on the cell screen. "It's him." She picked up the phone, said, "Hello," and then passed it on to me.

"Jarek, it's Mary. Did everything go okay?"

"Yeah, why wouldn't it?" he rushed to say, sounding short of breath. "The guys were drinking up a storm before I got there. Probably celebrating the fact they had all their gems and they could skip town for good. They were so wasted I had no problem wiggling what info we needed out of them."

"I'm Sorry it was such an intense evening for you, Jarek, but it's over. You should be proud of yourself. So, what mode of transportation have Demetri and Lewis chosen? Water or land?" I asked, assuming the men were still hanging out on Park Point somewhere. The stretch of land on this side of the Lift Bridge doesn't only have a marina, but a small airport as well. When I got my answer, I handed the phone back to Virginia. "Here. He wants to talk to you."

While Virginia spoke with her grandson, I rushed to the small metal lamp on her desk by the window where I had situated it an hour earlier. It was essential to our plans. I placed my hand on the light switch and clicked it on and off twice. Officer Fitzwell, standing by at the marina gate across the street, would know what the signal meant. A second later, a faint light from across the way flickered on and off. That had to be Fitzwell responding. He'd notify his fellow officers now. It was up to them to round up Demetri and Lewis.

When I stepped away from the window, Aunt Zoe walked over to me and gave me a hug. "We got 'em, Mary. Charice Hawthorne will be pleased to hear her daughter's killers are behind bars."

"They're not there yet," I replied, taking my light-weight jacket off the back of the chair I had been sitting in. "But she'll definitely be happy to hear the news. Look, I've got to go."

"So do I," Aunt Zoe reminded me, "Margaret and Lizzie are waiting for both of us."

I slipped on my jacket and zipped it up. "I'm not going to Lizzie's yet."

Aunt Zoe's eyebrows rose a bit. "Why not?"

"Trevor promised I could be there when they captured Demetri and Lewis."

"How did you swing that?"

"I shared what I knew and also came up with tonight's brilliant plan."

"Officer Fitzwell actually told you it was brilliant?"

I started towards the door, "No, not in so many words, but it was implied. Do me a favor, will yeah? When Virginia gets off the phone, tell her I'll talk to Jarek and her later."

~51~

I flew out of Virginia's fourth floor apartment, hustled to the stairwell, ran down six flights of stairs, rushed through the lobby, and raced across the street to meet up with Trevor, who had just pulled up in a police car. Let me tell you there's no comparison between the day I chased Trudy down one measly dorm hallway and the Olympic style athletics required of me tonight. Now I know why it's important for cops to stay in shape. They'd never catch any criminals if they didn't. My lungs burned. I thought they'd burst from my chest. Despite the pain I managed to take in enough oxygen to speak. "Trevor, have your fellow officers spotted them?"

"Not yet," he replied, standing by the open door on the passenger side of his squad car. "But we should be hearing something soon." As soon as I slid in, he closed my door and made a hasty retreat to the driver side. After buckling up, he turned on the car lights and sped off to the right. "By the way, great job with the signal. How did you think of that?"

"It came from a poem I memorized in high school."

"Huh?"

"I'll explain later when things aren't so tense."

When Trevor took off from the marina to go south instead of north, I assumed he'd turn around somewhere, but that wasn't the case. Something wasn't right. I tapped my hands together and squirmed in my seat. Why would he take us in the direction of Sky

Harbor Airport, when I specifically signaled the men would be escaping by boat? Unless—*Oh, Mary, you blew it.* I was trapped. My life was over. The end of my days had come sooner than I'd expected. I'd never see the inside of another classroom. No more little darlings staring up at me with their innocent eyes, eagerly waiting to accept what I dished out. Sweat beaded on my brow. There goes my chance to write a *New York Times* best seller novel. *Oh, crap.* What about Aunt Zoe? I'll never get to tell her how much she actually means to me even though she manages to irritate me a ton.

"You're sure acting jumpy, Mary. What's going on? Worried we won't catch up to those guys?"

"Ah, yeah, you could say that." Totally confused about the decency of the cop sitting next to me and whether I should bail out of the car or not, I decided to confront him head on while his hands were wrapped around his steering wheel, not his Glock, and before we reached the end of Park Point, only a stone's throw away. "Trevor, care to tell me why you're driving us towards the airport?"

"I thought I'd cover all the bases just in case Jarek misunderstood Lewis and Demetri's means of transportation."

"But ...he told me they planned to leave by water."

The cop glanced over at me. "You're definitely not a Park Point resident. Otherwise you'd know Sky Harbor doesn't just handle dry landing of small planes. Seaplanes take off and land there all the time."

I had to admit his explanation sounded plausible. "Whoa. You mean I screwed up?"

"No, I wouldn't say that." He applied the car's brakes and gently rolled up to the fencing surrounding the airport, and turned the lights off. "We'll get out here, and then slowly walk to the water, staying near the main building as much as possible."

"I don't think we have to be concerned about being spotted. The New Moon's just barely moved on."

Presuming Officer Fitzwell truly had my back, I prepared to slither out and face down whatever danger came my way. First step, quietly crack the door open. Second, swing legs out. Before I could follow through with step two, Trevor's hand clamped down on my left one still resting on the console. It felt intimidating. "Hold it," he ordered.

I closed the door. What's this cop up to? Have I underestimated him? Is he playing me for a fool? I put my faith in him thinking he wasn't part of the gem heist crew. Maybe that was a hasty decision on my part. One minute Trevor gains my trust completely and I go all soft, then bam seconds later he turns me into a doubting Thomas. I turned to face him. What's next, a gun pressed against my cranium?

Trevor must've felt the tenseness in my hand when he grabbed it. He quickly released it. "Don't go yet," he said, sounding official. "I'm not ready. I want to check to see if the Coast Guard's picked up any unusual boat traffic. No one's contacted me in a while."

I inhaled sharply. At some point here, I had to trust this cop completely. Make up your mind, Mary. What's it going to be? I picked trust. Hopefully, I wouldn't regret it. Trust's a huge priority in my book.

Trevor picked up his two-way radio to communicate with the others providing backup. His voice was strong and clear: one that would benefit theater or radio. I stayed glued to my seat, listening intently to what he shared. The instant he finished he opened his door. I followed suit.

"Okay, stay close. Don't go running off in another direction."

I promised I wouldn't. Why would I? I had no tools to defend myself with, not even Lizzie's flashlight, and I didn't know how the airport was laid out.

When we started to make our way to the water, I noticed a speck of light flash off the waves. "What's that," I whispered.

"Where? I don't see anything."

By the time I told him at two o'clock, the glint of light had disappeared. "I know I saw a light. I wasn't imagining it."

"Maybe someone was taking their dinghy back to their sailboat."

"You don't suppose Demetri and Lewis would try to sail out of here, do you?"

"Sailing's too slow. If anyone around here wants to outrun the police, they'd need a boat with at least a 300 horsepower engine or a plane." He turned inward a bit. "Let's head over to the shed on the right about four feet down. Those men would never suspect someone might be keeping an eye out for them there."

"You're right. It looks like it's about ready to fall down."

Trevor went ahead of me now, acting like a big brother wanting to protect his sister. I was okay with that. Let him handle the bad guys. I had done my share already. I'll just sit back and watch.

Two feet from the building everything changed. We heard noise above us and looked up. A seaplane circled above. A few minutes later it descended and landed about seventy yards out from where we stood. "Do you think it could be the getaway plane?" I asked.

"Could be."

"Well, I wish it could move a little faster. I can't stand the waiting."

"Be patient. We'll find out soon enough."

The moment the seaplane taxied towards the dock at our end, three men burst out of the shed. One of them hobbled like he had been badly wounded. I recognized him immediately. It was Jarek. Demetri and Lewis must've figured out he was working for the cops and decided to take him hostage. "Trevor, we've got to stop them. They've got the guy who helped us."

"Are you sure he's not involved with the heist?"

"Positive."

Trevor whipped out his gun and charged after them, "Stop!" he shouted, "You're under arrest!"

One of the men turned and fired as Trevor drew closer to the plane. Trevor yelled for me to drop to the ground, and then he fired back. Another bullet came whizzing by. Trevor let loose with an expletive, dropped his gun, grabbed his right arm, and fell to the ground.

I got up on my knees, crawled towards him, and collected his gun. I had never put one in my hands before. I never wanted to, too dangerous. I held it out in front of me and fired. There's no way I'd allow Demetri and Lewis to drag Jarek into this mess. They'd already killed Darcy.

One of my wild shots hit the guy to the left of Jarek in his butt. The men immediately let loose of Virginia's grandson's arms and scrambled onto the seaplane. I glanced back at Trevor. "They're getting away."

"No. They're not," he said, clutching his wounded arm, "The Coast Guard's blocking their path and the additional backup I requested should be arriving any second."

The police sirens I heard a few seconds ago off in the distance were growing louder. I turned to face Lake Superior again. Powerful searchlights popped on, covering the ground we stood on and the water. I handed Trevor his gun and scrambled to clear Jarek from the area.

"You know, when your friend gets patched up," Trevor shouted, "he'll be pulled in for questioning."

"He's not my friend," I yelled back, "But if you need to question more people, I'd suggest you start with Trudy Almquist."

~52~

As soon as the ambulances whisked Trevor and Jarek to the hospital to get patched up, Officer Murphy approached me and offered a ride back to the Del Rosa. I graciously accepted, not knowing how he'd treat me after our run-in concerning Fiona's presence in the underground garage. Luckily, I found his chit chat along the way quite comforting, not aggressive. Maybe the word had spread already among the cops how I helped Officer Fitzwell capture the gem thieves.

When we pulled up to the front of Lizzie's building, I asked Murphy if he'd like to come in for a cup of coffee. He declined. That was fine with me. I wanted to drive over to the hospital and check on Jarek and Trevor; if I called, nobody would release any information to me since I wasn't related to either man.

The second Officer Murphy took off I realized I couldn't just hop in Fiona and go. My purse containing driver's license and car keys sat in my cousin's apartment. So, I headed there instead.

Aunt Zoe gave me a bear hug the instant I walked in the door. "You look like you've been through a war zone, Mary."

My hands shot to my short hairdo. "I feel like it."

"Well, did your plan work?" Margaret asked, coming up alongside us, "Did the police capture Demetri and Lewis?"

"Yes. No one has to worry about them anymore."

Cousin Lizzie stepped out of her bedroom dressed in slippers and bathrobe. "Has anyone heard from, Jarek? I spoke to Virginia Bagley about ten minutes ago and she said he still hasn't shown up."

"That's right," I said, "She, hasn't heard the news yet. Aunt Zoe, call and tell her to meet me in the lobby right away."

Thankfully my aunt didn't waste time asking what happened. She picked up her small feet and quickly propelled them towards the kitchen phone.

Margaret moved closer to me. "What's going on?"

"Jarek's in the hospital. He's been injured."

The elderly woman's hand rested on her cheek. "Oh, my. Not severely I hope."

"As far as I could tell, no." I stepped away from the two women and went to collect my purse in the guest bedroom.

"Where did Mary go?" I heard Aunt Zoe say.

I strolled back into the living room, "I'm right here. Did Virginia agree to meet me downstairs?"

"She said she'd be right down."

"Then I'd better get going."

Aunt Zoe pointed to my purse. "Why are you taking that? Are you leaving the building again?"

I glanced at Margaret. "Can you please fill her in?"

"*Si*," and then she shooed me out the door.

***

When we got to the hospital, I asked the receptionist if she could tell me whether Trevor and Jarek had been taken to the emergency room or surgery. She picked up the phone and checked. "Officer Fitzwell is being sewn up," she informed me, "but Jarek Razinki's still in the emergency room."

After I escorted Virginia to the emergency room, I hunted for Trevor. I had to know how badly he was hurt. It didn't take long to find his room. A bunch of guys dressed in blues stood around the doorway of a room yakking away. Apparently he wasn't in too bad of shape if visitors were already lining up. I spun around and went to the lobby to wait for Virginia.

Epilogue

"Care for a cookie?" Aunt Zoe inquired, holding a plate full of humongous-sized chocolate chip cookies in her pudgy hand. "I made them myself."

"No thank you, I'll pass," Virginia said, turning her attention to me. "I can't thank you enough, Mary, for keeping what you knew about Jarek's drug problem to yourself. He's free to go back to Canada the end of summer if he wants to. After all we've been through, though, I'm hoping he'll want to stay put. We've got a lot of catching up to do."

I patted her hand. "I'm sure you do. How's his ankle?"

"He'll be off it for a while. He sprained it pretty bad when he tried to get away from those two thugs after leaving the bar." Virginia stood. "If you and Zoe ever take a trip up this way again, I want you to know my guest bedroom's always available."

"That's so kind of you," I said, escorting her to the door. "Say, Virginia, there's something I've been wondering about concerning your past."

Her facial expression turned sullen as she positioned herself in Lizzie's doorway. "Oh, dear, what's that?"

"Were you really a high school teacher?"

A broad smile pierced the somber look she held a second earlier. "Why, yes. I taught trigonometry and calculus. I'm sure you took those courses in high school, didn't you?"

"Ah, yeah," I lied too embarrassed to admit I barely survived Algebra classes. Math wasn't exactly my forte. After I shut the door, I returned to the living room and sat down in the one of the comfy French style chairs.

"Doesn't anyone want to sample my cookies?" Aunt Zoe asked, her bottom lip hanging a bit low.

"No," was the resounding response. "Maybe later."

"All right. I'll set the cookies on the kitchen counter then. We can have a late dessert of ice cream and cookies."

Margaret perched her wire-framed glasses higher up on her nose. Then she picked up her crochet hook, yarn, and the afghan she was finishing off for Virginia. "Have you heard how Officer Fitzwell's mending, Mary?"

"Only through the grapevine," referring to Officer Murphy. "He got hit in the shoulder."

"I've heard shoulder wounds can be fatal," she said, pulling a piece of yarn through crochet loops and tying it off, "What's his prognosis?"

"The bullet didn't hit a vessel or an artery."

"He's a very lucky man," she said.

I nodded. "Yes, he certainly is."

"Do you ladies definitely have to leave tomorrow?" Lizzie quizzed.

"Afraid so." I said, "This time of year there's a ton of requests for substitute teachers."

"I hate to see you go. I'm really going to miss having you three here."

"What about touring Glensheen Mansion?" Aunt Zoe asked, returning from the kitchen, "Couldn't we stick it out just one more day, Mary? I heard the interior and exterior of the mansion are exquisite. And don't forget, the place reeks of high-drama."

I rubbed the back of my neck. "Sorry to burst your bubble, but I think we've had enough mystery and intrigue to last us quite a spell."

Aunt Zoe pouted. "I guess so. Oh, well, there's always next year, right?" she added on a cheerier note.

I had a feeling she was going to say that.

"So, Niece, you never mentioned how much of a reward we got for finding the jewel thieves. Are we rolling in dough?"

How do I tell her our reward is based on only the value of the lone emerald we showed the jeweler, and that's already spoken for? "Um, ah, well. You see, it's like this—"

"Yes, yes, spit it out. Can we go out to dinner at least four times a week?"

"More like once a month if we're lucky."

Her mouth sagged. "What?"

"Auntie, you know how I hate to see you pout. Let me explain," I said, leaning forward in my chair, "Charice Hawthorne has decided to set up a scholarship at UMD in honor of Darcy. I told her we'd like to contribute to it."

"So, you gave her the whole amount?"

"Not quite. I gave her exactly five thousand six hundred, the remaining two hundred's for us to splurge on pizzas."

"Hmm? Well, at least you didn't tell her she didn't owe you anything for finding Darcy's murderer, or did you?"

I shared a smile. "Aunt Zoe, you worry too much. I accepted her payment. But if circumstances were different and we didn't have bills up the kazoo, I would've gladly rejected any attempt to pay me so more funds could go into the scholarship."

"That was a nice gesture," Cousin Lizzie said. "I'd like to donate money too. Make sure to write Charice's phone number down so I can contact her."

The phone rang and I offered to get it. "Hello?"

"Is this Mary Malone?"

"Yes."

"I was wondering if you'd like to go out to dinner tonight?"

I played coy. I hadn't spoken to Trevor since he got shot at the airport. "Is this Officer Murphy?"

"No, it's Officer Fitzwell. Trevor."

"Hmm, let me look at my calendar," I paused for a few seconds. "You're in luck. I can fit you in. What's the dress code, formal or informal?"

"Informal," he replied. "You do like Chinese cuisine, right?"

"I can take it or leave it." *Who was I kidding?* I loved Chinese, especially Leeann Chin's sweet and sour pork and lemon chicken.

Trevor sighed. "Has anyone ever told you you're exasperating?"

"Yes. I distinctly recall you telling me that. What time should I be ready?"

"Six."

"Okay, I'll wait for you in the parking lot. Bye." I rested the phone back in its cradle and twirled around. "Yippee."

"What's going on in there?" Aunt Zoe asked as she raced to the kitchen, "Is something on fire?"

"Yup," I replied excitedly, "me. Trevor's finally asked me out. I didn't think I'd ever see him again."

"Didn't I tell you from the very beginning he was right for you?"

"Yes, you did, but I was trying to keep my blinders on. I didn't want a sailor in every port."

Aunt Zoe flicked her hand. "Niece, you've still got a lot to learn when it comes to dating."

"I guess so."

She started to shove me towards the bedroom. "Well, go get ready."

"I will in just a sec," I set a hand on her shoulder, "but first I have a favor to ask. Would you mind painting my nails with that pumpkin shade you use?"

"Why I'd be delighted too. How about the lipstick? They go so well together."

Worried I'd scare Trevor off when he got here," I said, "Ah, I think the nail polish ought to do the trick. Thanks."

***

Trevor arrived on foot, promptly at six.

Surprised to see he came without a vehicle, I said, "Did you park down the road?"

He laughed. "Nope. The car is sitting in my driveway."

I glanced down at the flats I had on, which I rarely wear, wondering how far I'd get hoofing in them. "So, how long a hike do we have?"

"One block."

That's it? I felt the furrows in my forehead grow deeper. "But …but there's no restaurant on Park Point."

"Who said anything about a restaurant? I simply asked if you liked Chinese."

I stared at his deep set eyes. "I stand corrected." However, curious creature that I am, I inquired if we'd be heading to the right or to the left. The day Aunt Zoe and I took Winnie for a walk on the beach we tried to take note of the various houses along Minnesota Avenue. Maybe Trevor lives in one of the condos facing Lake Superior. What a spectacular view that would be.

"Once we get out of this parking lot," Trevor said, "We'll turn right and stick to this side of the street."

That shoots the condo theory. There are only houses on this side of the Avenue. Unless he has us cross the street further down. Which place could it be? Is it the one with the neatly mowed grass and all the red maples in the yard or the house with paint peeling off the trim, weeds galore and barely any grass? Oh, no. If it's on the other side, it could be the green house Aunt Zoe was so leery of walking behind to reach the beach. I guess I'll know soon enough.

Five minutes later we stood in front of Trevor's place. I couldn't believe it. He owned the gingerbread house Auntie and I wondered about. I remember her saying the joke would be on me if it was owned by someone my age. I covered my mouth to conceal a laugh.

Trevor noticed. "What, you don't like my taste in homes?"

"No, no. Your house's quaint. It's like one you'd see in a child's fairy tale book. The first time I saw it I thought it would be a fun place to come to beg for Tricks or Treats on Halloween."

"The neighbors refer to it as the 'Hansel and Gretel' house," he said, leading us to the porch, "I apologize for not having any candy sitting out here to entice you."

"No big deal. That's minor compared to what I forgot to do."

"Oh?"

"I didn't leave a trail of bread crumbs behind."

"Touché," Trevor said, as he unlocked the front door and waited for me to enter, "The woman's not only smart but witty."

I laughed. "Blame it on my ancestors." The second I stepped into Trevor's home I soaked in as much as I could. The interior was charming and well-kept, not at all like my brother's apartment, usually a total mess. Remembering I had my shoes on, I started to take them off.

"You don't have to do that, Mary. I vacuum regularly." He pointed to the dining room. "Why don't you take a seat in there. I'll be right with you. I hope you don't mind takeout?"

My kind of man. No kettles to do afterwards. Dishes, silverware, and napkins were already on the table. I stole a look under the tablecloth to see what kind of dining table he had, a card table. Smart guy. Easy to haul when you move to another location. I straightened up. "By the way, how's your shoulder doing?"

"Fine. Thanks for asking." He left the kitchen and came into the dining room carrying a tray, "Here we go." Trevor took serving spoons, several small white cartons, and something wrapped in wax paper off the tray and set it all in the middle of the table. "I forgot to ask which you'd prefer, beer or a wine cooler?"

"A wine cooler's fine, I'm not that crazy about beer."

While Trevor went back to the kitchen, I popped open the containers and peeked inside: fried rice, chow mein, sweet and sour chicken, and shrimp with broccoli. Yummy, the perfect dinner. My stomach went flip flop. Mom said the way to a woman's heart was through her stomach. *No, wait. That's not right.* It's a man's heart and stomach. Oh, well. I closed the cartons and opened the rolled up wax paper: eggs rolls, of course.

Trevor returned and handed me a wine cooler. Then he sat down with his beer. As he passed an egg roll to me, he said, "First of all I want to apologize for how rude I've been to you over the past couple of weeks. For a dog babysitter, you're one smart female."

I gave him a stern look. He was getting off on the wrong foot with me. Not a good sign.

He picked up on my reaction. "I'm kidding. I know you have a teaching degree and do substitute work in the cities."

That's better, I thought.

"Second, I want to thank you for partnering up with me to catch the jewel thieves."

"I'm sure your supervisor was pleased with your savvy understanding of the criminal mind."

Trevor beamed. "As a matter of fact he was. It definitely made up for the day I arrested you." He picked up the cartons of food and passed them to me. "Take as much as you want. I had a big lunch."

Funny, that's what I always say when I don't think I've made enough for company. I took two heaping spoonful's from each carton and left the rest for him. The guy needed it more than I did. Besides, wasn't I supposed to be dieting?

"So, Mary, now that I've got you all to myself, tell me where you came up with the idea for signaling me?"

I swallowed the egg roll still sitting in my mouth. "Sure. It came from a poem by Henry Wadsworth Longfellow, "Midnight Ride of Paul Revere.""

"Ah, yes. 'One if by land, two if by sea; and I on the opposite shore shall be…' I can't believe I missed that."

"You had more important things on your mind. So, has your superior heard anything from the lab on Darcy?" I inquired, shoving fried rice on my fork before it got too cold.

Trevor took a sip of beer. "Yes, and you were right. The medical examiner's report showed high levels of alcohol and amphetamines in her body. She was doped first and then tossed overboard."

"What about Trudy? Did she ever get pulled in for questioning?"

"Yup. I mulled over what you said at the airport and decided the department should act on it. Trudy thought she'd just get a slap on the wrist. I don't know where she got that idea. She may not have actually helped with the heist, but she was aware of the stolen gems and decided to keep some for herself. Not only that, she let Demetri and Lewis think Darcy knew where they were stashed."

"She sure chose the perfect place to hide the gems, in an old hassock in the manager's apartment. Who would ever think of looking there? I bet Trudy went crazy when she went to clean Virginia's apartment and the hassock had disappeared."

Trevor's face grew serious. "I don't feel sorry for her. If it weren't for her deceitful ways, Darcy Hawthorne would still be alive."

I was getting to like this man more and more. Not many men are willing to let down their guard, admit to a woman that they're right, and go out on a limb to prove it. Too bad we're leaving for the Cities tomorrow. I'd love to spend more time with him. Of course, I still had to resolve how I'd get Matt's Topaz back to the cities since Aunt Zoe doesn't drive. Maybe something could be arranged. I was about to let Trevor know how much I've enjoyed getting to know him when my cell phone rang. I tried to ignore it, but Trevor insisted I see who it was. I put my fork down and pulled the cell phone from my purse. "Hello? Oh, David, how are you?" I pushed my chair out and motioned to Trevor I'd be right back, and then I stepped into the kitchen to have a private conversation.

"I understand you're in Duluth," the undercover cop I had dated this past summer said. "I left several messages on your landline, but you didn't return my calls."

Perturbed that I hadn't heard from him in so long, I said, "Why didn't you try my cell phone?"

"I lost the number," David explained, "I finally called your mother to get it."

That explained how he knew I was in Duluth. Thanks Mom.

"When will you be back? I've got vacation time coming next week."

"Tomorrow."

"Great. How about going to Aamodt's Apple Orchard next Monday to celebrate your birthday? We can taste the wine, buy some caramel apples, and take a hot air balloon ride."

"Sounds good," I said, "See you then." I turned my phone off and went back to the dining room. "That was my brother," I explained, not wanting to destroy the evening's congenial atmosphere, "He needed a babysitter and wanted to know when I'd be back in town. So, where were we?"

Trevor's lips curved up. Obviously he swallowed my lie. "Talking about the jewel case while our food's growing cold," he said, piercing a piece of sweet and sour chicken with his fork and lifting it to my mouth, "I think eating instead would be nice. Here taste this."

"Mmmm, yum. It's quite tasty." I lifted my bottled wine cooler, "Compliments to the chef, whoever he or she is."

                                   ***

"Mary, guess what I'm going to do when we get home?" Aunt Zoe said from the back seat of Fiona.

"I haven't a clue."

"I'm going to sign up for driving lessons."

Heaven forbid, I thought, as my foot hit the brake pedal. Luckily, there were no cars following me. "Why would you want to do that? I drive you wherever you need to go?"

"Yes you do, but then things come up. Here we are in Duluth with two cars and only one licensed driver. It's a terrible predicament to be in. If I drove, you wouldn't be in this situation. Now you have to pay someone to bring one of the cars to the Cities for you."

"Actually, I don't. When we were leaving, Cousin Lizzie, handed me an envelope with money to purchase a bus ticket to Duluth. So, I can ride up and drive back. Pretty slick, huh?"

"Yeah. I guess. I suppose I won't be going with."

I raised one hand off the steering wheel. "Sorry, it's only enough to cover one ticket." And believe me, I was pleased. I could see Trevor without hearing her or anyone else's thoughts on the subject. "What do you think about another road trip next summer, ladies?"

"Where to?"

"North Carolina."

Margaret tapped her fingers on her lap. "Count me out. I'm too old to travel that far."

Aunt Zoe leaned her head over my seat. "Well, I'm not, but I agree it's a long distance. What's drawing you to North Carolina, Mary?"

"Emeralds."

Margaret suddenly nudged my arm. "Mary, you're not supposed to turn here. We need to go straight ahead to get on Interstate 35."

"Don't worry, I know what I'm doing this time," I said, pulling into a parking spot at Canal Park and eventually leading them to the empty horse carriages waiting for passengers.

"What's this all about," Aunt Zoe inquired, staring at the carriages in front of us.

"I thought we should do at least one fun thing before we head home. Everyone at the Foley's going to be dying to know what we did while we were in Duluth, especially Rod Thompson."

"Goodness gracious," Margaret exclaimed, patting a coal-black horse above its nostrils. "What a surprise. This takes me back to my childhood."

As soon as the three of us got situated in the carriage we selected, the driver turned to introduce herself. "Hi, I'm Patricia. Before we take off, would you ladies like your picture taken?"

"Of course," I said, passing my cell phone to her, "but before you snap it, make darn sure there's no criminal activity going on behind us."

Book Club Questions
Death of the Naked Lady

1. From the beginning of the story did you get the impression Mary would rather be on her own than depending on a roommate?
2. The elderly Margaret Grimshaw doesn't tell people what they want to hear, but rather gives them food for thought? What do you think of a person like her?
3. What obstacles did Mary have to overcome in order to take a trip to Duluth to do research for her novel?
4. After Mary's first encounter with Officer Fitzwell, do you think she meant what she said to Aunt Zoe about a woman needing more than a few days to figure out if a man's the real thing?
5. At what point did you decide Mary would take on the jewelry heist?
6. In Chapter 8 did you catch the first "red herring" Virginia and her jewelry?
7. How did you feel when Mary turned down Charice Hawthorne the first time she met her? Have you ever turned down someone when they asked a favor? Did you later regret your decision?
8. How did Mary feel when she found out the naked lady was Darcy? Was it reasonable for her to blame herself for Darcy's death?
9. Was it wise for Mary, an amateur sleuth, to keep certain information from the police regarding Darcy and the jewel heist? Did she make the right decision?
10. Did you suspect that the three men Mary and her companions encountered when they first arrived at the Del Rosa Apartment complex could be a clue?
11. Do you think Aunt Zoe and Mary had a right to be frazzled by what they saw on the beach or did they blow it out of proportion? What would you have done given the same situation on a beach in your area?
12. When Officer Fitzwell kept popping up at the weirdest times, did you think he might be involved with the jewel heist or just a "red herring"? How many times did Mary run into him in the story before she started sharing info with him?

13. Trudy kept lying every time she was questioned. Did you think she was involved with Darcy's murder or innocent?
14. How many "red herrings" did you find in the story?
15. Were Margaret and Aunt Zoe both helpful in solving Darcy's death and the jewel heist? Give examples.
16. How did you feel when you learned Aunt Zoe and Margaret had been tied up?
17. Did you ever suspect the missing jewels were hidden in Virginia's hassock she loaned to Cousin Lizzie? Where would you have chosen to hide them?

30722889R00155

Made in the USA
Middletown, DE
05 April 2016